The Complete Book of
MAGIC and WITCHCRAFT

THE
COMPLETE BOOK
OF

MAGIC
and
WITCHCRAFT

Leonard R. N. Ashley

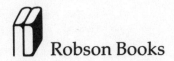

Robson Books

First published in Great Britain in 1996 by Robson Books Ltd, Bolsover House, 5-6 Clipstone Street, London W1P 8LE

British Library Cataloguing in Publication Data
A catalogue record for this title is available from the British Library

ISBN 1 86105 027 5

Printed in Great Britain by WBC Book Manufacturers Ltd., Bridgend, Mid-Glamorgan

Contents

Preface

WRITING this book has taken me to some unattractive places, among "wizards that peep and mutter," among the petty and the potty, the diabolical and the desperate, the sacrilegious and the fanatical. The search for facts has spread before me an amazing documentation of human pride and arrogance, frailty and ignorance, deception and delusion.

The result is presented for your entertainment and enlightenment. I hope it will also make you think. For one man's cherished beliefs and obsessive ambitions may strike another—particularly if he lives in a later more superficially sophisticated age—as revolting, vain, silly, frightening. But one should translate the excesses of an earlier age—avarice and vainglory, bigotry and stupidity, malice and self-deception—into the terms of one's own time. There are lessons to be learned from seeing how ready man is to blame the Devil or some other supernatural entity for the more despicable, hateful, life-destroying, irrational aspects of human nature.

Exploring this mysterious land has many a shock and many a surprise, for there seems to be nothing so foolish or so vile that someone—somewhere, at some time or other—has not attempted it. The hideous and their wretched victims are here together. Here is a man who gruesomely murdered some two hundred children to tell fortunes and to please the Evil One. Here is a Hungarian noblewoman who murdered dozens of serving girls in order to bathe in their blood. Here is a witch hunter who preyed on deranged old women and innocent young people and collected twenty shillings a head for sending them to horrible deaths. Here is a judge who sentenced nine hundred poor souls to violent deaths for witchcraft, the evidence having been obtained by excruciating tortures. (The families or heirs of victims were charged the expenses of torture.) Here are primitive and harmless superstitions derived from ignorance and what Karl Marx

ix

called "the idiocy of rural life," and also terrifying crimes and persecutions perpetrated by educated persons in the name of faith. Here are saints and demons and frauds and wonders. Here are sincere believers in the Old Religion and on the other side men of zeal armed with a text that dictates "thou shalt not suffer a witch to live." Here are charlatans and dupes, magicians and alchemists, diviners and divines, men ready to destroy the mind to gain some diabolical power and men ready to destroy the body to save the soul.

"I am human," wrote Terence, in the second century before Christ, "and nothing human is alien to me," not even man's seeking to contact the inhuman, or man's inhumanity to man. The history of magic and witchcraft is a colorful part of the record of human behavior. Here is some of the humor and horror to be found in it.

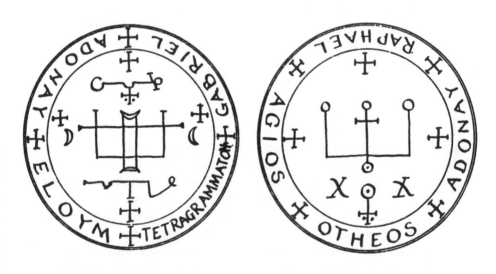

1
Magic and Sorcery

MAGIC is difficult to define with precision, but in all its aspects it is concerned with making reality conform to one's will. It attempts to exercise power over events and to produce marvels by compelling the intervention of supernatural forces or bringing into operation the occult forces of nature. It rewards those who have penetrated the secrets by enpowering them to make spirits do their bidding.

Remember that "occult" means simply "hidden." Thus magic can also involve not necessarily the supernatural but also the arcane, the secrets not known to ordinary or unlearned men, the merely mysterious. In some people's view, modern computers perform "magical" operations. To others, the telephone and the television—indeed simple electricity—are deep, dark mysteries; average people believe in them, use them, but cannot explain them.

Right up to and through the Renaissance, magicians were classed among what we should today call intellectuals. They were learned men, familiar with ancient lore and languages, with the obscure symbolism of signs and numbers. They read the stars and dabbled in the mysticism that surrounded alchemy. They were respected. In the early centuries of Christianity, magic was not considered an evil thing. In the world thought to be inhabited by men and angels and devils, men also believed in spirits neither good nor bad, spirits of the air, of fire, of the sea, of the mountains, of

1

the woods, of the winds. It was believed that if a person was sufficiently learned in the art of magic, he could summon and control these powers, make them do his bidding. Ariel in *The Tempest* was such a spirit; Prospero was such a magician.

It was only at the very end of the Middle Ages and particularly in the Renaissance enlightenment that animism lost its hold on men's minds. Then religion preached that all spirits that were not angels, doing the bidding of God, must be evil, doing the bidding of His Adversary, Satan. The Church decided that men who worked magic through spells must also be in league with the Devil.

Even then—it is worth noting—few magicians were persecuted as witches were (unless they had committed sex crimes). Witches were chiefly the poor, the friendless, the impotent, whereas magicians were gentlemen and scholars and—whether in league with the Devil or not—entitled to all the privileges of rank.

THE MAGIC OF ABRAMELIN

Abraham the Jew (1362–1460), better known as Abramelin the Mage, lived chiefly at Würzburg, Germany, but he had important clients all over Europe. He was credited with having produced two thousand spirit cavalrymen to aid Frederick, elector of Saxony, and to have assisted Pope John XXIII. (Not the one you are thinking of but an antipope who reigned 1410–1415.) Abramelin was universally believed to have saved John—for a price—from the clutches of the Council of Constance, which had seized and deposed him. Abramelin is also supposed to have helped an earl of Warwick escape from jail.

Abramelin claimed angels told him how to harness devils, to make armed men appear, to raise thunder, to tame a demon as a personal servant, and so on. He left his magic recipes to one son and his knowledge of the cabala to another and wrote (probably in Hebrew) a book on magic. It was translated into English by S. L. MacGregor Mathers from a French version in the Bibliothèque Nationale in Paris. It has been very influential among modern magicians.

MAGIC IN CHRISTIAN FOLKLORE

Hrabanus Maurus, an encyclopedist of the ninth century, stressed that magicians could not overcome the set laws of the universe: "Not for that reason ought anyone to believe that certain men can perform magic operations without the permission of God."

As a brief example of magic in Christian folklore, apparently by "the permission of God," take the legend of the priory of Christchurch. The priory lies in Dorset, England. The legend is that the church was intended to be built on top of a hill, overlooking a valley site that dated back to Saxon times. Every morning materials were carted up to the top, and the following morning, they were found back at the bottom again. The builders eventually faced the inevitable and began to erect the church in the valley.

As they worked, they were joined by a helpful but silent carpenter, who took neither pay nor meals but labored beside them every day. One day they made a mistake and cut a beam just too short to reach from one wall to the other. They thought they had ruined it, but the next morning, they found that the beam had grown to be just long enough, and the mysterious carpenter had vanished forever. They named the place for him: Christ-church.

THE NAMES OF GOD

Some of my Jewish students persist in writing the title of a Eugene O'Neill play *The Great G-d Brown* and referring to "the pagan g-ds of the Greeks." Their action reflects the ancient fear of the name of God. A pious attitude, for God's name not only should not be taken in vain but also should not be consigned to a piece of paper that may be defaced or debased. God's name is power.

But they do not really have to worry, for *G*, *O*, and *D* do not add up to God's Name, any more than *D*, *O*, and *G* spell the name of my dog Wolfram. God simply told the Jews, "I am," which is where we got *Yahweh* and *Jehovah*, and left it safe at that.

The Jewish tradition developed words of reverence and respect to stand in place of the ineffable name of the deity. Here they are:

EHEDEH	EL	EL ADONAI TZABAOTH
IOD	ELOHIM GIBER	ELOHIM TZABAOTH
TETRAGRAMMATON ELOHIM	ELOAH VA-DAATH	SHADDAI

These have come to be used in magic. With the Nine Names of God, it is alleged, you can work wonders, that is, minor miracles. For truly magical effects involving the exercise of divine creative power, you would need the accurate name of God.

But the secret name of God is known to us cabalists. My own religion sees nothing wrong in setting it down, so if you are ready, here it is. (If you don't want to know, skip to the next paragraph.) The secret Name of God is *Emeth*.

GOLEMS

With that secret name, you can do wonders. You can make a golem if you like, an artificial man. Rabbi Judah Lowe did in the sixteenth century, and they were able to show me his grave—the rabbi's, not the golem's—when I visited Prague. The golem comes back, according to legend, every thirty-three years, even if you destroy it.

As early as the eleventh century one Eleazar of Worms gave instructions on how to put together spare parts of corpses to make a man. But his monster didn't come to life (because he did not have the essential name I just gave you). Elisse of Chelm in the sixteenth century did know the Name; his golem worked but had to be destroyed because it ran amok (like Dr. Frankenstein's monster). The Prague golem was known in Toledo and in all the other European capitals of sorcery. Prague was famous for Rabbi Lowe and other Jewish sorcerers but also had its Christian contingent of magicians; a column was pointed out as the place a priest got in big trouble when he tried to get out of his pact with the Devil. The Jews not only had a golem but also a dybbuk (a demon who was especially fond of preying on dedicated students of the Torah). Ansky and others have written famous plays about the dybbuk.

A dybbuk, unlike a golem, which is confined to thirty-three-year intervals, can come at any time.

HOW STRONG A FOUNDATION

People once believed that human blood mixed with the mortar made buildings stronger, and at the urging of magicians, human sacrifices were immured in fortresses. Geronimo of Oran was buried alive in the walls of the fort at Algiers (September 18, 1569); on December 27, 1853, they recovered his skeleton, now on view in the cathedral there.

S. Baring-Gould in *Strange Survivals* (1892) writes:

When, in 1842, the remains of the Romano-Batavian temple were explored at Stinvezand, near Rysbergen [Rijsbergen, Netherlands], a singular mummy-like object was found in the foundation. This was doubtless a substitute for the human victim.

Often, however, magicians used the real thing, even for Christian churches. The way that witches and such have pursued personal enmities under the name of magic, and caused the deaths of many people, is a history in itself.

THE MAGIC OF THE UNCONSCIOUS

Novelist Colin Wilson, who has a deep interest in the occult, wrote a foreword in 1978 to *Ritual Magic: An Occult Primer* by David Conway (a pen name). In it, he presents this theory of magic:

> "Magical powers" originate in the unconscious mind. And the reason that we are very naturally sceptical about their existence is that what you call "you" and I call "me" is our *conscious* egos. . . . In most of us, the unconscious has adjusted itself to the routine of everyday life, and sees no good reason to make unusual efforts. . . .

Many others attest to the powers that reside in us, unused, and that enable those who have made "unusual efforts" to perform astonishing feats. Yogi ascetics are only one kind.

SAINTLY MAGIC

Hagiography (idealizing biography of saints) is full of stories of "magic" attributed to saints. Most of these fanciful tales are legendary, pious inventions that became associated with various saints usually long after death. (Indeed many saints—including the beloved Nicholas, Christopher, and George—may have been pious inventions themselves.) It is interesting to note how similar some of the miracles attributed to saints are to feats of sorcery. That magic was real, Saint Thomas Aquinas himself attests to:

> Certain learned men have declared that magic does not exist except in the belief of men who impute to witchcraft the natural effects whose causes are obscure. But this is contrary to all the

authority of the saints, who say that demons have power over the bodies and imaginations of men, when they are permitted by God.

Saint Columba, the Irish missionary to the wild Picts of Scotland, is said to have obtained entry to the barred fort of a pagan king by merely making the sign of the cross. Saint Martin of Tours, a Roman soldier, gave half his cloak to a beggar and that evening had a dream in which Christ appeared to him, wearing the half cloak and saying, "Martin covered me with this garment." Saint Elizabeth of Hungary, carrying bread to the poor, one winter day (which she had been forbidden to do by her husband), was confronted by him unexpectedly. He demanded to know what she was carrying in her apron, and she lied: "Roses." But when he forced her to unfold her apron, out fell roses.

A number of saints have been reported to levitate spontaneously, usually during ecstatic prayer states. These include Ignatius Loyola, Teresa of Avila, John of the Cross, Alphonsus Liguori, and many more. Most remarkable of these was Joseph of Copertino (1603–1663); at Christmas Mass in 1627, he astounded the congregation by floating up into the air. He was accused of black magic, but he got off when he actually flew before Pope Urban VIII. Even on his deathbed in 1663, Joseph floated above his bed until ordered by his superior to desist.

One of the most curious magical phenomena associated with saints is the liquefaction of long-dried-up blood. This is said to happen to vials of the blood of several saints, always in southern Italy, the most famous of whom is Saint Januarius (died A.D. 305), or San Gennaro to Italians. Donald Attwater, in *The Penguin Dictionary of Saints* (1965), has this to say:

> There is preserved in the cathedral at Naples a glass phial containing a substance said to be the dried blood of St Januarius. This relic is shown in public eighteen times a year, when, after a varying interval of time, the substance liquefies. This phenomenon has been carefully examined and seems unquestionably to take place; so far no fully satisfactory explanation of it is forthcoming.

Italian-Americans in New York celebrate the feast of San Gennaro every year on September 19 with a famous street fair. The saint's statue is carried in procession, and food, games, and entertainment stretch out over a ten-block section of Mulberry Street. No blood liquefies, but the saint is considered sufficiently honored by the pleasure enjoyed by 300,000 visitors.

MAGIC AND SCIENCE

As easily as magic could be confused with murder (Mother Lakeland may have poisoned her husband at Ipswich in 1645 but she was burned for killing him by witchcraft), it could also be confused with natural philosophy. Learned men could be students of both magic and science at once.

Arnaldus Villanovanus (1235–1312), for instance, moved from distilling to alchemy and from medicine to magic. He distributed amulets and seals as serious treatment, even to the pope, and he added the black arts to his sound advice on hygiene. Dominicans denounced him as a heretic, and he was lucky to escape death by fire, a fate many of his precious papers did not escape. Feared, he rose high and had the ear of princes. He became counselor to Frederick II, Holy Roman Emperor and king of the Two Sicilies, and to Jaime of Aragon. He was personal physician to three popes: Boniface VIII, Benedict XI, and Clement V. None of his masters seemed to reject his magic.

Another such curious combiner of magic and learning was Raymond Lully (1235–1315), called *Doctor Illuminatus*. Born in Palma, Majorca, where he is now buried, he was educated at the best continental universities of his time: Montpellier (renowned for medicine), Paris, Rome, Naples, and Palermo. He was a noted alchemist, a magician, reputed to be able to turn himself into a red cock. At the age of seventy, he was prominent at the court of Edward II, for whom he is said to have turned twenty-two tons of base metal into gold. Fired with an ambition to convert Islam, he studied Arabic with a Moorish slave, and as an octogenarian, he set out on his mission, only to die within a year or two. The legend that he was stoned to death at Bougie (modern Bejaia, Algeria) cannot be substantiated.

Or consider Sir George Ripley, born in Ripley, Yorkshire, an Augustinian monk who in the fifteenth century was canon of Bridlington; he died in a priory near Boston (the English one) about 1490.

Ripley was universally believed to have made gold alchemically for the Knights of St. John of Jerusalem and was famous in his time. As late as 1678 "Eugenius Philalethes" (who was probably Thomas Vaughan, brother of the mystic poet Henry Vaughan) revived Ripley's published work.

Should a man purported to have made gold out of base metal be regarded as a magician or a scientist? Or put to death, as was Marc-Antoine Bragadin (a Venetian alchemist beheaded as a sorcerer by Wilhelm II, duke of Bavaria)? Should such men have been confined to the madhouse or promoted to the academy?

The early scientists in their laboratories and the magicians in their magic circles (wearing a seamless robe of black, a cap of lead engraved with symbols of the Moon and Venus and Saturn, with a magic wand and a sword and a grimoire) were much confused in the public mind. And, indeed, their roles often overlapped.

ELECTROMAGNETISM

T. C. Lethbridge, Cambridge archaeologist and author of a study of ancient gods entitled "Gogmagog," in *Ghost and Ghoul* (1961), concluded that magic was akin to electromagnetism:

> Magic is the application of resonance, whether it takes the form of thought-reading, projecting images, prophesying, faith-healing, or causing inexplicable death and disaster to an enemy. . . .
>
> There is one thing about all this magic which seems to be constant. There must at some stage be a link between two minds. It may take such forms as a letter to a psychometrist, a spot of blood to the faith-healer or black magician, a hazel twig to the water-diviner, or a fixed locality to the projector of a ghost . . . a link of some sort must be established before the current of resonance will pass.

PICO

At one point humanist Giovanni Pico della Mirandola (1463–1494) invited "all the scientists of the world" to visit him at Rome and to debate any one or all of his nine hundred theses, among them many concerned with magic and witchcraft. As an occultist who had served Lorenzo the Magnificent and others, Pico considered that "magic is the most notable part of natural sciences," so Pope Innocent VIII forbade the debates on the grounds of heresy, instead appointing a commission to examine his ideas. Pico was under a cloud until 1493 when Pope Alexander VI, the last of the Schoolmen and a philosopher renowned all over Europe, absolved him from charges of heresy.

Alexander VI was not only a Borgia pope of execrable personal and political maneuverings (father of Cesare and Lucretia Borgia) but rumored to be a magician himself. If so, his luck ran out; many think his death in 1503 was due to his having drunk poisoned wine intended for his host, Cardinal da Corneto. Ironically, Pico too was poisoned—by his secretary—but not by mistake.

SAINT-SECAIRE

In Gascony they celebrated a kind of travesty mass called The Mass of Saint-Secaire, in which a rogue priest (assisted by his mistress or minion as acolyte) parodied the mass, everything reversed. It was said at night rather than before noon, it used a triangular Host instead of a round one, water instead of wine, etc. The sign of the cross was made not with the right hand but the left foot. Thought to bring death to enemies, it was frequently offered (and so was a counterspell worked up by the Church) in Gascony where pride, easily bruised honor, and easily lost tempers were proverbial.

GHOST DANCE MAGIC

The American Plains Indian was dependent on the buffalo for food, clothes, even shelter. When the buffalo began to vanish from the plains, under the reckless assault of white men, the Indians faced widespread starvation and disaster. Then in January 1889, a Paiute shaman named Wovoka announced that he had died and visited the Christian God in heaven and had been told that the Indians would be saved from destruction by the Ghost Dance Religion. If they performed the dance and did "no harm to anyone," their plains world would be restored to them. The buffalo would come back to life, as would their ancestors slain in wars with whites, and there would be no more hunger or sickness.

The new cult spread like wildfire, but it was not until it reached the Sioux in Nebraska and Dakota that new prophets began to urge retaliation against the whites. Indians were promised a magical "ghost shirt" that would protect them from white men's bullets.

Instead of allowing the excitement to run its course, white agents sent for the cavalry, and on December 29, 1890, at Wounded Knee Creek, South Dakota, the shameful massacre of three hundred men, women, and children occurred. One of the first to be killed was the fiery old shaman Sitting Bull.

RIGHT-HAND PATH AND LEFT-HAND PATH

Dennis Wheatley, a member of the Secret Planning Committee of Churchill's War Cabinet, later turned to writing popular novels with backgrounds of witchcraft and magic, which sold over 30 million copies in thirty different languages. In *The Devil and All His Works* (a 1971 history of demonism) he defined magic like this:

> Magical operations undertaken for an unselfish purpose belong to white magic, and those who perform them are followers of the Right-hand Path. Operations undertaken for personal ends belong to black magic, and those who perform them are followers of the Left-hand Path.
>
> A considerable number of people are born with psychic gifts. In most cases, when they become aware of this, they use them in minor ways, more usually for the harmless amusement of fortune-telling. As they have not made a deliberate study of magic, their powers are very limited and not having "crossed the abyss," they are not fully committed either to the Right-hand or the Left-hand Path.
>
> To achieve real power is quite a different matter, and a most arduous undertaking. It entails many years of preparation and an almost exclusive preoccupation with the supernatural.

MAGIC WORKS

Éliphas Lévi, a nineteenth-century occultist, asserted that "when anyone invokes the Devil with intentional ceremonies, the Devil comes, and is seen."

If you try hard enough, that's true.

This is no more than to say that anyone who believes sufficiently will experience what he seeks. Whether what is subjectively produced has also an objective reality the true believer cannot tell and perhaps does not care. You have, after all, the power within you to make yourself see anything you can imagine. Whether you should fully use that power or not is up to you.

But the power is *there*, as surely as you are.

MAGIC AND WORDS OF POWER

Magic is full of ambition. It promises power. It says it can make a man a "mighty god." It challenges fate and the laws of nature, attempting to remake the world "nearer to the heart's desire." It dares.

It deals in secret knowledge and words of power. Elsewhere I mention the secret name of God. Also powerful is the word *AGLA*, from *Aieth Gadol Leolam Adonai* ("The Lord will forever be great"). To banish demons that came to devour human hearts, King Solomon is supposed to have chanted *Lofam Solomon Iyouel Iyosemacui*. The Spaniards still say *Ojala ojal oja ojo* to get a husband. Johann Wier in *De Praestigiis Daemonum et Incantionibus ac Veneficiis* (1568) recommended for a toothache *Galbes galbat galdes galdat* (which, my friends say, works; try it) and *Irioni khirioni effer khuder fere* for hydrophobia (which I beg to doubt).

The magic circle for calling up demons.

Used with sigils (seals) and talismans and amulets inscribed with zodiacal symbols or the Tetragrammaton (four letters signifying the "I am" of Jehovah), or even on a scapular or blessed medal of a saint or on parchment inside the mezuzah at the door of a Jewish home or inside a prayer wheel in Tibet, words of power carry the hopes of millions and always have. With this, now just a joke, people used to think they could work miracles:

```
A B R A C A D A B R A
  B R A C A D A B R
    R A C A D A B
      A C A D A
        C A D
          A
```

It was magical, like the "Open Sesame" in *Ali Baba and the Forty Thieves* or "Shazzam" in a comic book—or the device on a door that opens it to you when you speak your name (provided your voice-print is in the computer's memory).

MAGIC MIRROR

In the British Museum you can see an obsidian mirror with an incredible history. How it reached London is not known, but it was definitely brought to Europe after Cortés got it from the Aztec magicians at Tenochtitlán, the capital of the great empire he and his *conquistadores* destroyed in Mexico. The mirror may be fourteenth century or earlier.

It was used by the great English astrologer Dr. John Dee (1527–1608), who listed it among his precious curiosities as "the Devil's Looking-glasse, a Stone." Other owners of the mirror included a seventeenth-century earl of Peterborough, Lady Elizabeth Germain (who died in 1769), a duke of Argyle (who bought it at auction in 1770), Horace Walpole (author of Gothic novels, who received it as a present from Lord Frederick Campbell), John Hugh Smith-Pigott, Lord Londesborough, Hollingworth Magniac, and Prince Alexander Soltykoff. The provenance is clear. What they used it for is obscure.

Dee is said to have employed the black mirror to perform famous feats in the late sixteenth century, sometimes in association with his friend and medium, Edward Kelley. They seem to have used it in 1581 when they were at Walton-le-Dale, Lancashire, searching for buried treasure. You can see their pictures in a rare old print recalling that event; it shows them in a graveyard, confronting a corpse in its shroud, which they have "materialized."

The British Musuem has other souvenirs of Dr. Dee, including some of his books and a disk of pure gold involved with a "vision" Kelley had at Kraków in 1584. Also displayed are three wax disks inscribed with magical figures and names; they were used under Dr. Dee's "shew stone," a crystal ball, which is still extant.

You do not need an obsidian mirror, of course, to try what Dr. Dee did in "scrying," for the top of a black marble clock or even a bowl of water (they say) will do quite as well; but this black mirror seems to me to have an aura about it, seems somehow to be charged with the physic energy of all the outstanding lives it touched, to retain some of the "power" that Cortés and Dr. Dee and others claimed to be able to find in it.

IS MAGIC IMMORAL?

In his master's thesis, "Five Ceremonial Magicians of Tudor-Stuart Drama," Robert J. Goltra, Jr., dealt with magicians in Christopher Marlowe's *Doctor Faustus*, Robert Greene's *Friar Bacon and Friar Bungay*, Anthony Munday's *John à Kent and John à Cumber*, the anonymous *John of Bordeaux*—all plays of the 1580–1590 period in England—and Shakespeare's *The Tempest* (1611). He found "at least three views" concerned with the morality of magic. These were what had come to be the orthodox view (magic was witchcraft and therefore forbidden), the less orthodox but commonly held view (magic was moral or immoral depending on the magician's source of assistance), and the unorthodox view ("presumably held by the goetians [black magicians], that no form of magic was immoral"). What's your view? Or do you not believe in magic at all?

MIRACLES AND MAGIC

In *Legends of the Panjab* (1884–1900) Richard Carnac Temple tells of "counterparts of saints," distinguishing between the miracle workers and the creators of magic. Miracles were good, magic evil. He writes:

Miracles may be defined as wonders legitimately performed, while magic embraces the class of illegitimate wonders. The actual deeds, whether the result of miraculous powers or magical arts, seem to be much the same. . . . It is good to work marvels miraculously, but very bad to arrive at the same result by magic.

This was the same way it was in Europe in the Age of Faith when saints were credited with and praised for miracles (usually performed for the benefit of others and principally the poor) while sorcerers were hated and feared for magic (usually performed for their own advantage).

STRANGE HERMETIC POWDER

Sir Kenelm Digby (1603–1665) traveled abroad both as naval commander in war and as diplomat in peace, and he brought home to England some great ideas from distinguished friends such as Descartes. He was one of the leading lights and a founding member of the Royal Society, but his undoubtedly important contribution to science—including the discovery that oxygen was essential to the life of plants—was accompanied by some very unscientific reasoning. Take his sympathetic powder, for example.

Sir Kenelm asserted that he had a wonderful recipe for an ointment that could cure wounds if applied not to the wound but to the weapon that made the wound. He also recommended a powder of "blue vitriol" that one applied not to the wounded person but to his bloodstained garments.

This imitative magic had a long history in the West but in this case was attributed to a mysterious Eastern source—and rotten wood:

> Strange Hermetic powder
> That wounds nine mile point blank would solder
> By skilful chemist at great cost
> Extracted from a rotten post. . . .

Perhaps the real source of the powder's "power" was that it left the wound alone, instead of applying the infection-breeding types of salve that were popular in Sir Kenelm's day.

ASTROLOGY AND HEAVENLY CAUSES

The most popular form of divination these days is astrology, in which it is popularly assumed that there is a *causal* connection between the stars and the lives of human beings—that is, that the stars and planets "influence" our actions. Not so. Not even the astrologers of ancient times argued for that. To them, as to every thinking person today, the idea that somehow distant heavenly bodies, reaching us across millions and billions of miles, could cause us to do this or that was incredible.

No, as Northrup Frye puts it, "Astrology is based on a conception of coincidence . . . a synchronic and acausal conception." Which means that the stars are arranged in such a way that there is a *pattern of coincidence* between them and human lives. Thus by studying those heavenly configurations and changes, we can understand more of terrestrial life and fate. Or so say astrologists.

MAGIC AND REALITY

Richard Cavendish suggests that magic is basically facing reality head-on:

Magic is a power-hunger pursuit and the obvious problem, in theory and frequently in practice, is that finding a positive value in evil can put a seal of approval on the worst of evil impulses. All the same, the attitude has something to be said for it, not as a method of explaining evil away by pretending it is something else, which ultimately will not do, but as a method of trying to deal with it which goes far beyond the confines of magical practice into more elevated philosophies, and eventually into the simple, homely advice to make the best of things.

HOW TO BECOME A SATANIST

Francesco Maria Guazzo, author of the authoritative *Compendium Maleficarum* (1608), tells us exactly what is involved in becoming a Satanist. You must:

1. speak your denial of the Christian faith;
2. get rebaptized, taking a new personal name in the name of the Devil;
3. have the traces of Christian baptism symbolically removed by the Devil's touch;
4. deny your godparents (who are given to help you grow in the Christian faith) and select two new sponsors (who will guide you in the Devil's ways);
5. make a gift of clothing to the Devil, betokening submission;
6. pledge allegiance to the Devil, taking the oath in the magic circle;

7. inscribe your new name in the Book of Death;

8. promise to sacrifice children to the Devil;

9. promise to pay annual tribute (usually black clothes) to the Devil;

10. receive the Devil's Mark, creating a secret and insensitive place on your body;

11. vow to the Devil to destroy holy relics and not reveal secrets of the *sabbat*.

If any group offers to sell you a Satanic Bible or enroll you in an atheist or materialist organization for a fee or fails to demand any or all of these requirements of you, be assured you are not dealing with Satan but just with some Church of the Quick Buck or something of that sort. Remember: not all con games are of the Devil nor frauds in his name!

MIND BENDING

There is nothing magical about hypnosis, now an approved scientific tool and not the mysterious "animal magnetism" of the days of Mesmer; and Transcendental Meditation and other manipulations of mind are commonplace.

But the history of magic and witchcraft is replete with extremes of hypnosis and self-hypnosis, hallucination and the power of suggestion, delusion and deception, "altered states," not all of them attributable to fasting or sexual excess, narcotic or so-called mind-expanding drugs, states of trance or ecstasy.

The alchemists were on the right track: The key to the metamorphosis of the mundane is first to transform the mind, and the mind suffers severe strain when operating at or beyond the borders of sanity.

Magic is a dangerous occupation, even if one does not think a protective circle drawn on the ground is essential. "Do what thou wilt" imposes heavy obligations. So do orthodox pronouncements forbidding dabbling with the forbidden or serving "other gods." Even if you do not fear prohibitions, you must be concerned about whether you can handle possible discoveries, within and without, for which nothing has prepared you. Even Saint Theresa's warning about "answered prayers" should give us pause. She cautioned against asking for things—you might get what you really shouldn't have or do not really need.

In the words of an old Latin phrase, *verbum sat sapienti*: "A word to the wise is sufficient."

TO CAST SPELLS WITH KNOTS

One can cast spells by tying knots. The Incas used the quipu—a cord with dependant cords in various colors, knotted in certain ways—to keep records or convey messages. From Scandinavian sorcerers one could buy cords with three knots in them: untie one, slight breeze; untie two, violent wind; untie three, tempest. Very useful for Vikings and other seafaring people.

Mohammed's sûra (chapter) CXIII in the Koran calls magicians' activities "the evil of [women who] are blowers on knots," and at the time of his revelation (commentators suggest) the Prophet was suffering bewitchment from an evil man and his daughters who were "tying eleven knots in a cord which they hid in a well." Here is the story as told by Sir E. A. Wallis in *Amulets and Talismans* (1968):

> The result was that the Prophet fell seriously ill and would undoubtedly have died had not God interfered. He sent down these Sûrahs to him, and also instructed the Archangel Gabriel [who often accompanied Mohammed as a sort of guardian angel] to tell him how to use them, and where the cord was hidden. Muhammed sent Ali to fetch the cord, and when it was brought he recited over the eleven knots the eleven verses of the two Sûrahs, and as he recited each line one of the knots untied itself; as soon as the last knot was loosed Muhammed was freed of his bewitchment, and recovered his normal health.

WOULD YOU LIKE TO WRITE IN YOUR
SPARE TIME FOR FUN, FAME, FORTUNE?

Writing is difficult. Many authors need curious stimuli. Some turn to drink. Thomas de Quincey, Wilkie Collins, Jean Cocteau, and others preferred opium. Byron found it helpful to keep a skull on his desk. Balzac wore a special robe when he was writing. Schopenhauer needed purple ink, or he could not write a line. One writer was helped by the smell of rotten apples, which he kept in his desk drawer. Ibsen stared at a picture of Strindberg over his desk and told himself: "He will be greater than I." Poverty has been a good goad.

In a mad book about Satanism, published in Grenoble in 1895, Domenico Margiotta alleges that Adriano Lemmi resorted to perhaps the most shocking stimulus of all. Lemmi (went the charge) "keeps constantly on his desk one of the hosts stolen from the Roman Catholic church and never writes a single line without having stabbed the Holy Eucharist with the pen called 'Calamus Transfigens' ["Piercing Reed"], which he maintains he received for this purpose from his familiar Sybacco, who appears to him with the horns of a bull and three eyes in his forehead."

ELDERBERRY WINE

Few people realize that the elderberry's name comes from Susannah and the Elders who spied on her while she bathed. The berries grow in a cluster upright until they begin to ripen; then the cluster reverses itself and hangs downward, as if in shame. Our forefathers said it hangs its head because it had given shelter to those prying elders.

With seven pounds of mashed elderberries and three gallons of water (plus a handful of raisins, several pounds of sugar, and some yeast) you can take the fruit of the tree and make elderberry wine, though it takes a year to do so and the result is not really worth the effort (in my view) unless you bolster it with brandy. On the other hand, with a wand of elder wood you can perform magic.

THE GIFT OF THE MAGI

The Magi were priests of the ancient Persian religion, which affirms that the supreme being Ahura Mazda (his name appears now mostly on light bulbs and rotary-motorized cars), created twins, reality and unreality. Magic bridges the two, complicating the religion of the Magi, which (Herodotus reported) had "no images of gods, no temples, no altars" and considered such things foolish. Later the Persians turned to the worship of Mithras (a god born of a virgin and resurrected after his death), and the astrologers and adepts gave way to more superstitious practitioners.

PETER OF ABANO

Peter of Abano (1250-1316) was the most famous magician of the very early fourteenth century, and also a famous physician, author of *Conciliator*

Differentium (1303). He argued that astrology was an essential part of the science of medicine, which the University of Paris and other august bodies of the time seemed to accept, and he brought into play a number of Arabic ideas from such doctors as ibn-Rushd (1126–1198), known as Averroës, that eventually were declared heresies by Pope Leo X.

One essentially heretical idea was astrology, for though Roger Bacon and many other scientists had accepted it completely, astrology was fatalistic, deprived man of his free will, and made him subject to the planetary influences. Whether it involved trafficking with demons or not, it put the emphasis not on God but on his creations, the stars and the planets. Saint Thomas Aquinas and many other influential teachers condemned astrology as leading to idolatry. The Church half believed in it and wholly feared it.

Peter of Abano himself (it is claimed) eventually abandoned belief in the stars. He may have been urged to this by having been twice hauled before the Inquisition on charges of practicing magic; he was acquitted at the first trial and died during the second. He is reported as having said that philosophy made him subtle, medicine made him rich, and astrology made him a charlatan.

He might have added that magic made him famous; to magic more than anything else he owed the reputation that caused him to have his statue erected in Padua and Urbino and his named recalled for long after his death.

RITUAL MAGIC

It is only possible here to suggest very briefly the incredible complexity of ritual magic, an art that requires long study and exact performance. But I can outline for you some of the things you need or must keep in mind to perform the ceremonies for some of the most common "intentions": namely achieving your ambition, success, or wealth; astral travel, divine reconciliation, or safe (ordinary) travel; studying for examination or safeguarding the home; disrupting friendship or attaining victory at arms.

To achieve your ambitions as described, you need the rite of Jupiter, auspicious stars (determined by study of astrology), blue hangings and garments, the help of Bethor, Chasmalim (as guardian angel), and the Archangel Zadkiel—and a number of symbols (unicorn, eagle, lion, dragon), metals (especially tin), gems (amethyst and sapphire), plants (oak, poplar, narcissus, agrimony), and perfumes (nutmeg, cinnamon, cloves, aloes, balm). You need incantations and magic implements and maybe sacrifices.

For astral travel, turn to the Moon, violet trappings, silver, crystal, pearl, quartz, hazel, almond, peony, dogs, geese, elephants, Phul and Gabriel, camphor, jasmine, white sandalwood (red is more common but useless here), and frankincense. The guardian angel needed here is Ishim.

For exams, try Saturn, and assemble indigo, civet, musk, crocodiles, crows, ash, yew, cypress, hemlock, lead, onyx, sapphire, a woman, Aratron the planetary spirit, Zaphael the archangel, and Aralim as guardian angel. There is a disagreement about colors. You could try yellow. Indigo may work better for you, though.

Causing discord or war is very serious indeed and needs the rite of Mars, with scarlet trappings, horses, wolves, bears, stags, a basilisk, rue, absinthe, a magic sword, lamb's tongue, iron implements, rubies, and Phaleg, Chamael, and the Seraphim.

So, if you and your friends, or just people you have heard about, are not getting truly magical results, maybe the proper tools are lacking—and, of course, the *timing* of magic and the *state of mind* of the magician and the *vibes* (as we might call them these says) must all be right. Ritual magic you may think is only for the credulous; most certainly it is not for the careless.

"DRAW A CIRCLE ROUND HIM THRICE"

Medieval magicians performed their rites within a magic circle (symbolic of protection, perfection, involvement, infinity) nine feet in diameter. This yielded the magical three times three and plenty of space to write Names of Power (in a band a foot wide) and place necessary bowls of water, herbs, crosses, the name of God anagrammatized, apt Biblical quotations, etc. The circle can be painted (ideally with paint containing elements of the philosopher's stone such as mercury and sulfur), made of a magnetized iron chain or (best of all) drawn with a magic sword.

This is convenient for me—I happen to live in a house with round towers nine feet in diameter inside—but inconvenient in a small apartment.

You do not need other circles outside the one I describe, despite what modern witches seem to think, unless you have assistants who need protection from the demon(s) to be summoned. Why not handle the work with no help? Demons are often easier to manage than assistants.

According to Éliphas Lévi, the circle drawn for evil magic (in that case absolutely drawn in the direction opposite the sun's movement) *must* be drawn with a magic sword. But there is really little use telling you how to make that useful object. Even if you had a magic sword, where would you get such other necessary supplies as strips of parchment (you could use goat's skin) nailed down with four nails from a criminal's coffin (the *Grand Grimoire* specifies a baby's coffin nails), vervain, chains from a gibbet, and candles of human fat in black wooden candlesticks?

THE RUNES

Runes were invented by Teutonic people as a crude way of writing messages, but they came in time to be considered powerful magic. They were thought to be able to keep the dead in their graves or to resurrect them, and each one had its name and its power.

The Saga of Egil, probably by Snorri Sturluson in the thirteenth century, tells how Egil, presented with an alehorn of poison drink, cut the ale runes on it, rubbed the runes with a drop of his own blood while he recited the magic incantation, and the horn "sprang asunder, and the drink spilled down into the straw."

At Björketorp in Sweden the runes that in Iceland protected Egil in Sweden protected a monument with the inscription:

I hid here magic runes, undisturbed by evil witchcraft. He shall die who destroys this monument.

The Swedes gave up the runes in the Middle Ages. The Icelanders passed a law in 1639 that anyone using the runes would be burned as a witch. But—in Germany in recent times—less civilized persons continued to attempt to use their magic. In the early twenties Adam Glauer (1875–1945), who liked to be called the Freiherr Rudolf von Sebottendorf, started a short-lived and virulently anti-Semitic organization called the German Orden, and Teutonic runes were part of their secret foolishness. This seems to have affected Heinrich Himmler, who chose *Sig* (the rune for "S") doubled as the symbol of his SS organization.

THE CRYSTAL BALL

If only from jokes and slang expressions, the average person knows that a crystal ball is used by some people to "see" the future. I think its so-called magic is in its ability to concentrate the mind of the "seer" (a bowl of water or any bright object or a number of other things would do as well) and permit him or her to look into his subconscious mind or even (some people think) to pick up "vibrations" from the "sitter" who is there to have a fortune told. To avoid the latter, some people have their fortunes read by proxies.

The holder for the ball is often inscribed with various magical symbols and names. Devotees treat the ball itself carefully, will let no one touch it lest they "charge" it wrong, and fortify it before they use it by making magical passes over it with the hands: with the right hand to render it stronger and more powerful, with the left hand to render it more sensitive. A good deal of this gesturing goes on before the ball is looked into.

Then in the ball, or in a kind of haze that comes between the "seer" and the ball after intense watching, one may see "clouds" of various hues and motions, and these are to be interpreted as follows:

white	favorable, auspicious
black	unfavorable, inauspicious
violet	
green	excellent, coming joy
blue	
red	
crimson	danger, trouble, illness
orange	deception, betrayal, slander
yellow	loss, trickery, unpleasant surprises

If the clouds are ascending, that is an affirmative answer to the question asked; if the clouds are descending, that is a negative response.

The basic book on this is John Melville's *Crystal-Gazing and the Wonder of Clairvoyance* (1920).

BLEEDING HOSTS MATERIALIZED?

Consecrated Hosts used in sorcery are usually stolen, but a man named Vintras used to materialize them, people claimed.

Pierre-Michel Vintras (1807–1875) was born Eugène Vintras and later was called Strathaniel ("Herald of God"). He was the author of an important *Oeuvre de la Miséricorde* ("Work of Compassion") and was well known for conducting magical ceremonies. The "fact" that at some of these ceremonies he used to materialize *bleeding* Hosts, in full view of everyone present, was often reported.

That people believed this was done, that they testified it was done before their very eyes and was not sleight of hand, is remarkable; and it is even more remarkable (I think) that the debates I have found in the literature of magic in France in the last century are not about whether he did that or not; they argue about whether he *ought* to have done that or not. His enemies call him not a trickster but a blasphemer; he is not accused of fakery but of evil magic.

Vintras with his shocking ceremonies surely was blaspheming in at least one way, for as early as Origen (185–255), who wrote in his *Homilies* that "scripture rightly prohibits the use of magic," the Church was moving ever farther away from exorcisms ("In My Name shall they cast out devils," Mark 16:17) and connecting magic only with the Evil One. "No good spirit obeys a magician," Origen warned.

EXURGENT MORTUI ET AD ME VENIUNT

"The dead arise and come to me," chants the necromancer. Incredible as it may seem, people once generally believed that the dead could be brought physically from their graves by magic, not the spirits (as in spiritualism) but the bodies. The artist and autobiographer Benvenuto Cellini claims soberly that a necromancer brought to him his dead mistress Angelica "for several minutes, materialized."

Just as Saul consulted the dead Samuel, in the *Epic of Gilgamesh* the hero evokes the ghost of his friend Enkidu. In the *Odyssey* the hero consults the dead soothsayer Tiresias. In Aeschylus' *The Persians* Atossa's calling up of the ghost of Darius the Great is regarded as perfectly possible and credible. The ghost of Constantine the Great (Michael Glycas wrote) appeared to his father, summoned by the magic of Santabarenus. Macbeth has the witches call up people yet unborn, the line of kings to be descended from Banquo (whom Macbeth has had murdered), including James VI of Scotland and I of England, sitting in Shakespeare's audience at a royal performance of the play.

As one of its tasks, the Society for Psychical Research has energetically weeded out fraudulent practitioners. But contemporary mediums have a self-serving rule: Touch a "manifestation," and the medium in a trance will die.

My favorite medium story involves a man invited to quiz the spirits at a séance. He asked if he could see his grandfather. After some impressive mumbo jumbo, the luminous figure hovered near. The young man was told, "I am your grandfather." He then asked if he could pose a question. Granted permission, he solemnly asked: "Grandfather, what are you *doing* here; you aren't dead!"

That was the end of that little séance.

2
Witchcraft

WITCHCRAFT differs from magic in two particulars. First, it is, above all, the people's magic. The witch did not pore over cabalistic screeds or ancient grimoires (magicians' manuals), draw on the ground elaborate circles filled with Hebraic inscriptions, or chant the many names of gods and devils. Usually she could not read or write at all. She had her little charms and spells, her amulets and fetishes, her herbal cures and secret potions, but essentially her magic was performed on a small scale. She could cure your headache, but she did not raise spirit armies.

Second, witchcraft—unlike magic, which was one of the learned arts— is considered the survival of an ancient form of worship, tens of thousands of years old. This "Old Religion," or worship of a Horned God, is said to have existed side by side with Christianity. (Not all historians agree on this theory, and even those who do have not worked out the connection between this "worship" and the village wise woman with her charmed herbal cures.) The great feasts of this supposed Horned God were four, all celebrated at midnight: February 1–2 (Candlemas); April 31–May 1 (May Day, Beltane, or Walpurgis); July 31–August 1 (Lammas); and October 31–November 1 (the eve of All Saints Day, or All Hallows Eve). The last of these has, of course, survived as the children's holiday, Halloween.

On these four nights, witches were said to leave their village homes by stealth, repair to the meeting place where they held their sabbat, or assembly, presided over by a man wearing the mask and skins of a goat and representing the Horned God. It was these meetings that Christian leaders interpreted as Satan worship.

In the early Middle Ages, sabbats were either not known to the authorities or were quietly overlooked. A woman charged with witchcraft— for casting a murrain (sickness) on a neighbor's cattle, say—was usually fined, reprimanded, and released. It was not until the fifteenth century, when the tensions of the highly charged Renaissance galvanized a sleeping Europe into activities of all sorts, that the really savage persecutions began. They were to continue for nearly three hundred years.

WITCH MASK OF DORSET

If anyone has an ooser for sale, I'd like to know. There were a great many of them around at one time, or so it is claimed. I suspect a few examples are still to be found somewhere.

An ooser was a horned mask, with a boss on the forehead where some people would locate the psychic "third eye," and was used to give the wearer the appearance of a devil or a heathen god. In seventh-century England, Theodore, archbishop of Canterbury (688–690), tried to root out their use:

> Whoever at the Kalends of January [Christmas season] goes about as a stag or bull; that is making himself into a wild animal and dressing in the skin of a herd animal, and putting on the heads of beasts; those who in such wise transform themselves into the appearance of a wild animal, penance for three years because this is devilish.

Doreen Valiente in *An ABC of Witchcraft Past & Present* (1973) draws our attention to *os* (god) in names such as Oswald (God-power), Osmund (God-protection), and so on. So the ooser may have been worn in imitation of *os*, or a heathen god.

The mask certainly suggests the Horned God of the witches. One of his titles, *Hu*, meaning "everywhere," explains the "Har, har, hou, hou" cries reported of witches dancing on the "goat field"—that is, the sabbat meeting place. His horns and cloven feet and tail are the probable origin of our modern concept of the Devil. The costume of the dancer who wore the ooser is similar to that seen in the most ancient cave paintings, where men are depicted cavorting in the skins of animals.

Valiente reports:

> As late as 1911, a Dorset newspaper carried a report of a man being charged with frightening some girls by chasing them when he was "dressed in a bullock's skin and wearing an ooser."

If you see another of those horned and horrible masks, let me know; I'd like to make sure it goes to those in Dorset to whose supposedly long tradition it belongs and does not simply hang on someone's wall as decoration.

APPLES

As one example of how ordinary things are related to sorcery, take the apple. Throughout history, apples have been thought of as having magical properties.

Remembering pre-Christian customs, English countrymen still "wassail" their apple trees and have many folk customs related to apples. Without any idea of the origin of the "game," children bob for apples on Halloween or tell the initial of the one they will marry by throwing apple peels.

One of the most terrifying moments of my childhood was when, in Walt Disney's *Snow White*, I saw the horrible old witch offer a shiny apple to our heroine. If you saw this cartoon as an impressionable child, I'll bet it scared you too.

Even more frightening, when seen through our eyes, is this report by one of the earliest good writers on witchcraft in England, Joseph Glanvill, author of *Sadducismus Triumphatus* (1681). He was Charles II's chaplain and a leading scientific mind of the period. He wrote:

> On Sunday, the 15th of November, 1657, about Three of the Clock in the Afternoon, Richard Jones, then a sprightly youth about twelve years old, Son of Henry Jones of Shepton Mallet in the County of Somerset, being in his Father's house alone, and perceiving one looking in at the Windows, went to the Door,

where one Jane Brooks of the same Town (but then by name unknown to this Boy) came to him. She desired him to give her a piece of close Bread, and gave him an Apple.

Soon after the boy suffered from fits and neighbors said he flew over the garden wall. He became the center of controversy: Was he bewitched? Jane Brooks's sister (who had once said "How do ye, my honey?" to the boy) escaped after close questioning, but Jane Brooks herself was sentenced to death by the Chard Assizes and hanged on March 26, 1658.

ALEX SANDERS

Seduced by his seventy-four-year-old grandmother in his teens, Alex Sanders says this started him off as a witch. His biography was called *King of the Witches*. He is credited with founding 107 covens.

NICHOLAS TROTT

Judge Trott told a Charleston, South Carolina, jury in 1703:

They that have given good proof of apparitions and witches have done service to the common cause of religion, for if there be such creatures as witches, then there are certainly spirits by whose aid and assistance they act, and by consequence there is another invisible world of spirits. . . . That there are creatures [such] as witches I make no doubt, neither do I think that they can be denied, without denying the truth of the Holy Scriptures, or most grossly perverting the sense of them.

If you believe in God, you believe in Satan, in angels, in devils—or so claimed such seventeenth-century experts as the clergyman Cotton Mather and King James I.

BABA YAGA

One of the most gruesome of European folktales involves the hideous Russian witch named Baba Yaga, who is said to live in a ramshackle cottage that moves around on chicken legs. It is surrounded by the skulls and bones of her victims, many of the children like those of the hag in Hansel and Gretel.

Baba Yaga is said not only to be a cannibal but also to have the power to turn you to stone with a glance. She secretly sucks the breasts of beautiful women while they sleep, rendering them shriveled and ugly. She eats children and consumes the souls of the dead. And at night Baba Yaga rides through the air not on a broom but on a blazing mortar.

"GIMME THAT OL' TIME RELIGION"

There are more survivals of paganism than you imagine, just disguised a little for Christian consumption. In medieval times, old statues of Venus and Cupid were sometimes equipped with halos and dubbed "Madonna and Child." Zoroastrianism gave us Easter eggs, and Teutonic animism produced Christmas trees.

In the United States many old customs still flourish and superstitions persist, even if not one person in a million who refuses to walk under a ladder knows that the bad luck is supposed to come from violating the Trinity or that the black cat who crosses your path may be a witch's familiar.

Some of the American customs came from England, and there they also still flourish. I have attended celebrations of the goddess Flora (turned into the Queen of the May) and "clipped a church" (the congregation stands around in a ring of power, holding hands, as the Romans did on the Feast of Lupercalia) and attended many harvest festivals (blessing the plow, decorating the church, strewing the church floors with hay, rush bearing). Our pagan ancestors would find it very familiar if they dropped in today. The rising from the dead in mummers' plays and the antics of morris dancers have very distant pagan origins. "Pace egging" (rolling Easter eggs) goes back to rolling the stone away from the tomb of Jesus.

I have seen the bonfires not only on Guy Fawkes' Day (November 5—when one of the conspirators who tried to blow up the houses of Parliament more than three hundred years ago is burned in effigy) but on Midsummer Eve (June 23). A string of bonfires—"good" fires? bone fires?—stretches across Cornwall's ancient duchy that night, and people jump over the flames for fertility, throwing in the "simples" and herbs of witches' concoctions.

London has not seen a maypole since the last century (and I believe they are still illegal in Massachusetts) but you can still dance around one in Devon. These days the garlands of Garland Day (in Abbotsbury, Dorset) wind up on the war memorial, but the pagan origins are still visible. In certain Yorkshire towns, the Devil's Knell is tolled each Christmas Eve—but some of the age-old customs are very much alive.

TO KEEP AWAY WITCHES

To keep witches out of your house, Hispanics in Texas suggest you kneel and recite this prayer three times in a low voice:

> Cuatro esquinas tiene mi casa
> Cuatro angeles que la adoran,
> Lucas, Marcos, Juan, y Mateo.
> Ni brujas, ni hechiceras,
> Ni hombre malchechor.
> En el Nombre del Padre,
> Y del Hijo, y del Espiritu Santo.

> Four corners has my house.
> Four angels adore it,
> Luke, Mark, John, and Matthew.
> Neither witches, nor charmers,
> Nor maleficent man [can harm me].
> In the Name of the Father,
> And of the Son, and of the Holy Ghost.

HOODOO

A hoodoo bag contains certain herbs, dirt (most effective if from a grave), maybe a piece of cloth (preferably red), even hair or fingernail clippings of the person to be hoodooed. To gain the power to hoodoo, a person has to sell his or her soul to the Devil, who appears for the purpose as a black bird at midnight on the darkest possible night.

Look around your house or apartment to be sure you have not been hoodooed. If there is a snake bone in your pillow or "wreathes" or "knots" in a feather pillow or a little bag tied to the tester of your bed, you have been hoodooed. Look for cards stacked over the door or a little doll with a pin in it or a loaf of bread with pitch on it or salt and pepper on your doorstep. Look for peculiar marks on your body, wounds that will not heal, a *gris-gris* (talisman) made of feathers or horsehair and other materials tied up with a red thread, or unusual knots in your horse's tail or mane, or pains in the wrists (if your wrists "open," you can "close" them by wearing bits of red flannel around your wrists). If you open your front door and there is a tiny coffin, with or without a hoodoo doll in it, you are in extremely bad trouble: This (in case you missed the other two) is your third and last warning that you have had the curse put upon you, and you are going to die.

You are not powerless, of course. You can get another hoodoo woman (other than the one who laid the curse) to take it off you—even to send it back whence it came. You can let a little blood or have teeth drawn (hoodoo often enters the teeth) or burn special candles (any color but red—red is the color of candle that brings down the curse on people) or say special prayers or destroy the hoodoo doll or bag with fire or running water. You can discover if people who have visited and have expressed sympathy with the trouble you have suffered are the actual cause of it or not. Just melt lead and cool it soon after their visit. If it cools smooth, they are friends; if it cools rough, they are "bad mouth" enemies.

Wear a silver coin on a string around your neck or get some other charm against falling victim to a hoodooer in future. Or become a hoodoo adept yourself, for protection!

TRANSVECTION

Goya's *Caprichios* shows witches on brooms sailing through the air. Many people used to think witches really did fly, and they testified to it under oath and under torture. Some learned men said it was impossible, but added that if witches thought they could fly, then that was proof enough that they had sold their souls to the Devil. Burn them anyway, said seventeenth-century Scots.

The earliest picture I can find of witches depicted as flying is by Ulrich Molitor, dated 1489, and shows them mounted on forked branches, rather like dowsing rods, not the brooms you see in pictures of Halloween witches. Soon popular art depicted witches aloft on sticks, tree trunks, pokers— anything phallic, in fact—but broomsticks predominated, since the broom was a symbol for a woman. Italian witches (*stregas*) traveled on mules. There are stories of the parking lot at sabbats containing he-goats (always black), dogs (black), and these days Rolls-Royces (also black).

The broomsticks were anointed with a special unguent. Witches on trial were always being asked for the recipe. The ointments usually would have excited the sexual organs, numbed the feet and hands, and made the witches "high," if not on their broomsticks, then on drugs. Hallucinogenic incense could also have had an effect.

Some people were just not buying the story. Gian Francesco Ponzinibio's *Tractatus Subtilis et Elegans de Lamiis* (the Lamia being a predatory witch that turns up frequently in Romantic literature) published in Venice in 1563 was neither subtle nor elegant in its dismissal of the whole idea of witches flying.

Martin Luther introduced a healthy Protestant skepticism. Of course witches did not fly to their sabbats, their *souls* were transported there, he said. Had he taken one step more and said they went there *in their minds*, I think he would have hit upon the truth.

Luther, however, was up against equally argumentative, dogmatic, and learned Biblical scholars ready to cite him chapter and verse. Did not Satan transport Jesus to the pinnacle of the Temple? Had not Christ gone straight up to Heaven on the day of the Ascension? Saints were occasionally levitated. So why not witches?

Witches kept confessing they flew, proof of a pact with the Devil. One seventeen-century verdict I like was: "Not guilty. No flying." Bishop François Sadoval in *Historie de Charles V* states that a witch was kind enough to give him a demonstration of flying, right in court. Taking her helpfulness into account, he pardoned her on the charge of witchcraft.

Today we talk more of teleportation and astral projection.

SWINGING WITCHES

Magic and witchcraft often demand highly excited states in the participants. Medieval witches sometimes used to be put into sacks and swung from trees to bring on ecstatic visions.

I know a New York wizard who used one of the rides at Coney Island for exactly this purpose. But the Cyclone and roller coasters in general made it "impossible to concentrate."

BLACK MASS

Over the centuries, black masses, travesties of Christian ritual, have been said for patrons as different as the fifteenth-century soldier Gilles de Retz and the eccentric nineteenth-century novelist William Beckford. The black mass, often undertaken by some renegade priest, has been recorded as early as the seventh century and is regarded by French historian Jules Michelet as a "peasant revolt against the church." Other scholars believe, as we have said elsewhere, that it was in reality a survival of ancient pagan religious forms.

It was usually practiced at night and in secret out of fear of Christian reprisal. Some members of the "congregation," called a coven, rubbed themselves with the juice of belladonna or deadly nightshade (the source of the modern drugs atropine and hyoscine), which is said to have given them the illusion of flying through the air to the rendezvous. This was always a lonely spot, preferably a ruined or deconsecrated church. There, torches and braziers of pitch burned balefully, adding to the smoky confusion.

Roman Catholic ritual is turned upside down, into sacrilege and blasphemy. In place of aspersion with holy water, the coven is sprinkled with urine. The kiss of peace, a ceremonial embrace among the officiating clergy at high mass, becomes a kiss on the posterior. The body of a nude woman is the "altar." Everything is black: the vestments, the hangings, the garments of the participants. Black bread and black wine (like the heather beer of the Picts) can be used, but a stolen Host is considered the most efficacious. Sometimes a toad is elevated and broken instead of the Host. Some authorities recommend a slice of black or red turnip. Often a goat or other animal is sacrificed.

Early in the fourteenth century, in an effort to free himself of money troubles, Philip IV of France attacked the rich and powerful Knights Templars with charges of witchcraft, sodomy (acts of homosexuality), and cannibalism. Under torture, the Grand Master, Jacques de Molay, and 140 knights confessed to such abominations as substituting the nude body of a young boy for that of a nude woman at the "altar" of a black mass, and on March 18, 1314, de Molay was burned at the stake. Since that day, the toad used at black masses has been called a "philippe," after the king.

Today a black mass in honor of the Horned God is most likely to be held in a suburban house or a city apartment. A pungent incense from the local "head shop" replaces the urine, subdued electric light illuminates the scene, and if a sacrifice is made, it is presumably carried out with neatness and decorum. The performance, however, is often expected to end in a sex party, much like the original.

WOMEN'S LIBERATION

Jules Michelet claimed the black mass was "the redemption of Eve from the curse Christianity had laid upon her," a liberation because "at the Sabbath woman fulfills every office," while women still cannot be ordained priests in many Christian churches.

But at the sabbat, Michelet points out, woman "is priest, and altar, and consecrated host, whereof all people communicate. In the last resort, is she not the very God of the Sacrifice as well?"

WITCH TREE

An example (which can stand for many) of how corruption of a word can give birth to a folk belief is to be found in the case of "witch hazel" or "witch wood," names for the mountain ash or rowan, long believed to have magical powers to defend against witchcraft.

But, as dialect shows us with the name "wick wood," these trees are not connected with witches but simply "alive." The Anglo-Saxon was *cwic-beám*, and that *cwic* ("alive") we still have, though you may never have noticed it, in expressions such as "cut to the quick" and "the quick and the dead."

The great Elizabethan herbalist Gerard (1597) refers to this: "This *Ornus* or great Ash is named . . . in English wilde Ash, *Quicken tree*, Quickbeame tree, and *Whicken tree*."

But the sacred grove of the Druids and other tree worshippers combined with the corruption of the language in English to make a witch tree out of an "alive tree," and in German also now magic is connected with the witch hazel, called *Zauberstrauch* ("magic shrub").

FASCINATING AND EVIL GLANCES

From the time before history, throughout the world, men have believed that witches and similar malefactors can injure with a glance. They call this the Evil Eye. In England women were burned at the stake for it. In Ireland witches with "eye-biting" powers were said to harm cattle. In Cornwall, as recently as a century ago, people bought "witch powders" to protect children or cattle that had been "overlooked" by someone possessed of the Evil Eye. A writer in *The Graphic* (December 1882) said that such witchcraft was more common in the West of Britain then that it was in Africa.

Fear of the Evil Eye is noted in many phallic and other amulets worn by Italian-Americans (and others) and is part and parcel of life in such places as southern Italy and Sicily. Montague Summers writes:

> Throughout Italy nobody is so feared as he who has this baleful influence, *mal d'occhio*. In the South *jettatura* [sic] is the common term. At the appearance of a person having this reputation the most crowded street in Naples will empty in a moment. The cry *Jettatore!* is heard. Everyone vanishes, rushing into shops, into churches, up entries, down side-alleys, helter-skelter, anywhere.

In Italian thinking, anyone can be born with this destructive gaze. The *jettatore*, writes Lawrence Di Stassi in 1981, "through no apparent fault of his own . . . is said to be born with eyes that damage whatever they see. Wherever he goes, he is feared." F. T. Elworthy in *The Evil Eye* (1895) tells of a hapless Polish father who believed that he possessed this unconscious power; he blinded himself rather than do harm to his children with his glance.

In popular belief, not even popes were spared the Evil Eye. Giovanni Maria Mastai-Ferrett (1792–1878), who reigned as Pope Pius IX, *Pio Nino*, was widely believed to have the *mal d'occhio*. In his last years, wherever he went in procession, the streets emptied; people who could not avoid his presence averted their eyes, crossed themselves (or their fingers), made the defensive sign by extending the first and fourth fingers and holding back the second and third and the thumb. Actually Pius IX was a devout prelate, much involved in the bitter battles in Italy between Church and State, and it was in his papacy that the doctrine of papal infallibility was declared. But infallible or not, Italians (and others) were terrified to look him in the eye.

THOSE SATANISTS DON'T COMMIT SACRILEGE

And they won't say a black mass. Gordon Wellesley in *Sex and the Occult* (1975) points out that "to the true follower of Lucifer the Host or the Crucifix means nothing, so to him there would be no point in violating them or committing sacrilege." A true Satanist has no interest in outraging Christians, Jews, or Muslims; he has his own "god" to serve.

But, you say, to *me* they are committing a sacrilege. However, it's God who is concerned in matters of that sort, and any good theologian will tell you without intention there can be no sin.

NAMES

You can do witchcraft using names; it's connected with numerology. In covens people often use just first names or adopted names. In some magical organizations, one is baptized in the name of the Devil (by some thought essential if one has previously been baptized a Christian) and given a new name. In others people take new names as, for example, people do upon entering certain religious orders.

Familiars usually have names, as you may have noted from the witches' scenes in *Macbeth* (where Greymalkin and others turn up), from the play *Bell, Book, and Candle* (where the cat has the old-fashioned name of Pyewacket), and so on, if not from the grimoire handbooks where cats are to be called Greedigut, Howffbacket, and such.

Other ceremonies require Egyptian or the ability to use the alphabets of the Rosicrucians or Masons, runes, the Ogham scratches (named after the Gaulish god of speech), even the Malachim alphabet or Celestial script.

BANISHING WITCHES

The Scots waved firebrands at Halloween and chanted:

> This is the night of Halloween.
> All the witches to be seen,

Some of them black, and some of them green,
And some of them like a randy quean [prostitute].
Halloween we fear will come.
Witchcraft will be done by some.
Burn your brand and let us see
Confusion to the witches be!

Cleansing by fire is an old practice but be careful: Certain candles can attract spirits.

SATAN'S MEMBER

Marguerite de Sare, aged seventeen, of Labourd, France, told inquisitor Pierre de Lancre, a famous expert on witchcraft, that the Devil's penis was "like a mule's, [he] having chosen to imitate that animal as best endowed by nature; that it was as long and thick as an arm." De Lancre commented:

Quite the opposite is told by [Henri] Bouget, who says that the witches he was prosecuting in the Franche-Comté have never seen one longer than a finger and correspondingly thin. All that can be said is that Satan serves the witches of Labourd better than he does the witches of Franche-Comté.

Sylvester Pierias wrote in 1521 that evidence was plentiful to suggest that the Devil's penis was bifurcated. Many witches spoke of this under torture and added that the Devil's semen was cold, his foreplay was clumsy, and his performance was painful.

De Lancre's *Tableau de l'Inconstance des Mauvais Anges* (1612) recorded this "eye-witness account" of a sabbat's orgiastic conclusion:

The Devil in the form of a goat, having his member in the rear, had intercourse with women by jiggling and shoving that thing against their belly. Marie de Marigrane, aged 15 years, resident of Biarritz, testified that she had often seen the Devil copulate with a group of women, whom she knew by forename and surname, and that it was the custom of the Devil to have intercourse with the beautiful women from the front and the ugly from the rear.

BATTLE DRESS

The Mau-Mau in Kenya and the blacks revolting against the Tshombe government of the Congo in midtwentieth century underwent witchcraft ceremonies to make them invulvernable to the bullets of the enemy. Then they ran berserk.

That old word "berserk" goes back to the Vikings who in "bear shirts" ran amok, also considering themselves impervious, invincible. Their mad eyes and terrifying screams as they attacked in a state of frenzy frightened their opponents.

Some British regiments still wear bearskin busbies, but the old British habit of painting soldiers blue to scare the enemy (that so shocked the invading Romans) has now been abandoned. It is impossible to say when the British stopped painting themselves to strike horror into their enemies, but we all know that warpaint (which also had a magical component) was used by the Amerindians.

SURFING WITCH

At Newbury in 1643 during the early days of the Civil War in England the Roundheads of Cromwell got a shock from a surfing witch. She was "taken by some of the Parliament Forces, as she was standing on a small planckboard and sayling on it over the River of Newbury."

GOOD WITCH

"Witch" originally meant a good witch. The Anglo-Saxon *wicca* means "a magician who weakens the power of evil." All witchcraft means to do good; the bad use of these powers is sorcery.

THE LEGACY OF WITCHCRAFT

Guazzo's influential *Compendium Maleficarum* (1608), an encyclopedia of witchcraft, spoke of "the contagion to children by their sinful parents" and the fact that witches introduced their offspring into the evil rites; indeed it was suggested that witchcraft was almost hereditary. Certainly many seventeenth-century documents attest to women dedicating their children to the Devil, or so they confessed.

Many people claim that witchcraft has run in their families for generations, and in America it is often believed that powers such as "second sight" are inherited. Of course, though most of the witches accused in England between 1556 and 1712 were women and children, the word "witch" can also mean a man; some fathers handed on the tradition and maybe even the talents to their sons.

In Africa it is generally believed that magical powers are inherited but only through the mother. Most American witches and even warlocks claim to derive their powers, if they believe them to have been "gifts," from their mothers.

The Rental of Sir Edward Moore (1677) tells us he had two tenants who were witches, Margaret Ley and her sister, the Widow Bridges. Their mother "who died thirty years agone," it is said, "was poor." When she died "she had nothing to leave" the girls but "her two spirits," familiars who assisted the daughters all through their lives. "God bless me," commented one writer, "and all mine from such legacies. Amen."

It is interesting to note that the executioners who put the witches to death were also in a trade handed down in families. Members of the famed Famille Samson served as Monsieur de Paris (official executioner and torturer) for seven consecutive generations, 1635–1889.

MACBETH'S NIGHT

Now o'er the one half world
Nature seems dead, and wicked dreams abuse
The curtain'd sleep; witchcraft celebrates
Pale Hecate's offerings; and wither'd murder,
Alarum'd by his sentinel the wolf,
Whose howl's his watch, thus with his stealthy pace,
With Tarquin's ravishing strides, towards his design
Moves like a ghost.
            —William Shakespeare

AKHELARRE

The above is the Basque word for sabbat which means "goat pasture." That's where these assemblages of witches were supposed to be held.

WELSH RABBITS

The eminent historian and naturalist Giraldus Cambrensis (Gerald de Barri, 1147–1223) recounts many marvels with a straight face, among them how witches turned into hares and, in this form, drank milk from the cattle.

URBAN BLIGHT

The sixteenth-century diary of Giancinto Gigli in the library of the Vatican tells an incredible story of machinations involved in the struggle for the papacy. It was a chancy time to be pope anyway; between 1590 and 1592, three different men wore the tiara.

Gigli was the nephew of Cardinal d'Ascensio, believed by some to have a good chance at the throne of Peter—if and when Urban VII should vacate it. Other people were anxious to hasten that along, too—by witchcraft if necessary.

Now, trying to encompass the death of a pope by witchcraft was tricky. But Urban VII seemed vulnerable, so it was worth a try.

They did a sort of dry run with the wax image of a woman. The woman died. Encouraged, they made one of the pope. But it would not melt. They tried again but realized they needed a stronger spell, one that used human blood.

The conspirators drew lots to see whose blood they would use. Gigli lost. He demurred. And he pointed out that Cardinal d'Ascensio was *his* uncle and that later on the conspirators might find themselves in a position where it would be useful to have him to intercede for them. Seeing the wisdom of this argument, all the conspirators could do was to draw lots a second time.

The intended blood-supply then proved no more willing than Gigli had been. In fact, he ran right off to the Holy Office (the Inquisition) and spilled the beans, naming all the conspirators.

They were immediately rounded up, quickly tried, condemned, and burned alive in the Campo dei Fiori for trying to bring about the death of the Vicar of Christ.

Urban died shortly afterward anyway. His successor was *not* Cardinal d'Ascensio.

QUALIFIED M.D.

The witch doctor in the New Hebrides is not considered fully prepared until he has captured a wild boar whose tusks have grown in a spiral. He then wears a tusk on a cord around his neck, much the way your doctor puts his diplomas on the wall. It inspires confidence.

THE WITCH OF ENDOR

The Witch of Endor was acceptable for King Samuel to visit, despite the law that "thou shalt not suffer a witch to live," because she was not a witch; she was a diviner.

The Scriptures call her *ba'alath ob* (mistress of a talisman), not *kashaph* (sorceress). The Hebrew words hint at her practice of cutting herself and using the blood ("the life itself") in the worship of Baal.

In *The Discoverie of Witchcraft* hard-headed Reginald Scot suggests the Biblical word meant simply "poisoner," not witch, an idea some later scholars have embraced.

SAINT PATRICK AND THE WITCHES

A fanciful story is recorded in Charles Kirkpatrick Sharpe's *A Historical Account of the Belief in Witchcraft in Scotland* (1884):

> About the year 338, the singular piety of St. Patrick, according to tradition, became so offensive to the devil, that he incensed the whole body of witches in Scotland against him. In a band they assailed the astonished saint, who fled toward the river Clyde,

near the mouth of which he found a little boat, wherein he immediately leapt, and set off for Ireland. It is well known that witches cannot cross a running stream in pursuit of their prey; but these tore a huge fragment of rock from an neighboring hill and hurled it after Patrick, taking, however, so bad an aim, that the mass fell harmless to the ground. . . .

It became, "with some additions from art," the fortress of Dumbarton.

A CAVEAT TO IRISH WITCHES

I pass along this warning to the half dozen Irish witches I happen to know personally.

So far as I can determine, the statute of the Irish Parliament of 1586 (passed to bring Irish law into line with that of the English) has never been repealed. Now, the English have given up punishing witches, but this Irish law threatens the pillory or imprisonment or both for the first offense and death as a felon for the second.

It also provides that the government can confiscate the witch's property, long a powerful encouragement in the rest of Europe to witch hunting.

GAY WITCHES

In the 1970s homosexuality, with sadomasochistic overtones, was combined in the published works of a New York "gay witch," Dr. Leo Martello, who claimed to come from a long line of Sicilian witches. He wrote several books publicized in *Gay* magazine, and rumors were rife that there were gay covens of witches dedicated to the androgynous god Baphomet. Other such covens were said to base their sex-magic rituals on what they could find out about the Knights Templars, whose Grand Master was burned for "abominable practices" in 1314.

Sybil Leek devotes a long chapter in one of her entertaining books on witchcraft to "Homosexuality and Witchcraft." In the 1980s the gay witch cult appears to be more active on the West Coast, especially in Los Angeles and San Francisco, somewhat dampened by fears of AIDS.

The Greeks (and some later peoples) believed that in the sex act, through the semen, "the virtues of the lover were transferred to the beloved." That quotation is from Gordon Wellesley's *Sex and the Occult* (1975) and he continues:

It was believed that this happened physically through the transmission of the semen which contained the essence of the soul, at least in part, for which the copulative act was necessary. This allegedly metaphysical explanation lent, in the eyes of the Greeks, a dignity to the homosexual act never ascribed to it by the prudery of later centuries. It refutes the suggestion that to the Greeks it [paederasty] was solely a form of sexual self-indulgence.

Today the slang vocabulary of child molesters—or at least of the minority of them who are gay—indicates that the concept of transfer of qualities (especially the desired ones of youth and beauty) are somehow still at the back of the minds of men who refer to boys as comestibles: "chicken," "twinkies," etc. As some Amerindians ate the heart of a brave enemy in an attempt to acquire, by sympathetic magic, some of the dead enemy's courage, so some men appear to be trying to "consume" the youth of their boyish companions. *Having* another person takes on quite a magical significance, and the term "sexual communion" an extraordinary and to many very offensive connotation.

INEXPENSIVE ROOM PURIFIER

Common salt sprinkled on the fire, they say, will drive evil spirits and witches right out of the room.

TEARS

Don't expect a witch to shed salt tears. First, witches are supposed to be very afraid of salt. Second, witches can never weep more than three tears at a time, the old books assert.

THE WITCH OF EDMONTON

In the seventeenth-century play *The Witch of Edmonton*, based on the true story of Elizabeth Sawyer, hanged for witchcraft in 1621, the witch character is made to describe herself as "poor, deformed, and ignorant," and to sell her soul to the Devil (who appears to her in the form of a dog) in order to get back at the locals who persecute her:

> Some call me witch;
> And being ignorant of myself, they go
> About to teach me how to be one.

The authors—Thomas Dekker, John Ford, and William Rowley—may have put their finger on an important truth here. For many of the despised hags who eventually "confessed" to being witches and trying to work evil on their neighbors may well have gotten the idea in the first place just because they were described in malicious rumors as crones in league with the Devil. "Poor, deformed, and ignorant," they may have hoped that witchcraft would enable them to get their own back.

GOSSIPS

Talk about male chauvinist pigs! One of the earliest books on European witchcraft explains why there are more female than male witches: Women can't keep a secret; they tell each other what they have learned. For every sorcerer, 10,000 sorceresses, they said.

COMMITTED TO MEMORY

Julius Caesar in *De Bello Gallico* mentions that the Druids in Britain were forbidden to write down the mysteries of their religion but had to retain them in memory and hand them down from one generation to another by word of mouth. Thus the ancient magical lore would be preserved pure, they thought.

Some of magic and witchcraft today reaches us just like that. Much may have been lost, but much is remembered as well.

WITCHES AND MAGIC IN ENGLAND

Witchcraft has a long history in England. Saint Augustine rapidly converted some British kings in the seventh century (and hence, in those feudal times, all their vassals), but he could not stamp out the Old Religion completely. As many claim, it's not dead yet.

In 685 Theodore, archbishop of Canterbury, felt it necessary to point out that it was un-Christian to sacrifice to demons. He also took exception to frequenting pagan temples and participating in pagan ceremonies. So Withraed, king of Kent in 690, fined subjects who sacrificed to demons. In 750 it was necessary for the archbishop of York to reiterate that. Also, the animists were still sacrificing to trees, and there was too much praying at wells.

Eventually holy wells were incorporated into Christianity, just as all those wild hermits of the West Country became "saints," and wells and annual well dressing and all that became as Christian as holy water.

King Alfred then arrived, and knowing his Bible, he condemned witches to death. By the tenth century, though, only fines were imposed. Then in 959 King Edgar condemned worship at wells, stone circles, and trees (especially oaks, alders, and rowans). Later King Canute tried a little to do away with *walcyries* ("choosers of the dead"). No success.

By then it was a thousand years since the birth of Christ. In 1008 King Aethelred forbade magic. But it kept on, especially in hard times; peril and pestilence drove people back to the old ways.

Nor did the arrival of William the Bastard from Normandy in 1066 by any means bring an end to Anglo-Saxon magic and witchcraft. *Au contraire*, it reinforced it with continental strains. William the Conqueror's son, William Rufus, may well have perished as a knowing sacrifice to the ancient "the king must die" tradition to ensure the continuance of his people. (But then again he may simply have fallen victim to a hunting accident. Historians differ.) Some claim Rufus was of the Old Religion, and mystery certainly surrounds his death. Ask why he is not buried in his tomb.

It was a distinguished Englishwoman, Dr. Margaret Murray, who theorized in *The Witch-Cult in Western Europe* (1921) and *The God of the Witches* (1933) about the vast extent of pagan survivals. It was she who first argued that witchcraft was simply *la vecchia religione* (as the Italians say) conceived of as the Devil's work by pious Christians. English scholars such as Mathers, Summers, Waite, and Gardner, to name a very few, have been fascinated by the occult, as have novelist Colin Wilson and the late Dame Frances Yates.

Finally, in this too brief survey, there were the notable French magician Alphonse Louis Constant (who went by the name "Éliphas Lévi") in the last century, and in the twentieth an Englishman, Aleister Crowley—or "The Great Beast," as he preferred to call himself after the beast mentioned in Revelations 13:18.

A BREATH OF MAGIC

Babies sometimes have oral moniliasis, or candidiosis, a fungus infection. Some people believe that they can be cured by taking them to a man who has the Power, who then simply breathes into the baby's mouth. (Presumably the disease then runs its course, and the baby is "cured.") The Power comes only to men who have never seen their fathers, the folk say.

FOLK CURE FOR ERYSIPELAS

In 1902 the *Journal of American Folklore* had an interesting article about the mountain folk's cures for burns, bruises, bleeding, and so on, some of which involved magical incantations. Afraid of being thought to be witches, or ridiculed by the unbelieving, the folk kept their incantations mostly to themselves, but the folklore collector did find out this:

> Erysipelas can be cured by taking a red hot brand from the fire, and passing it three times over the person's face, saying the words. ["clear out, brand, but never in. Be thou cold or hot, thou must cease to burn. May God guard thy blood, thy flesh, thy marrow, and thy bones, and every artery, great and small. They shall all be guarded and protected in the name of the Father, the Son, and the Holy Ghost."] This ordeal by fire was not fancied by some of the patients, so my witch told me; she sometimes put coals on a shovel, and waved it over the face, saying,

Three holy men went out walking,
They did bless the heat and the burning,
They blessed it that it might not increase,
They blessed it that it might quickly cease,
And guard against inflammation and mortification
In the name of the Father, the Son, and the Holy Ghost.

Their witch also claimed to be able to stop hemorrhaging, and she claimed "it was not necessary for her to see the patients; they might be far away. Only the first name must be known and pronounced exactly, also the side of the body from which the blood came, the right or left side; this was essential."

WITCHES' GARDENS

In another book of mine you will find many long-held and curious folk beliefs, and elsewhere in this present book I mention the idea that witches' gardens are bordered by red flowers. Like old English soldiers in their red coats, these red flowers "guard" the powerful herbs and botanicals the witches cultivate for their brews.

A SABBAT EVERY DAY

Popular belief has always been that the witches fly off on their broom sticks to their meeting (sabbat) only four times a year, but if we are to believe Sister Madeleine de Demandoulx de la Palud, whose alleged possession in 1611 in France was the subject of a detailed *Admirable History*, "there is a sabbat every day. . . . The witches are gathered together by the sound of a cornet which is blown by a devil."

WITCH WORDS

The words for witches and their activities are many, in English, German, Italian, Latin, and other languages. For example, the hex signs of our Pennsylvania Dutch go back to *Hexen* in German. Some of the strangest words are those given to us by Jordanes de Bergamo in 1470 in a work in which he listed: *bacularia* (because witches rode on broomsticks), *fascinatrix* (because witches had the Evil Eye), *herberia* (because witches used strange herbs in their potions), *maliarda* (because witches were maleficers, workers of evil), and *pixidaria* (because witches made magical ointment, which they kept in a little box similar to that in which the consecrated Host is kept, called a pyx).

THE BIBLE AND WITCHCRAFT

In addition to its poetry and piety and history and philosophy, the Bible has also been consulted in fortune-telling and magic. Bibliomancy used to be quite common, and people really believed that sticking a pin or a finger into the Bible at random would get them the Word of God like a fortune in a Chinese cookie. Designed to explain history and foster truth, the Bible has been used also to darken history and spawn superstition.

You would think that not only Exodus but antiwitchcraft texts in such books as Leviticus and Deuteronomy would put them off, but witches and magicians have sought power in the book, even in antiwitchcraft stories in I Samuel, II Kings, in Isaiah, and so on. They simply turned the message to their needs. Occultists have especially been interested in using the Book of Moses (the first five books of the Bible) and have added other books allegedly by the same author. They use Ezekiel and the Revelation of Saint John pretty much as found and feel free to interpret the rest.

Witches and magicians both are at once confused and stimulated by the Bible. The Old Testament seems at once to deny the existence of Hell and to be the basis of misinterpretations that have led worshippers into Satanism. The New Testament seems to approve of certain types of magic and has been used to condemn other types of heresies.

A *Canon Episcopi* ("Bishop's Rule") of the tenth century asserts that the belief in witches "who profess that in the dead of night . . . ride upon certain beasts with the pagan goddess Diana, and fly over vast tracts of country" is both stupid and heretical and then turns and says that such persons do indeed exist and not to believe in witches flying is to join them in their heresy. Likewise what is written in the Bible has been advanced as both the empowerment of witches and magicians and at the very same time embraced as our justification for destroying them, even one of our most potent weapons (the book of "bell, book, and candle") for doing so.

3
Magic and Witchcraft Around the World

AMONG the Arunta tribe (studied by Spencer and Gillen, 1927) evil spirits (*erintja* or *eruncha*) appear "when the victim is *alone in the dark*." In all cultures, people to some extent are verily alone and in the dark about a great many things; magic is therefore called in to help protect them and to counter the threat of the Unknown.

Even societies that prohibit magic have it practiced by their rebels. We have seen that Origen very early in Christianity asserted that "no good spirit obeys a magician" and went so far as to argue that "scripture rightly prohibits the use of magic" and such traffic with "apostate and evil spirits and foul demons." But from the time Christ Himself said, "In My Name shall they cast out devils," some Christians performed magic in the service of the Good, and some took an adversarial Left-Hand Path, unwilling to deprive

49

themselves of magical powers. In non-Christian societies the prohibitions and the practices were more or less similar.

Here now are a few items to suggest a broader scope than this present book can encompass, a few items that will remind us that magic exists all around the world, in all societies.

FIRE WALKING

You have heard before of people who could walk on fire without getting burned. You can even take courses on it now right here in America.

In the late eighteenth and early nineteenth centuries playing with fire was a major entertainment. There was Robert Powell, "the Fire King," who claimed to have mediumistic powers and "ate" hot coals "as natural as bread." There was Signora Josephina Giradelli, who walked barefoot on red-hot metal for the delectation of London audiences in 1814, and J. Xavier Chabert and his talented sister who walked on red-hot coals, put searing shovels to their tongues, and amazed London audiences of 1819 by entering an oven with a leg of lamb and not coming out until the leg of lamb was done to a turn.

In primitive societies walking on hot coals has been widely reported by anthropologists as part of native religious ceremonies and tests of bravery.

In connection with magic, some who have mastered the arts of playing with fire use them to impress audiences and gain greater belief in supposedly even more amazing spiritual powers. At the sabbat of Voodoo rites, says Pennethorne Hughes in *Witchcraft* (1952), adepts "can juggle with white-hot iron, dance in flames, smell ammonia, eat broken glass, and stir boiling water with their hands, without apparent pain or after-effects."

WORK CLOTHES

Sorcerers of Tibet, when appearing in public, comb their hair to cover their faces and wear aprons made of human bones over their magical robes.

"WE FEAR THE EVIL SPIRITS OF LIFE"

On his fifth expedition to Thule, Greenland, famed Danish explorer and ethnologist Knud Johan Viktor Rasmussen (1879–1933) was told this by an Iglulik Eskimo:

We explain nothing, we believe nothing, but in what I have just shown you lies our answer to all you ask.

We fear the weather spirit of earth, that we must fight against to wrest our food from land and sea. We fear Sila.

We fear death and hunger in the cold snow huts.

We fear Takananagapsaluk, the great woman down at the bottom of the sea, that rules over all the beasts of the sea.

We fear the sickness that we meet with daily all around us; not death, but the suffering. We fear the evil spirits of life, those of the air, of the sea and the earth, that can help wicked shamans to harm their fellow men.

We fear the souls of dead human beings and of the animals we have killed.

AZANDE WITCHES

Among the Azande tribe of Africa it is believed that one does not have to curse or cast spells or do anything at all to be a witch. They say a person may create witchcraft quite unwillingly, just because he or she has it in him.

BALEFUL BALOR

Balor, a giant warlock of Irish legend, was famed for being a cyclops. His one eye was an Evil Eye. He opened it only to scare the enemy, at which time it took four men on the battlefield to lift his eyelid. Like the glance of the mythical basilisk, Balor's glance froze you, rendered you paralyzed.

According to Celtic myth, this is what happened to this seemingly invincible giant. The god Lugh (still celebrated in Celtic lands at Lughnasa, a harvest festival) danced around Balor, chanting insulting remarks. Balor's curiosity was aroused, and he opened his big eye to see who could be so foolhardy. Instantly, avoiding Balor's glance, Lugh let go with his slingshot and got the warlock smack in the eye.

VOODOO AND TABOO

The explorer Soares de Souza in his description of Brazil reported in 1587 a number of deaths among the Tupinambás Indians we can attribute only to Voodoo. Merolla saw evidence of the same kind of thing in the Congo in the following century. In the eighteenth century the explorers in dark corners of the world constantly reported cases of what we might call Voodoo. In New Zealand, in the nineteenth century investigators commented on its prevalence, and similar reports came out of Africa, Haiti, and elsewhere.

Yet we had to wait until Walter Bradford Cannon brought out his book *Traumatic Shock* (1923) before we had a grasp on the physiology and psychology of Voodoo and the force of taboo. Fear can kill; belief that others can kill you by magic gives them the power to do so.

AZTEC MAGIC

The Aztecs lived in a world dominated by astrology; they believed that only magic could prevent the end of the world at the conclusion of the fifty-two-year cycles of their elaborate and surprisingly accurate calendar.

In addition to a crowded pantheon of fierce dieties, they also believed in ghosts (such as the *ciuapipiltin*, women who had died in childbirth and who haunted crossroads, able to paralyze any child who viewed them).

Their magic and their medicine were intricately mingled. A sick child might be held over a bowl of water, used somewhat like the magic mirror Merlin is credited with having introduced into Britain. If the face of the child reflected in the water appeared dark or shadowy, the soul had been stolen away.

The Aztecs knew a great deal about herbs and other medicines, but according to Warwick Bray in *Everyday Life of the Aztecs* (1968), a lot of their cures worked as much on magic as on a scientific basis: "Many of the remedies (like the morning dew dropped into the nostrils of children who snuffled) had a purely magical value."

MASKIM

In the complex demonology of the Sumerians, the *maskim* ("Ensnarers") were the worst of all the classes of demons. They disrupted nature even to the extent of putting the stars out of their courses, and they were implacable toward mankind:

> They are neither male nor female, those who stretch themselves out like chains, they do not take wives; they do not beget children; they are strangers to benevolence and heed neither prayers nor entreaties.

". . . AND NEVER THE TWAIN SHALL MEET"

Moses saw God in a burning bush and was able to strike water from the stone with his magic staff. In the "Great Miracle of Shrāvasti," the Buddha (to confound six heretical leaders who opposed him) caused fire to spring from his head (rather like the tongues of fire that descended upon the apostles in the upper room at Pentecost) and water to flow from his feet.

East and West, after all, are reachable one from the other, and if you go west far enough you wind up in the East, east far enough and you reach the West. Some ways, particularly in religion and magic, we are very much alike.

Our Western exorcisms require bell, book, and candle. In Tibet and Nepal they would call for a book (the Verbal Plane), a statue or a painting (the Physical Plane), and a *stupa* (relic mound, representing the Spiritual Plane). On our altars we burn candles; the Tibetans burn butter on theirs.

Maybe the East and the West are not so irreconcilable as Kipling thought. These days we are studying everything from each other's philosophies to each other's technologies and management systems.

AFRICAN SCULPTURE

For almost a century Western collectors have appreciated and acquired African sculpture. What they were encouraging Africans to sell—or stealing for them—were often religious objects, masks from magical dances, fetishes, carved idols. A tribe's principal god wound up in a New York gallery. Of course this is true of many artifacts now found in museums.

We have made off with the bronzes of Benin and the little gold weights of the Ashanti and a great deal of whatever was portable. One carving too large to be taken was made from a single tree and depicted three monkeys, twenty-two feet high. They guard the palace of the Sultan of Fumban. They were commissioned in the army and entered on the royal payroll as bodyguards.

In the Congo witch doctors treat patients suffering from stomach aches by putting medicine into a hole in a carved statue. We have even taken some of those. And figurines pierced with nails. You will see a number of magical figurines in musuem collections of ethnology as well as in art museums and galleries and private collections. A childless couple I know have a fertility god on their mantel, but they bought it without knowing what it was.

Even furniture can bear magical symbols or have magical uses. Idols of the Hamileke tribe are constructed in the form of chairs; you can sit in the arms of the protective spirit. I own a pair of ceremonial stools, originally provided for visitors; I gather the tribe didn't want to encourage them to get too comfortable and overstay their welcome.

The symbolism seen is often beautiful and speaks volumes to the initiated. Outsiders cannot fathom things like the keyhole-shaped doorways of the Mogroom tribe in Chad. The keyhole shape is supposed to keep out unwelcome visitors. My Chinese desk is heavily carved with dragons and good-luck symbols (including swastikas, which disturb my Jewish friends).

Next time you see native art, be respectful. That may be somebody's god.

MURDER FOR THE POWER

Occasionally the Satanist promises the Devil to sacrifice children to him. In some primitive societies it is believed that in order to become a witch one must murder a close relative. The Navaho witches had to kill a brother or a sister to get their power, the natives of the Marquesas Islands a father or grandfather.

DOWN-UNDER JUSTICE

The *kaidiche* (emu-feathered slippers) worn by witch doctors among the aborigines of Australia really work: Criminals see the footprints and die of fright.

PIGEON FANCIER

We are more likely to call "magic" the actions of those not of our faith. Mohammed is said to have had a familiar in the form of a pigeon that sat on his shoulder and whispered in his ear. Probably it was only a pet, or a symbol like the lion of Saint Jerome and the other animals associated with Christian saints and holy men. But legend says Mohammed's pigeon was the Archangel Gabriel.

My favorite legend about the Prophet (a wonderful man whose life you ought to read some time) concerns a cat that fell asleep on the sleeve of his garment as Mohammed sat at a table. Mohammed cut off the sleeve of the garment rather than disturb its rest. A similar story is told of Saint Malo.

AUTOPSY FINDING

"I once had the pleasure of interviewing Bokane, an African pygmy from the Ituri forest," wrote R. R. Marett in *Psychology and Folk-Lore* (1920), "and he told me how his people were wont to cut up a dead man in order to find out what had killed him. If in the course of this veritable post-mortem they lighted upon an arrow-head or a thorn, well, that had done it. If, however, nothing was found, then it must have been done by *oudah*, 'the mysterious.'"

Our Western doctors occasionally mark a chart "GOK," for "God Only Knows," which sometimes seems to be the only reasonable diagnosis.

MAGIC IN MEXICO

In the Florentine Codex, one of the few Mayan manuscripts that escaped the fire of the destructive first bishop of Oaxaca, a *nahualli* is mentioned: "He is a sorcerer, possesses seeds, and knows magnificent herbs; a witch doctor, he prophesies with cords."

The descendants of the Maya still have their medicines and their magic. The botanicals are spread out, often on bits of newspaper on the ground, at markets, and many are the powers attributed to the dried flowers and leaves and powders and twigs and what tourists regard as unrecognizable bits of nature. The magic is harder to find, but still there.

Among the Aztecs, Tezcatlipoca the creator god was also the god of the witches. He ruled the heavens, came by night, brought fire, could change himself into a jaguar, overthrew a rival god and (temporarily) ruled the universe. A perfect patron for witches, most of whom among the Aztecs were men. All were said to have been born with the gift, and some were believed to be able to transform themselves into animal form as Texcatlipoca did. They were called *nagual*. It was believed they could fly, enchant, cast spells, cure or cause death by sucking out the soul or introducing worms or stones into the victim's body. Today the descendants of the Aztecs still deal in herbs and hexes.

When the *conquistadores* came, they brought witchcraft and magic: What had been religion before became heresy, the old gods became devils. The Spanish also brought their lively tradition of *brujos* (witches) and black arts and added such concepts as that of the Evil Eye to the local repertoire.

The early missionaries saw witchcraft and demons everywhere and were certain that the old ways were superstitious, bloody, dealing with the Devil. What they failed to grasp was that in New World thinking, good and evil were not closed in some Manichean battle but intertwined, interdependent: Every god could be baleful or beneficent, everything fitted together.

The *indios* assimilated the new ideas and mixed them with the old; they would have father confessors and *curanderos* (witch doctors). I have seen copal burned as incense to pagan gods on the steps of the Church of Santo Tomás in Chichicastenango, Guatemala, while the Roman Catholic rites were going on inside. I have seen the *curanderos* operating in the church itself, before statues of *santos* and the Virgin. In religious processions in Mexico and farther south I have seen the Blessed Sacrament and Christian images carried in processions whose tail ends contained natives dressed as the ancient corn deities and others.

The old and the new, magic and Christianity, have simply been combined; and this is true, too, of the Christianity of Puerto Rico and Trinidad, Haiti and the Dominican Republic, and all the rest of Hispanic America.

The sabbats that were such a feature of the early colonial history of such provinces as Yucatán have gone underground, but a good deal of the Old Religion is there for anyone to see.

Today in Mexico the descendants of the Zapotecs have *hechiceras* who send out little *chizos* (stones, thorns, or other cursed particles) to trouble the bodies of their enemies. Or you can hire them to do it against your enemies, who will then have to turn to a *curandero* to break the spell.

The Tzotzils pray to Pukuj, the Mayan god of death, to harass their foes. Elsewhere there are evil *aires* to be combated with age-old prayers and ceremonies and the *tabayuku* (a sort of succubus) and *vampiros*.

Adivinas can make you a doll of *jonute de hule* (rubber tree bark), but at the same time evil magicians are manufacturing their dolls and sticking pins in them, tying red cords around their necks, and so on.

In both cases there is a liberal sprinkling with blood, albeit chicken blood, for both the *indígenes* and the Spanish have long traditions of gory gods and bloodletting.

Certain places such as Tepepán are known all over the country for their wondrous *brujos de naturaleza* (natural-born witches, as opposed to those of the Spanish tradition who sought their calling). Slightly more sophisticated centers have their spiritualist circles and dabblers in the occult arts. Before Francisco I. Madero became president of Mexico, he was commissioner for the First Spiritist Conference (1906) there, and spiritualist temples and curers abound both in places where foreigners have gathered (such as Guadalajara) and in more Mexican cities. Ever since Madero was assassinated (1913) he has been, like others who have died violent deaths—from Cuahtemoc, the last Aztec emperor, to less noble souls—available (Mexicans believe) as a "dark spirit" or guide to mediums.

William and Claudia Madsen in their highly recommended *Guide to Mexican Witchcraft* (1972) report interviews with a wide variety of practitioners and in a do-it-yourself section give recipes and instructions. Want to seduce a girl? Carry a dead hummingbird in your pocket. Or, if you can't get powdered human skull, put the leg of a beetle in her soda pop: guaranteed to drive her *loca*. Where to buy *piedra iman* (loadstone)? Try Puebla and Torreón. To keep a husband from running away, bury a live horned toad in a sealed jar under the house, or tie two large *chiles pasillas* together with a red ribbon and put them under his pillow. How to drive him *loco*? Put some of your dried menstrual blood in his coffee.

Here is one the Madsens do not guarantee:

A man who wants to kill his woman can bury the tooth of a rattlesnake at the spot where she urinates in the morning. That is supposed to make her dry up and die.

As for herbs and drugs, there are many books—and much that has never found its way into a book. The Mexicans gave us chocolate and chilis, which we now know affect the mind (chocolate contains a chemical that gives you a *high* when you are "in love") and the body in "magical" ways. Californian hippies (*jipes* in Mexico) discovered the hallucinations the Mexicans had been getting for a long time from morning-glory seeds and certain mushrooms that can (as Aldous Huxley put it) open the "doors of perception."

In New York, at least one pharmacy has for generations been selling such items as are used in European folklore and magic; now it has added a whole range of Hispanic herbs. In Hispanic neighborhoods the folklore of Puerto Rico and other places produces some exotic items, including the blue chalk you can apply before you sleep to protect you from the creatures of the night. *Botánicas* here offer a wide range of goods.

The *botánicas* of Mexico may be more informal but they offer *coatl xoxouhqui* ("green serpent," good for both gout and bewitching), *mixitl* (to crack the tongue to silence an enemy, to deaden the testicles), *tochtetepen* ("rabbit's leg," another paralyzer), and *tlapatl* (one of the daturas so prominent in European witchcraft).

MAORI MAGIC

The Maoris believe that *kaiwhatu* (a charm) defends you against witchcraft. They say that Rongo-mai and Ihenga, two legendary characters, brought it back from a journey to the underworld, along with some songs and the *whai* (what we call a "cat's-cradle").

OBEAH

There is no "white magic" or herbal cures in Obeah, witchcraft devoted entirely to getting back at your enemies. Obeah still flourishes in the Caribbean and elsewhere, despite a 1760 law defining it as a "Wicked Art of Negroes going under the Appelation of obeah-men and obeah-women pretending to have Communication with the Devil and other Evil Spirits."

A law against *pretending* to work evil!

THE IRNA

Among the Arunta tribe of Australia, the *irna* (pointing stick or bone) is used to bring evil and death upon a victim selected by the magician. First the magician has to take the stick or bone away into the bush, crouch over it, and charge it with curses. "May your heart be rent asunder," he repeats over and over.

He then hides the *irna* back home until he can creep out at night and, getting near enough to his victim to be able to discern his or her features, he repeatedly jerks the stick or bone over his shoulder and hurls curses under his breath. *Arungquiltha* (evil magic) is then supposed to strike the victim, who will sicken and die unless he suspects some such attack and calls in another magician to counter it. Meanwhile, the evil magician must hide the *irna*, because if others see him with an *irna* they will put him to death as a murderer.

CHINESE MAGIC

As I noted earlier, we in the West have put people into the foundations of buildings to give them strength; so the Chinese strengthened the Great Wall with the bodies of slaves. But the most striking example of this magical belief in practice was involved with the great bell of the temple of Ta Chung Su, which the emperor Yung Lo is said to have demanded be "strong" enough to be heard one hundred *li* (about thirty-seven miles) away. The tale goes that the bellmaker's own daughter, Ko Ai, was thrown or jumped into the molten metal to make the iron and brass and gold and silver fuse properly.

UNFROZEN CORPSES

This, from Ross Nichols, in Paul Christian's *History and Practice of Magic* (1963):

> In Tibet the object of reviving the corpse in a rite called *rolang* is to bite off its tongue whilst it is leaping in a violent dance. If this is not done the corpse kills the sorcerer who has revived it. This process must be distinguished from the animation of a corpse by a wandering spirit seeking embodiment, a process said to be accomplished by the *trong jug* rite in Tibet. The *jibbuk* [dybbuk] of Hebrew folk-belief is such a re-inhabited corpse; in this case it usually seems to be acting as a kind of medium for the re-estab-lishment of communications with this world by a departed human spirit. More horribly, West Africa, together with the other Voodoo regions of Haiti, Jamaica, British Guiana, Cuba and parts of South America, has its *zombies*, revived corpses acting as servants and slaves of the living.

STONE MAGIC

With the old Cornish language now extinct, place names that had ordinary meanings in Cornish have been given fanciful English form: Mousehole, Penny Come Quick, St. Just in Roseland. And to explain quite simple words, folklore comes up with odd stories: *The Merry Maidens* (*maen* for "stone") are nineteen stones about four feet high each, squatting in a field, but the legend has been invented that they were Cornish maidens turned to stone when they danced on a Sunday. Nearby are fifteen more stones called *The Pipers*, who supposedly played for those irreverent revels. The belief in magic, however, is enshrined in that tale.

In another area of Cornwall, where there are moors, *Men-an-Tol* is a five-foot stone with a hole in it, standing between two large boulders. (Christians came to call it the Devil's Eye.) In ancient times, sick children were "brackened" here to cure them by passing them nine times through the stone against the sun.

Elsewhere ancient people passed people through holes in trees for similar purposes. For example, the Bhil tribe in India passes a sick child seven times through a hole in a *palas* tree to effect an instant cure.

DEATH WISH

From M. Laird and R. A. K. Oldfield's *Expedition into the Interior of Africa* (1837):

Yesterday there was a procession of the wives of the late son of the king. . . . The women came down to the water-side. . . . They proceeded to drink poison, from a belief that they had *wished* their husband's death. . . . Out of sixty of these poor infatuated wretches, thirty-one of them died; while others, who vomited immediately, escaped death.

The belief that one can be guilty of another's death just by wishing the death to occur is also common in the West, and August Strindberg's *Brott och Brott* (*Crimes and Crimes*) is a play that reflects his own deeply held belief that one can be guilty of another person's death just by hoping for it.

MAGICAL FASTING

When people believed that there were demons resident in trees and streams, they also believed that certain foods contained such spirits. They attempted to purify themselves by fasting, refusing such foods as contained demons. They fasted also to placate the gods, to sacrifice to them, to earn credits by denying the human needs for sustenance, as it were, and thus approach the angels and demons (who never ate).

They were also aware that fasting could, in the long run, produce visions, and by what was called in Latin the *jejunium propheticum*, they sought to produce the ability to prophesy. In the early days of Christianity, some of the strangest visions, in which magic and religion were inextricably mixed, occurred to hermits and anchorites fasting in the desert, mortifying the body and attempting to strengthen the spiritual part of man. But the "prophetic fast" and the purification rites of shamans were calculated to increase power, not to weaken the individual.

FORBIDDING HEATHENISM

From the Laws of Canute, king of England (1017–1035), comes this:

We earnestly forbid every heathenism: Heathenism is, that men worship idols; that is, that they worship heathen gods, and the sun and the moon, fire or rivers, water-wells or stones, or forest trees of any kind; or love witchcraft, or promote *morth-work* in any wise.

THE MAGIC CIRCLE

The Crowthers in *The Secrets of Ancient Witchcraft* (1974) write:

The circle represents the borderland between this world and the domains of the gods. Since it [magic] is a fertility cult, it also represents the womb of Mother Earth.

The Crowthers worry about the dimensions of the magic circle—only nine feet across—but conclude that it is large enough to accommodate the thirteen members of a coven and speculate that for more people one might use a multiple of nine. Ceremonies in circles occur all around the world.

BIBLIOGRAPHY

For Western witchcraft you will need *The Book of Shadows*. It is not in print. Someone will give you a manuscript copy if you get to be a magician. Without a copy, you cannot work magic in the ancient tradition.

You may also have great trouble acquiring the following highly recommended and rare volumes: the *Sixth, Seventh, Eighth, Ninth, Tenth, Eleventh, Twelfth,* and *Thirteenth Book of Moses; The Little Book of Romanus; The Black Raven; The Spring Book; The Spiritual Shield; The Blessing of the Saints.* If you find *The Fiery Dragon*, be certain it is *The Authentic Fiery Dragon.* There are several grimoires (magicians' manuals) that tell you how to get demons to bring you books you will need, but these grimoires (never printed) are hard to find.

Eastern guide books are sometimes surprisingly similar.

REPTILE MAGIC

E. E. Evans-Pritchard lived right in the center of Africa from 1926 to 1930. He wrote *Witchcraft, Oracles and Magic Among the Azande,* which reports that it is *kere* (a bad omen) to see a certain kind of lizard, because this will foretell the death of a relative: "If you see the skin it has shed (or a python's slough) you will die."

In Central America, iguana meat is used in several potent magic recipes, and snakeskins are sometimes employed in magic as well. W. H. Goldie wrote of native New Zealand life in *Maori Medical Lore*:

> If a traveler should see a lizard in the path before him, he would know that the creature had not come there of its own accord, but had been sent by an enemy as an *aitua* (evil omen) to cause his death. He therefore at once kills the reptile, and craves a woman to step over it as it lies in the path. By this means the evil omen is averted.

REVERSE PSYCHOLOGY

If magic is the reverse of religion, understandably things work backward.

Many spells depend on reciting formulas backward. The authors of the *Malleus Maleficarum*, whom we will encounter in the next chapter, made it a point to stress that it was witchcraft if one put emphasis on the *manner* in which a spell was said. In some ritual magic one walks backward or otherwise reverses things.

The witch doctors of Africa's Kaguru tribe walk around on their hands. Among the Amba people witch doctors stand on their heads when not otherwise occupied or hang, naked, upside down from trees. They quench their thirst with salt. In fact, they do whatever they can backward. If you are going to try to reverse natural law, it only seems sensible to work backward.

SWEDISH MAGIC

From my very learned friend Erik Gunnemark in Sweden, some magic of West Gothia:

To understand all languages, catch a young swallow, roast it in honey, and eat it. Also . . .

To make dirty linen white, say I SAW A SWAN when you open the door to the laundry. (If you wanted it to remain dirty, you'd say I SAW A RAVEN.)

To banish the ague, say KULUMARIS KULUMARI KULUMAR KULUMA KULUM KULU KUL KU K.

He warns against whistling: "As a child I never whistled; it wasn't done—only godless people whistled. If I had whistled I would have 'called up the Devil!'" Singing early in the morning is also taboo. "The eagle will take you before the sun is down," Russians warned him. Erik quotes his father-in-law: "*E skata ska du inte hata,*" ("You shall not hate a magpie!") to the effect that you must never bother a magpie or destroy its nest ("If you do, expect to be dead within the year"), for magpies are "sacred birds in the Swedish countryside."

From southwestern Sweden (and apparently nowhere else) he reports that *tvesulning* is "a mortal sin," which means that one must not put two kinds of thing on one's bread. A ham open-faced sandwich, yes; a cheese open-faced sandwich, yes; but never ham and cheese. And he and his family and friends have revived an ancient custom of "running Gregor" on March 12.

> The trouble is that we must run barefoot when the ground is still
> frozen, sometimes covered with snow and ice—not pleasant at
> all. But if we run *three times* around the house or the compost
> heap we will get a good harvest and won't suffer from lice for
> the rest of the year.

He has all sorts of other folk beliefs to tell about, including one that seems to combine the pre-Christian and the Christian: All knives and scissors must be hidden and not used on Good Friday. Some superstitions far older than that persist in Sweden to this day, and some have been brought to America by Swedish immigrants of the nineteenth century.

"GET THEE BEHIND ME, SATAN!"

The Gialo "ghost women" of Kufara in the Libyan desert dress in heavy black robes to keep out the heat—an odd custom since the color black is supposed to absorb heat. Even odder, the "ghost women" drag six-foot trains behind them. Why? The trains obliterate the women's footprints, making it impossible for the Devil to creep up and tempt them into sin.

NATIVE GUILE

In Malaivi—or Nyasaland as it was then called (about 1934)—bands of *bamucapi* (witch finders) in Western suits and with Western methods of soft-soap and threat went around detecting black magicians by their reflections in mirrors. They forced witch doctors to give up their bloody robes, lizard skins, horns, and fetishes—and they used magic to keep them from returning to practice.

Each suspect was compelled to drink a soapy, reddish liquid which (he was assured) would, the moment he returned to practicing magic, cause him to swell up horribly and become so heavy that the people could not carry him to his grave.

Then the *bamucapi* moved on to the next villages, after selling the locals charms and magic powders—to protect them against evil magic, of course. The most expensive charms promised to assist the owner to cope with government officials (to whom, at last, the *bamucapi* themselves fell victim).

SJØNHVERFING

That Scandinavian word means "deceiving the eyes," and Scandinavian witches were supposed to have that power. In the Icelandic *Eyrbyggja Saga*, for instance, we find the tale of the witch Katla who protected her son Odd from men who wanted to revenge the fact that he had cut off the head of a woman.

When the men, including the bold Arnkell, arrived at Katla's house, all they could see was the old woman sitting on a dais, spinning. Odd, sitting beside her, she made invisible. The men went away, returned, and still could not see Odd; this time she was combing Odd's hair, but they saw only an old woman combing a goat. On a third trip the determined men thought they saw only a boar, but it was Odd asleep.

Arnkell was sure that they had had "a goatskin waved around our heads" but he could not conquer the magic of Katla until he found another witch, Geirrid, who was her match. As soon as Katla saw the blue cloak of Geirrid as she arrived with the men, Katla realized that her "deceiving the eyes" would not work on the second witch. Katla hid Odd under a dais, but as soon as Geirrid entered the house, she slipped a sealskin bag over Katla's head, rendering her powerless, and unerringly directed Arnkell and his friends to where Odd was hidden. Katla was stoned to death, and Odd was hanged.

LAPPLAND DRUMS

Lapps used to make magic drums from trees found in remote spots where the sun never shone. The heads were of reindeer hide painted with pictures of what Amerindians called the spirit animal, with the blood-red extract of alder bark used for paint. Decorated with bones and other objects, the drums were kept in a part of every Lapp's dwelling where women were never permitted to enter.

To tell what the future held, the male Lapp would place a brass ring or a little brass frog on top of the drum and watch how the object moved over the painted pictures as the drum was solemnly beaten. Though the conversion of

Lappland to Christianity led to the destruction of most of the old drums (a few remain in museums), new ones were made and used by every Lapp household down to nearly modern times.

In many other cultures the drum is used in magic to induce a trancelike state in which a shaman or priest may be able to get in touch with higher powers, but perhaps only in Lappland were drums ever beaten to watch magic little frogs hop to symbols in which the future could be divined.

LIKE PRODUCES LIKE

That is the basic principle of sympathetic magic, like Sir Kenelm Digby's wound ointment. It's what lies behind the practice of sticking pins in figures created to represent enemies and hoping thereby to injure or slay them.

If you make your image with something that has come in contact with the enemy or (even better) some part of the enemy himself (hair, nail clippings, even excrement), the magic will be that much more effective. Or employ contiguous magic, which attempts to injure the man through something he has touched, as when Australian aborigines put sharp pebbles or ground glass in the footprints left by an enemy.

The Ojibwa employ sympathetic magic to drive away evil from a community. When someone has a dream that some disaster—usually illness—is about to strike his village, he sends out messages to all the families involved, inviting them to assemble at a certain place and a certain time, usually his own house. A short distance away, a human-shaped figure of straw has been set up, dressed in male costume, to represent the impending trouble. The people eat, smoke tobacco to ask for a spiritual blessing on the enterprise, and at a signal from the dreamer, rush out at the straw man. First the men shoot it, then the women rush up and club it to bits, and finally the remains are heaped up and burned. This is believed to ward off the disease and thus save the health of the community.

CLOSE TO HOME

And lest you think that modern, learned, scientific societies are immune . . .

At a conference on geolinguistics in 1985, my colleague John Allee produced and handed around the audience a small figure from Greenland, carved from a tusk. The grotesque little image was a *tupalak*, he told us, and was used by the Greenlanders to cast a spell or place a curse. I noticed that the majority of my learned colleagues in linguistics, few or none of whom had any concern with magic or witchcraft, superstitiously gazed at the *tupalak* but resolutely refused to touch it.

HOW TO KEEP WITCHES AWAY

In New Mexico they say that if you will burn red pepper cores on a Friday you will keep witches out of your house.

The people of northern Italy seem to have had a different method. Rachel Harriet Busk in *The Folk-Lore of Rome* (1874) reports the following from a religious Roman woman with a highly superstitious husband:

> "He always kept a bag of particular herbs," I heard from her another time, "hung up over the door, all shred into the finest bits. As he was very angry if I touched them, I one day said, 'Why *do* you want that bundle of herbs kept just there?' and then he told me that it was because no witch could pass under them without having to count all the minute bits, and that though it was true she might do so by her arts without taking them down and handling them, it was yet so difficult when they were shred into such an infinite number that it was the best preservative possible against evil influences."

HAWAIIAN IDEAS

Until the last century there was a kingdom of Hawaii and in that society a system of taboos operated, hedging the royal family, the nobles, the priests with a magical circle of protection.

It was taboo to bathe in streams and springs set aside for the royal family or the priests or to touch pigs marked for sacrifice in the temples. It was taboo to stand in the presence of the king without permission, to approach him any way except on the knees, to step upon his shadow. Only royalty could wear yellow, only the priests red. Only royalty wore the exquisite mantles made from *oo* and *mamo* feathers.

Only the royal family and the nobility could eat turtle or squid or certain kinds of birds. No women could eat plantains, bananas, or coconuts, pork or certain kinds of fish. Never could men and women eat together.

At certain sacred times no food could be eaten at all, no canoe shoved off from the shore, no pigs or fowls utter a sound, and nobody but priests walk around in plain sight.

In this world of strict regulation, however, certain persons were thought to be able to work magic that could disrupt everything, and these persons were greatly feared. A kahuna anaana (one who prays his victims to death) was thought to be able to work magic against anyone provided only that he had a bit of something from the person, such as a lock of hair, a nail paring, even a drop of his spittle (sympathetic magic again). For this reason the king's spittoon-bearer was, in ancient Hawaii, a high-ranking and extremely trusted nobleman, assigned the vital job of safeguarding the king's spit.

Even in more recent times Hawaiians believed in *kilos* or sorcerers who were thought to be able to call up the spirits of the dead and sometimes to steal a living man's spirit from him while he was asleep.

HOW PEOPLE GET CONJURED

An informant told the *Journal of American Folklore* in 1900 how he was "conjured in May 1898, while hoeing cotton" with "some yaller dirt, and knew it was graveyard dirt." Searching his house in panic, he found "a bag under my door-step. I opened the bag and found some small roots about an inch long, some black hair, a piece of snake skin, and some graveyard dirt, dark-yaller, right off some coffin. . . ." He threw some red pepper around to purify the place and went right off to a "root-doctor" to have the spell removed, because "one root-doctor often works against another."

The informant was certain that professional help was needed to counter any spell that employed material as powerful as graveyard dirt, of which he said:

> Only root-doctors can git the graveyard dirt, they know what kind
> to git and when, the hants [ghosts] won't let everybody git it,
> they must git it through some kind of spell, for the graveyard dirt
> works trouble 'til it gits back inter the ground, and then [the
> spell] wears off. It must git down to the same depth it was took
> from, that is as deep as the coffin lid was from the surface of the
> ground.

TREES

Trees are associated with a great many magical beliefs and customs, some of which are carried down to our day. Here are just a few of the English folk beliefs about trees:

Apples. It's bad luck to pick all the apples in the orchard; some must be left on the trees for the fairies. It's called "the pixies' harvest." To go out and take the apples left for the pixies is called griggling or scraggling. Children who engage in such pranks then call at the farmer's house for some "goodies" or a penny, much like American children trick-or-treating on Halloween.

Ash. Want to know whether it will be a wet spring? Here's the old English rhyme; it refers to the leafing of the trees:

> If the oak's before the ash,
> You will only get a splash.
> If the ash preceeds the oak,
> You will surely get a soak.

Sap from the ash was used as an ointment on the newborn, a protection against witchcraft. The ash was closely connected with the Old Religion, and it was in a sacred grove of ash trees that the Druids conducted their religious ceremonies, so the ash became a part of many survivals of *wicca*, the ancient knowledge.

Bay. Tradition or superstition said that if you moved, you ought to take your bay tree with you, unless you wanted to leave behind your luck and your protection against witches.

Birch. A birch branch over the door advises a witch to visit elsewhere.

Blackthorn. To bring the blossoms of blackthorn indoors was thought to invite evil into one's house. The blossoms of mountain laurel are even more fraught with danger.

Cherry. Cherry trees in blossom may attract evil spirits, so it is best to have them blessed when they are in full bloom.

Elder. Some people advise elder wood for magic wands, and it used to be a common British practice to carry a cross-shaped elder bud in the pocket to ward off evil. But the elder bud had to be from a churchyard tree, or it didn't work. If you were a horseman, you carried a twig of elder to guard against saddle sores.

Hawthorn. There are many superstitions attached to the hawthorn and its blossoms, but one that seems to have disappeared entirely in Britain is the formerly widespread habit of making whistles for the children to blow (driving away evil spirits) at May Day celebrations, a time when witches were thought to be especially virulent.

Hazel. Hazel sticks used to drive the cattle were likely, people once thought, to guarantee that they would be fat and content. Willow was thought to hurt them.

Holly. Holly could keep away witches, and the English traditions of the Holly Boy and Ivy Girl—holly was a symbol of masculinity, ivy of clinging feminity—have gone, but we still use holly and ivy as Christmas decorations, even though we seldom or never recall their significance in the Old Religion.

It might be useful to remember, however, that holly may not be brought into the house any earlier than Christmas Eve (or bad luck will follow), and if you do not observe the ancient practice of keeping a piece of the yule log to start the next year's yuletide fire, then perhaps you have room even in a modern apartment for storing a few of Christmas' holly leaves. Tradition says they are to be saved and burned under the next year's Christmas pudding. It may not keep evil spirits away, but it does provide a charming bit of continuity from one year to the next.

With the more or less familiar holly, we will cut short what otherwise could be an extremely long list of superstitious beliefs in the magical powers of trees. Today you do not see the Dutch in New York horsewhipping their peach trees on Good Friday morning or yews and rowans in graveyards or even ash logs in the Christmas fireplace for protection against evil. Even with the few old customs we honor, we do not always get things right, forgetting such details as that hawthorn twigs have little power unless cut on Ascension Day.

AMERINDIAN MAGIC

Algonquian young men went through a sort of initiation ceremony just before attaining adulthood which was also seen, in one form or another, in many other Amerindian nations.

The young man retired to a specially built hut in an isolated place and there prayed and fasted until he was so purified the "spirits could see through him." At that point he was granted a dream in which a spirit guide appeared to him, bringing the secrets of hunting and curing disease, invulnerability to the weapons of enemies, and much more wisdom. Thereafter, awake, the young brave could use the wisdom and power to run his adult life and was expected to honor his guardian spirit throughout life.

THE OLDEST MAGICAL INSTRUCTIONS IN THE LIBRARY

The British Library has some two hundred tablets inscribed with the essence of Chaldean magic, charms, amulets, incantations, and more, all copied from the original texts set down for King Asurbanipal (884–860 B.C.) in Assyrian and Akkadian languages.

4

Witchcraft Trials

I
T took very little for someone to be accused of witchcraft. Perhaps he had walked past a neighbor's field the day before the cattle took sick of some ailment. Perhaps she had a soured and crabby nature, and people of her village did not like her. Perhaps a couple had prospered more than others in their town, and fellow townsmen were jealous.

But once the accusation was lodged, the whole process of condemnation seemed to roll forward of its own accord. The suspect was jailed and a watch kept on her—it was usually a her. She was questioned—and questioned and questioned and questioned. If the business took place in England or an English colony, no torture could be used (except pressing and then only if the accused refused to plead either guilty or not guilty), but she could be ducked in the village pond, or "swum" to see if she sank, and there was no law against keeping her awake for days on end. If she had been arrested anywhere on the continent of Europe, there were no restrictions at all; she could be broken on the wheel (which meant being strapped to a wheel and beaten systematically with an iron rod), racked, thumb-screwed, eye-gouged, burned, scourged until she confessed. What she had to confess to was not only her own guilt but that of other witches. And soon the persons she was named were arrested, too, and tortured to confess still other names.

It is from the confessions of these tormented wretches that most stories of black masses, Satan worship, broomstick flying, magic spells, soul selling, covens, and so on come. Much of what they "admitted" had been suggested to them by their interrogators.

Having "confessed" to witchcraft, the accused was then put through a travesty of a trial. Occasionally (not often) a confessed and repentent "witch" was allowed to go free, but only with a verdict of "not proven"—"innocent" was not allowed after such efforts. More often than not she was hanged, burned alive, drowned, or put to death in some other unspeakable way.

SATAN MIGHT SMILE

Henry Charles Lea in *The Inquisition of the Middle Ages* (reissued 1961) wrote of the persecution of witches:

Satan might well smile at the tribute to his power seen in the endless smoke of the holocausts. . . . Protestant and Catholic rivalled each other in the madness of the hour. A bishop of Geneva is said to have burned 500 witches within three months, a bishop of Bamburg 600, a bishop of Würzburg 900. The Inquisition evidently had worthy pupils. Paramo boasts that in a century and a half from the commencement of the sect, in 1404, the Holy Office had burned at least 30,000 witches who, if they had been left unpunished, would easily have brought the whole world to destruction.

THE SHAME OF SALEM

Superstition and stupidity, hand in hand with Puritan virtues of fortitude and piety, led to the shame of Salem in the spring of 1692.

The Salem witchcraft story, as we have stated elsewhere, is far from the goriest in the annals of witchcraft persecutions, but it has received a great deal of attention because, as an isolated colonial incident, it stood out starkly. And, of course, because parallels can be aptly drawn between the performances of our Puritan ancestors and our political and social contemporaries.

It all began in the home of a clergyman, the Rev. Samuel Parris. Some silly girls, no more or less superstitious than others of the time, were dropping egg whites into water, hoping to foretell thereby the occupation of their future husbands. (The idea was that the shapes formed would hint at the trades.) One egg white shaped up like a coffin, and the girl got hysterical.

The hysteria spread to other adolescents, girls developed false pregnancies, and eventually the whole town was in an uproar. Realizing that their antics were getting them attention, the girls began to make accusations of witchcraft.

The first charge was leveled at a Caribbean slave, Tituba. She had, in fact, filled the impressionable children with her own superstitious tales, but she was no witch. Unfortunately, she was a "heathen," and everyone "knew" that black slaves dabbled in all sorts of "hoodoo" and charms. Tituba had little defense against the testimony of the preacher's overwrought daughter, Elizabeth, and young Abigail Williams and their friends.

Pleased with their success and basking in the limelight, the girls denounced others. The girls claimed that they could detect witches simply by touching them. Arrest followed arrest. In this rigidly theocratic society one could not deny belief in the supernatural; that would be tantamount to denying the existence of God. So, people believed in the accusations—or said they did. The accusations broadened. Soon a kindly pastor, the Rev. George Burroughs, was executed for witchcraft, and the mania spread to nearby towns.

Incredibly, more than 150 people were arrested on serious charges, while the public—the superstitious and the sincere, the silly and the sadistic—allowed it to happen. The execution of Bridget Bishop in June 1692 was followed by the death of twenty others, three victims dying in prison before they could be killed. But unlike similar outbreaks of hysteria in Europe, those who confessed went free, among them Tituba the slave.

Then the witch hunters overreached themselves. They presumed to accuse the governor's wife. That caused the whole hideous structure to collapse.

It is only fair to note that even at the time some distinguished men, such as Thomas Battle and Increase Mather, thought the courts and the people were acting irrationally, and bravely said so. But Increase's son Cotton testified at the trial as an "expert witness" and the following year published his own book on witchcraft, *Wonders of the Invisible World*.

In 1697, the witch hunters began to regret their rashness, and Samuel Sewall, one of the presiding judges, posted a notice in his own meeting house: "Sensible . . . as to the Guilt contracted . . . at Salem . . . he

. . . Desires to take the Blame. . . ." Any relatives of the victims still around in 1711 received £600 in compensation. It was not really possible to make amends for the horror, but the witch hunters at least wanted to.

In more recent times the history of the dark days in Salem has been reexamined and reevaluated in the light of other forms of hysteria. In 1953 Arthur Miller produced his play *The Crucible*, using the Salem experience to examine guilt by association in the age of McCarthyism.

INNOCENT VIII AND THE INNOCENTS UNDER THE HAMMER OF THE WITCHES

The witch-hunting mania really began in 1484 with the issuance of the papal bull *Summis desiderantes* by Pope Innocent VIII. (Innocent may have been hoping to distract public attention from his own scandalous personal life and disastrous dabbling in Mediterranean politics, for he was anything but a pious and high-minded man.) The bull empowered two Dominican professors of theology, already at work in northern Germany hunting out "wretches [who] afflict and torment men and women," to

> proceed, according to the regulations of the Inquisition, against
> any persons of whatever rank and high estate, correcting, mulct-
> ing, imprisoning, punishing, as their crimes merit, those whom
> they have found guilty, the penalty being adapted to the offence.

The theologians were Fathers Jakob Sprenger and Heinrich Kramer, and the result of Innocent's bull was the publication of their notorious work on the nature of witchcraft and how its adherents were to be ferreted out: *Malleus Maleficarum, Hammer of the Witches*. It was to become the inspiration and guide for one of the ghastliest persecutions in history.

Summis desiderantes did not impose belief in witchcraft as dogma of the Church, but it certainly made disbelief in it more perilous. In Germany, many witchcraft trials began instantly, but there were repercussions in Italy as well; by 1510, 140 had been burned at Brescia, three hundred at Como. In France, suspected witches were questioned under torture—the soles of their feet were burned, and they were forced to swallow burning oil; eventually an eleven-year-old girl was burned to death. Backup directives were issued by Julius II and Paul III.

Soon the mania spread to England, where as a French writer says, "Henry VIII and Elizabeth persecuted sorcerers with extreme vigour, and we must not forget the sinister James I, who took the trouble to write with his own royal hand the treatise entitled *Daemonologia.*"

In the latter, the character Epistemon speaks for the King's point of view of mercy for innocents:

> EPISTEMON. The death by flames of fire is that most often laid upon them [witches and sorcerers]. . . .
>
> PHILOMATHUS. Think you that exception should be made or consideration taken in that they be, namely, male or female, of ripe or tender age, or by reason of their state, dignity, or degree, base or exalted?
>
> EPISTEMON. I adjudge that there must be no exception.

HOW'S THAT FOR GRATITUDE?

In the first secular witchcraft trial in France, in 1390, Jehane de Brigue was accused by a man named Ruilly—of having *saved his life* by the use of charms. A Paris court imprisoned her, tortured her into confession of witchcraft, and burned her, along with Ruilly's wife.

SADDUCISMUS TRIUMPHATUS

The Rev. Joseph Glanvill (1636–1680) was one of the original scientists in the Royal Society and one of the most important of seventeenth-century English writers on witchcraft. In his work *Sadducismus Triumphatus* (published 1681), we find stories like this sad tale:

> . . . at Stockholme a young woman accused her own Mother of being a Witch, and swore positively that she carried her away at night; whereupon both the Judges and Ministers of the Town exhorted her to Confession and Repentance. But she stiffly denied the Allegations, pleaded Innocence, and though they burnt another Witch before her face and lighted the Fire she herself was to burn in before her, yet she still justified her self, and continued to do so to the last, and continuing to do so, was burnt.
>
> She had indeed been a very bad Woman, but it seems this crime she was free from, for within a fortnight or three weeks

after, her Daughter which had accused her came to the Judges in open Court, weeping and howling, and confessed that she had wronged her Mother, and unjustly out of spleen she had against her for not gratifying her in a thing she desired, had charged her with that Crime which she was innocent of as the Child unborn. Whereupon the Judges gave order for her execution too.

GIVING THE DEVIL HIS DUE

"Whatever is not normal," wrote Nicholas Remy (1530–1612) in his much-consulted volume *Demonolatreiae* (1595), "is due to the Devil." With that excuse, Remy, a judge in Nancy, France, condemned to death an old beggar woman who had been angry when he refused her alms, for soon after that Remy's son died.

In a period of about ten years, Remy was personally responsible for— and boasted of—the deaths of some nine hundred other witches, an average of one a week. At his disposal there were nearly as many laws (one authority says eight hundred) against witches and very little protection for anyone accused of witchcraft. It was a world in which the majority of people were truly terrified of what a prayer after mass described vividly as "Satan and all the other wicked spirits who roam through the world seeking the ruin of souls."

THE SIGN OF THE BEAST

It is believed that Satanism is the reverse, a sort of mirror image, of Christianity.

Just as the baptism of a Christian was supposed to cleanse the body (and leave a indelible mark on the soul), so initiation into the Devil's Party would mark, or befoul, the body and the soul.

To find a witch, then, you looked for the Devil's mark. Perhaps the Devil had put a brand (a birthmark? a scar?) on the witch; perhaps where he touched the witch there would be an insensitive spot, detectable with a probing needle.

So suspects were shaved (removing all the hair also prevented amulets and such from being hidden on the body) and examined with great care. Every mole or imperfection was scrutinized.

Jacques Fontaine in 1611 wrote a treatise "on the marks of witches and actual possession taken by the Devil of men's bodies" and warned that examiners should be suspicious of ordinary things. "Those who say that it is difficult to distinguish marks of the Devil from natural imperfections, from boils or impetigo, show quite clearly that they are not competent doctors."

Sadistic clergymen and prying lawyers jabbed the suspects (often senile old women) with pins, probing for a spot that could not feel pain, often in areas where the victims felt the most embarrassment. On some witches examiners found marks they regarded as extra nipples; were these used to suckle familiars?

Even in England, where the judicial system ordinarily treated the accused as innocent until proved guilty, people suspected of witchcraft found themselves in the difficult position of having to prove their innocence. When you were "swum" as a test you were often tied, right thumb to left big toe and left thumb to right big toe, and then thrown into the water. If you *floated*, it proved that the Devil was buoying you up.

Speedy trial by prejudiced courts was followed too often by horrible death: You could be hanged, beheaded, burned alive, drowned, whatever was in fashion. Persons of high rank were sometimes hanged first and burned afterward, in consideration of their station. Gilles de Retz enjoyed this last privilege, despite his appalling crimes.

The Renaissance was the time of the Iron Maiden and other ingenious devices of torture. Or they could just ask you to pull a blessed ring out of a vat of boiling water; if the bandaged hand then healed in three days, you were a witch. Or they might hand you a bar of red-hot iron and ask you to carry it nine, or twelve, paces. . . . In an earlier day, they did that for ordinary crimes, too.

The connection between witch hunting and sadistic psychopathology needs more study. It is a vile record of human ferocity.

ELIZABETH DUNLOP'S CASE

Sir Walter Scott tells the story of Elizabeth Dunlop of Scotland. On November 8, 1576, she was tried for witchcraft and told the court that she dealt with a familiar who was really Thomas Reid (killed at the Battle of Pinkie, September 10, 1547, when an officer to the Laird of Blair).

She claimed, and all her neighbors agreed, that she only did petty sorcery and never anything but good deeds for the benefit of her friends. Whereupon she was "convict and burned" forthwith.

EVIDENCE

Jules Michelet's monumental study of medieval superstition, *Satanism and Witchcraft*, is full of incredible reports. Here is one in the translation of A. R. Allinson (1939):

> The procedure is of the simplest. To begin with, apply torture to the witnesses, and build up a travesty, a caricature of evidence, by dint of pain and terror. Then drag a confession from the accused by excruciating agonies, and believe this confession against the direct evidence of facts. For instance, a Sorceress confesses she had recently dug up a child's dead body from the churchyard, to use it in her magical compounds. Her husband says, 'Go to the churchyard and look; the child is there now.' The grave is opened, and the body found intact in its coffin. Yet the judge decides, against the testimony of his own eyes, that it is only an *appearance*, an illusion of Satan. He credits the woman's confession in preference to the actual fact,—and the poor creature is burned.

Why this judicial insanity? A hint from the first sentence of Michelet's chapter: "The Church always granted the judge and the accuser a right to the confiscated property of those condemned for Sorcery."

Behind the urge to be a witch is very often an insane desire for power and sheer greed; behind the persecution of witches, lie ecclesiastical and civil power gone mad—and greater greed.

THE EYES HAVE IT

Elizabeth Device was hanged as a witch in 1612 in Rochdale, England, on no other evidence except that she could look up with one eye and down with the other.

Isadore of Seville, the erudite medieval encyclopedist, solemnly wrote that you could easily spot a witch, because they have two pupils in each eye. No, that's not a mistranslation of his clumsy Latin; he really believed it.

THIRSTY WORK

Elspeth McEwen was burned to death in a tar barrel as a witch in 1697 at Kirkcudbright in Scotland. An old bill survives:

Payed to Robert Creighton . . . 8 shill[ings] Scots for beating the drum at Elspet[h] M'Queen's funeral, and to James Carsson his wife [James Carson's wife] thirteen shillings drunken by Elspet[h]s executioner at sev[er]all times.

A FEW FIRSTS

The Bible is the first significant book to suggest killing witches.

Tacitus was the first major historian to take ghosts seriously.

Agnes Ode was the first Englishwoman to be tried for sorcery (thirteenth century), and after she passed the carrying-a-hot-poker test, she was acquitted.

Angela de la Barthe was the first Frenchwoman to be tried as a witch. She was burned in 1274.

Agnes Waterhouse, the first woman to be hanged as a witch in England, was executed at Chelmsford, Essex, in 1566.

Alice Young was the first woman to die for witchcraft in the bloody assizes of Connecticut in 1647.

FRENCH JUSTICE

Henri Bouget, author of the *Discours des sorciers* (1602)—for a generation, it was *the* handbook for witchcraft trials—is credited with having condemned more than six hundred wretches in Burgundy, though the number may have been exaggerated because of the judicial eminence of the writer.

The book that supplanted the *Discours* was by Le Sieur de Bouvet, provost-marshal of the French army. The title translates as *Admirable Ways and Means of Investigating All Sorts of Crimes and Witchcraft* and appeared in 1659. Where Benedikt Carpzov gave Augustus of Saxony a mere seventeen methods of torture, Bouvet was far more inventive. The book is a sadist's dream.

It was Bouget who established the rule that the more the prisoner denied his guilt, the more he was to be punished. To Bouget, denial of guilt "was an especially good reason to continue the torture."

QUAKER JUSTICE

Leave it to sensible Quakers to distinguish between public opinion and fact. The 1684 verdict of a Pennsylvania jury on an old woman accused of witchcraft was that "the prisoner is guilty of the common fame of being a witch but not guilty as she stands indicted."

SPANISH LOGIC

Pedro Sanchez Cirvelo (1475–1560) was canon of Salamanca at a time when that university was drawing students from far and wide. In 1521 he published *Opus de Magica Superstitione* and in 1539 *Reproof of Superstitions and Witchcraft*, the first really important Spanish work on that subject. In this he maintained the odd contention that, although sorcery is *not* a heresy, the Inquisition ought to punish it as if it were.

But perhaps the Inquisition had enough on its hands with heresy, for witchcraft persecutions did not flourish in Spain—the one country in Europe that refused to be panicked into such mindless folly. In *Witchcraft* (1958) Geoffrey Parrinder writes:

When the secular authorities stimulated a witch-craze in Navarre in 1526, a congregation of the [Spanish] Inquisition seriously debated the root question of the reality of witchcraft, and the punishment to be applied. . . . They agreed that confession was not proof enough, and that in any case the witch should be dealt with by the Inquisition which would impose penance.

The Inquisition in Spain checked the popular and civil efforts to destroy witches and it protected their lives.

THE LAST WITCH EXECUTED IN SCOTLAND

The last Scottish witch to be executed was an old woman of the parish of Loth, condemned by Captain David Ross, "sheriff-depute," who believed that she had ridden upon her own daughter, transformed into a pony, and shod by the devil, which made the girl ever after lame."

The accused was asked to give the Lord's Prayer (in Gaelic), and when she got *one word wrong*, they burned her. The Witch's Stone still marks the spot where she died.

HOW MANY DIED?

It is curious that Salem, Massachusetts, should be so famous for witchcraft persecutions. Twenty-one persons died in the months the hysteria lasted. The total figures for all witchcraft executions during the entire colonial period for all thirteen American colonies was thirty-two.

During the same period in Germany, estimates of the deaths from witchcraft accusations have run as high as 300,000 (far too high, say modern authorities—even 100,000 is overgenerous), many from drowning, burning, or from torture to which the accused were routinely subjected. Even England, where torture was not permitted as punishment, the most conservative modern estimates run to 1,000 dead, and in Scotland the figure may have been three or four times that many. But what community is famous for witchhunts? Why, Salem, Massachusetts, of course.

SPECIAL TREATMENT

If you were a woman who had murdered her husband, or a counterfeiter, heretic, or one of a few other special groups who were condemned, you could be burned at the stake. Witches were burned at the stake partly because that was a purification for heresy and partly because of the fear that, if their bodies were buried, they would come out of their graves to hurt the living—like vampires.

DAME ALICE AND THE BISHOP

The history of Ireland includes a number of sensational trials for witchcraft, the most famous being that of Dame Alice Kyteler in the fourteenth century. It is the only Irish one in which torture was used in a prosecution for witchcraft.

Dame Alice came from a wealthy Norman family long settled in Kilkenny, and her money gained her a succession of husbands. The first was a banker, William Outlawe. He died—they said of poison—but that did not discourage Adam le Blund and Richard de Valle, both of whom also died after marrying her—also with poison suspected. Her fourth husband was Sir John le Poer, and the rumors flew that she had caught him by means of love philter and by other evil potions had deprived him of his senses.

Finally in 1324 the bishop of Ossory investigated, and a commission in Kilkenny reported that Dame Alice was reputed to be a member of a local group of sorcerers. These wizards denied the Christian faith and absented themselves from its sacraments, sacrificing animals to demons and distributing pieces of the animals' bodies at crossroads to a low-ranking demon they called the Son of Art. The demons in exchange gave them powers. They met nightly to conduct their ceremonies (some of them blasphemous parodies of Christian rituals) and to bring evil on their neighbors by the use of a witches' brew. The brew contained, among other ingredients, entrails of animals sacrificed to demons, herbs, bits of the shrouds of unbaptized infants or the brains and hair and nails of men's corpses, and other horrible things, all cooked up in the skull of a decapitated thief.

They put curses and spells even on their own husbands, it was alleged. The children of Dame Alice's first three husbands accused her of murdering their fathers by witchcraft and depriving them of their rightful inheritances. They said her present husband, Sir John, had lost all his hair and his strength and would have died had not a maidservant alerted him to his wife's witchcraft and showed him where he could find, locked away in her private chests, some of the ingredients of the witches' brew.

The hideous things found there were turned over to the authorities, but the accusers were unable to produce the incubus (named Art or Robin) with whom, they claimed, Dame Alice had sexual relations, or the big black dog, called Aethiops, an incubus and her familiar. Some witnesses did swear they

saw her in the streets "between compline and twilight" sweeping up all the
dirt toward her son William Outlawe's front door and chanting:

> "To the house of William, my son,
> Hie all the wealth of Kilkenny town."

A complicated power struggle ensued between the bishop and Dame
Alice's powerful relatives, which the bishop ultimately won. But Alice fled to
England, her son William, her accomplice in witchcraft, was too powerful to
punish except by a brief imprisonment, and the full brunt of the law fell on
Dame Alice's servant Petronilla.

The bishop had the girl flogged six times, forcing her to confess the
details of Alice's and William's obscene magical rites. She directed the
authorities to where, she said, Dame Alice kept her magical flying ointment
("wherewith she greased a staffe, upon which she ambled and galloped
through thick and thin, when and in what name she listed") and a desecrated
Host, on which the name of the Devil had replaced that of Jesus Christ.

This proof against Dame Alice served only to destroy Petronilla. When
it was added to her confessions, she was burned at the stake in Kilkenny on
November 3, 1324, the first instance of burning for heresy in Ireland.

The rest of the members, "the other heretics and sorcerers who
belonged to the pestilential Society of Robin, Son of Art," were (according to
an old report) rounded up and punished:

> the order of law being preserved, some of them were publicly
> burnt to death; others, confessing their crimes in the presence
> of all the people, in an upper garment are marked back and front
> with a cross after they had abjured the heresy, which is the cus-
> tom; others were solemnly whipped through the town and the
> market place; others were banished from the city and diocese;
> others, who evaded the jurisdiction of the Church, were excom-
> municated; while others again fled in fear and were never heard
> of after.

This tale of Dame Alice and her son amply illustrates the way that the
witchcraft laws were weighted against the poor.

WITCHCRAFT BANNED IN BOSTON

The four children of John Godwin said to be possessed by the Devil in Boston in 1688 were the subject of Cotton Mather's *Memorable Providences* published the next year. There were two boys (aged five and eleven) and two girls (aged seven and thirteen), and they alarmed the whole populace of Boston when they fell into "strange fits, beyond those that attend an epilepsy, or a catalepsy, or those that they call the diseases of astonishment." Whenever anyone wanted to get the children up in the morning, or put them to bed at night, or dress them, all Hell broke loose. They contorted their bodies so that they could not be dressed, they screamed and roared, they seem to go deaf and dumb or blind, and they twisted their heads "almost round."

Modern parents with obstreperous children might well suspect mere acting up or hyperactivity, but in seventeenth-century Boston there was only one explanation: "Nothing but a hellish witchcraft could be the origin of these maladies."

The cause was suspected to be Goody Glover, described as "a scandalous old woman," accused of having laid an "enchantment" on the children, having cursed them in her bad temper. She was just an old Irishwoman who could speak little English, but the fact that she could not say the Lord's Prayer in English was considered a sinister sign. When they searched her house, authorities produced "several small images, or puppets, or babies, made of rags and stuffed with goat's hair and other such ingredients." They said she confessed to hurting the children by wetting her finger and applying it to various places on the dolls. She apologized for being unable to say prayers in English; she said them, she explained, in Irish and—horrors! a Catholic?—in Latin.

Goody Glover was condemned to death by Judge Stoughton, deputy governor of Massachusetts, a figure who was to be more prominent later at the Salem witchcraft trials. After a second old woman was also condemned, things quieted down in Boston.

But Cotton Mather (1663–1728) was not content with that, and one of the most influential of his nearly four hundred books soon appeared as *Memorable Providences, Relating to Witchcraft and Possession* (1689). "I am resolved," Cotton Mather wrote, "after this [Boston incident] never to use but just one grain of patience with any man that shall go to impose upon me a denial of devils or of witches."

THE KING JAMES VERSION

James I of England is famous for the King James Version of the Bible. He ordered that translation, but of course it was not his work. He did write *Daemonologia*, a blast against Reginald Scot's *Discoverie of Witchcraft*, which called the black arts a mere "artful imposture." James defended the reality of witchcraft, because he was sure he knew, from personal experience, its widespread dangers.

In 1591, twelve years before he came to the English throne (he was then James VI of Scotland), a witchcraft conspiracy had come to light in the town of North Berwick. The women and men rounded up confessed to bizarre acts—going to sea in a sieve, causing a violent storm on the sea by drowning a baptised cat, and similar claims—and confessed that their purpose was to kill the king by causing his ship (he was returning from Denmark at the time with his new queen) to founder. At their trial, they swore that their leader was Francis Stewart, earl of Bothwell, son of a bastard son of James V (and thus the king's half first cousin).

James had always suspected his cousin of having designs on the throne, and the witches' confessions may have been an attempt to curry favor. If so, they did not know their James, for he had the group subjected to mangling and death, torturing one Dr. Fian until he was "less a man than a bleeding mass," and ordered a woman "burned in ashes quick [alive] to death."

Bothwell himself escaped being tried by fleeing to England, but at Christmastime the following year, he reappeared in Edinburgh and tried to get into Holyrood Palace, the king's residence, to demand a hearing. James cowered inside in terror and refused to admit his cousin, who eventually gave up and, fearful the king would have him secretly murdered, fled to Normandy and then Naples, where he remained for the rest of his life.

James meanwhile wrote *Daemonologia* and became king of England.

RADICAL VIEWS

The rule used to be that you couldn't take a valid confession actually on the rack. But five minutes before or after the rack was technically not under duress. Clever?

Peter Binsfield (1540–1603), author of a seminal Latin treatise on "malificers and sorcerers" of 1589, was willing to believe evidence obtained under duress, but despite "confessions" begged leave to doubt the reality of ailuranthropy (changing into a cat), cynanthropy (changing into a dog), and lepanthropy (changing into a hare). This position was regarded by other authorities of the time as wrongheaded and dangerous.

SWEDISH WITCHES

The Swedes were usually calmer than the French or the Germans when it came to witchcraft, but in 1670 at Mohra seventy women and fifteen children were executed for witchcraft and 136 children (aged nine to sixteen) were sentenced to "run the gauntlet and be whipped on their hands at the church door," some as often as once a week for a year. Later in that decade, between 1674 and 1677 some seventy persons were burned or beheaded in Sweden for witchcraft.

The severe sentences of the earlier part of the century in the reign of Gustavus Adolphus (1618) seem to have been aimed more at poisoners than witches. Queen Christina put a stop to sorcery trials. Still accusations spread, and executions at Mohra, just mentioned, led to forty-seven cases at Falun, more in Uppsala (an old stronghold of witchcraft), and Stockholm. The death sentence for witchcraft was abolished in Sweden in 1799.

Today, witchcraft is hardly active at all in Sweden (compared to Britain, for example) but the folk remedies and customs smack quite a bit of the pagan past.

MORE ON THE NORTH BERWICK WITCHES

At the trial of the witches in North Berwick, already mentioned, King James attended in person. At one point he was moved to yell at Agnes Simpson that she was lying in the dock.

She asked to talk with him privately and repeated word for word what James and his queen had said in bed on their wedding night. That convinced King James that she was a witch after all. So all the defendants, including Alice Simpson, were executed.

REALLY LAYING AN EGG

At the beginning and the end of the sixteenth century the normally placid Swiss had wild outbreaks of witch-burning: five hundred executed in Geneva in 1515 and three hundred executed in Bern 1591–1600, for instance. In 1474 in Basel, a fowl was sentenced to death for laying an egg. You see, it was a rooster.

A HIGH SCORE

In the quiet little Protestant town of Quedlinburg in Saxony in the year 1589, the population of 12,000 burned 133 witches on one single day. It would have been 137 witches, but four of the condemned were pretty young girls, and the executioner saved them, giving out that the Devil had spirited them away.

THE LAWGIVER

Benedikt Carpzov II (1595–1666), called the Lawgiver of Saxony, had two proud boasts: (1) that he had read the Bible fifty-three times and (2) that he had caused to be burned at the stake a total of twenty thousand witches.

Modern historians tend to be skeptical of such figures, even when not given as boasts. But plainly Carpzov gave it his best shot.

THE LAST

One of the most stringent laws ever enacted against "witchcraft, enchantments and sorceries" were Henry VIII's statute of 1542. Yet under that law only one single person was actually convicted, and he was pardoned. Under other laws, however, the accusations and killing continued, and in 1604 James I managed to get a law passed that made accusation of witchcraft virtually tantamount to conviction.

Under this law, one authority claims, over a period of some two hundred years, a total of 30,000 "judicial murders" for witchcraft were carried out. King James I once condemned a whole assizes for daring to acquit a woman accused of witchcraft.

About a dozen witches were executed in Northamptonshire in the first few years of the eighteenth century, and in 1716 a Mrs. Hicks and her daughter (aged nine) were hanged for witchcraft in Huntingdonshire. The laws against witchcraft were then repealed in the tenth year of the reign of George II (1736) when, according to Joseph Hayden's *Dictionary of Dates* (1841), "an ignorant person attempting to revive them" instituted a "bill against a poor old woman in Surrey for the practice of witchcraft."

The last execution for witchcraft in Scotland was in 1722, as we have described elsewhere. That did not end the persecution in the British Isles, however, for much hounding and torment went on clandestinely. In the 1750s in Hampshire, two oldsters were accidentally killed while their interrogators were "swimming" them in the village pond.

In the American colonies, trials for witchcraft were not confined to New England—although that is where they flourished—but Maryland is the only other mainland colony that actually executed a witch. In 1685, Rebecca Fowler was hanged for practicing "diabolical arts." Maryland was also the scene of the colonies' last witchcraft trial, in 1712, when a certain Virtue Violl was found not guilty of sorcery. The last execution for witchcraft in the British colonies was in Bermuda in 1730, when Sarah Bassett, a slave, was hanged for killing her master by spells.

In the Spanish-speaking parts of the Americas the persecution of witches continued much longer than in Europe, and the last person burned as a witch seems to have been a woman put to death in Peru in 1888.

In Germany in the seventeenth century, the bishop of Bamberg burned more than a hundred people for sorcery and perhaps as many as two hundred (accounts vary). Philip Adolf von Ehrenberg, a prince-bishop, and his cousin Johann Georg II Fuchs von Dornheim (the Axe Bishop) between them accounted for fifteen hundred dead. In 1627, the Germans built a big *Hexenhaus* to hold the accused until they could be tortured into confessions of witchcraft. The end of the eighteenth century saw the last important accusations of witchcraft. The age when Wolfenbüttel—and all too many other German cities—was "a forest of stakes" was finally over.

THE GUILT OF WITCHES

In times when a scapegoat was needed or when religion felt threatened, witchcraft became an abomination and a heresy, and toward it was directed all the righteous violence of the society. But was there really such a thing as a compact with the Devil?

Wallace Notestein's *History of Witchcraft in England from 1558 to 1718* (1911), leaning heavily on the court records, tends to agree with Reginald Scot's Elizabethan opinion (then unorthodox) that witchcraft is a delusion and that "witches" are more senile than Satanic. But such a viewpoint has been mocked as late as 1926. In that year Montague Summers published *History of Witchcraft and Demonology,* in which he says:

> A few authors have painted the mediaeval witch in pretty colours
> on satin. She has become a somewhat eccentric but kindly old
> lady, shrewd and perspicacious, with a knowledge of healing herbs
> and simples, ready to advise and aid her neighbors. . . . And
> so for no very definite reason she fell an easy prey to fanatic
> judges and ravening inquisitors, notoriously the most ignorant and
> stupid of mortals, who caught her, swum her in a river, tried her,
> tortured her, and finally burned her at the stake. . . .

Surely the truth is that some witches were decidedly antisocial, lawless, vengeful, murderers for hire, poisoners, terrorists, heretics, and some were indeed kindly old ladies with some old country recipes for healing. In either case, their treatment by the law was barbaric.

5
Amulets, Talismans, and Charms

TALISMANIC magic is one kind that most people have practiced at some time or other. Have you ever had a rabbit's foot or a "lucky coin" or any other object you carried around "just for luck"? Have you known anyone else who did?

Actually, many of the things we will be discussing are not talismans but amulets. Amulets ward off evil, whereas talismans attract good results. Just "knowing" one has something working for him helps to alleviate worry, creates confidence, and thus enhances the wearer's performance.

If you believe, as have many occultists such as Paracelsus and Colin Wilson, that magic is in the mind, then the wearer's personal attitude is the most important thing. But magicians believe that a true astral force or some other supernatural power can literally be put into an amulet or talisman and that it can function even if the wearer is wholly unaware of it.

Many people employ amulets and talismans as integral parts of orthodox religion: phylacteries and mezuzahs, crosses and medals. The Egyptians used scarabs and ankhs, the Africans use fetishes, the Mohammedans the Hand of Fatima and other devices.

Here are just a few examples of magical and ritual objects.

GRIS-GRIS

The African practice of making small idols or images of protecting spirits arrived in the Western Hemisphere along with slavery. Today, often still used in Voodoo and similar cults, they are worn as charms.

A.M.S.G.

The practice of the Society of Jesus is to put at the top of documents *A.M.D.G.*, which stands for *Ad Maiorem Dei Gloriam*, "To the Greater Glory of God." Others used *J.M.J.* ("Jesus, Mary, and Joseph") and similar devices.

Satanists use *A.M.S.G.* (*Ad Maiorem Satanae Gloriam*, "To the Greater Glory of Satan") on documents, in pentacles, on amulets and talismans, and so on. Sometimes *D.V.* (*Dei veri*, "The True God") is added.

FREE SERVICE

Occult tradition dictates that the maker of amulets and talismans must receive no fee for his services, though it is allowable for him who is to wear the amulet or talisman to provide the metal (usually silver or gold).

Thus getting your own metal disk and sending it out to be engraved by your local jeweler does not work, because you must pay him. Moreover, you will not know the precise moment when he gets to the work, and that is essential if you are to meditate on your intention and so help "charge" the amulet or talisman.

A CHRISTIAN CHARM

The *Malleus Maleficarum* allowed charms to Christians provided that no unknown names were used (lest these be of pagan gods or demons), no pact with the Devil, no belief in any power other than the power of God, nothing untrue or pagan (only the sign of the Cross for "passes"), and only Biblical phrases.

NOTHING BUT THE TOOTH

When you were a child, and lost a tooth, did you put it under your pillow to get a coin from the Tooth Fairy?

There are other strange superstitions about teeth, about babies born with a full set (who will be vampires or worse), about the order in which baby teeth are cut, about "wisdom" teeth, about horses' teeth hung around a child's neck to make the child's teeth strong (an old Scandinavian idea), and so on.

Did you know that the gypsies recommend that the first tooth a child loses must be thrown into a hollow tree? Clearly a tribute to the gods in the trees we used to worship.

Teeth that fall out after the age of seven should be saved; they can come in handy. If a child then has a severe toothache, a discarded tooth can be thrown into a stream. This recalls our ancient worship of the spirits in water.

Saved teeth come in handy when you have something to sell and no customers. Keep them in a little bag, along with the bones of a tree frog or toad or an ash twig. On market day, you simply rub the bag and wish and customers will then appear—if you believe strongly and if the bag has been properly prepared. (The main problem is getting the small bones clean. Bury them in a perforated container in an anthill; the ants will pick them quite clean.)

I have only once seen this ancient superstition alive in the modern world. At Caledonian Market, the outdoors antiques market at Bermondsey (part of London) in 1969, I saw an old man with his little bag and a deserted stall. He needed all the help he could get. His few goods looked a bit ratty, and it was very early on a very wet Friday.

I popped up behind him and asked, "Are there teeth and bones in your little bag?" He was startled, doubly so when I confessed that I got my information out of books.

"I didn't know things like that were in books," he said. "Perhaps a gypsy wrote that book, but he oughtn't to have done it."

I chatted awhile and eventually bought an old painting from under the stall that cleaned up fine and proved to be a fair copy of an original portrait of Lord Byron. The old man wrapped my purchase carefully in some old newspaper, and as I paid him, I jokingly remarked that one must never conclude a bargain on a Friday, for Friday (when Christ died) is unlucky.

"That's all very true, Guv," he responded, "but Caledonian Market is only open on a Friday, so what can a man do?"

What indeed? Well, a man can stick to his superstitions. In a way, his little magic bag did work. It brought me right over to his stall, and I was his first customer. As for me, I have my Byron portrait with a good story thrown in—not a bad bargain for £3.

THE LONDON CURSE

On a site in Princes Street, London, a piece of lead, perhaps once nailed to a door, was excavated. It read:

T[ITUS] EGNATIUS TYRANUS DEFIC [T]US EST ET P[UBLIUS] CICEREIUS
FELIX DEFICTUS E[S]T

It put a curse on Titus Egnatius Tyranus and Publius Cicereius Felix. One wonders whatever happened to them. If they *saw* the curse, it may well have had its effect.

LINES (AND CIRCLES) FROM CHRISTOPHER MARLOWE

These metaphysics of magicians
And necromantic books are heavenly:
Lines, circles, scenes, letters and characters:
Ay, these are those that Faustus most desires.
O, what a world of profit and delight,
Of power, of honour, of omnipotence
Is promised to the studious artisan!
—*The Tragical History of Doctor Faustus*

A TALISMAN

In the will of Napoleon III (1808–1873), that emperor of the French left to his son "as a talisman the seal I used to wear attached to my watch."

THE PRIEST'S HAND

Eric Maple, active in the Society for Psychical Research and the author of numerous books and radio talks, writes in *The Complete Book of Witchcraft and Demonology* (1966):

> During the Protestant ascendancy, no sport was more popular, if we except witch hunting, than hounding to death those Jesuit priests who attempted to keep alight the candle of Roman Catholic faith in Britain. These priests were usually to be found in the homes of the old Catholic families, often hidden in secret rooms ["priest holes"] and passages. When caught they were often tortured and condemned to the dreadful punishment reserved for male traitors: partial hanging, castration, disembowelling and finally decapitation.
>
> In the reign of Charles I, Father Edward Arrowsmith [1585–1628], a Jesuit, was tried and executed for the mere fact of being a Romish priest, but before dying, asked those nearest to him, to sever his hand after death, declaring that with the aid of this talisman, they would have the power to work miracles.

The hand did, in fact, get credit for many curses and "miracles" over the next three hundred years and the *Dictionary of National Biography* noted that it "is preserved as a relic" in Newton-le-Willows, Yorkshire.

COSMETICS

In the sense that cosmetics are supposed to "draw" people to you, by making you look more beautiful, they are rather talismanic, and some ancient recipes mix magic with their ingredients, charms with charm.

Cosmetics are said to have been invented (along with astronomy and astrology, metal workng and armaments, magic and witchcraft) by "the Watchers," two hundred angels under the command of Azazel who descended to earth (at Mount Hermon) and married the daughters of men, according to the apocryplial Book of Enoch (first century B.C.). What they taught of magic cosmetics is among the most closely guarded secrets of the adepts in magical arts. Few covens, in fact, know of the powers attributed to body painting and perfuming for magical ceremonies.

Magical cosmetics are supposed to be a sort of warpaint in the battle the Satanists wage. If these "recipes" are indeed of ancient origin, then early adepts were well aware of the exact chemicals that cause human sexual excitement, for that seems to be the principle result of using them. (They also affect animals; it is reliably reported that when Aleister Crowley wore his perfumed ointment, the horses started and neighed as he walked by them in the street.)

CURSES

Superstitious people feared the curses of witches and magicians, and maleficers risked the curses of Church authorities. Plato, however, wrote in his *Laws* that the most effective of all curses was that of the parent on the child. "The curses of parents," you may care to remind your obstreperous offspring, "are mighty against their children as no others are."

GAINING THE FAVOR OF A JUDGE

When MacGregor Mathers obtained a court order to prevent Aleister Crowley from publishing the secrets of the Order of the Golden Dawn (1910), "The Beast" appealed the decision, and this is the talisman he used— borrowed from Chapter 19 of Mathers' own translation of *The Sacred Magic of Abramelin*—to get a judge to reverse the order of the court:

```
A L M A N A H
L
M A R E
A A L B E H A
N
A R E H A I L
H                A
```

If you are ever on trial, try writing these letters on parchment. They worked for Crowley—at least, he did get the order reversed.

BASMALA

The *basmala* is the Arabic formula for "In the Name of Allah, the Merciful, the Compassionate." In Arabic that is nineteen letters, equal to the *zabaniah* (company of angels under Malik).

Write it sixty-one times and wear it, and if you are barren, you will become fruitful. Write it six hundred times and wear it, and you will gain great honor among men. Or so it is claimed.

FETISH

The word *fetish* these days, as casually used by Europeans, generally refers to something with sexual significance, but it came originally from an old Portuguese word for "false" and is related to the current word for sorcerer: *feiticeiro*. It's primary meaning is still occult: any artifact or natural object held by its owner to possess supernatural powers.

ANTIDOTE

Secretum Secretorum ("Secret of Secrets") was a medieval magic book falsely attributed to Aristotle. It says that a bezoar stone prevents epilepsy in children. A bezoar is a mineral lump or concretion, like a gallstone, found in the stomachs of ruminants, particularly goats and deer. Epilepsy was only one of its uses. Ground up, it was prescribed as a cure for leprosy and fever, and carried about (preferably in a gold box) it was regarded as a preventive for plague—a true amulet.

But by far the commonest use of the bezoar was as a universal antidote for poison. When a Spanish nobleman tried to sell one to Charles IX of France, the king summoned his court physician, who happened to be Ambroise Paré, "the father of surgery," and asked if it really worked. Paré, a man famed for his common sense, said it wasn't possible for any single substance to be an antidote to all poisons, so the king tried an experiment. One of his cooks was about to be executed for theft; Charles offered to let the man go free if he would subject himself to a trial of the bezoar, and when the condemned man eagerly agreed, he was given the poison (corrosive sublimate) to swallow followed by some of the ground-up stone. The poor man died seven hours later "with great torment and exclamation," bleeding from every opening of the body. Charles burned the rest of the bezoar.

A CHARM IS A SIN

The Greek fishermen who seek for sponges around Tarpon Springs, Florida, know that their deeply held Christian faith forbids such superstitions as they have inherited from a pre-Christian past, but they manage to combine the old and the new. For example, they will not set out to sea on a Tuesday (Tuesday is an ill-fated day to begin any enterprise) nor begin the fishing season before Epiphany. They believe that if a storm is brewing at sea, they can protect themselves from its fury by carving a cross on the mast of the ship and sticking the knife into it.

Folklore in America (selected by T. P. Coffin and Hennig Cohen) adds:

> This saves them from the fury of the storm. The person who
> performs this charm is committing a sin and must do some form
> of penance. The fishermen do not hesitate, however, to resort to
> this charm when in danger.

Anthropologists all over the world notice that fishermen may not use magic in unthreatening situations (like fishing in a lagoon) but resort to magic in danger.

KNIVES TO MEND

Among many people, knives are considered potent devices to use with charms. The Greek seamen above stick one in the mast to cause a high wind to die down. English seamen do the very same thing for the opposite purpose—to call up a wind when they are becalmed, or to change a foul wind to a fair one.

The Scots are particularly fond of knife superstitions. Carrying one in your pocket will prevent the fairies from abducting you at night. (Fairies are afraid of cold iron.) A recently killed deer must be stored overnight with a knife stuck into it, or the fairies will carry *it* off. When you enter the house of a fairy or a witch, you must stick a knife in the door, which will prevent the owner from closing it; once you are safely outside again, you remove the knife and go your way. If, on an otherwise calm day, you see an eddy of wind whisking up dust and straw, that means the fairies are carrying people off, and you must throw a knife at the eddy; that will force them to release their captives.

THE MUMMY'S CURSE?

Ancient Egyptians considered the pharaoh's person sacred and tried hard to protect it in death as in life. Their priests were clever, and they were vengeful; they used to put a picture of their enemies on the soles of their sandals, so that they could tread on them at every step. It was believed that the priests laid a curse on anyone who disturbed the sacred bones of a dead king.

If so, such curses did not work very well, for one after another, the tombs of pharaohs, no matter how carefully sealed and guarded, were broken into by grave robbers and rifled. Only one pharaonic tomb came down to the twentieth century intact.

On November 4, 1922, after seven years of searching, archaeologist Howard Carter discovered and opened the tomb of Tutankhamen, who had lived in the fourteenth century B.C. It was overwhelming. There was the mummy of the boy-god-king, adorned with about a hundred pieces of fabulous jewelry and (a poignant touch) a wreath of faded flowers, perhaps a last token from his young wife. The rest was a storehouse of treasures. The discovery made "King Tut," an obscure boy who had reigned ineffectually for only a few years, the best-known pharaoh in history.

But when Lord Carnarvon (1866–1923), Carter's patron, died of pneumonia during the excavation of the tomb, rumors started that he had been a victim of a pharaoh's curse. Subsequently, other members of the expedition died from various causes, mostly natural. Out of these unlikely ingredients—for no one could even point to a curse inscribed on the tomb—sensation-mongering newspapers created the myth of an ancient curse against anyone who disturbed the bones of the dead king.

It's hard to see why, if there was a curse, it didn't take Howard Carter first. He lived until 1939 and was sixty-six at the time of his death.

WANT TO TRY YOUR HAND?

A talismanic ring of the ninth century in the British Museum bears this inscription in runes:

AERKRIUFLTKRIURIPONGLAESTAEPON

Nobody has ever been able to interpret it.

TEMPLE OF THE TOOTH

Kandy was once the capital of a separate kingdom but is now the jewel of Sri Lanka, formerly Ceylon.

Among its many marvels is the Temple of the Tooth, one of the most sacred shrines of Buddhism. It is said to contain one tooth of Gautama himself, smuggled into the country by a princess who hid the relic in her elaborate hairdo.

At one time the Christians desecrated the temple, burned the relic, and threw the ashes into the sea. But Buddhists asserted that the tooth the Christians destroyed was a fake, that the real tooth of the founder of one of the world's great religions had been secretly saved.

Today, in a replacement temple the tooth is on display at the heart of a magnificent shrine.

I have seen the cloak of Mohammed in the treasures of Topkapi, palace of the Ottoman emperors, now a museum in Istanbul. I have seen relics of Jesus Christ, such as the Shroud of Turin. But these are "second-class" relics, simply associated with those men; the tooth is a "first-class" relic, a part of the Buddha himself.

If there can be magical power in things "charged" or blessed or touched by holy men, it is natural to believe that a piece of the person himself will have great power. Think of the blood of saints, for example, and, on a secular level, even the awe with which one regards the bloodstained shirt of Charles I, a lock of Napoleon's hair, a star's autograph.

THE SORCERER'S CURSE

Poussinière, sentenced to be burned at the stake in Fougères, France, said just before he died that the steeple of the church of St. Sulpice, nearby, would tilt that very day. It did, and for hundreds of years it has stood with its tip a foot and a half out of plumb.

INCANTATION AGAINST NIGHTMARES

Hang over your bed a crucifix or a stone with a natural hole in it. Before lying down to sleep recite these verses:

> St. George, St. George, Our Lady's knight,
> He walked by day, so he did by night:
> Until such times as he her found,
> He her beat and he her bound,
> Until her troth to him he plight,
> He would not come to her that night.

TREES AND STONES

Tree worship was denounced in Aelfric's "Homily on the Passion of St. Bartholomew the Apostle":

> It is not allowed to any Christian man to fetch his health from
> any stone, nor from any tree.

Note Aelfric doesn't say you *can't* do that—just that you *must* not. The English were a long time giving up the worship of trees.

In *Ancient Laws and Institutes of England,* Thorpe quotes the *Canones Edgari* to the effect that "tree-worshiping and stone-worshipping and that devil's craft hereby children are drawn through the earth" are expressly forbidden.

That last requires some explanation. Ancient custom had a child crawl three Fridays (the day of the Crucifixion, a nice tie-in of the New Religion with the Old) successively, silently, through an arch of brambles. Until fairly recent times Swedish women in labor were passed through *elfenlöcher*, holes in trees.

But we no longer worship trees, knock on wood.

THE CROSS

The Cross is of course a common symbol in post-Christian amulets, etc. The sign of the Cross has substituted for a number of the "passes" magicians used to make with their hands. Appearing often in missals and other religious books, it once convinced the ignorant that magical symbols were used in Roman Catholic rituals. Even Satanists use the symbol, though it ought to be neutral for them.

The cross surmounts many churches, including St. Paul's Cathedral in London. But the architect Sir Christopher Wren wanted a pineapple there.

SACRED STONES

Throughout history certain precious and semiprecious stones have been thought to have magical powers.

In Iceland jet, or black amber, is carried as a protection. In Africa, certain stones often form part of the pack buried under an enemy's threshold to put a curse on him. In medieval Europe, jet was used to test virginity (I am uncertain how) and burned to drive away evil spirits.

The breastplate of the High Priest of the Jews was composed of a number of precious and semiprecious stones, each believed to have its own special power. (I discussed these in *The Wonderful World of Superstition, Prophecy, and Luck* [1984], so I will not repeat their meanings here.)

It was inevitable that heavenly powers should be attributed to such stones as fell from the "pavement of Heaven" to earth. Tondriau and Villeneuve in their *Dictionary of Devils and Demons* stray a little from their subject to discuss aerolite, defined as a "piece of a star which has fallen to earth." But meteorites and such have been less used in magic than stones mined from the earth.

Among stones believed to protect the wearer are amber (against poison), amethyst (against drunkenness), coral (against violence), jade (against nightmares), topaz (against injury), turquoise (against assassination), and zircon (for many uses).

To bring or retain love people have worn beryl, emerald and lapis. Moonstones, onyx, and opal are unlucky for most people, though opal (it is said) will warn the unlucky wearer by becoming cloudy.

Millions of people still concern themselves with birthstones, and in my book on superstition, prophecy, and luck, of course, I gave a list of them. Here let me amplify it a little by commenting on each of the stones.

January	**garnet**	gives constancy, sincerity, friendliness, frankness, generosity.
February	**amethyst**	cures alcoholism, creates contentment, draws favor of superiors.
March	**aquamarine**	gives hope and confidence, cheers up the unhappy.
April	**diamond**	reconciles lovers, gives constancy, fidelity, innocence.
May	**emerald**	strenthens love and intelligence, eloquence, popularity.
June	**pearl**	gives purity, fidelity, gentleness, tears of joy or sorrow.
July	**ruby**	gives boldness, anger, loyalty, charity, cruelty, courage, misery.
August	**sardonyx**	gives intellectual power, can be used in magical rites.
September	**sapphire**	gives loyalty, justice, truth, peace, contentment, humility.
October	**tourmaline**	gives vitality, potency, vigor, exhilaration, excitement.
November	**topaz**	gives sobriety, fidelity, love, draws honor or wealth, cures anger.
December	**turquoise**	prevents assassinations or accidental death, brings safety.

If you think pearls are unlucky, (as many people do), you can wear alexandrite. This variety of beryl changes color and so seems in some people's minds to combine the advantages of other stones it can resemble: sapphire, emerald, amethyst. The reason that ruby's characteristics seem at odds with each other is that rubies are believed to alter their appearance, and when they do, they bring on the negative: the cruel and uncontrolled side of the individual comes out.

It is considered unlucky to wear a stone of a month other than one's birth month, but jade or crystal are reckoned as exceptions. Anyone can gain luck by wearing jade or crystal. Jade is for persons of the highest morality; crystal is likelier to create a better morality in a person by sharpening the intellect, directing it toward a better harmony. Anyone can wear beryl to attract the opposite sex, jet to protect against fears and apparitions, zircon to promote sound sleep and good health and to protect on journeys.

Opal, once thought unlucky for anyone not born in October, is now passed by very often even by them, tourmaline being chosen instead, but October people can wear opal safely if they will just discard it should it grow dull (unlucky).

Probably the most revered stone in the world is the "black stone," set in silver, and built into the Ka'abah at Mecca. A pilgrimage to that site is the dream of every Muslim in the world, and every year a great many people of the Islamic world make their way there. Some say that this black stone was once part of the Temple of Solomon.

HERESY

The Inquisition sitting at Saragossa, Spain, in 1585 solemnly declared that keeping a dead man's finger as a good luck charm was a heresy.

SWEDISH CUSTOM

Besides keeping on or near one's self certain things to bring good luck or protection, there is also the matter of sacrificing material to God or the Devil.

Sacha Segal Scarlet in a *Key to Stockholm* (1960) says that "a tradition that is dying out is at Christmas for the children to carry a bowl of rice porridge to the attic for the Robin Goodfellow [Devil] or goblin of the dwelling. Possibly the family cats regret that this custom is now so little observed."

From the earliest times people sacrificed animals. The Germans used to offer reindeer, their most valuable livestock. The Greeks poured wine on the ground. Melchizedech, king of Salem and priest of the Most High God, substituted bread and wine for animal sacrifice and set the tradition now followed by the Christians. This custom of offering human food to the gods is seen in many religions around the world, and the "rice porridge" offered to Swedish goblins is part of this.

WHAT'S IN A NAME?

Names play an important part on amulets and talismans, and many have an inscription beginning "in the Name of" followed by names or *Shemoth* (substitute names) of God or demons or archangels.

A name in magic is regarded as a part of the person who bears it and is often used just as a lock of hair or some nail clipping would be. Magicians were believed to exert power over spirits and demons by knowing their names; once they had drawn their magic circle (containing the names of God) to protect themselves, they would summon up the supernatural beings and force them, by the use of their names, to do the bidding of mortals.

In black magic, many names are reversed or anagrammatized.

Never put your own name or an amulet or talisman, but put as much of "yourself" as possible into its manufacture and keep it with you continually to increase and derive the most benefit from its power—even if you are not sure you believe in its efficacy.

SPIT

Baseball pitchers spit on the ball. Laborers spit on their hands. People spit on the ground to seal a bargain. Enemies spit at you in derision or contempt.

Spit is magical. Voodoo magicians spit on their little effigies to "give them life." Christ used spit to work miracles of healing.

A Dr. Gregory, lecturing to the British Association (Oxford, 1894), explained how he and the chief of the warlike Masai tribe of Africa made peace after a disagreement: "We spat on each other."

Spitting is messier than shaking hands (which comes from the old custom of showing you were holding no weapon) but better in that it transfers a part of yourself to the other. Blood brothers the easy and painless way!

People also spit on money "for luck" and on charms, kiss "good luck" pieces, and so on. Did you ever wonder why? Now you know.

THE STAR THAT ISN'T DAVID'S

Common on amulets and talismans, as in pentagrams, etc., is the six-pointed "star of David," honored by the Jews and dishonored by Hitler who tried to make it a badge of inferiority.

It was King Solomon, not King David, however, who had a seal ring with this ancient star on it; engraved with "the real Name of God," it was supposed to give him power over demons. It's lost; he was buried with it.

Cabalists adopted the six-pointed star because it incorporated the symbol for fire, a triangle resting on its base, and that for water, a triangle on its point.

They called it the Seal of Solomon and used it for talismans and put it on their equipment, such as their magic robes. It is found as a sign of power in the magical books ascribed in the Middle Ages to Solomon himself. These have been "adapted" and reprinted. Useless. Magicians insist they must be in manuscript.

This "Jewish" symbol is seen in Christian churches (sometimes combined with the Greek *alpha* and *omega*, suggesting the beginning and the end) and on magicians' hats from places as far apart as Wales and Algeria, Nepal (where it is combined with a sword as an insignia of the king) and Mexico.

NIGHT MAGIC

Lenormant's *Chaldean Magic* (1877) and similar historical studies of the Sumerians and the Babylonians and Assyrians, demonstrate something of the age-old nature of magic.

A Chaldean magical tablet yields a talisman to keep demons out of your house. It translates thus:

> Talisman, Talisman,
> Boundary that cannot be taken away,
> Boundary that the gods cannot pass,
> Barrier immovable,
> Which is opposed to malevolence
> Whether it be a wicked *utuq*,

> A wicked *alal*, a wicked *gilgum*,
> A wicked god, a wicked *maskim*,
> A phantom, a spector,
> A vampire, an incubus,
> A succubus, a nightmare,
> May the barrier of the god Ea
> Stop him.

Perhaps a little more translation will help. *Utuq*, *alal*, and *gilgum* are kinds of demons; *maskim* are seven subterranean demons. You know the others. As I say elsewhere, a vampire is not really a demon (being undead) but is in some manner related to demons associated with the bloodthirsty Moloch. The nightmare used to be thought of as a kind of animal demon or hag who tormented people during their sleep, as did incubi and succubi. Ea was the god of wisdom.

"Now I lay me down to sleep. . . ." The night has always held terrors for people and is the Devil's time of day, as it were. Chaldean demons also appeared at night. Against them they used such a *teletē* (Greek for "rite"), while an amulet gave passive protection.

Today people use a four-leaf clover, the pompom from a European sailor's hat, the *fascinum* (winged phallus, some of which were found in the ruins of Pompeii and seemed to have done little good there), and so on.

As O. Henry said on his deathbed, we do not want to go home in the dark.

MORE STONES

Precious and semiprecious stones were thought to have medicinal as well as magical powers; medicine and magic were closely intertwined anyway, like the snakes on the *caduceus*. One Roman emperor drank up a fortune in crushed rubies and other precious gems in a futile effort to cure a fatal disease. In Shakespeare rulers dissolve pearls in wine, another expensive drink.

But any odd-shaped stone found on or in the ground or fallen from heaven could be put to use, and was. Islan had the Seal of the Snake, a stone handy for love charms. The *quirin*, or "traitor's stone" (found in the nest of a lapwing), was a primitive sodium pentathol: Place it on the forehead of a sleeping man, and he will tell the truth, confess secrets.

Don't forget the larger stones: the rune stones of Scandinavia, the ogham-inscribed stones of Ireland, the massive monuments of the Druids, the Stone of Scone (on which all British monarchs have been crowned since it was stolen from the Scots in 1306). The Stone of Scone is Scottish sandstone and not from the Holy Land, but many believed it was Jacob's Pillow, the stone on which he rested his head as he dreamed of the angels ascending the stairs into heaven. No amount of argument could convince people that other stones were not also full of magic and had, in a sense which Shakespeare did not intend, "sermons" in them.

CHARMING FACTS

It was characteristic of magicians to associate charms with astrological matters. In fact, charms can only be effectively made at certain astrologically correct times. Here in brief is a good deal of the "correspondence":

Aries	Diamond	Axe	Iron	Mars	1987, 1994, 2001, 2008
Taurus	Emerald	Owl	Silver	Moon	1984, 1991, 1998, 2005
Gemini	Agate	Caduceus	Silver	Mercury	1983, 1990, 1997, 2004
Cancer	Ruby	Anchor	Silver	Moon	1984, 1991, 1998, 2005
Leo	Sardonyx	Heart	Gold	Sun	1981, 1988, 1995, 2002
Virgo	Sapphire	Spider	Silver	Mercury	1983, 1990, 1997, 2004
Libra	Opal	Scales	Copper	Venus	1982, 1989, 1996, 2003
Scorpio	Topaz	Tau	Iron	Mars	1987, 1994, 2001, 2008
Sagittarius	Turquoise	Arrowhead	Tin	Jupiter	1986, 1993, 2000, 2007
Capricorn	Garnet	Cat	Lead	Saturn	1985, 1992, 1999, 2006
Aquarius	Amethyst	Key	Lead	Saturn	1985, 1992, 1999, 2006
Pisces	Bloodstone	Fish	Tin	Jupiter	1986, 1993, 2000, 2007

There you have your birth signs, with their birthstones and symbols, metals and planets, and the years in the current cycle (of the sun 1981–2016), in which "your" planet will be most influential.

You can use general charms, such as a cross or acorn (the latter in tin and copper is supposed to maintain vigor or regain a wayward lover) or a silver skull (but ruby eyes are vulgar) but you are promised most "power" and "protection" if you wear the appropriately made and appropriate charms listed above. It is considered very bad luck to wear the charm of another astrological sign; Gemini's caduceus is really bad news for anyone else, as is Libra's opal, and so on. Most people, if they wear charms at all, wear silver or gold, but less than half the people will benefit from this. Tell your loved one that cheaper tin or lead may be best for you.

An amulet or talisman must be made or bought (if you have to) on the appropriate day. Otherwise, forget it. Here are the planets that rule the days of the week:

Sun	Sunday	Leo
Moon	Monday	Cancer
Mars	Tuesday	Aries, Scorpio
Mercury	Wednesday	Gemini, Virgo
Jupiter	Thursday	Sagittarius, Pisces
Venus	Friday	Libra, Taurus
Saturn	Saturday	Capricorn, Aquarius

You can choose your sign by the day of the year on which you were born (mine is Sagittarius) or the day of the week on which you were born (mine would still be Sagittarius, or Pisces). Every day of the week has both "positive (even-numbered) and "negative" (odd-numbered) hours. If you know the exact time of your birth and the latitude and longitude of the place you were born, astrologers promise your horoscope will be more accurate.

Once you have chosen the right sign and charm, and you have decided to be a little fancier than just carrying a coin with your date of birth on it (be sure it's really copper, silver, or gold)—to make assurance doubly sure make or buy your amulet, talisman, or charm at one of these hours (when the planet of the day is most influential): 1 A.M., 8 A.M., 3 P.M., 10 P.M.

Never wear a ring that has belonged to a dead person without having the stone reset, not even on a chain around your neck. Women can make broaches out of old rings.

Now, all this sounds very complicated. It is. But if you are going to wear something, whether is be an Egyptian ankh, a religious medal, a cross, a gris-gris, an amulet, a talisman, or whatever, consider this: If you are superstitious enough to wear it with magic in mind, you ought to be scrupulous enough to do it right.

TO HAVE PROPHETIC DREAMS

Get up between 3 and 4 A.M. any morning in June, go out silently, and pick one full-blown red rose. Take it back to your room and "fumigate" it over a brazier in which you are burning sulfur and brimstone; let it have at least five full minutes of this. Write the name of the person you love and your own name on a clean sheet of paper and fold the rose in it. Seal the paper with three wax seals and bury it under the tree from which the rose was gathered. Over the spot trace the letter A (for *Amor*, "love").

On July 6 at midnight, dig up the rose wrapped in paper, take it to your room, and put it under your pillow. Sleep on it for three successive nights. "You will enjoy dreams of great portent."

HOW TO RUIN A DINNER PARTY

"Take the four feet of a mole and slip them under the tablecloth without being seen. The guests will not fail to come to blows." The magician who called himself Paul Christian offers this "as a joke."

HOW TO WIN AT GAMBLING

In *The History and Practice of Magic* by the above author, this hope is held out to habitual losers:

Would you like to *win at gambling?* . . . On the first Thursday of the new moon, at the hour of Jupiter, before the sun rises, write these words [in dog Latin] on virgin parchment: *"Non licet ponare in egarbona quia pretium sanguinis."* Then take a viper's head, and put it in the middle of the writing; fold the four corners of the parchment over the head and, whenever you wish to gamble, attach the whole to your left arm with a red silk ribbon, and no one else but you will win.

If you don't wish to put all your eggs in this basket, Paul Christian has eight more to suggest. He adds: "Whichever of these methods you choose, never forget to keep a tenth part of what you win for the poor. If you forget this precept, instead of winning you will lose."

PASS IT ON

An extremely nasty and (one hopes) now abandoned practice was to "get rid" of venereal disease by having sex with another person and "passing it on." This kind of magical idea is to be found in many cultures. In Haiti, for example, if you are ill, you leave food at a crossroad; anyone who finds and eats your food gets your illness, taking it away from you.

RELICS

The Roman Catholic Church has long recognized the use of relics as devotionals—objects which, because of their physical connection with a saint or someone of great piety or inspirational conduct, increase in Christians a sense of veneration. Devotion to a particular saint—which does not mean worship anymore than devotion to the memory of some personal acquaintance does—can be aided by viewing or touching a relic of that saint. Relics give a sense of closeness.

Relics fall into three classes. First-class relics are actual remains of a person: the skull of Saint Catherine of Siena (with two front teeth missing as a result of the Devil having pushed her down a flight of stone steps), the arm of Saint Francis Xavier that was sent to Rome after the rest of him was buried in Goa, the tiny bits of bone that are placed in an altar when one is consecrated. Second-class relics are objects that were used by the saint in life: clothing, crucifixes, books. A third-class relic is one that has merely been touched by one of the other relics.

Over the authenticity of relics there has been a great deal of dispute. Relic faking was an old art even in the Middle Ages, but in the Age of Faith, people set great store by the fragment of the True Cross that was exhibited in their local church or by a reliquary containing the Crown of Thorns, and so on. A nail purportedly from the True Cross was built into the jewel-encrusted crown of the Hapsburgs. Pieces of the True Cross itself (found, according to tradition, by Saint Helena, mother of Constantine the Great) were to be seen in many Western churches.

People made hazardous pilgrimages to pray at shrines where relics of famous saints were on display or where the saints were buried—the tombs provided with apertures so that the faithful could reach inside and touch the corpse. Wealthy persons gladly bought bones or tattered garments that were sworn to as "genuine relics" of this martyr or that renowned bishop and had bejeweled reliquaries made to contain them. The cathedral at Chartres once housed garments supposed to have been worn by the Blesed Virgin at the hour of Christ's birth; brought from Constantinople, they survived an accidental fire in the Middle Ages, only to be destroyed on purpose during the French Revolution.

Frenchman Roger Peyrefitte discussed the relic problem in his satiric novel *The Keys of Saint Peter* (1957). The urbane but saintly Cardinal Bellaro is speaking:

> "A great many *outré* relics were destroyed during the religious wars or the French Revolution. Thus, for example, a sneeze of the Holy Ghost, a sigh uttered by St. Joseph while he was sawing wood, the bones of the fish that Christ multiplied, the tail of His ass, the rays of the Star of the Three Magi, a feather of the Angel Gabriel, the candle of Arras which burned without ever being consumed. Some equally curious relics still exist in Italy, but . . . the march of enlightenment is beginning to be felt; St. John the Baptist has sixty fingers, but formerly he had more than a coral reef; St. Giulia has forty heads but once had more than the hydra of Lerna; St. Agatha has five breasts, but used to have almost as many as Diana of Ephesus. A few more centuries and our saints will have one head, two hands and two arms, like the rest of us."

Whatever the intentions of the Church authorities in encouraging the veneration of relics, there is no doubt that some people misused them. Instead of making them devotional aids, they regarded the relics as having magic power in their own right. Relics were often stolen to be used in magical incantations or midnight orgies, to prophesy by or to raise spirits of the dead. Many genuinely devout—but simple—people misunderstood the idea of veneration and felt that if they simply touched the relic, the object itself would miraculously do what they wanted done.

In all too many cases, the relic of a holy man became an amulet, a talisman, or a charm.

ABRAXAS STONES

Certain pre-Christian and early Christian cults believed in gnosis, spiritual truth obtainable by faith alone. Gnostic sects used the term "abraxas" to denote the hierarchy of spirits collectively that emanated from a supreme being.

The letters of the word "abraxas" in Greek add up to the number 365, and thus it was believed that there were 365 orders of these spirits. "Abraxas" has frequently been found on ancient talismanic stones, which were thus called abraxas stones. It is thought that the word "abraxas" may have been the origin of the talismanic formula "abracadabra"—although some cabalists claim that it is made up of the Hebrew *Ab* (Father), *Ben* (Son), and *Ruach Acadsch* (Holy Spirit).

THE EVIL EYE

The famous author W. Somerset Maugham used on the cover of his books and on the gates of his fabulous Villa Mauresque on the French Riviera a symbol from the East designed to ward off the Evil Eye.

Did you notice it on the door of one of the buildings in the long-running TV comedy *M*A*S*H*?

On the cover of his books Rudyard Kipling used an ancient symbol for good luck employed by peoples as different as the Indians in America and the Indians in India. Later, the old symbol acquired a tragic new meaning. It was the swastika.

SKULLS

The skull (thought to contain the "personality") has become more than any other part of the body associated with the spirit of the departed. A skull above two crossed bones represents the dead. When the Gravedigger unearthed Yorick's skull in *Hamlet*, he brought back to Hamlet a rush of memories of that jester and his own youth.

The Vikings drank from the skulls of their enemies. Necromancers used them in their black ceremonies.

Some Christian chapels, as *memento mori*, are entirely "decorated" with skulls and bones. They have a peculiar fascination for Hispanics, but in France and Germany also bones are gruesomely displayed; in Hallstadt, Austria, bodies are disinterred after ten years and the skulls bleached and arranged in rows with identifying inscriptions. In Ireland, an oath taken on a skull was considered inviolate.

Headhunters of the Amazon and Africa place their collections of skulls both outside and inside their houses. In Taiwan human skulls were lined up to indicate position and were regarded as wealth. In Sarawak the government, after banning headhunting as barbarous, had to set up a kind of lending library of skulls; headhunters could "check out" an old skull instead of acquiring a new one, renting it for age-old ceremonial rites.

The witch doctors of Africa wear necklaces of skulls. The chief of the Sanem tribe of Papua sleeps with the skull of an enemy as a pillow, to acquire the bravery of the dead. In Tibet skulls are frequently used in magic.

In the West we display the skulls of heroes and saints. The skull of Saint Valentine is shown on Valentine's Day each year in the Church of Santa Maria Cosmedin in Rome—and some believe that if you gaze on it you will keep the brow of your loved one free of frowns for a year.

We used to keep skulls on our desks to remind us of death. Mary Queen of Scots had a watch in the form of a skull; she carried it around in her hand to keep her mind on the passing of time and the inevitability of death. A few people kept the skulls of their departed love ones, and in the Azera tribe of New Guinea, widows can wear no adornments but the skulls of their dead husbands. Mourning rings and Victorian jewelry made of human hair are a milder Western version of the same custom.

The bush people of Maleluka, New Hebrides, use human skulls to make memorial scuptures; they entertain them with spirit-puppets in their funeral ceremonies. The natives of the Nicobar Islands, in the Bay of Bengal, annually dig up the skulls of their dead relatives and, dressing them in colorful rugs, invite them to a four-day feast at which they are the guests of honor. These customs seek to propitiate the dead. Where the New Hebrideans seek to induce the dead to do them favors, the Nicobar Islanders merely hope to get the dead relatives into such a good, relaxed mood that they will not trouble the living for another year.

In some old illustrations you will see skulls used as candlesticks. No serious magician would use so powerful a thing in such a way nor depict such a thing on an amulet or talisman.

MAGIC MUSIC

I have always thought of Wagner's *Parsifal* as "Mounted Boredom and the Holy Grail," although it is full of cabalistic lore and symbolism. So is the charming *Magic Flute* of Mozart (he and his librettist, the actor Emmanuel Schikaneder, were Freemasons).

TO BRING MONEY

A necktie with small portraits of Adam Smith on it is beginning to be seen worn by economists of the more conservative stripe. They might try this talisman instead: a ring with a piece of red chalcedony in it engraved with the picture of a man holding a scepter. The ancients swore it brought wealth.

RESTIVE PERSON

French novelist Nicholas Edmé Réstif de la Bretonne (1734–1806) recalled in his autobiography a conjuring incident of his youth. A boy named François Courtcou found an old almanac in which there was a description of how "a Shepherd may call up the Devil." He talked young Nicholas into trying it. When the Devil appeared, Nicholas was shaking so hard he could not write down the "pact" that Courtcou kept shouting he was "getting" from the hoarse voice that was heard. Forty years later, Nicholas still remembered the occasion vividly, but by that time he had come to the conclusion that François was drunk and engaging in a little ventriloquism. Or perhaps, as the credulous Montague Summers believed, Courtcou may just have "attracted some of the very lowest of spirits."

WORKING EVIL WITH A TALISMAN

The amulet is supposed to ward off bad forces, the talisman, to attract good forces. But Francis Barrett in his confused but presumably authoritative book *The Magus, or Celestial Intelligencer* (1801), argues that a talisman can draw bad forces and so can be used to work evil against someone.

As a talisman of silver (made of the Moon's favorite metal and in the right phase of the Moon) can bring health and respect, so a talisman of lead (the metal associated with the maleficent planet Saturn) if engraved with messages of power at the right aspect of the planet and buried near an enemy's house, can bring evil upon him.

CURE FOR HYDROPHOBIA

Write HAX, PAX, MAX, DEUS ADMAX on a slice of apple and eat it. *Deus* ("god") and *pax* ("peace") are real Latin words but the rest are nonsense syllables.

CHARM AGAINST SCORPION BITES

Try pinning forget-me-nots to your clothes.

CURE FOR A DISLOCATED JOINT

As we have noted elsewhere, magical formulas were frequently attributed to famous persons, from Vergil to Agrippa and Paracelsus. Here is a set of nonsense syllables said to be from "Cato," which could mean Cato the Elder (234–149 B.C.), his famous great-grandson, Cato the Younger (95–46 B.C.), or even "Dionysius Cato," whose name is attached to 164 moral precepts of the fourth century A.D.

Whoever this "Cato" was, he advises victims of dislocation to step within the pentacle and chant:

"HUAT HANAT HUAT, ISTA PISTA SISTA, DOMINABO DAMNAUSTRATA."

CONCLUSION

Whether you wear a bracelet of elephant's hair or an asofetida bag or (as Honoré de Balzac did all his life) a talisman of a square of numbers that add up to fifteen in all directions, good luck!

Charlemagne's talisman was a large sapphire said to contain bits of the

True Cross and to have been given to the emperor by Harun al-Rashid, famed caliph of Bagdad. It was supposed to protect the wearer and symbolized the Protectorship of Jerusalem and the Holy Sepulcher.

Charlemagne always wore it, and when he was buried, sitting upright on his throne in full imperial regalia, it went to the grave with him. Then 186 years later Otto III opened the tomb. He placed the head of Charlemagne in a jewel-encrusted golden reliquary (now in the cathedral at Aachen, Germany), and the talisman went into a church treasury. Napoleon got his hands on it in 1804, and after his death it reached the cathedral treasury at Rheims. It remains there to this day, though Kaiser Wilhelm II did try to buy it.

Harun died of apoplexy (809) very soon after having given Charlemagne this nice present, and the caliph's successors repudiated what the gift was said to represent politically. From the disagreement eventually arose the Crusades.

HOW TO SPOT A THIEF

There are amulets against being robbed, but among the Tome tribe of Africa you hardly need them, for thieves can be spotted easily. They wear talismans to give them good luck in their burglaries.

COUNTRY MATTERS

Witches were supposed to be kept from cattle if one put around the cattle's horns or necks wreaths of rowan tied with red threads. (The witches were especially deterred by braids: They supposedly had to count the threads before attempting to harm the animals.) Witches were also to be put off by farm machinery and carts painted in bright colors—once again red was a favorite.

These precautions, with rowan in the barns and perhaps "spectacles" or "butterfly wings" designs painted on the wagons (actually magical symbols to ward off the Evil Eye) pretty much protected the cattle in England. The horse brasses that Americans today so avidly collect in Britain (and which are being imitated at a great rate today) often had symbols on them, which suggested that they might be amulets against evil, and bells on the harness were certainly aimed at annoying any spirits that might want to injure the teams.

"Collars of holly and bittersweet saved horses from witchcraft, and whips with holly-wood handles were favoured by Fenland coachmen after dark," writes Margaret Baker, an authority on *Folklore and Customs of Rural England*.

WALL STREET REPORT

If civilization lasts long enough for people to look back at our time as a distant past, some of the things we do casually they may consider bizarre.

In Iceland in ancient times a falcon's claw was hung over the fireplace to protect homes from disaster. Do we not have some equally strange ideas?

A friend of mine, a very successful executive in a big, no-nonsense corporation, has for years kept a "lucky tie." He says it got him through his early important job interviews, and he has worn it at similar occasions ever since.

"A security blanket," readers of psychoanalytical works (or Charles Schulz's *Peanuts*) will say. The tie gave him the confidence to make a good impression; his self-assurance helped to get him the jobs.

But now that my friend has reached the top, he still keeps the tie. He does not, I suppose, have to face any more interviews: then why the tie? He says he keeps it "out of gratitude" and because "I wouldn't feel right throwing it away; and who knows what would happen?" Would someone else pick it up and take over his company?

He laughed at the foolishness of his skyscraper not admitting it had a thirteenth floor, but I think my friend believes in magic.

Have we changed so much from the American Indians who ate the hearts of their enemies, hoping to gain their courage? Are we, in the age of "smart missiles," much different from the ancient Britons who rubbed the stones for their slingshots in the brains of slain foes, to make the missiles "smarter"?

A PRECIOUS OPAL

Pliny the Elder (A.D. 23–79) in his *Natural History* recorded 20,000 facts that he considered worth noting. From this mine of information, one gem: Rather than let his precious opal fall into the hands of Mark Antony, the senator Nonius chose exile from Rome.

From the earliest times opals were valuable but risky to own. The Norse *Edda* tells of gems made from the eyes of children, probably opals, and it has always been the gem associated with the eyes. In Venice during the great plagues of the Middle Ages, those who wore the opals were said to see them grow bright when they caught the dread disease, only to fade with the death of the wearer.

George Stimpson, in *A Book About a Thousand Things*, says that "much of the modern superstition no doubt owes its origin to Sir Walter Scott's story entitled *Anne of Geierstein*, published in 1829, where the opal is represented as an unlucky stone, inviting misfortune and unhappiness to the possessor."

Albertus Magnus, great thirteenth century saint, theologian (Thomas Aquinas was his pupil), and eventually bishop of Ratisbon, was a firm believer in the power of opals. According to *The Book of Secrets* (supposedly compiled by one of his students):

Take the stone which is called *Ophthalamus* [opal], and wrap it in the leaf of the laurel, or Bay tree; and it is called *Lapis Obtalmicus*, whose colour is not named for it is of many colours. And it is of such virtue that it blindeth the sights of them that stand about. Constantius [an eleventh century monk] carrying this in his hand was made invisible by it.

The sixteenth century writer Stephen Bateman agreed with Albertus about this quality of the opal: It "dimmeth other men's eyes so that in a manner it maketh them blind, so that they may not see what is done before them, so that it is said to be the patron of thieves."

THE TALISMAN

In Sir Walter Scott's *The Talisman* (1825), Saladin saves the life of Richard the Lion-Hearted with a snakestone or madstone that draws the poison out of a wound, the "talisman" of the title.

Perhaps Scott got the idea from the Lockhart family in Lanarkshire, which preserves such a good-luck talisman called a "Lee penny" brought back by their ancestor, Sir Simon Lockhart, from the Crusades.

Belief in the efficacy of snakestones to draw out the poison was common in early America, too. Some Amerindian peoples were said to use them as antivenins, and Abraham Lincoln himself took his oldest son, Robert, from Springfield to Terre Haute, Indiana, to have a madstone applied for snakebite. Robert at least survived.

THE MIRACLE OF HOLY CROSS ABBEY

Holy Cross Abbey, in Tipperary County, Ireland, was so named because it boasted a piece of the True Cross. The story is told of a certain woman who, "tortured by magical spells," was cured by wrapping around her stomach a scarf that had touched the relic.

"Suddenly she vomited small pieces of cloth and wood," wrote Patrick Byrne in *Witchcraft in Ireland* (1967), "and for a whole month she spat out from her body such things. . . . This he [the abbot] took care to set down in writing."

"YE OF LITTLE FAITH . . ."

Some say that all power of amulets and talismans, including the power to make you well, comes from faith. So, throw away Blue Cross, Medicare, pills and potions, and think straight! Cancel your insurance policies and get a few amulets.

To be on the safe side, get a talisman of the Sun (engraved on a plaque of very pure gold), made on a Sunday at the proper time, and consecrated with the fumes of cinnamon, frankincense, saffron, and red laurel, burned with laurel and heliotrope stalks in an earthen vessel. That protects against fires.

But if you dream of a purple cloth, get ready to see a doctor; you are going to be very ill.

LONGEVITY

For a long life, why not try a talisman on a disk of wood from a macrozamia tree? These trees grow in the Tambourine Mountains of Queensland, Australia, and are among the oldest living things on earth.

TRAIN YOUR MEMORY

Many magicians complain that though, in complicated rituals, one can consult a sort of manual as one goes along, one is not supposed to keep a drawing of an amulet or tailsman to copy. One is supposed to re-create it from memory—"alphabet of the Magi," Hebrew letters, and all! You must not copy amulets out of books!

IT FIGURES

There's one cabalistic amulet that you should never see anyone wearing. Hung around the neck, if donned before sunrise on Sunday, it is supposed to make the wearer invisible.

6

Recipes and Formulas

FOLKLORE tells us of many strange recipes and remedies. Some of these concoctions really do work, because they contain useful medicines that our forefathers discovered. Aspirin (in the form of willow bark), digitalis (foxglove extract), atropine and hyoscine (belladonna) are all ancient medicines. Some of these discoveries were aided by magical beliefs, such as the belief in signatures, which suggested that a plant with, say, a heart-shaped leaf or flower might be good for heart disease. And some worked only because the remedies were administered with magical incantations, and the recipients were convinced of their efficacy.

In addition to taking the medicine—often bitter or disgusting to convince you it really was doing you some good—you could also transfer the trouble to some other person or animal, or even a tree or a stone. It was just a matter of knowing what magical words to say.

Some people, especially "wise women," specialized in folk medicine, including the magical. If they used their "powers" for good and took no recompense for cures, they were "white witches." If they dealt in poisons and love philters and such and did evil, they were "black witches." At one time *wicca* meant both wisdom and magic.

Wicca it was that told you that this or that mysterious potion had to be made up only when the astrological aspects were right for it, that this or that ointment had to be applied with appropriate chanting and only at the correct time—and never with the "poison finger," the forefinger. *Wicca* it was that claimed to have inherited wisdom of herbs and botanicals, charms and curses, and that its practitioners were powerful because of birth order or "gifted" ancestors or other special circumstances. These wise men or women could tell you that, since the house leek was a potent charm against your house catching fire, its creamy juice was also (naturally) good to soothe burns. They it was who, taking no chances, applied their remedies with a combination of mysterious mumbo jumbo from the Old Religion and also the potent "in the Name of the Father, the Son, and the Holy Ghost" of the New Religion.

Folk medicine drifted into folk magic. When one drew three rushes (not two) through the mouth of a child suffering from thrush (because *rush* sounds like *thrush*) and then threw the rushes into a stream so that the disease would be washed away with them, then that was magic. Similarly, when goose grease was thought not to be worth applying to the chest of a child suffering from a cold unless the grease was on a *heart-shaped* piece of paper, or a poultice was considered not worth trying unless it was tied on with a *red* rag, or a bitter draft had to be taken only after uttering an incantation, then one had superstition, not just medicine.

If the flowers of eyebright were used to make a medieval Murine, if the patient had to eat food given to him or her only by a woman whose name had not changed when she married, if you had to keep the sharp instrument that had cut you bright and shiny until your wound healed (rust would lead to the wound "going bad"), there you had sympathetic magic and superstition.

"WHITE WITCH" REMEDIES

As we have just said, much of the pharmacopoeia of the witches or "wise women" was based on sympathetic magic and the doctrine of signatures. Some of the witches' remedies were eventually recognized as very beneficial; comfrey root, used in casts for broken bones (hence its alternate names "knitback" and "boneset"), now turns out to contain allantoin, a crystalline substitute that promotes bone growth. Some still sound merely superstitious to us. And some ideas have caused regettable damage, such as the recommendation that alabaster chips be used in certain compounds, which caused large chunks of alabaster to be whacked off church monuments—the most convenient supply.

Naturally belief in the efficacy of the medicine or the powers of the physician has always been a major factor in recovery. A framed diploma or a necklace of skulls helps a great deal. Being the seventh son of a seventh son doesn't hurt either, because belief in the natural powers of such a person is widespread. Crones are popular too.

A sick person can hang up a kind of "magnet" to attract away his disease—a stone with a hole in it, a peeled onion, a doll woven of straw—or sprinkle a little holy water around or ride a piebald horse or say a charm.

Or he can take his bed to the cow loft and breathe in its ammoniac odors of dung. (Dung was also considered good in various poultices—King Charles II on his deathbed was smeared with pigeon dung and God knows what else.) To staunch bleeding, he can get the blacksmith to touch him or wrap the wound in cobwebs. For virility he can eat some mandrake root (don't let them pass off bryony on you), or adopt any one of the many rural remedies entertainingly described by Margaret Baker in her *Folklore and Customs of Rural England* (1974).

Here are a few of the ways of country magic:

Warts: Prick each wart with a new pin and then drive the pin into an ash tree (transferring the disease to the tree) as you say:

> Ashen tree, ashen tree,
> Pray buy these warts of me.

Or you can cut as many notches in a stick of elder as you have warts and bury it. As the stick decays, the warts vanish.

Jaundice. Eat nine lice on a piece of bread and butter.

Tuberculosis. Before modern methods were adopted, "an emulsion of snails dissolved in salt was taken with cream and sugar, or the patient made to sleep over the cowhouse. . . . 'Hetherd-broth' of adder-flesh and chicken was taken in Lancashire," reports Ms. Baker. Other sufferers employed "lungs of oak," the lichen *Sticta pulmonaria*, found on the oak trees. Or—sympathetic magic again—the lungs of a healthy sheep were bound to the patient's feet.

Arthritis and rheumatism. The skin of an eel or snake, worn as a garter, keeps you supple and prevents cramp; a stolen dried potato or a cross-shaped bud from a churchyard elder helps. Beekeepers attribute their freedom from rheumatism to the stings they receive (another remedy that has received scientific imprimation). Beating with a holly spray has been tried or carrying the dried front feet of a mole in the pocket nearest the afflicted limb. Of course, aspirin is often recommended; we don't know exactly how that works, either—but it was first synthesized (by an unknown chemist at Friedrich Bayer and Company, Elberfeld, Germany, in 1899) from willow bark, an old "wise woman's" remedy.

BLOODY GOOD MEDICINE

Baths in human blood were recommended by ancient witches as cures for numerous illnesses from leprosy to epilepsy. Blood baths were also supposed to keep one from aging. The Countess Elizabeth Bathory (d. 1614) is reputed to have taken such baths to preserve her good looks. Her agents lured young peasant girls to her castle with the promise of well-paid jobs, only to turn them over to the countess to be "milked" of blood until they died. Estimates of the number of her victims run from thirty-seven to six hundred. She died in prison and entered Hungarian vampire legend as one of the "undead."

MAGICAL POISON

One of the most powerful (and peculiar) magical poisons calls for, among its ingredients, the finger whorls from twins.

MAGICAL FLYING OINTMENT PRESCRIPTIONS

With tongue in check, Reginald Scot (1538–1599) wrote the *Discoverie of Witchcraft*; from Scot's book are recipes for which many sought in his time. Take . . .

the fat of yoong children, and seeth it with water in a brasen vessell, reserving the thickest of that which remaineth boiled in the bottome, which they laie up and keep until occasion serveth to use it. They put hereunto [add] Eleeoselinum, Aconitum, Frondes populeas and Soote.

sium, acarum vulgare, pentaphyllon, the blood of a flitter mouse [bat], solanum somniferum and oleum. They stampe all these togither, and then they rubbe all parts of their bodys exceedinglie till they look red and be verie hot, so as the pores may be opened and their flesh soluble and loose. They joine herewithall either fat, or oil in steed thereof, that the force of the ointment maie the rather pearse inwardly and so be more effectuall.

Scot goes on to say that on a moonlight night then "they seeme to be carried in the aire to feasting, singing, dansing, kissing culling and other acts of venerie with such youthes as they love and desire most" but attributes it not to magic but to the drugs' actions on their imaginations "so vehement that almost all that part of the braine wherein the memorie consisteth is full of such conceipts."

Another traditional English recipe for flying ointment undoubtedly "worked," considering that the first and principal of its nine ingredients was *Cannabis indica.*

ALL-PURPOSE INCANTATION AGAINST DISEASE

These words are from Albertus Magnus himself. Step within the pentacle (five-pointed star) and recite: OFANO, OBLAMO, OSPERGO. HOLA NOA MASSA. LUX, BEFF, CLEMATI, ADONAI. CLEONA, FLORIT. PAX, SAX, SARAX. AFA AFACA NOSTRA. CERUM, HEAIUM, LADA FRIUM. (A mixture of real and nonsense Latin.)

OLD MEASUREMENTS

In making up old magical cures, you may need to know that a noggin is a quarter of a pint and that two kilderkins are a firkin and a runlet a scant kilderkin and that four firkins make a tun. Also, a cubit is 18 inches (or twice a span), a pace is exactly two and a half feet, se'nnight is a week and a fortnight (a word still in use in Britain) is two weeks.

The British still weigh in stones but Americans need to be told that's 14 pounds, and everyone needs to be told that a clove is a half a stone, a burthen is one stone more than a firkin, a kip is half a ton (not tun), a pennyweight is 24 grains, and a hundredweight—in a nation where public schools are private schools—is not 100 pounds but 112 pounds.

Add to that some Scots forms. Two mutchkins of liquid equal a chopin, two chopins equal a Scots pint (about nine-tenths of an English pint), and eight Scots pints equal a Scots gallon. In dry measurements, four lippies (or forpits) equal a peck, four pecks to the firlot, four firlots to the boll, and sixteen bolls to the chalder. A chalder is equal to about ninety-six American bushels, which of course differ slightly from English bushels. In Scotland heavy loads were weighed at the public weighing machine called a trone; trone weight was based on a pound that equaled anything between 21 and 28 ounces, and therefore 3,000 trones weight was the nearest Scots equivalent to the ton.

STAR CHILD

Star Child, a firm in Whitby, Yorkshire—a kind of modern day John Wellington Wells—conducted a mail-order business in magicians' supplies; ash wands (hazel wands were too hard to dry "in this coastal climate"), herbs, resins, balsams, oils, spices, incenses, Solomonic swords, Athame (black-hilted) and white-hilted daggers, tridents and burins, and other "Magical tools." Their catalog announced that they could not undertake to "consecrate Magical tools for you," but they provided virgin parchments (for talismans and other things), beeswax (for candles and *fifth-fath* dolls), Chinese wash (for purifying the threshold and magic circle), and an anointing oil based on an old recipe.

The catalogs and sales of Star Child were evidence of a lively interest in witchcraft in Britain and overseas, especially among young people.

Here is Star Child's recipe for Elfin Incense. Whereas Aztec Incense is "powerful . . . slightly dark . . . useful in works of sacrifice and sex magic, not for the weak-hearted," and Incense of Saturn "may bring unpleasant surprises," Elfin Incense "conjures up the dark wooded country-side and the folk tales of the Elves and Fairies who peopled our land in the distant past." Here's how to make Elfin Incense:

Break up 2 parts of *Rhus aromatica* (fragrant sumac) and grind together with 1 part juniper berries, mix in 2 parts willow bark, 2 parts red sandalwood, and as much honey as you like.

For Ruthvah, the Perfume of Immortality, the most famous of occult perfumes (also called Satyr and Perfume of the Eternal Triad) you need more expensive ingredients, but you may think it worth the money. Mix 1 part real ambergris (*Kether*), 2 parts real musk (*Chokmah*), 3 parts real civet oil (*Binah*). But some people swear by its effectiveness. This perfume was supposed to have been used not only by the beauties of ancient Arabia but by Aleister Crowley. Crowley wrote:

It must be rubbed on the body, particularly at the roots of the hair, where the skin is not too tightly stretched, so thoroughly that the subtle perfume [!] is not detected, or even suspected, of others. The user is thus armed with a most powerful weapon, the more potent for being secret, against the deepest elements in the nature of those whom it is wished to attract. They obey, and they are all the more certainly compelled to obey, because they do not know they are being commanded.

Worth a try? Crowley's own success with women and men was astounding, but I must tell you that a friend in New Orleans to whom I gave the recipe, at his request, was soon after murdered.

RHEUMATISM CURE

For rheumatism, patients are seated in St. Fillan's chair, a stone seat in Renfrewshire, Scotland, and dragged down the hill by their heels.

MODERNIZING MEDICINE

In *The Lost Gods of England* (1957), Bruce Branston demonstrates how physicians in the Middle Ages took the ancient magical formulas and adapted them to Christianity for use in whispering them into the patient's ear. Here's the Old High German charm for a sprain from the tenth century:

Balder and Woden rode to the wood where Balder's foal wrenched its foot when Woden charmed as he well knew how: as for bone-wrench so for blood-wrench so for limb-wrench: Bone to bone, blood to blood, limb to limbs as if they were glued.

For Christian consumption this becomes:

Our Lord rode his foal's foot slade [slipped] down he lighted: bone to bone, sinue to sinue, blood to blood, flesh to flesh, in the name of the Father, Son, and Holy Ghost.

The old Germans also used phylacteries; Orthodox Jews still strap on these little boxes every day to pray. Inside are little bits of parchment on which Old Testament verses are written. The Germans employed an odd combination of heathen charms and Biblical texts, and the use of medical amulets along with the potions and powders is as old as the Assyrians.

A CUSTOM FROM CUMBERLAND

Cumberland has always been a little strange; it did not become a part of England until 1157 and is still rather offbeat, strongly northern, slightly Scots. Its people proudly cling to their ancient traditions.

Here's one that ought to be more widely adopted: Cumberland Rum Butter. Just melt half a pound of butter (the goodness of life) with a pound of brown sugar (the sweetness of life), a generous amount of rum (the spirit). On top sprinkle nutmeg (the spice of life).

Now you are ready for the birth of a baby. When visitors come to see the new infant, give each a taste of the Rum Butter, preferably on a homemade oatcake. The visitor then leaves a coin for the child. When the Rum Butter is all gone, the coins are put into the dish, which is never cleaned out (thus money will *stick* to the baby, and it will never be poor).

"THE FLAGON WITH THE DRAGON HOLDS THE BREW THAT IS TRUE"

One piece of witch's paraphernalia that must never be bought is the cup. The chalice must always be a present from another member of the craft.

FOLLOW THE SCRIPT

Hugh Dalziel Duncan, *Communication and Social Order* (1962), reminds us that, if not used exactly right, the sacred, powerful words of magic can fail to produce the desired effect—worse, they can turn the tables on the magician and bring harm to him who would harm others. Duncan writes:

Magic spells must be handed down, without change. The slightest alteration from the original pattern would be fatal.

DEFENSE AGAINST WITCHES

If you can draw even one drop of a witch's blood, her spells are rendered harmless. "For the time being," the instructions add.

CHARM AGAINST AGUE, FEVER, OR WITCHCRAFT

The *Transactions of the Devonshire Association* (1899) offer this old incantation from the West Country of England:

When Jesus saw the Cross thare to be crucified Pilate said unto him "what aileth thee? Why shakest thou/ hast thou fever, ague or witchcraft?" Jesus said unto him "I have neither fever, ague nor witchcraft but shake for thy sins. Whosoever carryeth this in his mind or in writing shall never have neither fever, ague nor witch- craft. In the name of the father and of the Son and of the holy ghost. Amen Amen."

ANOTHER CURE FOR DISEASE

"Diseases can be cured by wearing a girdle of ferns gathered on St. John's Eve, at midnight, and arranged in such a way as to form the magic character HVTY." This is from Jacques Collin de Plancy (1793–1887), *Dictionary of Witchcraft*.

HOW TO LOCATE THE GUILTY PARTY

Cornelius Agrippa in one of his books describes how to detect a thief or other criminal from a group of innocent people. The diviner takes a sieve (in the fifteenth century these were flat circular utensils), grips it with a pair of pincers or tongs, which in turn are held in place by the middle fingers of two assistants—that is, it is suspended in air by a very slight grip. The diviner then says these six words:

"DIES, MIES, JESCHET, BENEDOEFET, DOWIMA, FNITEMAUS."

The conjuration is followed by the reading of the names of the suspects. When the guilty party's name is read, the sieve—"by the help of the demon," says Agrippa—will turn.

MOTHER DEMDIKE'S METHOD

From the *Wonderful Discovery of Witches in the County of Lancaster* (1613), here is the standard sympathetic-magic way of attacking an enemy as described by a woman burned as a witch for using it:

> The speediest way to take a man's life away by witchcraft is to make a picture [figurine] of clay, like unto the shape of the person whom they mean to kill, and dry it thoroughly. And when you would have them to be ill in any one place more than another, then take a thorn or pin and prick it in that part of the picture you would so have to be ill. And when you would have any part of the body to consume away, then take that part of the picture and burn it. And so thereupon by that means the body shall die.

THE BASIC CAKES RECIPE AND ITS USE

In one of Shakespeare's plays a merry group replies to the puritanical Malvolio that just because he is dour and depressed there is no reason there should be no cakes and ale.

Cakes and ale are features of the *esabat* (frequent meeting of witches, more informal and less infrequent than a sabbat). They are also in evidence in the Cakes and Wine ceremony, which the coven conducts somewhat along the lines of Holy Communion of the Christians.

The wine is usually sweet (often sherry or white), and the cakes are made of whole meal, salt, honey, wine, oil and (sometimes) blood. They are crescent-shaped, in honor of the Moon Goddess, the Great Mother, the female principle.

When making the cakes, the witch recites this incantation:

> I do not bake the meal nor the salt, nor do I cook the honey and the oil with the wine. I bake the blood and the body and the soul of the Great Aradia that she shall know neither rest nor peace and ever be in cruel suffering till she grant the fulfillment

of my innermost desires. If the grace be granted, O Aradia, in
honor of thee I will hold a feast. We will drain the goblet deep,
    We will wildly dance and leap.
And if thou grantest the grace which I desire, then, when the
dance is wildest, we shall extinguish the lamps and love freely,
caring neither for age nor kin.

It is worth noting that where religion propitiates, magic threatens and
compels.

A LOVE POTION

William Butler Yeats was a great student of the occult and of Irish
folklore, and in a book on Irish fairy tales and folk tales he says that lovers

can make love-potions by drying and grinding into powder the
liver of a black cat. Mixed with tea, and poured from a black
teapot, it is infallible.

LOVE MAGIC

In Malaysia they take sand from the footprint of a beloved and fry it.
This is supposed to make him or her itch with desire.
    The Arabs write certain characters in oil on the palm of their hands,
then rub the hand furtively on the face in the presence of the beloved.
Irresistible.
    American girls recite the alphabet while twisting the stem of an apple;
when the stem comes off, the initial of the beloved is revealed. (Boys named
Zachary don't have much of a chance.) Or you can peel an apple in one long
continuous strip and throw the peel over your left shoulder; whatever letter
it forms should be the initial of your future lover's name. Or you can jump
rope while reciting the alphabet:

    Ice-cream soda, cream on top,
    Tell me the name of my sweetheart.
    A, B, C, D, . . .

You will miss on the letter of your lover's name. If you reach Z, start over.
    Mary and Herbert Knapp in their charming book on the folklore of
American children, *One Potato, Two Potato* (1976), give instructions for

what they call the "wiggle-waggle" paper predictor and many other American children's devices for telling fortunes. The most frequently asked question is "Does he/she love me?" or something about dating or marriage.

If you want something more complex than "loves me, loves me not" plucking of the daisy's petals, try this chant, quoted by the Knapps, of a Mississippi girl counting the seeds from her apple:

> One I love, two I love, three I love, I say.
> Four I love with all my heart,
> Five I'll cast away.
> Six he loves, seven she loves,
> Eight they both love.
> Nine he comes, ten he tarries,
> Eleven he courts, twelve he marries.

ANOTHER LOVE RECIPE

On a Friday sew into a green silk bag a mixture of vervain, southernwood, and orris root, crushed between sandstones. Wear the bag pinned to your undergarments, next to the skin.

CHINESE RECIPE

The Chinese say, "Respect spiritual beings—but keep aloof from them." If you decide to ignore this sage advice, here's a good trick: Collect as many scorpions as you can find and put them in a jar. Screw the lid on tight and leave them for a year. (Well, a long time.) The scorpions will eat each other until there is only one left. Thus you get a really terrific poisonous creature to set on an enemy.

This is *ku*, reverse magic. *Ku* also means rubbing out an enemy by making a straw effigy and pouring water over it (to drown him), sticking pins in it, and so on.

HOW TO DIG UP THE INGREDIENTS

Iris foetidissima, or stinking gladdon, is called for in many recipes. Like a mandrake (whose "shriek" when pulled up was supposed to drive men crazy), it is difficult to collect. If you cannot tie it to a dog's tail and have him pull it up when you are out of earshot, draw a circle round it three times with a double-edged sword (which bears some resemblance to a crucifix) and be sure to leave in place of the pulled-up plant a flat wheat cake (the kind King Alfred let burn). This is payment to the forces of nature—not a replacement for gladdon but a kind of real-estate tax.

MAGIC OF THE BOOK

Christians used to (many still do) use their Bibles for fortune-telling. Open it at random and put your finger on a message. In Islam the superstitious eat the ink in which certain texts of the Koran are written, hoping thereby to absorb the message.

HOW LONG WILL YOU LIVE?

You can get a good horoscope. You can summon a demon and ask him. You can make a pact with the Devil for a stated period, at the end of which you can count on going—dragged off like Faust, if necessary. You can use any one of a number of methods to get an answer to this important question, provided you are sure you want to know. Think about it.

Here are two methods, one Mexican, one Muslim.

The Mexicans used to put their arms around a certain pillar in the temple at Mitla and measure the distance between their fingertips. That indicates how long they will live. I have tried this and was pleased to discover that, in exchange for having arms so short that I always have to have my shirtsleeves shortened an inch, I am going to live to a ripe old age.

The Muslim system is more complicated and varies with the time of year.

In the first month, close your eyes at midnight, say "God is One" (in Arabic) ten times; then open your eyes quickly and look immediately at the moon. If it looks black, you will die soon. In the fifth and sixth months you can only ask the question fruitfully on Wednesday nights, and you must use a lamp, not the moon. In all other months, gaze at a cloudless sky or at water in a bowl. If they have a reddish tinge, you will die soon.

The Muslims have no system (besides astrology) for long-range forecasting; you have to keep checking.

FOR THE CRAMP

The Devil is tying a knot in my leg.
Mark, Luke, and John, unloose it, I beg.
Crosses three we make to ease us:
Two for thieves and one for Jesus.

CURE FOR DRUNKENNESS

Wear on a piece of paper or parchment, hung from a string around the neck: IAEO, IEALO, IOELET, SABAOTH, ITHOTH BAE. (Mostly nonsense syllables.)

MAGICAL DEFENSE

Write on a parchment and carry with you everywhere this:

DULLIX, IX, UX.
YEA, YOU CAN'T COME OVER PONTIO.
PONTIO IS ABOVE PILATO.

No, I can't figure it out, either!

HOUSE PROTECTION CHARM FROM LANCASHIRE

Lancashire folklore preserves this potent charm against all harm. Over the door write:

Sun, Moon, Mars, Mercury, Jupiter, Venus, Saturn, trine, sextile, dragon's head, dragon's tail, I charge ye all to gard this house from all evil spirits whatever, and gard it from all desorders, and from aney thing being taken wrangasly, and give this famaly good ealth and welth.

INCONCEIVABLE

Fron an ancient grimoire, here is a recipe for curing barrenness:

If a woman may not conceive. Take an Harts horne, turned into powder, and let it be mixed with a cows gall; let the woman keepe it about her . . . and she shall conceive.

It might be classed as folk medicine if the user were expected to swallow it, but since she is enjoined to "keepe it about her," it is clearly magic.

AN ANCIENT CHARM AGAINST MARSH FEVER

Nail three horseshoes to your bedpost with a heavy crucifix (Holy Crok, formerly the Hammer of Thor) and you have the Christian God, Wod (Wotan), and Lok (Loki) all working to protect you if you chant as you do so:

FATHER, SON AND HOLY GHOST
NAIL THE DEVIL TO THIS POST.
THRICE I SMITE WITH HOLY CROK,
WITH THIS MELL I THRICE DO KNOCK,
ONE FOR GOD, AND ONE FOR WOD, AND ONE FOR LOK.

HELP FOR THE AFFLICTED

Remember Sax Rohmer, creator of the improbable Dr. Fu Manchu? He found this in a seventeenth-century chapbook and copied it out. I hand it on to you:

To help a Person under an ill Tongue, and make the Witch appear, or the Effect cease:
Cut off some of the Party's Hair, just at the Nape of the Neck, clip it small and burn it to a Powder, put the Powder in Sal-Armoniack, write the Party's Name you suspect [that is, of casting the spell] backwards, and put the Paper, dipt in *Aqua Vitæ*

[brandy], into the other two, then set it over a gentle Fire; let the Party afflicted sit by it, and dilligently watch that it run not over to catch flame, speaking no Word, whatsoever Noise is heard, but take Notice of what Voice or Roaring is heard in the Chimney, or any part of the Room, and then write how often you hear it, and fix before each writing this Character [he shows a crescent moon]—and if the Party who afflicts you appear not Visible, though you may know the Voice, repeat it again, and if she appear in no visible Shape, it may make her Charm impotent, and give relief to the afflicted Party.

KILLING OINTMENT

On the subject of witchcraft, Johann Wier (1516–1588) was extraordinarily reasonable for his time, pressing for medical examinations of the accused. As a pupil of Cornelius Agrippa, he had been initiated into the healing arts, but he knew their darker side as well. Here, from him, is potent medicine indeed:

> Hemlock, juice of aconite,
> Poplar leaves and roots bind tight.
> Watercress and add to oil
> Baby's fat and let it boil.
> Bat's blood, belladonna too
> Will kill off those who bother you.

ANY WEDNESDAY

Some people have been pestering me for the formula for invisibility. If I give it to you, will you promise to—disappear?

The *Grimoire Verum* is an eighteenth-century fake purporting to be the work of Alibeck the Egyptian, 1517. It's based on *The Key of Solomon* (very ancient already by the time it got on the list of books banned by the Inquisition, in 1559), but itself not prohibited. Here are its instructions:

Take the head of a dead man and put a black bean in its mouth, one up each nostril, one in each ear, one in each eye. That's seven. Then trace a magic pattern of your own devising on the dead man's head with your fingers. Bury the head in the ground, face up. Each day before sunrise, water the place with good brandy. On the eighth day a spirit will interrupt and ask what you are doing. Reply: "I am watering my plant." Do not permit the spirit to water it, though it will ask to do so.

It will show you the pattern you have traced on the head, proving it is a spirit and a good one. *Then* you can permit it to water the place.

On the ninth day the plants will sprout. When the beans finally appear, pick them and place one in your mouth. When you look in the mirror you will not see yourself, for the beans "carry the invisibility of the dead and buried head." *Do not, in your surprise, swallow the beans*; you can only become visible again by removing them from your mouth.

If this fails to make you invisible, it may be because you did not plant at the right time. That's any Wednesday, Mercury's day, before sunrise.

ITCHING POWDER

In Haiti a powerful itching powder is made from the plant called creeping cowage. When "baptized" with an incantation, it is said to irritate the eyes and skin so much it will drive a person crazy.

GARLIC

I'm a garlic freak, and I have good company. Homer called garlic a god, the Chinese have revered it for 4,000 years, and the Egyptians were so sure it gave strength that they fed it to their pyramid-builders.

Garlic occurs often in recipes for invisibility, but I insist on heliotrope, instead. What's the use of being invisible if people can detect you by the garlic on your breath?

TAKE A TRIP

In *Ingoldsby Legends* R. H. Barham (1788–1845) gives a lighthearted description of witches flying off to the sabbat.

> Hey Cockalorum! my Broomstick gay!
> We must rush back ere the dawn of the day,
> Hey up the chimney! away! away!
> Old Goody Price mounts in a trice,

In showing her legs she is not very nice;
Old Goody Jones, all skin and bones,
Follows 'like winking.'—Away go the crones.

Sound like fun? Here, according to a grimoire, is how to get the same results: "Into a well-covered receptacle place the following:

100 grams of lard
5 grams of superior hashish
a pinch of hellebore root
a pinch of crushed sunflower seeds."

Then: "Fill the container with flowers, hemp, and poppy. Let it simmer over water for about two hours. Remove from the heat and uncover."

Before retiring one is supposed to smear this stuff all over, including under the armpits. Then—presumably in sleep—one "flies."

HOW TO GET TO THE OTHER SIDE

From *De Mirabilis Naturae* (1730), translated for your convenience:

Communication with the other world is easy . . . all that you
need is a bell made from an alloy of lead, tin, iron, copper,
mercury, silver, and gold. Inscribe on it: ADONAI, JESUS, TET-
RAGRAMMATON. Then place it for seven days in the middle
of a ditch in a cemetery.

THE HAND OF GLORY

Possibly the most famous charm in the history of magic is the Hand of Glory, which, if properly made, is supposed to paralyze all spectators, so that the possessor of the Hand can rob them freely or do whatever he wants to them.

The process begins when the would-be sorcerer obtains either the right or left hand of a criminal who has been gibbeted—that is, left hanging on the gallows to rot. It is then wrapped in a piece of winding sheet, pickled in an earthenware pot, and dried in the sun. Finally the grease extracted from it is combined with virgin wax and Lapland sesame to make a candle, which is placed in the mummified hand (as in a candlestick), and lighted. As long as the candle flame burns, the spell operates.

Burglars, supposedly protected by the Hand, have been caught in the act of robbing a house. So the spell seems to be more famous than efficacious.

SIMPLE CURSES

Perhaps the simplest curses are those effected by sticking a candle or an onion with pins. The Italian witches claim to get good results with *la ghirlanda delle streghe*: the "witches' garland" is simply a piece of rope in which knots are tied, each accompanied by the repetition of the curse and the sticking of a black feather into the knot. For best results, the witches' garland should then be hidden in the victim's mattress.

THE CURSE OF BREADALBANE

At a Scottish site at Killin, on Loch Tay, stood a castle where the earl of Breadalbane had a witch put to death. She, in her last throes, cursed the earldom, vowing that the title would not pass from father to son for seven generations.

On May 18, 1923, a correspondent wrote to the editor of the London *Times* to point out that the curse had been fulfilled: For seven generations the earldom had not passed from father to son, and the latest earl, whose obituary had recently appeared in the paper, was succeeded by a distant cousin.

The curse seems to have run its course. The present earl (born 1919) succeeded his father (born 1889) in 1959.

THE LORD MAYOR'S CURSE

Daniel Cohen in *Curses, Hexes and Spells* (1974) notes: "In 1521 the Mayor of Lincoln published a formal curse against those who had taken the records and books of the Common Council."

We are not informed what the result of the curse was.

MAGIC STONE

Considered "the food of the Immortals," green jade is also said to be good for you, if you powder it and eat it.

SOMETHING ABOUT PLANTS

Out in the witch's garden (with its white circle in the center to honor the Moon Goddess) there are a lot of plants, some nice, some nasty. Angelica's name suggests the former, and indeed it is worn around the neck to protect children from spells, much as asafetida or camphor used to be worn to protect against disease. Daffodils bring gold, and ginseng, as a tonic, is almost worth its weight in gold; it is reputed to aid digestion, improve the mind, tone up the system, and on and on—but make sure the root you take is seven years old exactly.

Anything with spikes or thorns on it (briar, holly, thistle, thorn) belongs to the Devil. Anything that smells good is good.

An oak was sacred to a Druid. Rowan trees drive off evil spirits. Hazel wands are good for dowsing. Plant a juniper to keep the witches away and a conifer for a Teutonic god to live in.

To be on the safe side, apologize to a tree before you cut it down. Never ever bring an "insulted" tree in for Christmas.

Dillweed, mallow flowers, and horehound keep evil at bay. Bay is unlucky. Hemlock, chestnut, and hawthorn are also unlucky.

The "promethean plant," when mixed with the gall of four animals makes a great "beverage of hate" to use against enemies.

There are two plants called the devil's eye—one for each eye, perhaps. There's also devil's milk, devil's oatmeal, devil's beard, etc. Devil's bit is mandrake, a sovereign remedy.

Place the roots of wild carrots (Queen Anne's lace) under your pillow, and you will dream of your future.

Four-leaf clovers are lucky; everyone knows that. But did you know that fern seed can make you invisible and that mustard seed can protect the front and back doors against unwelcome and unlucky visitors, or that barberry plants (my house has a hedge of them) are supposed to ward off demons?

Low John the Conqueror is a good luck plant used in Voodoo. High John the Conqueror is used for good luck charms in Mexico.

Put belladonna on your horse to make him strong, but only on *Walpurgisnacht* (the evening preceding May Day), or there will be trouble. When you cut belladonna, let a black hen loose to distract the devil; no other color will do. Cut hazel wands for divining on the first night of the full moon, but never cut them from the east side of the plant.

Peas should be eaten only on Thursday (in honor of Thor), but at any time you can rub pea vines on jilted lovers to console them. If you should find nine peas in one pod, put it on the windowsill, and if, when you hear footsteps, you hold your breath, your future husband will appear.

And then there's "the primrose path." Never bring fewer than thirteen primroses into your house. (Never bring in flowering hawthorn at all, never.) But better still, leave the primroses outside to ward off witches. Also good for this are all evil-smelling weeds (except a few dedicated to the Devil) and such things as flax in flower. Burn juniper berries to keep out witches.

Anemones tell witches when people are coming. Witches plant clumps of purple (violets, sorcerer's periwinkle, lilac) to bring money, grow morning glories to protect them (the seeds are also hallucinogenic), and lay in St. John's wort (good boiled in wine to stop vomiting of blood) for the neighbors. They need lots of herbs; recipes like them to be combined in groups of as many as seven or nine, always odd numbers. Sun worshippers like yellow flowers on Mondays. . . .

There are, of course, also appropriate times for gathering simples and herbs: the waxing or waning of the moon, and so on. Any farmer's almanac will tell you the auspicious times for planting, whether you practice witchcraft or not.

CLASSIC RECIPE

From those famous witches, in Shakespeare's *Macbeth*:

> Double, double toil and trouble;
> Fire burn, and cauldron bubble. . . .
> Eye of newt and toe of frog,
> Wool of bat and tongue of dog. . . .
> Finger of birth-strangled babe,
> Ditch-deliver'd by a drab,
> Make the gruel thick and slab. . . .

SOME OLD UN-RELIABLES

Henbane poisoning (a witch's standby) is supposedly cured by the juice of purslane mixed with white wine. If a fishbone sticks in your throat, put your feet in a bath of cold water. Painless childbirth is obtained by fumigating the house with dried eagles' droppings thrown on burning embers. To make your hair grow, mix mouse droppings with roasted bees, burned chestnuts, or beans burned to ashes, held together with attar of roses. To cure shingles and other skin eruptions, eat leeks cooked with barley flour and oil.

If you hold a stalk of nettle and another of millefoil in your hand, you will be "impervious to fear," but they must be picked when the Sun is in Leo (July 19 to August 23). Agnus castus (an ornamental shrub of the verbena family) protects virginity and when added to "smallage [wild celery] and sage in salt water" makes a liniment which, applied to the back of the head, brings people out of comas.

If you want to know how a sick person is going to make out, simply approach his bed with a sprig of verbena *in your left hand*. When you ask him how he feels, if he says "unwell," he will get better; if he says "well," he is in danger of death. If he says, "What are you doing with a sprig of verbena?" the whole thing is best forgotten.

CALCAREOUS AGGREGATED SKELETONS OF DEFUNCT CORALLIGENOUS ZOOPHYTES

That's coral, venerated in ancient India, worn (says Pliny) on the war helmets and weapons of the Gauls, put around the neck of Roman children to protect them (and later used on teething rings and rattles for babies), perfect material for an Italian amulet against the Evil Eye, considered for that purpose (by the Persians) even better than the eye of a sheep whose throat has been cut. Like jade, it can (it is said) detect poison in food or drink. It can cure bleeding and defend you against losing your virility, being struck by lightning, many other misfortunes.

It's just what the doctor ordered, if the doctor is John Schroeder (1660), for purifying the blood: Crush it to a powder and ingest it. Also good (except the black kind) for making you merry, curing fluxes of the belly and malfunctions of the womb, runny eyes, ulcers, fits and convulsions, among other things. Albertus Magnus added, "It stemmeth anon blood, putteth away the foolishness of him that beareth it, and giveth wisdom. . . . And it is good against tempests, and perils of floods."

SORCERERS IN THE SOUK

Edward Mace, writing of a holiday in Rabat, Morocco, in 1975:

If you are out of snake skins, dead bats or rats' tails, the sorcerers in the souk [suq, the marketplace] in the Spanish quarter is the place to go. . . . We bought kurin [cummin?] and saffron there and nutmegs, pine nuts and musk, weighed out for us on a chemist's balance from huge, conical mounds. The sorcerer, sitting among bowls of dried rose petals, produced from an astonishingly questionable jar a black raisin which, placed on the tongue for half an hour, induces a deep drunkenness from which few recover.

I have seen similar "pharmacies" in other countries. In one place I asked the seller, "Will this work if I take it but do not say the *words*?" "I do not know, señor," he replied. "I have never taken it without the words."

We must respect these "crude native remedies." One of them was "Jesuit's bark"—quinine. But I never would patronize the lady in Jalisco, Mexico, who can, by all local accounts, put more hair on your head. I was afraid the witch would shrink my head to fit the hair I already have.

GETTING BACK AT THE WITCH

Robert Herrick tells us how to revenge ourselves on the hag who has taken some hair or nail clippings of us and cast a spell to hurt us:

> To House the Hag, you must doe this:
> Commix with Meale a little Pisse
> Of him bewitcht: then forthwith make
> A little Wafer or a Cake;
> And this rawly bak't will bring
> The old Hag in. No surer thing.

"IT'S LOVE THAT MAKES THE WORLD GO ROUND. . . ."

Suppose you have added up the numerological values of your first name and your birth date (don't forget to add 3, the magic number) and you "know" therefore the "number" of the boy or girl who is just right for you. Now you have the number. How are you going to attract him or her?

You could make a wax figure and go through a lot of burying and unburying of it, and many other—often disgusting—actions. You could pray to Venus. You could tie a wryneck (a variety of woodpecker) to a wheel and turn it, "turning the affections" of your intended. You could sneak your fingernail parings—or a few drops of your bathwater—into his or her food.

You could slip the object of your affections a maddening drug, from datura to laurel, or something more subtle, such as lettuce or cinnamon. You might dare to call on the devil Asmodeus, but that's very risky.

It used to be a crime to "provoke another to unlawful love" by magic, as bad as ruining people's sex lives by tying knots in cords and all that. First offense (under laws of 1563 and 1604 in England) you got a year in jail. Second offense? The law of 1563 got you life and in 1604 they made it death. The crime was increasing.

TYING THE KNOT: HOW TO MAKE A LOVE KNOT AND HOW TO UNDO A HATE KNOT

From a magical papyrus of ancient Egypt:

You take a band of linen of 16 threads, 4 of white, 4 of green, 4 of blue, 4 of red, and make them into one band, and stain them with the blood of a hoopoe [a European bird, often used in magic perhaps because of its eye-catching crest], and you bind it with a scarab in its attitude of the sun-god, drowned, being wrapped in byssus [a fine-woolen cloth], and you bind it to the body of the boy who has the vessel and it will work quickly.

Later and simpler methods were developed to make people fall in love. There was even an antilove (or at least anticopulation) black magic trick called knotting the cord.

You attend a marriage ceremony and hang around at the back, rather like the bad fairy not invited to the christening in "Sleeping Beauty." While the couple are taking their vows, you secretly tie knots in a cord. Virgil's *Eighth Eclogue* suggests "three colors in three knots," which sounds good, if a little difficult to do surreptitiously.

Roman Emperor Theodosius the Great (346–395) and King Philip Augustus of France (1165–1223) are but two of the many personages unmanned for marriage (they said) by knots. Arranged marriages for political purposes may have accounted for other impotence among the high-born.

Pliny was sure it was a danger, but he told how to break the spell: Rub the threshold of the marriage chamber with wolf fat. Sounds slippery, but you are *not* to step on the threshold when you carry the bride over it anyway.

Or you can make yourself immune to knots by filling your pockets with salt and urinating just before you enter the church (not in the graveyard, though—you might make a dangerous enemy). Or while you are picking out the bride's wedding ring, get one for the groom, too. Make sure it is gold and "contains the right eye of a weasel."

RAISING THE DEVIL

Here is the German formula for raising the Devil, who arrives in the form of a he-goat. This conjuration takes a loud voice that rises to a terrific scream on the final commands for the "King, King" to come.

> *Lalle, Bachea, Magotte, Baphia, Dajam,*
> *Vagoth Henech Ammi Nagaz, Adomator*
> *Raphael Immanuel Christus Tetragrammaton*
> *Agra Jod Loi. König. König!*

Once again, Haining's *The Necromancers* is helpful. If this doesn't work, he has a second one "to be read backward except the last two words," which are *"Komm! Komm!"* That should do it. The formula given to dismiss the Devil, Haining says, "would evidently make almost anybody go away."

ALCHEMICAL FORMULAS

Strictly speaking, alchemists were the research scientists of their day, exploring the properties of various minerals and chemicals, mastering the art of changing matter by combination, distillation, calcination (reducing a mineral to powder), fixation, and other techniques.

The ultimate goal of alchemy was to make or discover the philosopher's stone, sometimes called the elixir, a substance that was believed capable of turning base metals (lead, tin, mercury, iron, copper) into gold or silver. "The belief that it could be obtained only by divine grace and favour," writes E. J. Holmyard in *Alchemy* (1957), "led to the development of esoteric or mystical alchemy, and this gradually developed into a devotional system where the mundane transmutation of metals became merely symbolic of the transformation of sinful man into a perfect being through prayer and submission to the will of God."

It was all too easy for this mystic aspect of alchemy to become tainted with sorcery, for astrology to replace trust in God, for prayer to turn into incantation and ritual magic—especially when the alchemist's patron was impatient. Gilles de Retz turned first to alchemy to recoup his squandered fortune; then when the transmutation did not occur, he hurried on to a particularly vile form of black magic. The same impatience beset Augustus the Strong of Saxony, as we will see below, but with happier outcome.

One of the objects of the alchemist's search was the alkahest, a universal solvent, which was said to exist. (Old joke: If it dissolves everything, what do you keep it in?)

The alkahest could be made from sweat, spit, worms, and so on, but the best raw material was blood. A true magic formula, for blood represents life itself, and spitting is in widespread use in spells.

Many formulas for making the philosopher's stone were developed over the centuries, all immensely complicated and tiresome to read about. Here is one, much simplified. You start by purging the original material (not specified) with water from the Black Sea, distilling the result into what is known as mercurial water, and dividing that into five portions, two of which are set aside. The other three portions of mercurial water are added to one twelfth of their weight in virgin gold (gold that has never been used for mundane purposes), put through another distilling process in an alembic (a primitive pot still), and when they have formed a solid amalgam, one of the reserved two portions is added to the mixture, followed by the other, in seven installments. The container is then sealed and kept warm for forty-seven days, and at the end of that time—if all has gone well—the result should be the long-sought substance, of a beautiful purple color. In theory the alchemist could then set about turning base metal into gold. Other formulas are even longer and more tedious.

Here is a recipe for making gold that does not require the elixir. It is from the magical Sanskrit *Atherao Veda*, but there is more of metallurgy about it than of magic:

Take the following ingredients: twenty parts of platinum, the same amount of silver, plus 240 parts of brass, and obtain also 120 parts of nickel. Melt these separately in different crucibles. They are then to be combined when in the molten condition. This alloy is then poured into moulds to cool. Then use the metal.

Alchemy had many sources: ancient Egypt, where men were said to have made some mysterious oxide to use in the worship of Osiris, which effected wonderful cures and transmuted metals; China, where they studied the chemical and mystic properties of gold, cinnabar, and other materials; Babylon; Arabia, where learned scholars discovered caustic alkalis; Spain, where Christians had their closest contact with Arabic and Jewish lore.

By the late Middle Ages, when alchemy was flirting with magic, it began to get a bad name, and yet it hung on. Henry V banned it from England in 1404, but his son granted licenses to various alchemists to practice their craft and actually employed one himself. So, it is said, did Elizabeth I. James IV of Scotland (1473–1513) was interested in alchemy, as was Holy Roman Emperor Rudolf II (1552–1612). Charles II, according to Holmyard, "had an alchemical laboratory built under the royal bedchamber with access by a private staircase." Learned men found it attractive, too: Roger Bacon, Saint Thomas Aquinas, Sir Thomas Browne, John Evelyn, and even Sir Isaac Newton.

The elixir has been reported found on a number of occasions. In 1648, one Johann Richthausen demonstrated the art of transmuting metals in the presence of his emperor, Ferdinand III (1608–1657); with one grain of his magic powder, he changed two and a half pounds of mercury into gold, which the emperor had struck into medals. (They no longer exist, but see illustration of what one looked like.) In 1676, during the reign of Ferdinand's son, Leopold I, a monk named Wenzel Seyler—again in the imperial presence—changed both tin and copper into gold. Leopold made Seyler a baron and had a medal struck from the "gold" that carried Leopold's image on one side and on the other a bit of verse: *Aus Wenzel Seylers Pulvers Macht/Bin ich von Zinn zu Gold gemacht* ("By the power of Wenzel Seyler's powder, I have been changed from tin to gold").

That medal too disappeared, but the result of a later "transmutation" by Seyler, a medallion, survived until 1888, when it was examined by a chemist. Unfortunately for believers in alchemy—if any still existed—the medallion turned out to be decidedly brassy in color and to have a specific gravity of only 12.67—6.63 short of the specific gravity of gold.

This medal was minted in 1648 in honor of an alchemical demonstration in Prague before Emperor Ferdinand III—supposedly of the gold that, everyone was convinced, had been created out of base metal.

There were other "successful" alchemists, including a number of learned men, but after the 1780s, when the Royal Society sent chemist Joseph Black to investigate the claims of a certain James Price, interest languished. Price had reportedly changed mercury into gold by adding a white powder to it, mixing it in a flux of borax and niter, and heating the results in a crucible, which he stirred with an iron rod. The results assayed out as the purest silver. Price later performed the same "transmutation" with different quantities and produced gold. But when Black arrived to test out the process in person, Price swallowed prussic acid and died before the chemist's eyes. It turned out that Price was not only a fraud, but a little mad into the bargain.

And then we come to the case of Frederick Augustus I (1670–1733), called the Strong, elector of Saxony and off-again-on-again king of Poland. Augustus had luxurious tastes and no urge to stint his personal pleasures. He caused his capital city, Dresden, to erect many gorgeous (and expensive) baroque buildings, and founded a famed art collection. He was particularly fond of porcelain, then obtainable only from China at enormous expense, and indulged himself lavishly in buying it. (He also conducted some expensive wars, chiefly in his efforts to retain the Polish crown.) Inevitably he ran out of funds. To recoup, he hired a young alchemist, one Johann

Friedrich Böttger (1682–1719), to find the philosopher's stone and make gold.

Böttger was kept virtually a prisoner and nagged regularly by the impatient Augustus. But the great discovery remained elusive as ever. One evening, as the story goes, when the harassed Böttger was entertaining a friend in his quarters, he poured out the tale of his troubles. The friend was sympathetic, but he thought Böttger was going at things the wrong way. "Even if you find the elixir," he pointed out to the alchemist, "Augustus will simply take the gold and spend it on porcelain. I say, forget about learning how to make gold. Learn how to make porcelain."

Böttger thought it over and decided that was a good idea. Abandoning the alchemical search, he learned how to make porcelain. In 1710, in partnership with Count Ehrenfried Walter von Tschirnhaus and under the patronage of Augustus, he established the Royal Saxon Porcelain Manufactory at Meissen. In a few short years the names "Meissen" and "Dresden china" were synonymous with exquisite ceramics. Over the centuries the manufacture of fine porcelain has brought Saxony more wealth than it could have acquired with a thousand philosopher's stones.

KILLING RECIPE

Get a specimen of your victim's urine. Buy a hen's egg without haggling over the price, and on some Tuesday or Saturday night take the egg to some deserted place where you will not be disturbed. With a circular incision at the broad end, extract the white only. Add the urine to the yolk in the eggshell and, saying the name of the victim, close up the end of the shell with a small piece of virgin parchment. Bury the egg in the ground and leave without looking back.

The only thing then that can prevent the victim from dying of jaundice is the discovery and destruction of the egg, burned by the same hand that buried it. If the egg is allowed to rot in the ground, the victim will die within the year.

SOVEREIGN CURES FOR EVERYTHING

Remember the fad for copper bracelets "for rheumatism"? Magic? In fact, the copper bracelets worked because people thought they would. Earlier copper bracelets "cured" cholera, typhoid, and other ills, and guarded against the dangers of impure water. Faith can move mountains!

In case you'd like to be the first on your block with a new fad, note that silver is supposed to cure or relieve epilepsy, platinum keeps you from being constipated, tin is recommended for worms, lead improves the complexion (but don't ingest it—it killed off the Roman patrician class, which used lead pots, and threatens our poor infants who eat leaded paint in tenements), iron builds the blood, and gold can help you to sleep at nights (keep it in Swiss banks).

Whoever said that "diamonds are a girl's best friend" dwelt too much in the world of practicality. Diamonds are "unconquerable" (Greek: *adamas*) and impart courage and faith. They are connected in arcane lore with Aries and in the popular mind only with buxom blonds having "more fun."

INCENSE FOR SUCCESS

Mix together these ingredients (powdered if necessary) by weight:

sandalwood	30 percent
myrrh	10 percent
patchouli leaf	5 percent
orris root	5 percent
cinnamon	10 percent
frankincense	40 percent

Add a dash of saltpeter. Burn with incantations for your desire.

THE ELIXIR

And even the search for the philosopher's stone was intimately connected with the search for the elixir of life, for youth, a search that continues today with "life extension" plans using procaine and other drugs. The count of St.-Germain (supposed to have lived hundreds of years under a series of names) suggested an extract of senna, "St.-Germain tea," the vitamin C of its day. Arnaldus Villanovanus recommended alcohol (our word *whiskey* means "water of life"). Our grandparents liked patent medicine, of which alcohol was always a main ingredient (even those labeled "temperence beverages"), and tonics and cordials of various sorts. The Irish philosopher Bishop Berkeley praised tar-water as a panacea. Sir Francis Bacon recommended smelling freshly turned earth, the very clay of which God made us. The Countess Bathory (as I say elsewhere) bathed in the blood of countless maidens. Others swallowed blood, urine, gold.

In *The Alchemists*, F. S. Taylor gives the recipe for Dr. Stevens' Water, a seventeenth-century potion guaranteed to preserve life and make a man "seem young in his old age."

To a gallon of "Good Gascon Wine" (red), add a dram each of ginger, cinnamon, nutmeg, cloves, fennel seed, caraway seed, oregano, and galingale. Then throw in a generous handful each of sage, mint, wild marjoram, wild thyme, thyme, pellitory (a southern European herb), rosemary, red rose petals, pennyroyal, mint, camomile, and lavender. The herbs are bruised, the spices ground, and the liquid (once the solid ingredients have been allowed to soak in it for twelve hours or more) is thrice distilled. The distillate should be taken in small but very regular doses.

This certainly sounds more healthful than the "eye of newt" preparations we are usually offered. And don't be like the Scottish clergyman who is said to have concocted in his youth an elixir of life, but was afraid to swallow it. Thirty years later, he felt he was old enough and brave enough to try it. But by then it had evaporated.

RULERSHIP

A rule of magic is "as above, so below." From the most ancient times, the planets were said to rule terrestrial destinies and powers. Days of the week were named for the seven "planets" then known: Sun Day, Moon Day, Mars Day, Mercury Day, Jove Day, Venus Day, and Saturn Day. We can still see the remnants of these in the English Sunday, Monday, and Saturday and in the French Mardi (Tuesday), Mercredi (Wednesday), Jeudi (Thursday), and Vendredi (Friday). The magician learned and exploited celestial rulership over people, plants, metals, and minerals—everything.

Magic rituals must be conducted at astrologically correct times and with instruments, incenses, and plants correct for the ruling planet. For example, a love potion demands herbs controlled by Venus. Periwinkle's blue flower is described in the book attributed to Albertus Magnus as the best ingredient for a love potion, but it must be gathered at a date and day and hour dictated by astrology. It is ignorance of rulership and such arcane matters, say magicians, that render totally useless the concoctions thrown together by amateurs.

7
"All Manner of Folk"

WITCHES and magicians both tend to be people who are a little set apart from the rest of us—bolder, more learned, more restless, more confident, sometimes more wicked, but always imbued with a strong sense of self and a belief that the rules that govern ordinary people do not apply to them. The great English jurist Lord Coke hit on their basic quality when he legally defined witchcraft. Sorcerers, he said, are *determined* to work their will.

French historian Grillot de Givry writes in *Witchcraft, Magic and Alchemy* (first published in America in 1931):

> Some skillfull sorcerers knew the art of calling up the Devil or the subordinate demons of the vast infernal army. . . . Other sorcerers, known as necromancers, could call up apparitions of the dead. . . . There were sorcerers whom we should now class as "intellectuals." They were called sorcerers because what we mean

by "learned man" did not then exist. . . . There were monks, even, to whom the name of sorcerer was applied, both Roger Bacon and Albertus Magnus. . . . There were also sorcerer-monarchs like Henry III [of France] and his mother, Catherine de Médicis, and, strangest of all, sorcerer-Popes, Pope Honorius in the seventh century, and Pope Silvester II in the eleventh century, were considered, rightly or wrongly, to be sorcerers. . . .

In this chapter we shall meet some of these strange people, who considered themselves, or were considered by others, or laid claim to being, magicians and witches. And some others, who preyed on them.

DOUBLE GLOUCESTER

Humphrey, duke of Gloucester, brother of the ill-fated Henry VI, had a wife who was very curious about when the king would die. Some people said she was trying to hasten that event and that she had a wax figure of the king by her fireplace, hoping that, as it melted, the life of the king would drain away.

The duchess of Gloucester was tried and on flimsy evidence, she and her "accomplices" were all convicted. One woman from the town of Ely was burned. A canon of Westminster was confined to the Tower, where he died. Another "accomplice" was hanged, drawn, and quartered at Tyburn. Of course you couldn't treat the wife of "Good Duke Humphrey" in that way, so her punishment was this: On three successive days she carried a tall wax candle to the high altars of St. Paul's, Christ Church, and St. Michael's, three London parish churches. There, in the presence of the lord mayor and aldermen of London, she did her penance. Then she was sent off to the worst place they could think of, the Isle of Man.

The locals there believe that she haunts the Isle of Man to this day.

SIMON PURE AND SIMON NOT SO PURE

In Acts 8:9–12 and 8:18–24 the Bible tells the story of Simon, a magician, who in former times had "bewitched" the people of Samaria and had paraded himself as "some great one." Simon was baptized a Christian and became a follower of Philip, but when Peter and John arrived in Samaria and began to heal by the power of the Holy Ghost, Simon was so impressed that he offered them money if they would confer on him the same gifts. Peter rebuked him, saying, "Thy money perish with thee, because thou has thought that the gift of God may be purchased with money." Simon thereupon repented and asked Peter to pray for him. From this incident we have our word "simony," for the buying or selling of church offices.

That is all that the Bible itself says about this Simon, but some later works, especially the apocryphal *Acts of Saint Peter*, tell us of a certain Simon Magus, who supposedly appeared in Rome during the reign of the Emperor Claudius (A.D. 41–54), and these two Simons may—or may not—have been the same person.

Simon Magus was an evil sorcerer, who won many followers by performing acts of magic. He survived into the reign of Nero (54–68) and when Peter arrived in Rome, they became rivals. As the story goes, Nero demanded that Simon demonstrate his vaunted powers at high noon before a gathering of Roman citizens, and the magician agreed.

When a great crowd, among them Peter himself, had gathered in the imperial forum, Simon took center stage, magic staff in hand. His first act was to stand the staff upright and tell it to wait for him. It remained where he had placed it, erect. Then, having bowed to the emperor and his court, Simon stretched out his arms and began to rise into the air.

Higher and higher he rose until he was level with the top of the shrine of Juno Moneta (where Roman money was coined). At that point, Peter knelt down and made the sign of the cross in the air, and the spell was broken. The magician's staff toppled over, and Simon's body came crashing to earth.

Since Peter's original name was Simon, this can be said to be the magical duel of the two Simons. And Peter himself was martyred shortly afterward, during the Neronian persecutions.

PARACELSUS

His real name is impressive enough: Theophrastus Philippus Aurealus Bombastus von Hohenheim. But for this sixteenth-century physician and occultist, it was not enough. Considering himself equal in greatness to the ancient Roman writer on medicine, Aulus Cornelius Celsus, he named himself Paracelsus ("alongside Celsus").

Paracelsus was one of the most multitalented men of his time (1493–1541), a universal scientist, discover of zinc, a man deeply involved in very ancient magic and in the most advanced science of his time, alchemist and chemist, magician and physician, mystic and pioneer in medicine, metallurgy, pharmacy, and just about everything else.

His was a brilliant but not at all a humble personality. He went to the University of Basel at sixteen, became a physician and town doctor of the city, and outraged all the other medical professors by advocating new methods and attacking the old-fashioned, even superstitious beliefs of the great doctors of the past, such as Galen and Avicenna. It was time, he said, to observe rather than to believe, to experiment (as he did) very boldly with new compounds and new concepts, and, of course, to recognize genius (his).

They drove him out of Basel in 1529, and thereafter he led a life of wandering and conflict. He published a long list of works on subjects ranging from mineralogy (which he had early studied in the Tyrol) to magic. He died in Salzburg in 1541.

Quite apart from his innovations in pharmacy and medicine, he believed in an earth peopled below and above with gnomes and spirits. He forged some strange kind of link between the scientific emphasis on observable fact and the magical stress on the invisible world. Thus this extraordinary mind, one of the most advanced of the Renaissance, not only launched medical treatment and research on their way to modern empirical science, but fostered the most ancient mystical and magical beliefs.

A SCOTS SORCERER

Thomas Weir, born sometime around 1600, was the chief officer of the town guard of Edinburgh and one of its most respected citizens. A pillar of the Establishment, a "saint" of the very strict and upstanding sect known as the Bowhead Saints, Weir had served as a soldier on the side of Parliament in the Civil War, where he was distinguished for his cruelty toward Royalists and was known far and wide for his devout Presbyterian piety and his extraordinary gifts for moving extempore prayer. Thus, when Weir, at the age of seventy, suddenly and voluntarily confessed that he practiced the black arts as a magician, owned a magic staff, and was full of "blackness and darkness, brimstone and burning to the bottom of Hell," the provost (mayor) of Edinburgh was embarrassed and astonished.

And yet this "pillar" proceeded to add that he had for years committed incest with his sister—from the time she was in her teens until she reached fifty, at which point he was disgusted with her age and wrinkles—and had had carnal knowledge of Margaret Bourdon (the daughter of his dead wife), Bessie Weems (a serving girl, over a period of twenty years), and had "polluted himself" with various sheep, cows, and his own mare. When doctors and ministers tried to help the old man, he cursed their efforts to save his soul from perdition.

On April 29, 1670, Thomas and his sister appeared before the court, charged with sexual offenses. Weir was convicted of four—incest (two counts), fornication, and bestiality. He was sentenced to be strangled to death and his body to be burned, his black sorcerer's staff along with him. Jane offered the court a free confession that she was guilty of incest with her brother and "most especially [of] consulting witches, necromancers, and devils," keeping a familiar that not only assisted her in evil but also spun extraordinary quantities of wool for her. She was more helpful to the court than it wanted her to be, for the details were frightening. She was sentenced to be hanged in the Grassmarket, a street in central Edinburgh.

But despite her cooperation at the trial, when the day of execution arrived, Jane put up a battle royal. She struggled with her guards, threatened to remove all her clothes and shock the spectators, stuck her head between two steps of the scaffold, and was very difficult to pry loose. Worse, she said she had no remorse for her sins. They hanged her anyway.

As long as the two lived, some people were willing to dismiss the confessions as the results of madness or senile decay, but once the Weirs were dead, their reputation as sorcerers grew and spread. Thomas Weir's house, called Bow Head, stayed uninhabited for a century or more, while rumors of hauntings pervaded the city. It was said that other inhabitants of the street often heard, at night, the sound of a spinning wheel. . . .

ACCORDING TO RULE

Margaret Rule (whose story is vividly recounted by Cotton Mather) was prosecuted as a witch in Boston in 1693.

She reported that the Devil forced her to swear fealty on a big red book, by which she must have meant the lettering. It was not uncommon for grimoires to be printed in red—they were said to burn the eyes if gazed at too long—but they were always bound in black.

BOULLAN'S ATROCITIES

The abbé Boullan (born in France in 1824) claimed to be John the Baptist "returned to earth" and the "reincarnation of the prophet Elijah." He was, in fact, one of the most despicable of nineteenth-century magicians.

Jean-Antoine Boullan took holy orders at the age of twenty-five and almost immediately set out to "exorcize the Roman Catholic Church." As part of this campaign he performed the black mass (for which he was briefly jailed in Rome) and committed other sacriliges.

Early in his pastoral work, Father Boullan became the confessor of a nun named Sister Adele Chevalier. She became his mistress, and they had several children, at least one of which he was widely believed to have sacrificed in a demonic ceremony. With his mistress the nun, he founded a Society for the Reparation of Souls and engaged in blasphemous rites, offering to exorcise demons from nuns by administering the consecrated Host smeared with human excrement. Later he headed the Church of Carmel, and some people who were taken in by his apparent piety flocked to his "services," among them famed French novelist Joris Karl Huysmans (1848–1907).

A couple of Rosicrucians showed him up as a Satanist. Stanislaus de Guita and Oswald Wirth infiltrated the Church of Carmel and learned what Father Boullan was doing. They wrote a book, *The Temple of Satan*, which exposed his attempts to call up incubi and succubi, to practice sex magic, to exorcise with excrement and to practice Satanism. They labeled Father Boullan as a "pontiff of infamy, a base idol of the mystical Sodom . . . an evil sorcerer." This ended Boullan's career, and he died in disgrace.

AGRIPPA, THE CABALISTIC PHILOSOPHER

It is very difficult for moderns to understand a man like Heinrich Cornelius Agrippa von Nettesheim (1486–1535), philosopher, physician, magician, and more. Although he spent time in exile and even in jail for debt, his ideas influenced the study of the occult for generations.

His life was remarkable. Born in Cologne without good prospects, by the age of twenty he was well launched on a career in diplomacy and was sent on a secret mission to Paris by the Emperor Maximilian I. Then suddenly we find him entering the academic profession, lecturing on theology and occultism. His opinions so angered the church that he found himself right out of a job. He returned to diplomacy for a while, then acquired a medical degree from the University of Pavia. But soon he was in trouble again for his beliefs, this time for daring to defend a woman accused of witchcraft.

In Fribourg, Switzerland, he became so famous as a physician that the Queen Mother summoned him to France to be her personal doctor. When she wouldn't pay his salary, he went to Antwerp as historiographer to Charles

V, but soon the salary there was refused too. After more adventures—including being arrested as he passed through France for complaining about how badly the Queen Mother had treated him earlier—he found his way to Grenoble, where he died on February 18, 1535.

Agrippa gained a reputation as a magician for his *De occulta philosophia* (1531). He owned a black dog named Monsieur to which he was much attached; the animal ate at his table and slept on his bed, and though friends testified that it was a perfectly ordinary dog and could be walked on a leash, gossip said that Monsieur was Agrippa's familiar demon.

Agrippa believed in magic as a way of gaining deeper knowledge of God and nature. His ideas combined the ancient mysteries and the new Lutheranism, science and superstition, the cabala and Catholicism, and many other elements, and his influence was to prove greater in later times than during his exciting life.

AUGUST STRINDBERG

"Strindberg still remains," wrote Eugene O'Neill in 1924, "the most modern of moderns," but this great Scandinavian playwright (with Ibsen, a founder of the modern drama) had some very old-fashioned ideas, too, among them alchemy and black magic. Dabbling in the latter poisoned his later life.

Strindberg believed he could will things to happen and felt deep remorse when he reconsidered willing his child ill, not ill enough to die but problem enough to reconcile the parents.

He wrote that "there are crimes and crimes," some of which the law cannot punish but which nonetheless bring guilt, and in one play Strindberg traces the fate of a man who wills the death of his only child. Like all the fifty volumes of his work, this is partly autobiographical.

In the mad, mystical mind of this modern dramatist and old-fashioned alchemist were mingled the most advanced ideas and some of the oldest superstitions.

PAPAL SORCERERS

A number of popes have, at one time or another, been accused of practicing sorcery. Benedict XIII (1394–1423, actually an antipope, not to be confused with the real Benedict XIII, 1724–1730) was said to hold "continuous traffic with spirits" and to keep "two demons . . . in a little bag" for personal use and to search "everywhere for books on magic." Gregory VII (1081–1084) was pronounced a sorcerer by the Synod of Bressanone, June 25, 1080. Honorius I (d.638) was anathematized (formally cursed) forty-two years after his death. Benedict IX (1032–1048) bought his way to the papacy at the age of twenty, was twice deposed for profligacy, and ended up as antipope to Clement II. Antipope John XXIII (as I have said elsewhere) was reputed to have employed Abramelin to save him from the Council of Constance (1414–1417). Alexander VI (1492–1503), one of the two Borgia popes, bought his way to the papacy, fathered Cesare and Lucretia Borgia, and devoted himself entirely to expanding the temporal power of the papacy and the wealth of his own family.

But all the above men were involved in political clashes. Honorius and Gregory VII were austere reformers, opposed by worldly cardinals (Gregory was canonized in 1606); antipopes were the result of disputed papal elections; and pontiffs who lived scandalous private lives eventually shocked even people who had adopted lascivious life-styles of their own. In the struggles to control the papacy, charges of sorcery were freely employed— much as charges of "communist" and "pinko" were freely employed during the Senator McCarthy era. Usually there was nothing back of them except a desire to get rid of the accused.

But the label "sorcerer" has been pasted on others, less political, too. Leo III (795–816) is supposed to have authored a manual of magic called *Enchiridion*, which he sent to Charlemagne. Honorius III (1216–1227) also has a book of magic attributed to him, a new version of the *Black Book*, but it might also have been the work of antipope Honorius II (1061–1064) or of some Honorius who was not a pope at all.

But the pope about whom the most fanciful tales are told was Sylvester II (999–1003). Prior to his election, he had been known as Gerbert, and he was the foremost scholar in Europe. He invented an elaborate abacus and celestial and terrestrial globes for the teaching of mathematics and astronomy. He is credited with construction of a remarkable sundial at Magdeburg and several pipe organs. A devoted bibliophile, he collected manuscripts from all over Europe, especially of classical (secular) Latin authors, and created one of the great libraries of the Middle Ages. He devoted his short papacy to diplomacy, reconciling quarreling prelates and advancing old rivals and confirming their appointments.

But genuine achievements were not enough apparently, for after his death, fabulous tales began to circulate about Sylvester. He was supposed to have been a powerful magician and to have won the papacy by his spells. (He did have pull; his former pupil, later Holy Roman Emperor Otto III, obtained the See for him.) He was supposed to have had a love adventure in Spain. It was claimed that he had sold his soul to the devil and received in return a magic statue that made prophecies, one of them being that Sylvester himself should not die, "except at Jerusalem."

As the story goes, he was saying Mass one day in Rome and was taken ill. He remembered the prophecy and asked for the name of the church he was in; he was told "Holy Cross of Jerusalem." He knew then that he was going to die, and he did.

MAGICIANS AND SCIENTISTS

Johannes Heidenberg (1462–1516) was abbot of the Benedictine monastery of Trittenheim, West Germany. He was a theologian, and since magic was then regarded as one of the learned arts, he drifted into the study of it. He maintained that there were three kinds of magic—natural, cabalistic, and black—and pored over the works of the great Dominican, Albertus Magnus (1193–1280), who had also dabbled in magic.

His fellow monks were impressed at first by Heidenberg's writings; then (perhaps because witchcraft persecutions were then beginning to rage throughout southern Germany) they became uneasy and burned their abbot's books. Heidenberg left for Würzburg and continued his arcane studies. In *Stenography* he taught not shorthand but the art of raising demons, and he greatly influenced such magician-scientists as Agrippa and Paracelsus.

"In magic," wrote Heidenberg, "it is the practice that is dangerous, not the knowledge," and the great Albertus is said to have agreed with him:

> Every science is good in itself, but its operation is good or evil
> according to the end to which it is directed. . . . Magic is neith-
> er forbidden nor evil, since through knowledge of it, one can
> avoid evil and do good. . . . Magic . . . is useful knowledge,
> but very dangerous when one gets to know nature in depth.

However they did it, Heidenberg and his cohorts delved into pharmacy and psychology, magic and mesmerism, physics and medicine, philosophy and the occult. And along the way they laid the foundations for any number of later sciences.

WILLIAM JAMES

The great American psychologist (*Principles of Psychology* and *The Varieties of Religious Experience*) and philosopher (*The Will to Believe* and *Some Problems of Philosophy*) said every hallucination was "as good, and true a sensation as if there were a real object there. The object happens *not* to be there, that is all."

SAINT ALFONSO MARIA DE' LIGUORI'S ADVICE

The founder of the Congregation of the Most Holy Redeemer, known as the Redemptorists (1696–1787), says that in breaking a pact in which you sold your soul to the Devil you must repent and make restitution to any persons you have injured, adding in his *Moral Theology*, Book III (one of seventy volumes on his works), that if the Devil has given you any books, amulets, talismans, or what-have-you, you must burn them but, if he holds the document of your deed of gift of the soul—Bishop Liguori had been a prominent trial lawyer before he entered the priesthood—you don't need to get it back to burn it; just tell the Devil you recant.

But for all the sophistry in such reasoning, Liguori was best known for the simplicity and dignity of his sermons, understandable by the least sophisticated of his peasant flock.

ROGER BACON

Roger Bacon (1214?–1294?) was famous as a student of the occult, though he was, in fact, a scientist. (Even as late as Shakespeare's time, Bacon was portrayed by dramatist Robert Greene as a magician.) A Franciscan, he was the author of a *Treatise on the Secret Works of Nature and Art*; his experiments (detailed in his *Mirror of Alchemy*) laid some foundations for chemistry and physics, including studies of the rainbow and magnets.

It was widely believed that he had created some sort of golem, or Frankenstein's monster, and a brazen head that could speak. Pope Clement IV asked to read his work, and Bacon sent him his *Opus Majus*, a kind of encyclopedia, but it only seems to have got Bacon in trouble, for the head of the Franciscan order denounced him for "suspect novelties," put him under house arrest, and forbade the reading of the *Opus*. What could you do with a man who was inventing the magnifying glass, fiddling around with gunpowder, studying astrology as well as astronomy, and working on an elixir of life, except to throw him in jail and ban his books? His ideas about a lighter-than-air flying machine alone were enough to show he was in league with the Devil.

DOCTOR FAUSTUS

Faust is so widely known as a legendary figure, the subject of drama, epic verse, and opera, that most people assume he was a figment of someone's imagination. But a magician named Georg (later Johann) Faust actually did live from about 1480 to 1541.

He was born probably in Knittlingen in Baden-Württemberg, southwestern Germany. He learned the black arts in Kraków, then led the life of a wandering magician, traveling to various cities in Germany accompanied by a performing horse and dog. He called himself Magister (Master) Georgius Sabellicus (Sabine) Faustus (lucky) Junior. He told fortunes and cast horoscopes. He laid claim to occult knowledge and power, such as the ability to restore lost works of Plato and Aristotle and to perform the same miracles as Jesus.

Some of his contemporaries denounced him as a charlatan and mountebank, notably Johann Wier, who called Faust a drunken vagabond of "unspeakable deceit, many lies, and great effect." But the religious reformers of the day took the magician seriously. Melanchthon feared him as "a disgraceful beast and sewer of many devils" and considered the horse and dog his familiars. Johann Gast, a well-known divine, claims to have taken a meal with Faust at which these creatures were attendants. Luther himself declared that Faust had worked sorceries against him, which he only overcame by God's help.

One morning in 1541, at Staufen in his native Württemberg, Faust was found in his room, lying on his face, dead. His neck had been wrung as if by superhuman force. It is said that the corpse, though repeatedly laid out on its bier face up, was five times discovered to have been turned face down.

Out of this material, men's imagination constructed the story of a learned man who sold his soul to the devil Mephistopheles (or Mephisto) in return for youth, love, and universal knowledge, then was claimed by Mephistopheles and carried off to Hell. The first book to carry the story was printed in Frankfurt in 1587, and from there it became Marlowe's play *Doctor Faustus* (1588), Goethe's great dramatic poem *Faust* (1808 and 1832), a drawing by Rembrandt, and countless operas, symphonies, tone poems, overtures, and other musical pieces.

For a drunken mountebank, it was quite an apotheosis.

THE PRINCE OF SORCERERS

The title, common in his lifetime, was really too grand for Louis Gaufridi, a handsome priest of Provence, whose real offenses were chiefly sexual. He fell in love with a twelve-year-old nun, seduced her with the help of a charm which he carried in a walnut, and "married" her in the name of the Devil (because he couldn't marry her in the name of God).

But he ran into an accusation of witchcraft by a fellow resident of his mistress' convent, a hysterical woman named Louise Capeau, and was brought to trial by Church authorities. They assigned an exorcist to his mistress (Madeleine de Mandols de La Palud), and he claimed to have driven 666 devils out of her. They forced Gaufridi to confess in court to a story of obscenities, blasphemies, and heresies. Madeleine, now "unpossess-ed" of the Devil, gave evidence that Gaufridi had said black masses, and Capeau testified that she could see the Devil, in the shape of a toad, sitting on the priest's shoulder.

Father Gaufridi was burned at the stake on April 30, 1611, at Aix-les-Bains. They put Madeleine away safely, lest she bring more embarrassment to Church and civil authorities; first she was set to chopping wood for charity, later (1653) they feared her more and put her in perpetual cloister. Louise Capeau went free. She accused a lot more people and managed to get another person burned at the stake. That victim was a little blind girl named Honorée.

MACDUFF

Shakespeare's *Macbeth* is not only full of witches, prophecies, spells, incantations, and ghosts. It also contains the brave Macduff who, in revenge for Macbeth's many crimes, including the murder of Macduff's wife and children, kills Macbeth. Macduff, having had a Cesarean birth, was considered "not of woman born" and thus of mystic origin. In Scotland to this day, Macduff figures in occult lore.

In Fifeshire there is the base of what used to be a Celtic cross named for the Macduffs. The cross itself has long since disappeared, demolished in the Reformation as papistical, but the site remains haunted to this day.

In medieval times Macduff's Cross had been a place of sanctuary. Anyone could run to it, hold onto it, and be safe from retribution for murder, provided he arranged to pay blood money to the relatives; some say the price of a life was nine bulls and a heifer.

The story goes that the relatives of one murdered man were too angry to respect this tradition or accept this payment. They chased the murderer to the cross, dragged him off it, and killed him on the spot. At a place called Nine Wells (the 3 times 3 is interesting), they washed the blood off their hands. The site of the cross is said to be haunted by the ghost of the murderer, who was entitled to sanctuary and got only vengefulness.

THE MONKS OF MEDMENHAM

Near West Wycombe, not far from London, stood a Cistercian abbey which, by the eighteenth century, had fallen into ruins; by then it belonged to young Francis Duffield, who had come under the influence of the madcap Sir Francis Dashwood (1708–1781).

Sir Francis inherited great wealth in his teens and was devoting himself to a life of aesthetic debauchery. He founded the Friars of St. Francis with himself as prior and Duffield, several poets (Whitehead, Selwyn, Potter), politicians (John Wilkes and the Earl of Sandwich), and others as rollicking members. They staged orgies in a specially designed cave, had black masses said in a Satanic chapel, and were generally known as the Hell-Fire Club.

Over the doorway the "monks" inscribed *Fay ce que voudras* ("Do what thou wilt"), the motto of the Abbey of Thelema in Rabelais' *Gargantua*. Later Aleister Crowley, who tried as hard to be wicked as Dashwood and Duffield did, picked up the motto and the name of the abbey for his own orgiastic organization.

In time Sir Francis succeeded his uncle as Lord le Despencer (1762) and became postmaster general and chancellor of the Exchequer. The "monks" broke up, having scandalized all England.

At one point Lord Sandwich found himself arguing in the Lords for the impeachment of Wilkes (who had been Lord Mayor of London and held other political offices) on the grounds of blasphemies at the abbey, outrages of which Sandwich was especially knowledgeable because he himself had participated in them.

THE WITCH-FINDER GENERAL

During the turmoil of the Civil War in England, Matthew Hopkins of Ipswich appeared in Essex (1645–1647) as a witch finder. He did what Americans call a land-office business, at 20 shillings for every witch he identified to the authorities.

He looked for "a mark whereof no evident Reason in Nature can be given," and he often found one. (Looking for the devil's mark like this was common; in Scotland "common prickers," as they were called, were numerous enough to form a kind of union.) Thus the fact of witchcraft was considered proved if the suspect had a mole on her back or under the armpits or lip or on her private parts. Some said the mark was red like a flea bite, some said brown like a mole, some said blue like a nip, and *The Highland Papers* report that at the trial of one Kate Moore a white spot was found. It was "the devil's mark" if, probed with a pin, it was insensible. The pins could be up to three inches long and some had pins that retracted into the handles so that "pricking" could be faked.

With this "pricking" method, Hopkins found hundreds of witches in Chelmsford and Bury St. Edmunds in July and August 1645. He also used interrogation; English inquisitors were not permitted to torture suspects with instruments, but they could keep them awake for several nights in a row, and this worked perfectly well. They could also test to see if a bound suspect would float if thrown into water. If you did not sink, you were a witch—the Devil kept you afloat; the water would not receive you.

Hopkins operated with great success for about four years but then fell under suspicion himself, so cleverly had he made the populace aware of witchcraft. He was tied up and given the water test. He either floated (in which case he was executed as a witch) or sank (and was drowned). Nobody is quite sure which, but he died. And that was the ironic end of the witch-finder general.

GERALD B. GARDNER

One of the most knowledgeable and respected of modern witches was Gerald B. Gardner (1884–1964). After some years in the East, Gardner retired as a wealthy man and began to devote himself to the occult—

theosophy, Rosicrucianism, and particularly a coven of witches in the New Forest. The group called itself the Craft of the Wise. When witchcraft laws were repealed in England, the group, which had hitherto been secret, surfaced and in the ensuing publicity, drew many would-be witches and magicians to their organization.

Gardner impressed a great deal of his strong personality on British witchcraft. His *Witchcraft Today* (1954) is a refreshingly rational attempt to divorce the reputation of the Old Religion from that of Satanism, black arts, and blood sacrifices, devil worship and malicious acts.

> If I were permitted to disclose all their rituals, I think it would
> be easy to prove that witches are not·diabolists; but the oaths
> are solemn and the witches are my friends. I would not hurt their
> feelings. They have secrets which to them are sacred. They have
> good reason for this secrecy.

The press called him Britain's Chief Witch, and occasionally he referred to himself as King of the Witches. He founded the Witchcraft Museum at Castletown on the Isle of Man, and he was unquestionably more knowledgeable about witchcraft than many self-proclaimed wizards who had been taken up by the popular press.

TWO INQUISITORS

Pierre de Lancre was a relative of the great Montaigne. In 1608 King Henry IV of France appointed Lancre to investigate the outbreak of witchcraft among the Basques, and he promtly sent six hundred people to their deaths for sorcery. He thus became a recognized expert on the sabbat, lycanthropy (werewolves), and similar matters, and he published a big book in Paris in 1612, disagreeing with those who urged moderation. Lancre claimed to have found *une Royne du Sabbat* in *chasque village*—"a Queen of the Sabbat" in "every village."

At the same time, Alonzo Salazar de Frias, sent to quell an outbreak of witchcraft in Cigarramundi, reported to the Inquisition in Spain that he had examined the evidence of 1,800 people (including 1,384 children) and after eight months of investigation decided that there was no evidence whatever of dealing with the Devil.

He had experimented by alternately sending word that he was coming (to investigate witchcraft in a certain village) and arriving unannounced. In the former case, there were always ample accusations ready when he reached the village in question, and in the latter, none. He concluded therefore, and so reported to the Inquisition, that "there were neither witches nor bewitched until they were talked and written about." The Holy Office did not go so far as to deny the existence of witchcraft, but it followed Salazar's council in insisting on adequate evidence of evil actions (such as out-and-out poisoning) before it allowed a suspect to be condemned.

MELMOTH THE WANDERER

The apex of the Gothic novel is often considered to be *Melmoth the Wanderer* (1820), written by an eccentric and mysterious Irish clergyman named Charles Robert Maturin (1782–1824).

Melmoth is a gruesomely horripilative tale of an Irish gentleman who has sold his soul to the Devil for a long life and, wearying of it, dejectedly wanders among the ruined men whom fate has cast down, vainly hoping that one of them may be foolish enough to take over Melmoth's pact and free him from the terrible burden.

Balzac ventured to rank the novel with the works of Molière, Goethe, and Byron (creators of *Don Juan, Faust*, and *Manfred*) as contributing authentic and enduring allegorical figures to modern literature. (People tended to lose their literary judgment in those days when horror was involved.)

In the story, the term of the agreement with the Devil runs out, and the Wanderer disappears; all that is left is his scarf, caught on a crag some distance from the brink of a great cliff that juts out into the tumultuous ocean. But in Balzac's continuation, *Melmoth Reconciled*, the Wanderer finds a villain willing to assume his fearful responsibility and goes to his own death without fear of eternal damnation.

As the century closed, a descendant of Maturin, Oscar Fingal O'Flahertie Wills Wilde, found himself in jail, his brilliant writing career blasted by homosexual scandal and disgrace. When he was released from Reading Gaol, Wilde fled to Paris, where, to hide his identity and shame, he took the name "Sebastian Melmoth." As Sebastian Melmoth, Wilde lived out his last few years.

HENRY III OF FRANCE

The third son of Henry II and Catherine de Médicis, Henry (reigned 1574–1589) was widely reputed during his lifetime to be a sorcerer—as was his formidable mother. At his castle of Vincennes, in a wood east of Paris, he studied the black arts under various magicians, who had been summoned there for that purpose.

His reign was a bloody one. Two years before he came to the throne, he had helped instigate the infamous St. Bartholomew's Day massacre of French Protestants, and in the religious wars that followed his ascension, many Frenchmen died for one faith or the other. And despite his personal inclinations, he allowed 30,000 people to be executed for witchcraft.

After his assassination at the hands of a Dominican priest, his retreat at Vincennes was examined. In the keep servants found "the dressed skin of a child."

HEARTS

Mention of Henry III, whose heart was buried separately from the rest of him, reminds us of some of the others whose hearts were connected with superstition.

Take Blanche Parry (1507–1589), governess of Elizabeth I. She was buried in St. Margaret's Church, Westminster, in two pieces. Her heart was separated lest it burst with "love of the queen."

King Robert Bruce (1274–1329) died of leprosy in Scotland, but his henchman Sir James Douglas, called the Black Douglas (1286–1330), undertook to carry his embalmed heart to Palestine to be buried in Jerusalem. He died fighting the Moors in Spain, so Bruce's heart went back to Scotland and was buried in Melrose Abbey. Bruce's body was buried in Dunfermline Abbey.

The old idea that the heart was the seat of emotions (still recalled on valentines) led to many superstitions and occasional use in witchcraft. A pig's or sheep's heart, stuck full of pins or thorns, served the same purpose as a wax image—brought a curse on one's enemy.

SWEDENBORG

Emmanuel Swedenborg was born in Stockholm in 1688. He died in London on March 29, 1772—as he had predicted he would.

In 1743 he had a vision of a magician in a purple robe—a vision that was repeated the next year. From this apparition and from necromancy (he called up the spirits of men such as Virgil and Martin Luther), he claimed to have derived a rich store of occult information.

He turned to spititualism and pneumatology (hypnotism) and added a reputation as clairvoyant and prophet to one as scientist (his interests ranged from anatomy and astronomy to zoology). He had visions of historical events and of the end of history, the Last Judgment. He lived in an "illuminated" world, peopled with visible angels and informed by visions.

He never preached or attempted to establish a church, but after his death his followers founded the Church of the New Jerusalem, thus fulfilling another of his prophecies, that his influence would long outlast his life.

THE ROSY CROSS

Johann Valentin Andreä (1586–1654) published *Fama Fraternitatis* ("Report of Brotherhood," 1614) under the pseudonym of Christian Rosen-kreuz, and there may possibly have been a person of this name (1378–1484?) who is often credited with founding the Rosicrucians. It is alleged that he returned to his native Germany with the wisdom of the East, recruited eight disciples, and sent them to eight different countries to spread the secret lore. More than a century after the death of the first Rosenkreuz, his body was said to have been found uncorrupted in a mysterious octagonal tomb and accompanied by occult papers that are the basis of modern secret societies.

Other Rosicrucian organizations claim even more ancient origins, tracing them all the way back to pharaonic Egypt and asserting that over the centuries many of the world's greatest sages have owed their knowledge to the occult symbols of the rose and the cross, the pyramid, and the swastika.

If the *Fama Fraternitatis* and the book published the next year by the same author, *Confessio Rosae Crucis* ("Testimony of the Rosy Cross"), are to be believed, then Rosicrucianism did derive its symbolism and lore from the East, especially from Arab lands, but probably not from Egyptian mysteries.

There is some sort of connection between the Rosicrucians (variously called Brothers of the Rosy Cross, Knights of the Rosy Cross, and Philosophers of the Rosy Cross) and another secret society that claims very ancient origins, Freemasonry. Even the authoritative A. E. Waite (*Real History of the Rosicrucians*, 1887) and H. S. Lewis' respected *Rosicrucian Questions and Answers* (1929) have by no means answered all the questions or convinced everyone of the true history.

Complicating the matter still further, the European Rosicrucians, who were known as the Illuminati, have only very vague connections with the theosophical teachings of the American AMORC (Ancient and Mystical Order of the Rosy Cross). The latter group is not really ancient at all, having been founded in California in 1915 by H. S. Lewis, author of books on such matters as Atlantis and the so-called secrets of the pyramids. It is not really very mystical either, certainly not secret, since it advertises itself widely in magazines.

A competing American organization, *Fraternitas Rosae Crucis*, was founded by R. Swinburne Clymer and is advertised not as the modern inheritor of the secrets of the pyramids but of the clandestine brotherhood that (they claim) numbered among its members such well-known names as Plato, Jesus Christ, and Benjamin Franklin.

Competing with Lewis and Clymer is the society of Rosicrucians founded in New York by G. E. S. De Witow, author of *The Temple in the Clouds*, and the Rosicrucian Fellowship. The fellowship, the richest Rosicrucian group, headquartered at Oceanside, California, was founded by Max Heindel, a former ship's engineer. Directed by astral orders, he said, he wrote *The Rosicrucian Cosmo-Conception* (1908), and his brand of esoterica, combining astrology, Christianity, vegetarianism, and faith healing has many attractions for American occultists. When the founders of some of these groups died, their families continued their work—and often their lawsuits.

At the moment Rosicrucians of all groups seem to be doing very well, whether they are teaching the authentic doctrines of ancient Rosicrucian masters or just pretending to have learned secrets from the magic of Tibet, from aliens visiting from other planets, or whatever. Meanwhile, the John Birch Society is said to fear that the Illuminati are still with us and plotting—with four hundred members sworn to the deepest secrecy—to take over the world by black magic.

MIRIAM

Maria Prophetissa (also known as Mary the Jewess) of the fourth century was thought by her contemporaries in Alexandria to be none other than Miriam, the sister of Moses. Cooks of today will be amused to hear that her alchemical pots and pans are supposed to have given rise to the *bain-marie* ("bath of Mary"), the very useful double boiler.

GEORGE GIFFORD

In *Dialogue Concerning Witches* (1593) George Gifford, a clergyman who died in 1620, condemned *white* magic!

"These cunning men and women with charms, seeming to do good," he wrote, "ought to be rooted out."

ABRAMELIN

Abramelin, also called Abraham the Jew, as I said earlier, is supposed to have been a fifteenth-century magician, the author of *The Book of Sacred Magic* (1458), said to have been delivered to his son Lamech. The modern edition (translated by S. L. M. Mathers) is *The Sacred Magic of Abramelin the Mage.*

In this book, Abramelin recounts many journeys he took about the then known world in search of magical enlightenment: Egypt, Arabia, Greece, Hungary, Austria, Constantinople. In Prague, he encountered "a wicked man named Antony," who rendered himself invisible, flew through the air, entered rooms through the keyhole, knew everyone's secrets "and once he told me things that God alone could know." In Lintz a young woman anointed "the principle pulses of my feet and hands" with an unguent that was supposed to enable him to fly, and he did indeed have the sensation of flying through the air and seeing wonders, but he woke up depressed and with a headache.

Later, this same young woman, at Abramelin's request, rubbed herself with the same unguent in order to travel two hundred miles to visit a friend of his and bring back news. She fell to the ground and lay insensible for three hours, then woke up and told him what she had learned of the friend. Alas, when he checked with the friend, her story was "entirely contrary to his profession." He therefore concluded that "what she had told me was a simple dream, and that this unguent was a causer of phantastic sleep." Thus, though Abramelin was a believer in magic and demonology, he was no fool.

His book offers readers cabalistic magic squares that will purportedly perform such feats as raising tempests, causing spirits to appear, changing men into animals and vice versa, procuring visions, raising the dead, rousing love or hate, demolishing buildings, walking under water, and even making stage performances appear.

COUNT OF ST.-GERMAIN

When a man calling himself the count of St.-Germain turned up in Paris in 1748, looking about thirty, he claimed he was two thousand years old. Was he an Alsatian Jew or a Portuguese with a whale of a good line? Or was he a man who had discovered the elixir of life? Did he die in 1784 in Schleswig, or was he the "Major Fraser" who appeared in the 1850s claiming to be St.-Germain? Or perhaps he was the gentleman who turned up on top of Mount Shasta, California, in this century making the same claim? Many people insist they have met him, including Madame Elena Blavatsky (1831–1891) and Annie Besant (1847–1933).

He told eighteenth-century Parisians that he had known Henry IV (1553–1610). If that was true, then perhaps he was also the man who scared Catherine de Médicis to death in 1589, for she was Henry's mother-in-law. An astrologer had told Catherine (1519–1589) "to beware of St.-Germain," so the queen carefully avoided the Faubourg St.-Germain, a district of Paris. Then she fell ill and sent for a priest to hear her confession. He appeared and announced that his name was St.-Germain, and she dropped dead.

But back to our St.-Germain. When he arrived in France, it was probably from Germany. But was he a Jew? A Jesuit? The heir or illegitimate son of Frederick II Rákóczky of Hungary? Nobody knew much except that he was mysterious and liked it that way.

He told the court that he had developed an elixir to keep him thirty forever. He graced many dinner tables, but would never eat; he said he never touched food but lived on his magic elixir. He did add that he had partaken of one wedding dinner—the one that Christ attended at Cana. He opened a scientific laboratory outside St.-Antoine to various society visitors, but no one could figure out what he was doing. Even when the king of

France gave him laboratory space at Versailles, they were no wiser. Nor Charles of Hesse-Cassel later.

St.-Germain became a confidant of Louis XV and a favorite of the king's mistress, Madame de Pompadour. In a society in which gossip was the leading indoor sport, he heard much and repeated nothing. He never invited anyone to his home, took nobody into his confidence. He said he was a Mason but had forgotten the signs.

He got involved in diplomatic intrigues and went on several confidential missions for the French king, journeying mysteriously to Vienna, Constantinople, Moscow, and other exotic capitals. In Paris, he made lots of friends, mostly ladies. They kept him so busy (he told Casanova, also an agent of Louis XV) that he didn't have time to invent the steamboat, but he would get to that in the next century. Meanwhile, he distributed to them a wash that took away wrinkles and warned Marie Antoinette of the impending revolution (she didn't believe him).

In 1760, a spell of unpopularity caught up with him, and he moved to London for two years, perhaps serving as a spy for the English government. From there he traveled to Russia, where he served in the army of Catherine the Great as "General Welldone." In 1770 he was back in Paris for four years, until his final move to Schleswig, where he went into the magic business with Landgrave Charles of Hesse-Cassel. In 1784 he died.

Or did he? Not according to "Major Fraser," Madame Blavatsky, Annie Besant, and some others.

THE QUEEN OF VOODOO

Marie Laveau, a mulatto born in New Orleans near the end of the eighteenth century, was the most colorful of the Voodoo queens of that fascinating city. She was living in a rickety shanty on Lake Pontchartrain when a rich white family appealed to her to save their son from being convicted of a crime. Marie put three peppers in her mouth and prayed in the cathedral for a while, then placed the peppers under the judge's bench. The young man, despite all the testimony against him, got off scot-free. The grateful white family gave her a cottage on St. Ann Street, between Rampart and Burgundy streets in the Old Quarter.

For more difficult cases she had a "magic" shawl (which she claimed the Emperor of China had sent to her) and innumerable gris-gris charms, African fetishes, and Catholic religious articles. She could make people fall in and out of love. She could tell fortunes. She gave spiritual advice and material help. She was even said (having failed to get him out of jail on a charge of murder) to have poisoned Antoine Cambre, the bouncer at the Louisiana Ballroom, at his request, to prevent him from having to face hanging; she used a bowl of the gumbo she frequently brought along when she made her regular charitable visitations to the city prison.

On June 7, 1869, when she was over seventy, Marie Laveau was replaced as Voodoo queen of New Orleans by Malvina Latour, who performed such astounding public exorcisms as that of the chaplain of the Louisiana legislature, who coughed up a live black mouse and was thereafter wholly cured. But never again was anyone to be so relied upon or so feared as was Marie Laveau in her prime. She died about 1875, but is still remembered as one of the most outstanding characters in the checkered history of the French Quarter.

BERNARDO DI COMO

When the inquisitor Bernardo di Como came along at the very beginning of the sixteenth century, he argued that witchcraft had flourished in Como, Italy, for as much as 150 years and something drastic had to be done about it. To accomplish this, he was prepared to write his own rules and to act as he pleased, whatever the advice of lay experts and councils.

One of his problems was that learned opinion of the time often tended to the belief that the sabbat was a delusion: Witches did not really fly off to these obscene orgies but, under the influence of drugs or delusions, just thought that they did so. If the sabbat was not real, how could the witches be punished for attending it?

In his magisterial history, *The Inquisition of the Middle Ages* (1887), Henry Charles Lea writes that Bernardo di Como "triumphantly adduced the fact that numerous persons had been burned for attending the Sabbat, which could not have been done without the assent of the pope, and this was sufficient proof that the heresy was real, for the Church punishes only manifest crimes." So, Bernardo burned hundreds more.

"THE BLACK POPE"

Anton Szandor LaVey is the head of the Church of Satan. He believes that the mass proper desexualizes and dehumanizes true pagan beliefs, and thus is a parody—hence the black mass is only a parody of a parody. He complains that "all of the books about the Devil have been written by the agents of God," whereas real Satanists refuse to be defined by the Church.

In the manifesto of his Church of Satan he writes:

> It would be an over-simplification to say that every successful man and woman on earth is, without knowing it, a practicing Satanist, but the thirst for earthly success and its ensuing realization are certainly grounds for Saint Peter turning thumbs down. . . . If the love of money is the root of all evil; then we must at least assume the most powerful men on earth to be the most Satanic. . . .

APOLLONIUS OF TYANA, MAGICIAN EXTRAORDINAIRE

One of the most famous magicians of the ancient world was Apollonius of Tyana (in Cappadocia, now part of Turkey), the date of whose birth is unknown but which may have been in the reign of the Roman emperor Caligula (37 A.D.–41). In any case, he enters history with a vengeance in the reign of the emperor Nerva (96–98), with a terrific reputation as Pythagorean philosopher and miracle worker. In his biography, written by Flavius Philostratus, a third-century philosopher and literary man, Apollonius is said to have arrived in Rome heralded by word that he had rid Antioch of scorpions by imitative magic (he buried a bronze scorpion in the city), rid Ephesus of plague (by encouraging the inhabitants to stone the spirits who brought it), and rid Corinth of a vampire.

In *Anatomy of Melancholy,* author Robert Burton featured the vampire tale in the English tradition, and John Keats picked it up for his poem *Lamia.* The story goes that Menippus, a young student of Apollonius, was irresistably drawn to a very beautiful woman in Corinth. They married, but on the wedding night Apollonius entered Menippus' house, revealed to him that she was a *lamia* (vampiric serpent woman of Greek folklore), and caused her to vanish.

Apollonius in Rome became a part of the literary circle around Julia Domna, the wife of the emperor Septimus Severus and mother of Caracalla. It is said that Apollonius annoyed the emperor by being called *deus* (god) and was brought to trial. As a preparation for that, it is reported, they cut his hair (attempting to diminish his power, as Delilah did with Samson), but his magic seems to have remained unaffected, for legend asserts that he vanished from the courtroom, never to be seen again.

THE MAHDI

Mohammed Ahmed ibn-Seyyid Abdallah (1843–1885), a member of the mystic Sufi sect of Islam, moved from the civil service to the slave trade and eventually proclaimed himself the Mahdi (Messiah).

In the 1880s he and his dervishes battled the Egyptians and the British for control of the Sudan. On November 4, 1883, he defeated an Egyptian army led by a British general named William Hicks, known as Hicks Pasha. On January 26, 1885, the Mahdi captured Khartoum, and his men (though orders were to take the British general alive) killed Charles George "Chinese" Gordon and delivered his head to the Mahdi.

This helped to fulfill the prophecy that the Mahdi and Gordon would meet "face to face." Gordon's face "bore a cheerful smile," it was reported. The Mahdi was impressed that Gordon had a space between his two front teeth such as was prophesied that the Muslim Messiah would have.

Four months later, on June 22, the Mahdi himself died. When the British army under Kitchener finally retook Khartoum in 1898, they looted for days and blew up the tomb of the Mahdi, having first thrown his body into the Nile and shipped off his head to Cairo. The head (or skull) was eventually buried at Wadi Halfa, Sudan.

Kitchener, who was responsible for this indignity inflicted on the self-proclaimed Messiah of Islam, was told that he would be punished by being drowned at sea and yet his body would be consumed in flames. Some eighteen years later Kitchener was drowned in the sinking of H.M.S. *Hampshire* off the Orkneys on June 5, 1916. There is some question about whether the body was recovered and cremated.

Harold T. Wilkins in *Strange Mysteries of Time and Space* (1959) reports: "The Mahdi's formerly blown-up house, rebuilt, is one no Sudanese, *today*, will stay in. It is haunted by *afreets*, and a British Commissioner went mad in it."

Is the Madhi, a Sufi magician, still at work?

IAMBLICHUS

Anyone who has tried to carry the nuances of one language over to another recognizes the seed of truth in the Italian proverb "A translator is a traitor," which equates "translator" (*traduttore*) with "traitor" (*traditore*).

Greek philosopher Iamblichus argued that this is especially true of magic formulas and incantations.

Iamblichus (250–325), the founder of the Syrian Neoplatonism (which he tried to reconcile with Chaldean magic and pagan religions), was himself a magician of no mean talents. But even he, he said, could not translate his spells into other tongues, because translation alters the letters and hence the numerology; the magic words lose their power.

CALVIN

John Calvin fulminated against relics, mocking the French king who built Sainte-Chapelle to contain the Crown of Thorns. Or one of them. There were so many "real" Crowns in existence, Calvin scoffed that "it must have been a hedge." Bits of the True Cross, he said, would form "a full load for a good ship." In his treatise on relics (1543) he vehemently attacked the "anthill of bones" assembled by the faithful and the foolishness of a superstitious belief in the "magical" powers of relics.

THE MONSTER

Gilles de Laval de Retz (1404–1440) came from a distinguished Breton family; he was the grandson of De Guesclin (1320–1380), constable of France. He distinguished himself in the Hundred Years War, fighting beside Joan of Arc, and for his exploits he was made a marshal of France at the age of twenty-three. He was incredibly wealthy.

The Maid, his comrade-in-arms, went on to be burned as a witch and later canonized. Gilles too was executed for witchcraft, but he is recalled as a devil of depravity.

He lived sumptuously at Tiffauges and Machecoal, his castles on the border of Brittany, spending lavishly on books (then a big-ticket item), on gold and silver and velvet and jewels. Even his immense wealth could not survive such extravagance and he soon ran into debt. To recoup, he turned to alchemy, and when the philosopher's stone failed to materialize, he went on to magic. He brought the magician Francesco Prelati from Florence to teach him the black arts and sold his soul (they said) to the Devil.

Soon children began to disappear from peasant villages roundabout, young boys mostly. Stories began to circulate that they had been carried off by agents of Baron de Retz, but Gilles was too powerful for ordinary people to combat. Complaints went to ecclesiastical authorities, but still men hesitated. Then Gilles, for some reason, carried off a priest and held him prisoner, and this deed made him liable to action by the Church authorities. He was arrested and brought before an ecclesiastical court.

At first he was haughty and scornful, called his accusers simoniacs, and cursed them. But on the third day he broke down and confessed. He had indeed engaged in forbidden practices, he said, not only dealings with Satan but inspeakable cruelties to the children he had had kidnapped—sodomizing them, then cutting their throats and offering up their hearts and cut-off hands as part of the ritual he practiced. Sometimes he had them torn open so that he could predict the future by the condition of their entrails.

After this terrible confession, he burst into tears and prayed for mercy, but the court found him guilty and turned him over to the secular authorities for punishment. On October 26, 1440, he was hanged and his body partially burned. His servants were burned alive.

In her 1933 book, *The God of the Witches*, Dr. Margaret Murray suggested that all this was a trumped-up story, that Gilles was actually a ritual sacrifice along divine-victim lines and that he connived with certain church and secular authorities to make his execution seem plausible. Unfortunately for this theory, since then, Gilles's Breton castles have been excavated, and in the ruins nearly two hundred little skeletons have been found.

ALEISTER CROWLEY

Reputedly the most sinister of modern proponents of magic is the Englishman Aleister Crowley (1875–1947). As a child, he is supposed to have begun experimenting with animal sacrifice at the age of twelve, when he killed a kitten. He himself boasts, "Before I touched my teens, I was already aware that I was THE BEAST whose number is 666," a reference to Revelations 13:18. For the rest of his life, he liked to refer to himself as "the Great Beast" or its Greek equivalent, "Therion," and used the number 666 as a kind of signature.

A brilliant student at Cambridge, Crowley was first drawn to a serious study of magic by a clash with the master (dean) of St. John's College. The master had forbidden Crowley to put on a bawdy play, and in revenge Crowley and some friends made a wax image of the man and prepared to drive a needle through its heart; instead, Crowley's hand slipped, and the needle pierced the figure's leg. The following day, the master fell and broke his ankle.

In 1898, fresh out of Cambridge, Crowley joined the Order of the Golden Dawn and began to clash with that organization's other stormy petrel, S. L. MacGregor Mathers. Mathers managed to get Crowley expelled—or the rites were too tame for him, stories differ—and he withdrew to a lonely house in Scotland to continue magical experiments in private. When complaints were raised by neighbors about the strange goings on at Crowley's place, he retaliated by placing the complainers under a curse, causing two servants to commit suicide and a parish worker to turn alcoholic. (Or so it was claimed.) A butcher, who had received a check from Crowley covered with demonic signs, subsequently cut himself severely. (When Mathers died in 1918, it was claimed that Crowley had killed him by magic.)

In 1912, Crowley joined a German group called Ordo Templi Orientis ("Order of the Eastern Temple") and became head of its British section. When World War I broke out, he removed to the United States and spent the war years writing German propaganda. In 1920, having acquired some disciples and mistresses, he moved to Cefalu on the northern coast of Sicily.

There he set up what he called the Abbey of Thelema. (In Greek, *thelema* means "will, choice," so the place seems to have been named for Crowley's favorite motto: "Do what thou wilt shall be the whole of the law.") At the abbey he and his followers indulged in animal sacrifices, black masses, worship of Satan, and orgies and drug taking and sex. (Crowley was bisexual.) One follower is supposed to have died after drinking the blood of a sacrificed cat. Finally, in 1923, rumors began to circulate in the region that children had been sacrificed as well as animals. Crowley was expelled from Italy.

Dennis Wheatley in *The Devil and All His Works* (1971) relates a story of Crowley's attempt—successful, if Wheatley's information is not romancing—to raise the god Pan. The attempt is reported to have killed a follower and sent Crowley himself to a mental hospital for four months. If the tale is true, it presumably happened after the Sicily period and before the Great Beast returned to England to write *Magick in Theory and Practice*, an exposition of his ideas on the occult.

But from there on it was all downhill for Crowley. He tried but failed to break his addiction to heroin. His following fell away (the world had more important things to think about in the thirties and forties) and finally in 1947 he died. A black mass was performed at his funeral, concluding with a hymn to Pan.

Interest in Crowley revived somewhat during the 1960s, when anything that was unconventional won approval from some people and "wickedness" seemed glamorous and original. But this phase appears not to have lasted, and today—his "shocking" behavior dismissed as mere childish attention-getting—he is of interest chiefly to historians of magic.

8

A Few Frauds

IN the annals of fraud there may be few more egregious examples than can be found among pretended magicians and purported witches, false prophets and quack alchemists, humbug astrologers, flim-flam hocus-pocus. It would be hard to beat the nerve of the Frenchman who forged and sold to another Frenchman the supposed autographs of many characters in history, including Julius Caesar and Adam and Eve—all in French. It would be hard to beat the victim's credulity, too.

But deception has been a major element in magic for a long time, and not only in stage magic, which is mere sleight of hand, admitted but entertaining trickery. Men with pretensions to true sorcery have not hesitated to claim fantastic results, in order to impress other men with their esoteric knowledge and skill.

In this age of test-tube babies, can we believe that Paracelsus (1493–1541) actually created a little man (*homunculus*) in an alchemist's alembic? How about the eighteenth-century Abbé Geloni and Count Francis Joseph Küffstein, who claimed that, after only five weeks' work in the laboratory, they had produced ten *homunculi*: king, queen, architect, monk, miner, nun, knight, seraph, red spirit, blue spirit? Magic? Science? Ballyhoo?

Here are a few of the representative and interesting frauds in magic and witchcraft, some false ideas, and a zany or two.

THE GRAND FRAUD

Men didn't like him much; Giovanni Jacopo Casanova, who met him, said he was "short and badly hung." But women adored him. Baroness Oberkirch said he had "indescribable eyes" and then went on to describe them. Carlyle called him "Great Quack Face" and "King of Liars," and Dr. Howard W. Haggard said he was "one of the most successful charlatans of faith healing."

He may have been born Giuseppe Balsamo of Palermo, but the name he made famous was adopted from a Sicilian uncle: Cagliostro. He was "the last of the magicians" and perhaps the bravest fraud of them all.

A familiar figure at the glittering courts of Europe and in secret circles of Freemasonry, Cagliostro seems to have had some real psychic powers; when they failed, he faked. He invented the title "Count Alessandro di Cagliostro," and with his beautiful wife, Lorenza Feliciani, he traveled about to Egypt, Arabia, Persia, Rhodes, Malta, and many countries of Europe, dispensing love philters and elixirs of life, forging documents, healing, telling fortunes, treating rheumatism in a "magic" chair, changing coarse fabrics to "silk" and pebbles to "gold." In Paris, he got involved in the scandal of the queen's diamond necklace, though in this case he was only a pawn of the real defrauder, the countess of de la Motte.

Later he translated the names of Louis XVI and Marie Antoinette into "the language of the Magi," and by numerology predicted that they would both be beheaded. His friends urged him to warn the royal family, but he declined. First, he said, they would certainly not believe him. Second, if it were fated, how could warning them alter anything?

Through all the vicissitudes of his incredible life, Cagliostro maintained, in the spirit of Freemasonry, that the mystery was for the good of all. He wrote: "I am oppressed! I am accused! I am calumniated! Have I deserved this fate? . . . I probe my conscience; and there I find the peace which men deny me! I have traveled a great deal. . . . I have everywhere shown myself to be the friend of my fellow men. My knowledge, my time, my fortune have been employed in the relief of distress." He made a large fortune, let it be said, for all this "relief of distress" and spent it chiefly on show.

Despite the reason he gave for not warning the French monarchs, Cagliostro constantly tried to tamper with his own fate. But it caught up with him on April 7, 1791, when he was condemned by the Inquisition in Rome. Lorenza, whose cleverness and charm had more than once got him out of previous scrapes, could do nothing this time; she was compelled to "confess" her part in his swindles and sent off to a convent for life. Eventually Cagliostro's sentence was commuted to life—in a prison cell of the Castel Sant'Angelo. He tried to escape and was cast into a deep dungeon. There in 1795 his jailer strangled him.

Some said that was not the last of Cagliostro's influence. Gérard Encausse (1863–1916), known as Papus in magical circles, was born in Spain of a French father and a gypsy mother, who said she was descended from Cagliostro and had inherited his powers. Papus combined science (a medical degree and inventions) with the occult (he was clairvoyant to Czar Nicholas II for fifteen years) and excelled in magic. Cagliostro would have been proud of Papus. Others say Cagliostro was reincarnated as Aleister Crowley, and undoubtedly there were force and fakery in both.

TALL STORY

Nekhtnebf was one of the last native kings of Egypt (c. 358 B.C.). When a big navy was on the way to attack his kingdom, he put toy ships into a large bowl of Nile water and fought a battle in which the enemy toys were sunk. The real ships also were supposed to have perished.

The next time he tried it, his own ships' representations sank. Taking the hint, Nekhtnebf shaved his head and beard, put on rags, and with an immense fortune in gold and jewels ran off to Pella, Macedonia.

There he bought a nice house and set himself up as an Egyptian magician. One of his customers was the wife of Philip II of Macedon, Olympias. He convinced the queen that the god Ammon wished to visit her amorously by night.

Disguised as the god, Nekhtnebf then came at night and made love to the lady, who a reasonable time afterward gave birth to—Alexander the Great.

They do say that Alexander wasn't much like his father, King Philip.

MATHEMATICIAN AND ASTROLOGER

"James Hallett, Mathematician and Astrologer, New House, Chichester [England], Curer of All Diseases."

That's the inscription on a magical box of the eighteenth century that still exists. A sampler (dated June 20, 1791) testifies to one of Hallett's miraculous cures, but in the box when it was opened in modern times were found—two nutmeg halves.

Ladies and Gntleman waited on at their own Houſes, on the ſhorteſt notice.

⁎ Nativitics caſt for the Cure of Witcheraft and cthe Diſeaſes that are hard to be cured,

Advertisement of James Hallett, "Curer of Witchcraft" (1795).

PANACEAS

Magic and witchcraft or at least suggestions of the occult sciences were often used to give glamour (a word that means "magic") to all sorts of fraudulent cures and quack devices. Cagliostrio sold beds for painless childbirth. James Graham kept a Temple of Health in London (1779) that contained a sumptuous "celestial bed" guaranteed to produce conception. George O. Barnes of Kentucky preached that only the Devil caused disease, and this view is shared by many faith healers from the "bone setters" Valentine Greatrakes and "Crazy Sal" Mapp to Mary Baker Eddy.

In this country, where nostrums and tonics were hard-sell peddled with great success, there has been (and to a lesser extent still is) an especially promising market for every kind of cure from cancer to baldness and "loss of virility."

In his entertaining *Golden Age of Quackery* (1959), Stewart Holbrook describes the newspaper ads that touted some of them:

> There was no hedging about it, no qualification: Dr. King's New Discovery was the only Sure Cure for Consumption on earth; and for this reason "It Strikes Terror to the Doctors." There was Dr. Rupert Wells's Radiatized Fluid for Cancer. ("It will cure you at home without pain, plaster or operation.") Dr. Tucker had a specific for epilepsy. So did Dr. Kline and Dr. Grant. If the trouble had to do with kidney or liver, you need only to step into the nearest drugstore for a bottle of Dr. Kilmer's Swamp Root, which cured Bright's disease, Catarrh of the Bladder, Gravel, and trifles like Dropsy.

Consumer protection laws, beginning with the landmark Federal Pure Food and Drug Act of 1906, have put a halt to such advertising and driven many of these magical "cures" off the market. Nowadays, even people who frequent fortune-tellers and never miss the daily horoscope in the newspaper are likely to seek out a qualified physician when they are ill.

But there remain some, even today, who will pay large sums of money to con men for "magic earth" and "electrical belts," for treatment in machines that guarantee to drive out disease as the magician's wand was supposed to drive out demons, in short, who still believe in spells and incantations.

MARY TOFTS

At Godalming, Surrey, in 1726, Mary Tofts caused a sensation by announcing that she was giving birth to rabbits. King George I sent a royal physician, Sir Richard Manningham, to investigate, and her fraud was detected. William Hogarth depicted the lady in all the pangs of this incredible labor in his picture *Credulity, Superstition, and Fanaticism* (1762).

If you think we moderns are more sophisticated, examine the Amity-ville story of the seventies and its popular sequels. These impostures breed like rabbits.

"KATTERFELTO, WITH HIS HAIR ON END"

And here, for all of the miracle workers and spellbinders out there in Videoland, is an impressive example of fakery—an inspiration in Gustavus Katterfelto.

The self-proclaimed "Greatest Philosopher Since Isaac Newton" took London by storm. The eighteenth century was an age of patent nostrums, crank ideas, and pseudomedical nonsense. In 1755, when a disastrous earthquake shook Lisbon—and the complacency of Europeans—Katterfelto actually sold pills "for the earthquake." He cashed in on the plague (1782) and advertized a "solar microscope" to detect disease. To his "technological" approach he added the occult; his two "Morocco black cats" were known as the Doctor's Devils, and he did nothing to dispel the rumor that they were not pets but familiars. With them, and the patter, he peddled flu cures at five shillings a bottle in an age when the taverns literally guaranteed "drunk for a penny, dead drunk for tuppence."

His customers included George III and the largest royal family in British history. William Cowper mentioned him in his long poem *The Task* as one of the oddities of that flamboyant age:

> And Katterfelto, with his hair on end
> At his own wonders, wandering for his bread.

The vogue faded, and fashionable London was off on some other foolishness. Katterfelto wound up as a mountebank and cheap street conjuror, and died penniless in 1799.

LEVITATION

As we have seen elsewhere, many saints have been reported to float a foot or more off the ground—a phenomenon called levitation. People were also said to levitate when possessed of the Devil, and, of course, witches were supposed to fly off to sabbats on broomsticks.

Levitation was also attributed to various magicians and mediums, the

most famous being the nineteenth-century notable medium D. D. Home.
One English lord described in detail how he saw Home float out one window
of a séance room and in at another.

On the stage the trick has been duplicated by a number of performers.
Harry Kellar did it this way:

> A woman lay on a couch. She rose slowly in the air. Kellar was
> able to pass a hoop over the entire length of her body, "proving"
> that no wires were being used and that nothing was supporting
> her. Then in full sight of the audience she floated down until she
> rested once more on the couch.

The secret of the trick was that the top of the couch was detachable and
connected to an iron bar worked by a pulley from backstage. Draperies
concealed the rigid platform. The bar was painted so as to match the
background perfectly and be undetectable from the audience. A U-bend in
the bar enabled the solid hoop to be flipped backward and forward so that,
from out front, the audience would "see" that it passed right over the
reclining body. Then the hoop was drawn back again, and the platform was
lowered.

Indian magicians perform the trick in much the same way, usually with a
piece of drapery to cover the supporting rod.

A CONFESSED FRAUD

All too many innocent persons have been sent to the gallows for
witchcraft or necromancy by means of lying testimony. All too seldom has
the fraud been discovered in time. But in England in 1632, it did happen.

A man named Edmund Robinson—apparently out of no motive except
malice toward his neighbors and perhaps a desire to have power over
them—decided to lay charges of witchcraft. He taught his eleven-year-old
son to tell a story: "In the fields he [the boy] had met with two dogs, which
he urged to hunt a hare. They would not budge; and he in revenge tied them
to a bush and whipped them; when suddenly one of them was transformed
into an old woman and the other into a child, a witch and her imp."

The Robinson boy told this story, and it was so well received that the
youngster became a local phenomenon. Robinson then began to tell people
that his son could detect a witch at a glance, and he took the boy around to
various local churches, where he was placed on a bench after the service and

told to pick out the witches. He named seventeen persons, who were then arrested, tried at the local assizes, and found guilty of witchcraft.

The judge in the case, however, was skeptical. He postponed the sentence of hanging and sent four of the condemned "witches" to London, to be examined by the king's physicians (one of whom was William Harvey, who later discovered the circulation of the blood) and then by Charles I himself. These august personages could find no evidence that the accused had practiced black arts, so they summoned the Robinson boy and questioned him.

He broke down, confessed that it was all a fraud, and admitted his father's part in the affair. The seventeen were pardoned. It is not known what happened to Robinson.

LAMBE TO THE SLAUGHTER

In seventeenth century England, a certain Dr. John Lambe was convicted of practicing "execrable arts"—afflicting Thomas Lord Windsor with a terrible wasting disease by magic (or perhaps poison). Ordinarily that would have been enough to get him hanged, but he was "the duke's devil," which was to say that he had the protection of the first duke of Buckingham (1592–1628), boyfriend of the homosexual king, James I.

So John Lambe was not hanged, but he was sent to jail for fifteen years. In jail he continued to practice his astrology and other occult business and was allowed to have clients visit him and collect his fat fees. But eventually Buckingham began to lose confidence in Lambe.

Like all high rollers who depend on public credulity for their success, once his principal backer had defected, he went downhill fast. First he was deprived of the use of his jail cell as a consulting room, which lost him his clientele. Then, upon his release in 1640, he was set upon by the mob with cries of "Kill the wizard! . . . Kill the poisoner!" They caught him as he was on his way to the theater and beat him to death.

EGYPTIAN MAGIC TRICKS

The Egyptian priests understood the place of "magic" in overawing superstitious followers, and they often resorted to trickery to impose on the worshippers.

At the Temple of Luxor a fire lighted on the ancient altar, which was hollow, expanded the air within. This heated air forced water from a jar into a bucket. The bucket sank, which pulled a rope, and this caused a precisely hung door to swing open mysteriously. It may sound like Rube Goldberg, but its effect on superstitious worshippers must have been tremendous.

I. G. Edmonds in his book on stage magic, *The Magic Makers* (1976), tells of a trick performed by a famous Egyptian magician in the days of Cheops. Summoned to perform before the pharaoh, Teta offered to cut off the head of an animal and restore it again. When the king agreed, Teta brought forth a goose and beheaded it, laying the head on one end of the table and the body on the other.

> At his magical command, the two moved together. The severed head rejoined the body. The goose got up on its feet and cackled.
> Then, to prove his mastery of magic, Teta performed the trick on another bird. . . .
> The fact is that any magician can perform this simple trick—and through the centuries most magicians have. . . . All the trick requires is a trained bird and a carved wooden head and neck.

While the magician was pretending to cut off the head, the bird tucked its head under its wing. The magician palmed the realistically painted head and then laid it at the far end of the table. A few more passes, the "severed" head was again palmed, and the bird raised up its real head.

Egyptian priests were reported to have performed many feats of "magic" to impress the king and the common people—feats which modern stage magicians have no trouble duplicating. They caused ghostly images to appear on walls or in columns of smoke, which could be done by reflecting light off a mirrored surface through a hole in the ceiling of the temple. They hollowed out statues—at least one of these hollow images has been found—so that a priest could slip inside and cause the statue to "speak." Trumpets were made to play by remote control. Tubes, painted black so they could not be seen in the dark temple interior, led from an air bladder to the trumpet's mouthpiece; the priest stepped on the bladder, and air was forced through the instrument, blasting a long note.

They understood the function of air pressure in stopping the flow of liquids, and they used it in the bottle trick, in which three or four different liquids are made to flow from a single vessel. The bottle, specially made with several different (hidden) compartments each with a tiny air hole, is held so that the hand covers all the holes except one; the tilted bottle pours water, then the hand is clandestinely shifted to uncover a different hole, and wine emerges, and so on. Thus a priest could "change" water into wine and wine into milk and perhaps milk into beer.

Today most of these illusions are part of the repertoire of conjurors and stage magicians, used for pure entertainment. But how many other credulous people, aside from Egyptians, have they fooled, down through the ages, into thinking some charlatan was performing true magic?

9

Familiar Demons and Demon Familiars

MAGIC and witchcraft were worked, it was believed, not by the sorcerer or witch himself but by demons who did their masters' bidding. Magicians, who were powerful and learned men and knew the secret names of God and of the major Devils in Hell, forced these great spirits to submit to them. But witches were not thought to be so gifted. Poor, ignorant folk—and usually women at that—they could only make limited bargains with Satan. In return for their souls, he would give them a minor demon or imp, a "familiar," who would perform small magical chores like causing sickness or curing it.

Some demonologists argued that the Devil could not create something out of nothing, as God could, but he and his minions could change forms. An imp might appear as a dog or a black cat or a pet crow. However this changed form could never be perfect; some "imperfection" would eventually betray the evil spirit within. Interrogators, hoping to unmask witches, looked at the suspect's pet and asked about mysterious strangers who might have been seen in her company.

Tradition told of the Devil having appeared in tangible form to many people, even to Jesus Christ. The temptations of Saint Anthony in the desert involved evil spirits, which appeared to him in various forms, especially as a

192

beautiful maiden. Hagiography was full of instances of the Devil appearing as a dwarf or a giant, as a beautiful and tempting person or a hideous monstrosity, of demons part human and part animal. Had not Martin Luther himself mentioned the Devil sixty-seven times in his *Greater Catechism* (and Christ only sixty-three times) and thrown his inkwell at the Devil when His Satanic Majesty dared to appear in Luther's study?

Our ancestors fully believed that evil spirits roamed the earth in dangerously deceptive human and animal forms.

HOW TO SELL YOUR SOUL

Here is how, according to seventeenth-century Germans, you sell your soul to the Devil.

On a piece of virgin parchment write in your own blood:

I promise GREAT DEMON to repay him in seven years for all he shall give me.
In witness whereof, I sign my name——————.

Then begin the invocation, holding the bit of parchment, within the magic circle:

LUCIFER, Emperor, Master of All Rebellious Spirits, I beseech thee be favorable to me in the calling upon thy GREAT MINISTER which I make, desiring to make a pact with him.

BEELZEBUB, Prince, I pray thee also, to protect me in my undertaking.

ASTAROTH, Count, be propitious to me and cause that this night the GREAT DEMON appear to me in human form and without any evil smell, and that he grant me, by means of the pact which I shall deliver to him, all the treasures of which I have need.

GREAT DEMON, I beseech thee, leave thy dwelling, in whatever part of the world you may be, to come to speak with me; if not, I shall thereto compel thee by the power of the mighty words of the Great Key of Solomon, whereof he made use to force the rebellious spirits to accept his pact.

Appear then instantly or I shall continually torment thee with the mighty words of the Key: *Aglon, Tetragrammaton, Vaycheon,*

Stimulamathon, Erohares, Retrasammathon, Clyoran, Icion, Esition, Existien, Eryona, Onera, Erasyn, Moyn, Meffias, Soter, Emmanuel, Sabaoth, Adonai, I call you. Amen.

The Demon will then appear and demand the written promise of payment after seven years time, "that I may do with thee, body and soul, what shall please me."

The pact is then thrown to the Demon outside the circle, taken up and away, and commences in effect.

FAMILIARS

Pope Gregory IX (1147–1241) issued a bull to the German hierarchy explaining how the Devil took animal forms, and Reginald Scot in his *Discoverie of Witchcraft* recorded the English superstition that imps or little devils or demons could take animal form and that witches kept them as pets, feeding them human milk or blood, occasionally bits of chicken.

In the trials for witchcraft, familiars are often alleged to have accompanied witches, and some witches confessed (or made up lies) about familiar spirits, even giving their names and descriptions.

Some poor old women who had nothing but a house cat or faithful dog as a companion were accused of being witches and had their pets used as "evidence" against them. Gray cats and black dogs were especially suspect, and people were frightened if a black cat even crossed their path. But two animal forms were said to be avoided by demons, the lamb and the dove, because of the Christian Agnus Dei (lamb of God) and Paraclete (Holy Ghost in the form of a dove).

Nonetheless, the Devil himself is supposed to have appeared to a witch named Agnes Webster (tried at Aberdeen in 1597) "in the liknes of a lamb, quhom thou callis thy god, and bletit on the, and thaireftir spak to the," though as a black and deformed lamb.

In fact, it was believed that the devils (superior evil spirits) and demons (under their jurisdiction) could take on any animal form whatsoever, even that of a human being living or dead. So when you saw a ghost, you could not always be sure that it was, indeed, the ghost of some soul departed or the Devil tempting you, and when you saw an animal, you could never be quite sure that it was not an evil force in disguise. Just as angels came to earth in human form, so could fallen angels.

INNOCENT AMUSEMENT

Giovanni Battista Cibo (1432–1492), who reigned as Pope Innocent VIII, believed that humans can mate with demons. He declared: "It has actually come to our knowledge and we are deeply grieved to hear that many persons of both sexes, completely forgetful of the salvation of their souls and straying far from the Catholic Faith, have [had intercourse] with evil spirits, both incubi and succubi." An incubus was a male demon who preyed on women, a succubus a female demon who preyed on men—thought nowadays to be the personifications of nightmares and sexual dreams.

CAVE CANEM!

The Devil has a black dog, and many demons and familiars are said to appear in canine form, an ironic comment on "man's best friend." In Goethe's *Faust* Mephistopheles first appears as a dog.

Dogs are common in Christian legends of saints too. Saint Roch, ill of the plague, was nursed by a dog. Saint John of the Cross was freed from prison by one. Saint Christopher was sometimes depicted with the head of a dog. Saint John Bosco (1815–1888) had a self-appointed guard dog named Grigio, which appeared one day when John was being set on by a robber, drove off the thief, and remained. But dogs are even commoner in pagan myth and demonology.

In ancient Britain a pack of hounds accompanied Gwynn ap Nudd (the god of the underworld) hunting souls. In Norse myth, Garm is the hound of Hell; in Greek myth, the many-headed Cerberus guards the shore of Styx. In Hindu myth, there are sun dogs and moon dogs (a twenty-four-hour patrol) of Yama, the god of death. In Persian myth, a dog guards the afterlife.

The Iroquois, Huron, Ojibway, Seminole, and other Native American groups all have a dog guarding their Hells; so do the Koryaks of Siberia.

The Chinese *p'eng hen* (black dogs without tails) are thought to be demons. The Muslims have a demonic black dog, and English tradition had the Black Dog of Newgate (the prison area), which consorted with "blacke conditioned people" and dwelt in the "bosom of traytors, murtherers, theives, cut-purses, cunny-catchers [coney-catchers, con men], and the like."

The Devil is said to have left Judas Iscariot in the form of a black dog, to have attacked Saint Stanislas Kostka in that form, and to have appeared in this form to many saints and anchorites. Some alchemists had big black dogs for pets that followed them everywhere and were popularly assumed to be familiars.

Dogs have been gods as well as devils. Set ruled Upper Egypt as a greyhound with a forked tail. Anubis, the Egyptian god of death, took a doglike jackal form. Hecate, queen of the witches, rejoiced in "the barking of dogs" and was accompanied by many a harpy or *empusa* or other vengeful night creature, some of whom took the form of bitches.

At the beginning of the eleventh century there was even a dog who reigned for three years in Norway. It was said he could speak several Norwegian words; in any case, all royal acts were signed with his paw. This King Sueining (or Saur) was thought by some Norwegians to be "the soul of a great lord of the past . . . reincarnated in the body of this dog" (as reported in Fernand Mery's *Life, History and Magic of the Dog*, 1970).

DEMON LETTER WRITER

If you want your love letters (or business letters, if you are more prosaic) to meet with wonderful success, you can enlist the aid of demons this way:

Take a sheet of virgin parchment (the real animal skin) and cover it on both sides with this invocation in black ink:

ADAMA, EVAH, EVEN AS THE ALL-POWERFUL CREATOR DID UNITE YOU IN THE EARTHLY PARADISE WITH A HOLY, MUTUAL AND INDIS-SOLUBLE LINK, SO MAY THE HEART OF THOSE TO WHOM I WRITE BE FAVOURABLE TO ME, AND BE ABLE TO REFUSE ME NOTHING:

✡ ELY   ✡ ELY   ✡ ELY.

Then you burn the parchment and add the ashes to the ink with which you write the letters you wish to make irresistible.

Paul Christian's *History and Practice of Magic* recommends you add to the ink ("which has never been used before") seven drops of milk from a mother suckling her firstborn and a pinch of powdered lodestone and suggests you write with a new quill pen sharpened with a never-used knife.

IN PERSON

At the beginning of Book V of his *Historia Sui Temporis* the medieval writer Raoul Glaber describes someone whose appearance you might want to be warned about: "At the foot of my bed I saw a little monster in human form. As far as I can remember, he had a thin neck and face, very black eyes, a narrow wrinkled forehead, a flat nose, a wide mouth with swollen lips, a short tapered chin, a goatee. . . . " And that's what a demon looks like.

MOURNFUL NUMBERS

According to James David Besser (in *The New Republic* of July 25, 1981), writing about the Moral Majority and the media evangelists on Station WABS ("We Always Broadcast Salvation") and so on, the Devil is still very active. "Satan," says the Rev. Jerry Falwell, "would love to silence the voice of the 'Old Time Gospel Hour,'" and the Devil has programs of his own. Besser reports: "David Weber warns that zip codes, Social Security numbers, and government computers are among the tools the Antichrist will soon use to identify his followers, who have been marked with the number 666. Already, he says, uniform product codes on food packages contain the dangerous digits." Hate campaigns count the letters in the name of Ronald Wilson Reagan.

GROTESQUE CREATURES

I remember my astonishment as a teenager when I found in my college library, at McGill University, a book with color plates purporting to portray the faces of various demons. Apparently people could not only call demons up; they could also get them down, drawing their likenesses.

The medieval imagination especially rejoiced in grotesques, and in the Middle Ages believed in the existence of extremely odd combinations of human and animal characteristics, in gargoyles and other monsters. In the Renaissance, Shakespeare had Othello charm Desdemona with his tales of

> . . . Cannibals that each other eat,
> The Anthropophagi, and men whose heads
> Do grow beneath their shoulders.

These latter were the Blemmyae that the historian Pliny placed in Libya and were (probably) men who hid behind shields so that their heads could not be seen in battle. How to explain the belief, though, in creatures such as the Astomi (whom Pliny said did not eat but subsisted entirely on smelling fruit and flowers, and could be killed by bad odors), the Sciopods (one-legged people who spent "their days lying on their backs protecting their heads from the sun with a single great foot"), and men with the heads of dogs, etc.? But none of the pygmies and giants and monsters are as grotesque and incredible as the demons.

Alphonse de Spina in *Fortalicium Fidei* ("Fortress of Faith," 1476) grouped demons in ten classes: Fates, Poltergeists, Incubi and Succubi, "Armies or Hordes," Familiars, Nightmares, Disguised Demons, Demons attacking saintly men, Demons who persuaded old women to go to the sabbat, and Demons created by "copulation" of human and inhuman creatures. The *Fortalicium,* however, denied the existence of this last class.

Satan ("Adversary") is the chief of the fallen angels in Hell, and demoted seraphim and cherubim there include various princes. Matthew gives Beelzebub ("Lord of the Flies") the title of Prince of Hell. Other princes are Mammon, Asmodeus, Belial, and Astaroth. De Spina says that 133,306,668 angels became devils. One of the discomforts of Hell: overcrowding.

TITLE OF RESPECT

Because God is called the Most High, the Devil is called the Most Low. Further information is presumably available from the public relations officer of Hell; his name is Nybras. It may be cold comfort to p.r. reps to learn that "he is treated as an inferior demon, prophet, and charlatan."

MOTHER REDCAP

The London *Sunday Chronicle* of September 9, 1928, published a startling story of a modern witch, Mother Redcap, who lived in a little village only fourteen miles from the University of Cambridge:

One day a black man called, produced a book and asked her to sign her name in it. The woman signed the book [not knowing what it was, which in true occult tradition, would invalidate the bargain], and the mysterious stranger then told her she would be the mistress of five imps who would carry out her orders. Shortly afterwards the woman was seen out accompanied by a rat, a cat, a toad, a ferret, and a mouse. Everybody believed she was a witch, and many people visited her to obtain cures.

The story, though only a typical piece of Sunday supplement sensationalism, does point up the dangers of a lonely old woman keeping pets. Mother Redcap, thanks to living in a relatively enlightened age, was left in peace, but how many similar old women, over the centuries, have found themselves paying dearly for the crime of giving house room to a cat?

FOREIGN DEVILS

The list of strange demons spoken of in other cultures is long, but just as a sample we may mention *Shui-mu Niang-niang* (the Chinese water demons who cause great rivers to flood), the Sumerian *Maskim* (the worst of all the seven classes of demons, "neither male nor female . . . they do not beget children . . . they are strangers to benevolence and heed neither prayers nor entreaties"), the *mutua* or *batwa* of Africa (pygmies about four feet tall, with one eye, webbed feet, and those on backward—if you see one, you die), and the *yara-ma* or *yara-ma-yha-who* of the Pacific Coast of Australia (also four feet tall, but with red and green scales—they can swallow a human being whole, dropping on him or her out of the trees).

DEMONIC ENERGY

Acts 19:11–16 tells the story of some vagabond exorcists who had seen Paul cast out demons of disease in Jesus' name and thought they would try their hand at it. Accordingly they went to work on some patients, ordering the possessing demons to leave and adding, "We adjure you by Jesus whom Paul preacheth."

One of the patients—or his demon—retorted, "Jesus I know, and Paul I know, but who are *ye*?" Then he leaped on them and knocked them about so severely that they "fled out of that house naked and wounded."

Exorcising is best left to professionals.

LUCIFER

Actually, there is no Lucifer.

The name "Lucifer" ("light bringer" in Latin) occurs once in the Bible (Isaiah 14:12), the King James Version calling him "Lucifer, son of the morning" and the Douai Version rendering it as "Lucifer, who didst rise in the morning." According to the Millers' *Harper's Bible Dictionary* (1961), this is a translation of the Hebrew "shining one," which refers not to fallen angels but to the king of Babylon, who boasted pridefully that he would ascend to Heaven and challenge God. But the Biblical attack might also refer to the Assyrian king Sargon II, father of Sennacherib. In any case, there is no devil named Lucifer, nor is this another term for Satan.

The Middle Ages were wrong. Lucifer is not Satan.

Tondriau and Villaneuve's *Dictionary of Devils and Demons* (1972) is also confused. They identify Lucifer (or Lucibel) as the most beautiful of the angels, "transformed for rebelliousness into a hairy monster and he became known as Satan" but then proceed to say that "Lucifer tempts men through vanity, while Satan tempts them through lust" and later that Lucifer is "King of Hell, superior even to Satan."

The authors are mistaken. It's true that the name "Lucifer" does turn up in medieval lists of demons or devils. But he never had any more reality than, say, Mammon ("riches"), another "person" created out of a misunderstanding of terminology. Sometimes men invented names for persons actually unnamed in the Bible: Dives and Lazarus, the Magi (Caspar, Melchior, Balthasar), the centurion whose spear pierced the side of Christ (Longinus), the "good thief" (Dismas). Lucifer is not even one of those— Lucifer is just a word mistaken for a name.

TAKING NO CHANCES

Readwald, king of the East Angles (died 627), was converted to the new religion (said Saint Bede in his ecclesiastical history) but was cautious not to abandon the Old Religion. He erected a church in which Mass was said at the high altar but on either side sacrifices were offered to the Devil. Early Christian churches often had Old Religion symbols decorating them as well as Christian symbols, especially at the north door. From the north, ancient Hebrews believed, came evil.

As Machiavelli (some swear) remarked on his deathbed when asked to abjure the Devil and all his works and pomps: "At a time like this I cannot afford to make enemies."

A DIFFERENT VISION

The Satan of Hieronymus Bosch is neither kingly (he has a kettle on his head) nor ordinary (he is shown as a creature with the head of a day-old chick impassively devouring people who emerge whole at the other end).

INFERNAL LEGIONS

Whereas de Spina, as we have seen, listed ten species of demons, Peter Binsfield (1540–1607) in his Latin treatise on "maleficers and sorcerers" connected seven demons with the Seven Deadly Sins. Lucifer was pride. Mammon (according to Biblical precedent) was avarice. Asmodeus, long associated with dissipation, was lust. Satan was anger. Beelzebub was confused with the watchman of Hell (Behemoth) and connected with his sin, gluttony. Leviathan, who as Lilith seduced Adam and as a serpent tempted Eve, was envy. Belphegor (the Moabite's Baal of Mount Phegor) was sloth.

Francisco Maria Guazzo and others arranged them a different way: demons of the upper atmosphere (not in touch with mankind), demons of our terrestrial plane (in the forests, the seas, the earth beneath our feet), demons of the day and demons of the night. Saint Athanasius averred that "the world is full of demons," but I suspect at least some were invented to fit those neat categories that medieval people liked to construct, paralleling with ranks of demons the Thrones, Dominions, Principalities, and so on, of the archangels and angels.

Creatures of disorder created by the desire for neatness!

THE DEVIL IN DISGUISE

When the Devil appeared to Saint Juliana of Izmir (303), he appeared in the shape of an angel. When he appeared to the old hag in the seventeenth-century play *The Witch of Edmonton*, he appeared as a dog and said his name was Tom.

SALT OF THE EARTH

In Derbyshire, England, people used to swear on salt, not the Bible. It is used at baptism and on the dead. It keeps away witches and (if you spill some and throw it over your left shoulder) the Devil. The Devil never serves salt at infernal banquets.

A MESSAGE FOR THE PREACHER

A Lutheran pastor named Carolstad preaching at Basel, Switzerland, on December 22, 1541, said the Devil appeared to him and told him he would not live through Christmas. He died by strangulation on December 25, 1541.

DOUBLE DEALING

The Bavarian painter Haizmann (died 1700) sold his soul to the Devil. In 1677 he went to Church authorities for help in breaking his bargain with the Devil and was exorcized. He drew portraits of the Devil who, he swore, appeared to him seven times as a dragon, a black dog, and in other shapes. Ecclesiastical authorities were convinced of the truth of his story and were delighted to have these Identikit likenesses of a Most Wanted personality, but Sigmund Freud long after used Haizmann's case as a *locus classicus* of paranoid schizophrenia.

MORE MALE CHAUVINIST PREJUDICE

The Kekchi Indians do a devil dance to banish the king of devils, who held court at Metnal (the Mayan Hell). Thomas Gann in the *London Illustrated News*, in 1926, reported this king "collected an army, consisting of his wife, his father and mother, four minor devils, a boar, five sows, a monkey, and Death." When Gann told his informant that this was impossible because he (as an anthropologist specializing in the Maya) knew there were no women in the Mayan Hell, the old informant replied *Ah Tat, Ma Xupal Ma Metnal*. I regret to tell the ladies that translates: "If there were no women, there would be no hell."

AMDUSCIAS

We've had Dr. John and the Night-Trippers and quite a few other pop groups more or less dabbling in the occult, right up to *nuevo wavo* punk. If any new group needs a moniker, I suggest that of Amduscias. He is grand duke of Hell, commands twenty-eight legions of demons, and is the patron of deafening noise.

LIVING ALONE IS PERILOUS

There has been a sharp upswing in America of people living alone. The Talmud advises: "It is indiscreet for one to sleep in a house as the sole occupant, for Lilith will seize him." Further, it warns: "Never go out alone on Wednesday or Saturday nights, for demons are abroad then, and eighteen legions of them, commanded by Agrath the daughter of Machlath, seek whom they may devour."

DEMONS IN THE DICE

In German tradition, the Devil is supposed to have invented dice, and in some old trials for witchcraft he was referred to as the Dicer, but the idea that dice are somehow diabolical and un-Christian goes back to Saint Cyprian (A.D. 200–258), who condemned them as inspired by the Devil.

In German folklore Jacob Grimm (1785–1863) found references to devils or demons living inside dice; that's why people bowed to dice on picking them up.

In India they say that Dvapara, an evil spirit, lies inside the dice and that you will always win with dice made from dead man's bones. In many other cultures dice are associated with magical things, often related to ancient forms of divination. They were part of the equipment (in the form of *urim* and *thurim*) provided in the magical breastplate of the High Priest of the Jews.

Dice may have been used first for magic and only later came to be playthings, used for gambling. It is, of course, magic to spit on the dice before throwing them.

THE IMP OF LINCOLN

High up in the choir of Lincoln Cathedral in England perches a half-human, half-animal creature that, legend says, was once not a carved statue but one of the little devils out of Hell.

The story is that in the thirteenth century the Devil sent two imps to bother the builders and clergy of Lincoln. One flew into the cathedral and pestered the bishop, knocked down the dean, and really raised Hell with the verger. The angels told him to cease and desist. "Stop me if you can!" he impishly replied.

So he was turned to stone, and to this day you can see him, about a foot high, way up in a cleft between two arches.

Gargoyles and similar creatures were a common decoration in medieval cathedrals; look for them even in modern imitations of such ancient buildings. You will see them perched, lurking, even "mooning" worshippers below in many otherwise sedate churches. But the Imp of Lincoln is the only one I know of that (at least legend claims) was once a real live devil.

THE DEVIL'S HELP

According to William Perkins, writing in 1608, all witches are in league with the Devil. "A witch is a magician who, either by open or secret league, wittingly and willingly consenteth to use the aid and assistance of the devil in the working of wonders." What, then, could be a so-called white witch? Without the Devil's help, there can be no witchcraft; what you have in "white magic" is nothing more than primitive pharmacy.

HOW A HELL FIRE CLUB WAS DISBANDED

The famous English Hell Fire Club had a counterpart in Ireland.

A story is told of a curate visiting Dublin who expressed a desire to attend a meeting of this notorious group and was invited to a lavish banquet. He expressed surprise that a black cat was given the place of honor and served first. The members assured him that was because the cat was "the oldest member."

"No," said the curate, "it is because the black cat is the Devil."

Their secret discovered, the members said they would kill the curate and gave him a few moments to say his prayers before being dispatched. As he did so, the cat turned into a demon and flew away, taking the roof of the building with him.

The prayers the curate had said were not for himself but an exorcism.

"FRIAR" RUSH

A German folktale, translated into English in 1568 as *Friar Rush*, told of the Devil sending a demon in human form up to earth, where he was admitted to a monastery to work as a scullion. He tempted the monks to gluttony, wantonness, and anger, but then was discovered and thrown out into the great world where he became a mischievous hobgoblin.

What he represented is clearer when you see his German name: *Bruder Rausch*. *Bruder* mistakenly suggested "Friar" (friars, who are ordained priests, are correctly addressed as "Father") but *Rausch* (drunkenness) is the clue; that's what drove the monks to sin.

HERE'S WHAT TO CALL YOUR CAT OR DOG

Oliver Cromwell is said to have had a familiar called Grimoald. Matthew Hopkins (*Discovery of Witches*, 1647) identified these familiars in the case of Elizabeth Clark: Holt ("a white kitling," or kitten), Jamara ("a fat spaniel without any legs at all" who "sucked blood from her body"), Vinegar Tom ("like a long-legged greyhound, with a head like an ox, with a long tail and broad [spaced] eyes" who could turn into a four-year-old child "without a head" and vanish), Sack and Sugar ("like a black rabbit"), and Newes ("like a polecat"). No Newes is good news.

WEREWOLF

Werewolves have been a standard bit of horror fare. Here's a story from 1590.

Peter Stubb (or Stump) of Bedburg, Germany, possessed a belt given him by the Devil, which enabled him to turn into a wolf at will. It was bad enough when the werewolf killed and ate cattle and sheep, murdered thirteen children and two pregnant women, and got his sister pregnant (though he had several "concubines" and a succubus the Devil sent him for his off hours), but when he killed and ate his own son, the populace had had enough.

Pursued across the countryside by irate citizens, lycanthropic Peter shed the wolfskin belt and turned back into an ordinary person. But they caught him, tortured him, and killed him, along with his daughter and mistress.

DRIVING OUT THE DEVIL

Recently a mother was arrested and jailed in New York City for having burned her infant child to death in an oven. She wanted, she said, to drive the devil out of him. Driving out demons has long been an excuse for abominable cruelties to the young.

From ancient times on, a child who cried too much—or too little—was considered a changeling or possessed of a demon; the least it could expect, even if it was still in its cradle, was a daily beating. Sometimes children were beaten regularly, whether they had misbehaved or not, just on general principles. Royalty was not excepted. The little dauphin who became Louis XIII when he was eight years old was beaten every morning from the age of two on. "I would rather do without so much obeisance and honor," he said once, "if they wouldn't have me whipped."

Infants were swaddled at birth—tightly wrapped from neck to feet so that they could not move—in order to prevent them from falling prey to evil tendencies. In this condition they were like little logs of wood, and servants sometimes played catch with them. When they reached the age of one or two, they were often strapped to chairs to prevent them from crawling on the floor "like an animal." And at night, they were told ghost stories and monster stories and bogeyman stories to terrify them into being good (and not bothering mother).

This was not enough for some, however. In 1771 a "holy man" appeared in Russia, claiming to be the brother of Jesus Christ and preaching a doctrine of avoiding sin (and especially sexual sin) by castrating young boys. He established a sect called the Skopsti, "the castraters."

In the 1920s in France, a woman calling herself the Holy Mother advocated severe beatings for children to make them good. She was tried at Bordeaux in 1926, but the outcome of her trial is not known to me.

In the United States a few years ago, a couple were jailed for having killed their two children by savage beatings to "discipline" them; interviewed in jail, they were outraged at the state for the treatment accorded them and had plans (on their release) only for moving to another state, having more children, and "disciplining" *them.*

When an adult mistreats a child to drive the demon out of it, you wonder in whom the demon really resides.

A REAL DEFINITION OF WITCH HUNTING

Jean Bodin (1529–1576), author of *République* and *Demonomanie des Sorciers* (ten editions up to 1604), argued that "not one sorcerer in a million would ever be accused or punished if one were to follow the regular legal practices" but thought also that anything was allowable in the face of the great threat that the populace felt, "and popular rumor is practically never wrong."

Bodin thought Satan had "a profound knowledge of all things" and could create beings. But is he not to be combated with justice and rationality and not ideas such as "suspicion is sufficient justification for torture"?

BAPHOMET

The church of St.-Merri in Paris has a representation of the demon Baphomet on its facade, and Aleister Crowley had his photo taken with this as a background, for Baphomet since the time of the Knights Templars has been regarded as useful in sex magic, one of Crowley's interests.

Some think Baphomet ought to be depicted as a herm (all head and phallus) and others suggest the Eternal Father, three-sided, three-genitaled, horned. Some wanted him to have the head of Mohammed or a hermaphroditic body because they thought the Knights Templars were getting heresies and homosexual practices from Islam. New York covens of gay witches worship him in the form that is a combination of kitsch and Ken Russell's *Lisztomania.*

NUMBERS GAME

The Talmud says there are 7,405,926 demons. Since the number of demons is fixed, every increase in the world's population improves our changes against the demonic enemy.

STAY TUCKED IN

Medieval Jews believed that a sick or dying man was especially vulnerable to demons if a hand, arm, foot, or leg stuck out from under the covers of the bed.

ARMENIAN GIANTS WERE ONCE DEMONS

The Armenians have such expressions as *devi ooj ounie* (he's as strong as a *dev*), *devi bes goudeh* (he eats like a *dev*), *devi hasag ounie* (he's as tall as a *dev*). A *dev* is a kind of giant, but formerly it was a demon who, in the form of a wild beast or snake or other horrible creature, terrified mankind. "There were giants in the earth in those days," says Genesis and it must have been to such demons the children of Adam and Eve were wed.

So we all must have some demonic relatives. Any genealogist will tell you there are strange creatures perched up in the family tree, and among ours are giants and demons.

A CALENDAR OF DEMONS

Watch out for the following in these months:

January: Belial, demon of pederasty, disorder, the Beast 666.
February: Leviathan, who in different sexes seduced both Adam and Eve.
March: Satan (the Adversary of God), not a demon but the Devil himself.
April: Astarte, not a demon but the Phoenician goddess of beauty.

May: Lucifer (the bringer of Light—the enemy's god of light became the Devil of the Jews), prince of Darkness, a fallen angel.

June: Baalberith, master of marriages, secretary and librarian of Hell.

July: Beelzebub (lord of the Flies), prince of Hell, master of the Living.

August: Astaroth, treasurer of Hell, grand duke of the Western Part of Hell.

September: Thamuz, the demon who is credited with inventing artillery and the Inquisition.

October: Baal, grand duke of Guile, a Phoenician god turned Christian demon.

November: Hecate, queen of the witches, a moon goddess gone wrong.

December: Moloch, Ammonite god turned Christian demon.

DEMON MATRIARCH

The Plantagenet kings of England were descended from William the Conqueror on the female side of the family and the counts of Anjou on the male, and their family name is taken from the plantagenista, or broom, which Geoffrey of Anjou wore in his helmet. The counts of Anjou, it was well known, were the offspring of a demon.

Their ancestor, Count Fulke, probably in the tenth century, went off on a journey and came home with a mysterious wife, Melusine. The couple seemed happy and produced four fine children, but the count was bothered by the fact that his wife would never remain in church through the Consecration of the mass, the solemn moment when bread and wine are changed to Christ's body and blood. One day, he gave orders for his knights to detain Melusine by force. She stood in the chapel, with two of her children on one side and two on the other. When it came time for the Consecration, she made as if to leave, but the knights stood on her dress and tried to hold her arms. But as the Host was elevated, she gave a terrible scream, wrenched herself free, and seizing the two children on her left, flew out of the chapel window.

This revealed the fact that Melusine was a demon. Her children inherited her demon blood, and thus England was ruled for 331 years by descendants of the Devil himself.

DEMON, STAY 'WAY FROM MY DOOR

Diners in Chinese restaurants are familiar with the traditional Chinese symbols of luck, longevity, prosperity. But you may not be aware that the character *shen*, hung over a doorway, prevents evil spirits from entering.

The Greeks use blue paint around doors and windows for the same purpose. So do some Frenchmen. In New Paltz, New York, there is a row of restored seventeenth-century French Huguenot houses, some of whose rooms are painted blue for good luck—despite the fact that blue is the most difficult color to obtain from vegetable dyes and in this case had to be wrung drop by drop from blueberries.

THE GEOGRAPHY OF DJINNS

The genies live in Ginnistan, banished there, legend says, by Taymour-al, a Persian prince. They are named for Gian ben Gian (Gian son of Gian), another Persian ruler; he was the first to discover there are two kinds. The good ones are *peris*, the bad ones are *dives*. The principal city of Ginnistan is Schadou Kiam. The country has two great deserts: Badiat-Goldare (Desert of Monsters) and Bidiat-Tealgim (Desert of Fairies); in the latter the *safar* (cold wind of the dead) never blows.

DEAD DOG

Here, you see, on Marston Moor outside York, a seventeenth-century soldier dispatch (with a magic silver bullet) a large poodle named Boy. But Boy was no ordinary pet. The gift of Lord Arundel to Prince Rupert, Boy was popularly believed to be a familiar, and it took "a valliant soldier, who had skill in Necromancy" to do him in. He is shown being mourned by a witch, not Prince Rupert, which is an error, but the Roundheads didn't worry about that and rejoiced that some magic helping the Cavalier cause in the English Civil War had been effectively countered.

ASMODEUS

Tales of the demon Asmodeus can be traced back at least as far as Aeshma Daeva, an ancient Persian deity who represented anger and devastation. Asmodeus appears in the apocryphal Book of Tobit (Chapters 3 and 7), written some time around 250 B.C. In the story, he falls in love with Sarah, daughter of Raguel, and is fiercely jealous of her seven husbands, whom he kills, one right after the other, on their wedding nights. When Sarah decides to marry her cousin Tobias, Tobias is afraid, but he follows the advice of the Archangel Raphael, who tells him to take the heart and gall of a fish and burn them in the bridal chamber. The odor drives the demon away.

Asmodeus flees to Egypt, where he is taken prisoner by Raphael. In time he escapes and now resides in Hell, from which he will come if called by certain rituals and sacrifices.

Asmodeus is depicted as having three heads (a bull, a man with fiery breath, a ram), and some Jewish writers say he is the chief demon of the *Shedim* (demons with vicious claws, haunting ruins and deserts). Traditional tales say that King Solomon forced him, by magic, to construct the First Temple. Later he is said to have dethroned Solomon and taken his place, committing the sins attributed to the king.

Demonologists of the Middle Ages tried hard to organize the denizens of the infernal world in the ranks of their own society, creating princes, dukes, and other officers of Hell. They made Asmodeus a sort of casino

manager, but sorcerers would say he is far more frightening—and useful—
than that. They call upon him to prosper adultery and wreck marriages, and
conversely, blame him for impotence and infidelity.

"CRAZY, AS NUTS AS THEY COME"

Stephen Cooper, defending Ronald K. Crumpley on a charge of
murdering two men and attempting to murder seven others on a November
19, 1980, rampage in Greenwich Village, New York City, said his client was
"crazy, as nuts as they come," and a defense psychiatrist testified that
Crumpley, an ex-transit policeman, was convinced that "demons in the guise
of homosexuals" were stalking him, and he was "merely protecting the
nation and himself" by destroying gay men.

Found not responsible by reason of mental illness, Crumpley, who
previously had done nothing much worse than stealing credit cards, was
turned over to the state for psychiatric treatment. The demons, if any, go
free.

THE CHURCH AND THE DEVIL

If God made everything, why did he make the Devil? If God is good,
why did he make evil?

Saint Thomas Aquinas, the Angelic Doctor, argues that evil is merely
"the absence of a due and necessary good"—so *God didn't make evil.* But we
still need someone to blame it on. If God is anthropomorphized as a
venerable old man with a long beard and a short temper, why not the Devil
as an anthropomorphized scapegoat? With a tail.

The Holy Office (this is the official name for what is better known as the
Inquisition), or Sacred Congregation for the Doctrine of the Faith (new
name), has announced: "The existence of the devil's world is revealed as a
fact of dogma in the Gospel" and is "a central tenet of the faith of the Church
and of its concept of redemption." To doubt the existence of the Devil and
his demons—to call the Devil just a convenient figment of our imaginations
or a useful poetic way of putting things—is "to trouble people's souls."

Rosette Dubal has psychoanalyzed him. Her *Psychoanalysis of the
Devil* (1953) puts the Devil on the Freudian couch and shows him up as a
wicked father figure, the embodiment of natural forces, the personification of

the libido. In Freudian analysis, he does not come through as the most interesting person around—as he unfortunately does in Milton's *Paradise Lost*.

Poor Old Nick! Now science wants to make him into a libido, and the Church won't let him retire, despite his advanced age!

A CHRISTIAN DEVIL DANCE

The *diabala* (devil dance) of Bolivian Indians presented at the Oduro Mission is not a remnant of pagan religion but is performed on the Feast of the Virgin of Sacavon for Christian purposes and is made up by the Indians out of bits of post-Conquest Hispanic culture. The dancers wear a headdress influenced by animal forms but also by the shape of Roman helmets in pictures of the Crucifixion that the padres showed them.

HARD TO HANDEL

Every time composer Domenico Scarlatti heard the music of Handel, he crossed himself. He believed (as some did of Paganini, the violin virtuoso) that such art was achieved with the help of the Devil.

"IN MY NAME SHALL THEY CAST OUT DEVILS"

This, from Mark 16:17, is only one of more than a hundred references to the Devil, devils, and demons in the Bible.

THE END OF THE DEVIL

In a parody of kissing the pope's shoe or the bishop's ring or the king's hands, it was rumored the sabbat witches performed the *osculum infame* on the Devil's posterior. The Knights Templars were accused of similar indecencies. One poor person on trial for witchcraft insisted she had "never seen the Devil from the rear." By the time this filtered through the confused mind of Caesarius of Heisterback, this appeared in his *Miraculorum* as the assertion that the Devil has no buttocks.

EVIL SPIRITS MUST BE FED

Mary Henrietta Kingsley (1862–1900) was a daring and indefatigable explorer of what used to be called the Dark Continent and at considerable personal risk went into the wilds to study the fetish of West Africa, starting in 1893. Among her interesting discoveries about "fourteen levels of the spirit world" is this about African familiars:

> It is held that a person who has the power of bewitching others has in his possession, under his control, a non-human spirit, and this non-human spirit is, in the case of witches, of a malevolent class. The spirit, among the true Negro Tschwi, is kept in a *suhman.* . . . I have reason to believe that among the true Negroes this malevolent spirit is kept in an external home as a general rule; still it has so close an inter-communion with the other souls of its owner, that if they get weakened it can injure them so as to cause his death. Among all the Bantu tribes I know, this spirit is kept in the witch's own inside; and it is held that it is liable to kill him, if he keeps it unemployed, *unfed,* too long. You will hear—when someone has been injured who does not seem to have merited injury in any particular way, someone who has not given any other person reason to hate him, or when a series of minor accidents and a run of ill-luck comes to a village— "Ah, someone is feeding his witchpower"; and means are, of course, taken to find out who that someone is, and put an end to him.

THE RITE OF EXORCISM

From the earliest times, people attempted exorcism, the driving out of devils and demons. It remains an integral part of baptism and certain other sacraments, but in recent times the Roman Catholic Church has much reduced the practice, and some Protestant sects have abandoned it entirely. The modern approach is to attribute cases of "possession" (with *glossolalia,* "speaking in tongues," violence, and so on) to psychopathology and to

THE REALM OF FAERIE

Fairies may have originated in spirits of nature or memories of earlier races that man drove away into hiding or unbaptized persons who belonged neither in Heaven nor in Hell. But whatever the source of the belief they have always been thought to live in an retreated underground realm—from which they ventured forth only warily among the sons of men.

Twelfth-century English chroniclers present as fact the story of the Green Children, a boy and a girl who somehow escaped the realm of Faerie and found themselves among the peasants at Wolfpitts in Suffolk. The children were lost, weeping in some foreign tongue, and oddly dressed— and green. They were taken to the home of Sir Richard de Calne and cared for but could eat nothing that was not green. In fact, the boy sickened on human food and died. The girl started with green beans and worked her way up to regular English cooking, learned the language, and gradually lost her green color, though she remained (as fairies are supposed to) "very wanton and lascivious." Eventually she was married to a human at King's Lynn in Norfolk.

Fairies, being half human to begin with (the other half being variously described as angelic or devilish), presumably can mate with earthlings. Perhaps those of us humans with "second sight," who can actually see the fairies with their bodies of "congealled Air" and perhaps even wings, have some strain of faerie in them and are distantly descended from marriages between our world and the realm of Faerie.

In 1556 a Dorset man, John Walsh, accused of witchcraft, swore that he could tell if a person was bewitched because "he knew it partly by the fairies, and saith that there be three kinds of fairies, white, green, and black, which, when he is disposed to use he speaketh to them upon hills whereas there is great heaps of earth, as namely in Dorsetshire." *The Examination of John Walsh* said one could consult fairies between twelve and one at noon or night but to be very careful of the black fairies, because "the black fairies be the worst."

Other old historians told of how the swineherd of William Peverell and others found entrances to the subterranean worlds of the fairies and elves and consorted with them in their kingdoms.

But these days, the folk wisdom or credulity that enabled sixteenth-century peasants to chat with the fairies of Dorset hills has gone forever. Our "little green people" now are expected in spaceships.

THE FAIRY BANNER

Dunvegan Castle on the Isle of Skye is the ancestral home of the McLeods, and it has been occupied by that family for more than eleven centuries. It is said to be protected by a fairy banner that, if waved in time of danger, will bring the hosts of fairies to the aid of the McLeods.

Other castles house many treasures, from the horn of Old King Cole to relics of the regal and damnable personages of Britain's past, but none but the castle of the McLeods' boasts such supernatural support, from a boggart, a special kind of supernatural creature we might now call a bogeyman.

FROM THE FAIRIES

Fairies work at night. Santa Claus comes during the night to pile presents under the Christmas tree. When baby teeth fall out, children put them under their pillows, to find money there in the morning, the gift of the Tooth Fairy.

The statue of Sir James M. Barrie's immortal Peter Pan was erected in the darkness of a single night in order to convince London children it had been put there by the fairies. When a duplicate was put up in Perth, Australia, it too was erected overnight and for the same reason.

FAIRY FASHIONS

Fairies always wear a long red mantle with a pointed hood; but witches do too. The Devil usually wears black, but in Scotland he has also been reported to wear green. Serious sorcerers need elaborate robes of different colors for different purposes and seasons, just as the chasubles worn by priests vary in color depending upon the occasion: red for the feasts of martyrs, purple or black for requiems, white or gold for solemn feasts, and so on. Leprechauns wear green. Most serious witchcraft is performed stark naked. Brownies wear brown, sometimes. Norwegian elves are blue but naked; maybe it's the cold. In the Faroes, elves wear a gray costume and black hats.

BRIDGET CLEARY

In March 1894, County Tipperary, one Bridget Cleary disappeared. When her burned and battered body was found, her husband Michael, her father, and seven other men—all but one of them relatives—were charged with her murder.

It seems that Michael Cleary and his relatives thought Bridget was a witch or a changeling—a fairy who had taken over the real Bridget Cleary's place. The mother of Michael Cleary "used to go to the fairies," and it was feared Bridget had too.

Yeats records this ancient belief in his *Irish Fairy and Folk Tales*: "Sometimes the fairies fancy mortals, and carry them away into their own country, leaving instead some sickly fairy child," or even marry mortals, keeping their supernatural nature a secret or revealing it only to a few—often under the threat of fire, of which they are afraid.

Trying to get Bridget to confess, Michael and his family forced her to take herbs and milk, tried countercharms, threw around a mixture of urine and chicken feces to get rid of the spells, and called in the parish priest to say mass in the house. (He later claimed he had no idea that witchcraft was suspected or he "would have given information to the police at once.") When those measures failed to force a confession from her, they threw oil from the lamp on her, burned her face, abdomen, and arm, and tortured her over the fire. But the woman died proclaiming that she was the real Bridget Cleary.

At the trial, the relatives told their strange story of superstition and murder. All were found guilty of manslaughter and sentenced to penal servitude. Michael Cleary got twenty years.

That was Ireland's last trial for witchcraft—or, rather, murder for witchcraft.

SYLPH CONSCIOUSNESS

Sylphs, salamanders, undines, and gnomes were elemental creatures, occupying (respectively) air, fire, water, and earth. They were believed to stand halfway between men and the immortals, being mortal in that they could eat and drink, become sick, beget children, and die, and being supernatural in that their bodies were transparent, they could move with great speed, and they could foretell the future.

Louis the Pious, son of the emperor Charlemagne, by royal edict banished from France all "sylphs." William Woods' *History of the Devil* (1975) comments:

> By forbidding them to appear, Louis was presumably forbidding people to see them—whereupon they were no longer seen. . . . [but] Charlemagne's world of faerie, almost contemporaneous with that of Arthur in Britain, has not died in France even today.

IGNIS FATUUS

The will-o'-the-wisp may lead you to destruction, like *ellylldan*, tiny little elves, only a foot high, that can appear and offer you a very unpleasant choice: either a flight through the air or a voyage upon the ground. If you choose the former, you are whisked up into the air and sped along only to be dropped from a great height; if you elect terra firma, you are dragged at great speed through briars and over jagged rocks, and dumped off one of the cliffs or precipices that the *ellylldan* call home. The twinkling lights of Will may be only the ghostly candles that are leading some soul to the grave—maybe yours.

In *Folklore in America* (1966) Coffin and Cohen write: "The Negroes are also very much afraid of the will-o'-the-wisp, or *ignis fatuus*. They believe that on a dark night it leads its victim, who is obliged to follow, either in the river, where he is drowned, or in bushes of thorns, which will tear him to pieces, the jack-o'-lantern exclaiming all the time, 'Aïe, aïe, mo gagnin toi'— 'Aïe, aïe, I have you.'"

They are not the only ones who are frightened. The *ignis fatuus* of marsh gas has led untold numbers of modern viewers to call the local sheriff to report invasions by flying saucers and little men.

WHERE FAIRIES CAME FROM

The *moira* (fate) of ancient Greece became the *Fata scribunda* (Fates who write down the destiny of each newborn child) of the Romans. The *Encyclopaedia Britannica* makes an striking point in a 1971 article on "fate":

This use of *fata* had an interesting development. When the neuter
gender became extinct in spoken Latin, its plural came to be
thought of as a feminine singular; hence Italian *fata*, French *fée*.
The Fates had become a fairy.

HOW TO GET A FAIRY

The Ashmolean Museum in Oxford was founded by an antiquarian with
a lifelong interest in the occult, so it may be no surprise that among its rare
manuscripts is a fifteenth-century description of "An excellent way to get a
Fayrie." Here it is:

> First get a broad square christall or Venus glasse, in length and
> breadth 3 inches; then lay that glasse or chrystall in the blood
> of a white Heene, 3 Wednesdays or 3 Fridays, then take it out
> and wash it with Holy Water and fumigate it [with incense]. Then
> take 3 hazel sticks or wands of a years growth, peel them fayre
> and white and make them so long as you write the spirits or
> fayries which you call 3 times on every sticke, being made flatt
> on one side. Then bury them under some hill, wheras you sup-
> pose fayries haunt, the Wednesday before you call her, and the
> Friday following, take them up and call her at 8, 3, and 10 of the
> clock which be good planets and hours, but when you call, be
> of cleane life and turn thy face towards the east, and when you
> have her, bind her to that stone or glasse.

This manuscript says you can summon up your own fairy at will,
whether to give you secret information, endow a child with a good fate,
protect an area, or even give you the precious diamond that some fairies are
supposed to have in the middle of their forehead.

ANOTHER RECIPE

Raymond Lamont Brown's *Book of Witchcraft* (1971) does not say where
he found this "Charm to See the Fairies":

> A pint of Sallet oyle and put it in a vial glasse; and first wash it
> with rose water; the flowers to be gathered towards the east.

Wash it till the oyle becomes white, and put it into the glasse, and then put thereto the budds of hollyhocke, the flowers of ma[r]ygolds the flowers or toppes of wild thyme, the budds of young hazle, and the thyme must be gathered near the side of a hill where fairies are used to be; and take the grasse of a fairy throne; then all these put into the glasse and set it to dissolve three days in the sunne and keep it for thy use.

Note that in the case of both recipes, you have first to know where the fairies are found.

WOMEN OF FAIRYLAND

Many noble houses were lucky enough to have an elf or fairy attached to each member of the family to help and guide them through life. Robert, count of Lusignan, even married a woman who was half human and half fairy: Her father was Elinas, king of Albanie (which could be Albania or Scotland), and her mother was Pressina *le Fay.*

In Ireland and the highlands of Scotland, the *bean sith* (women of fairyland) used to wail and lament under the windows of a house under their protection just before a member of the family was to die.

We call them banshees.

THE AIRMAN'S ELVES

Gremlins are clearly a twentieth-century creation, dating from the early days of flying, but exactly when they first appeared, or who coined the name, is not known and probably never will be.

The Dictionary of Phrase and Fable traces these "imaginary elves whom the R.A.F. in World War II blamed for all inexplicable failures in aeroplanes" back to the thirties, to "a Squadron of Bomber Command serving on the North West Frontier in India." Actually gremlins were known earlier than that.

Horror-story writer Roald Dahl claimed to have invented the term, but to refute him, B. J. Watson wrote to the *Radio Times* (December 1, 1979) to say that gremlins were mentioned a couple of times, by name, in a poem published in *The Aeroplane* (April 10, 1929), when Dahl was just entering his teens.

The late Eric Partridge, expert on all kinds of British slang and contributor of the RAF words to *Forces' Slang, 1939–1945* (1948), noted that "gremlins" had become Standard English. But when it was still slang, as Watson pointed out, it meant a creature that could bring good or evil; gremlins were "responsible for *all* unaccountable happenings—good or bad." Now gremlins—except in Australia, where the word describes a very young surfer, especially a showoff—bring pilots only bad news.

FAIRY NAMES AND NATURES

Novelist Gillian Edwards covers the incredible history of fairy lore in *Hobgoblin and Sweet Puck* (1974) and not only touches on fates and fays and fairies, elves and oafs and imps and urchins, but also dwarfs, gnomes, knockers, bugs, bogles, bogeys, boggarts, brownies, hobs, goblins, and hobgoblins, pookas, pucks, pixies, Queen Mab, Robin Goodfellow, Carabosse, the Elf-Queen, and other personages, from fetches to will-o'-the-wisps and gremlins. To this list Reginald Scot (of the famous *Discoverie of Witches*, 1584) would add "Bull-beggars, Spirits, Witches, . . . Hags, . . . Satyrs, Pans, . . . Sylens, Kit-wi-the-Can[dle]stick, Tritons, Centaurs, Gyants, . . . Calcars, Conjurors, Nymphs, Changelings, Incubus, . . . the Spoorn, the [Night]Mare, the Man-in-the-Oak, the Hell-wain, the Fired-rake [dragon], the Puckle, Tom-thombe, . . . Tom-tumbler, Boneless [and other bogeymen], and such other Bugs, that we are afraid of our shadow."

If your name is Alvin, it goes back to *aelf-wine* (friend of the fairies), and of course similarly derived names such as Oberon and Auberon and Aubrey were "fairy" names. There was a queen of England called Elfleda, and Alfred the Great had a daughter named Elfrida ("threatening elf"); were they fairy princesses?

PROTECTION

To avoid being *led willed* by will-o'-the-wisps, turn your left stocking inside out, or your cloak inside out, and put it on again. The old magical reverse! Usually a reverse (such as the Lord's Prayer or the Stations of the Cross backward) produces an evil result; this produces a good one.

SMALL TRUTHS

"How much is written of Pigme's, Fairies, Nymphs, Apparitions, which tho not the tenth Part true, yet could not spring of Nothing!"

That, in a nutshell, is the opinion of Robert Kirk, as found in his essay of 1691 entitled, in part, *Secret Commonwealth, an Essay of the Nature and Actions of the Subterranean (and, for the most Part) Invisible People, heretofioir going under the name of Elves, Faunes and Fairies, or the lyke, among the Low-Country Scots as they are described by those who have Second Sight* . . .

FAIRY POSSESSIONS

Everyone has heard of fairy gold (said to be found at the end of a rainbow), which vanishes when men try to take it home. But mankind has managed, it is said, to hold onto some fairy possessions. In the Victoria and Albert Museum in London you can see a glass vessel called the Luck of Eden Hall, reputed to have been stolen from the fairies by the Musgrave family in the old days. The intrepid Otto, count of Oldenburg, was said to have stolen the Oldenburg horn from the fairies; in Denmark, the church at Aagerup, Zealand, has a golden chalice stolen from the fairies.

But possession of anything belonging to them is uncertain; magical fairy things are likely to disappear as quickly as they appeared.

If you ever visit the fairies or elves, try to steal something (they are always stealing things from us) but be sure not to accept any refreshment. If you eat with them, you will not be able to return to our world.

FAIRY LORE

The legends about fairies and elves and such creatures may actually derive from exaggerated accounts by primitive peoples of strange nearby tribes with whom they had little communication. The fairies' hatred of iron, for example, may represent race memory of conquest of a Bronze Age people by invaders possessing iron weapons.

Early folklore got a big boost from the collections of the Brothers

Grimm (*Kinder- und Hausmärchen* in 1812–1814 and *Deutsche Mythologie* of 1835 started a whole school), and in England pioneers in folklore often wrote up and published old stories of the "little people": Peter Roberts' *Cambrian* [Welsh] *Popular Antiquities* in 1815, Thomas Keightley's *The Fairy Mythology* of 1828 (greatly expanded in 1850), and so on. Others found in the lore of fairies and elves and goblins some of our earliest memories and some of our most lasting and widespread oral literature.

By the way, it has been unlucky for you to be reading the word "fairy" here at all, which explains the section title, "The Good Neighbors." *They* like us to call them that, or "the little people," or some such name.

LITTLE RED MEN

The Europeans have their leprechauns and gnomes and fairies. In the New World we have our "little people" as well. A case in point is described in *Dictionary of Bahamian English* (1982):

> LITTLE RED MEN . . . *n.* mythical creatures said to inhabit the island of Andros: 1966. The little Red Men are about two feet high, have three fingers on each hand, and are "bright" or

Malicious little creatures crying "Hobyah! Hobyah! Hobyah!" are drawn by John D. Barton for More English Fairy Tales *(1894) collected by Joseph Jacobs. "Hob" means "devil."*

light-skinned. They wear long beards and black velvet waistcoats, but no trousers. They protect animals and try to keep humans out of the Andros interior and other isolated areas. They are said to come to the aid of birds or animals wounded by hunters. To show friendship and good will, Out Islanders hold up three fingers over their heads while walking through the high bush. . . .

SOCKS WITH WHITE TOES

Today there are some socks manufactured with white toes because of an ancient Irish belief that they will keep you from being tripped up by the "little people."

DON'T DAWDLE

In Britain the fairies come out to dance at night. If they do not find a well-swept hearth to dance on, they may dance in a ring outdoors. Where they dance, the grass withers and is called briza or dawdle. If you walk across it, you will get very drowsy and may fall into a sleep from which you will never wake, but if you leave a wad of cheese there (the favorite food of elves and fairies), you will gain their help. In Ireland it is considered mad to disturb the fairy rings marked on the grass.

Elsewhere, especially in Northern Europe, there are similar creatures called *duergar, nokke, droich, pixies, nixies,* and *kobbolds* (the latter related to the mineral cobalt).

THOMAS THE RHYMER

Fairies liked to carry off human beings to fairyland. Tales abound in Scotland and Ireland of young men or boys who, returning home late, happen to pass by a fairy mound when the door is open and see the revelries going on within; they are thereupon whisked away by the fairies and never heard from again.

Or fairies may steal away a human baby and leave a malevolent changeling in its place. Or they may simply invite some amenable human to visit them and later send him away, laden with extraordinary powers. The most famous real person to whom this is supposed to have happened was Thomas of Erceldoune (now Earlston) in Berwickshire, Scotland. Thomas was known as Thomas the Rhymer from the surviving fragments of rhymed prophecy attributed to his name.

His most famous prognostication concerned a great storm that was to sweep over Scotland March 20, 1286. But when the day came, it dawned clear and sunny, and people began to laugh at Thomas. But while they were still jeering, a messenger arrived with news: King Alexander III had died in an accident, leaving no heir.

"This is the storm of which I spoke," Thomas said, and indeed for the next century and longer Scotland was racked by dynastic wars and English invasion.

Thomas figures frequently in literature. Both Sir Walter Scott, in *The Bride of Lammermoor*, and Robert Louis Stevenson, in *The Master of Ballantrae*, have used prophecies of the Rhymer as plot devices. In 1921, the British government itself caused one of Thomas's prophecies to come true. He is supposed to have predicted this:

> . . . Whate'er betide
> Haig shall be Haig of Bemersyde.

The government purchased the estate of Bemersyde, which had been in the possession of the Haigs since the twelfth century but had recently passed into other hands, and donated it to the military leader of World War I, Field Marshal Sir Douglas Haig.

11

Magic and Witchcraft in the Modern World

THERE are very likely more active covens today then there have ever been before. Superstition is rife. Éliphas Lévi was the leading expert on ritual magic of the nineteenth century, yet in his whole life he attended only three such ceremonies. These days, in many cities in the world, you can do that well in a single weekend.

The present is marked by a great deal of the heritage of magic and witchcraft. We may think that we are less superstitious than our ancestors, but in many respects we are exactly the same. At the moment there is no witch hunt such as marred dark ages long past, but no one can deny that magic and witchcraft, though largely underground, are widespread in the modern world.

In fact, the modern world has produced newsletters for witches and mail-order magical daggers (though they come unconsecrated). There are far more covens in the United States today than in the seventeenth century, and more people (whether they will admit it publicly or not) are more guided by astrology than by conventional religion. Moreover, along with the cranks and

228

crackpots, there is a highly educated and respectable segment of the population that increasingly believes that "there may be something in" occult happenings. The future, it is safe to say, holds surprises, and in the strange history of magic and witchcraft there may be hints.

HALLUCINATIONS

Many drugs used in witches' brew are reported to be able to cause visual or auditory hallucinations. You may start "seeing things" if you ingest any of these: amantadine, amphetamines, amyl nitrite, antihistamines, aspirin, atropinelike drugs (one of the witches' standbys), barbiturates, benzodiazepines, bromides, carbamazepine, cephalexin, cephaloglycin, chloroquine, cycloserine, digitalis (which witches brewed from foxglove), digoxin, disulfiram, ephedrine, furosemide, griseofulvin, haloperidol, hydroxychloroquine, indomethacin, isosorbide, levodopa, nialamide, oxphenbutazone, pargyline, pentazocine, phenothiazines, phenylbutazone, primidone, propranolol, quinine, various sedatives, sulfonamides, tetracyclines, tricyclic antidepressants (such as chlorpromazine), and tripelennamine. You may have auditory hallucinations as a result of amphetamines, aspirin, digitalis, diphenhydramine, indomethacin, morphine, and pentazocine.

Many of the "results" obtained in ritual magic may be attributed to the ingestion of such drugs, drunk or inhaled during the ceremonies. Or they may have been caused by the presence of nightshade and the burning of henbane and similar hallucinogens, or merely to the ill effects of burning charcoal in a closed room.

The "temple" that the Order of the Golden Dawn used had little room for the participants in the ceremonies, and some people were undoubtedly ill affected by the heat and the smoke. Also, some of the people used drugs. One cannot be too careful about the ingredients of magic oils applied to the body, either. Magic is supposed to deal in realities, not fantasies, objective results and not subjective hallucinations. An astral trip and a drug trip are not the same thing at all.

WITCH WEDDINGS

My researches show that ancient witch weddings were long on celebration but short on ceremony. One Spanish witch wedding ritual is simply (in translation): "This woman is good for you; take this woman."

Today, witch weddings are too much influenced, I think, by the do-it-yourself variation introduced by the hippies into their weddings in the sixties. I notice that the crowns of flowers are not even the correct combinations (to real witches flowers have individual powers and uses and are not to be thrown together haphazardly), and, of course, the inevitable circle is usually of the wrong size.

In today's Alexandrian circles of witches, the ceremony includes the old practice of the bride being spreadeagled naked in the circle and the groom mounting her naked. But spectators are required to look the other way while that goes on, and the actual consummation of the marriage is conducted later, in private. If the Alexandrians had known more of ancient witchcraft, they would have had the Horned God deflower the bride before the groom lay with her, a practice that long was honored and even came down to Christian times disguised as *le droit de seigneur* or *jus primae noctis*. I believe modern witches are too selfish or sophisticated for that.

WHITE WITCHES

One of the best writers on witchcraft, Christina Hole, has this to say in her brief but excellent *Witchcraft in England* (1947):

The white witch, or wiseman, was the protector of the community, as his criminal opponent [the black witch] was its enemy. Like the black witch, he relied on magic, but he used it principally for benevolent purposes, to cure diseases, to defeat spells, detect thieves, or find stolen goods, and to protect his neighbours from every kind of ill. His influence at all times was very great, and is not yet entirely extinct. On the whole, perhaps, his activities did more good than harm. When doctors were few and not very highly skilled he was often able to cure simple ailments by the use of herbs and common sense, garnished with charms. He was the natural repository of the traditional lore of the countryside, which was not always so foolish as we tend to think today. . . .

One of the worst writers on the subject, the so-called Black Pope of San Francisco's Church of Satan (a materialist and hedonist organization), denounces white witches vehemently. In "Gay Witch" Leo Martello's *Weird Ways of Witchcraft* (1972) he is quoted thus:

They're tea shoppe witches, plump little women sitting around threatening to turn each other into toads. Most of them are neo-pagan Christians and they toy with the same notions other religions have, skulking around under a burden of guilt and afraid of being called evil.

The Satanist "religion of the flesh, the mundane, the carnal" seems to me to be a selfish and rather silly version of the Left-Hand Path, since the very essence of witchcraft involves a sense of community and unselfishness: "Do what thou wilt, so long as thou harm none other."

"MORMONS PULL PLUG ON MTV IN 1985"

Under the above headline, datelined Provo, Utah, comes this story about new restrictions on students at Brigham Young University:

Mormon bishops have pulled the plug on MTV [a TV channel showing rock music videos] for students living in church-approved housing, after condemning the popular cable music channel for containing "sex, drugs, witchcraft and the bizarre."

ARADIA

One of the most important books in the modern history of witchcraft is the *vangelo*, or gospel, of Italian witchcraft, written out by an Italian witch called Maddalena and published in 1899 as *Aradia: or the Gospel of the Witches*.

Charles G. Leland, the publisher, was aware of the survival into modern times of very ancient practices of an Old Religion, which he felt had long been a significant force in Western culture, whether on the surface of society or underground. Until the history and nature of that Old Religion are understood, he maintained, the history of the Establishment cannot be complete.

CONVICTED OF NOT PERFORMING WITCHCRAFT

Many gypsies in years gone by were executed for performing magic, but today we fine or jail them for pretending to do so. At the Portsmouth quarter

sessions in 1939, Bessy Birch, a gypsy, was accused—under witchcraft laws
that went all the way back to George II—of getting money and jewelry from
a woman by falsely saying that as a gypsy she could take away the curse on
the jewelry.

THE NECRONOMICON

The American fantasy writer H. P. Lovecraft and some of his followers
used as the basis of some short stories an imaginary grimoire which Lovecraft
called *Necronomicon*. Some people thought or hoped that such a book really
did exist and, *presto!*, someone came up with one. Unfortunately, this
Necronomicon was not only a forgery but a forgery based on a forgery,
because its modern authors had "ripped off" the *Fourth Book* attributed to
(by not authored by) Agrippa.

COURSES OF WITCHCRAFT

Many witches believe that they are not permitted to charge for teaching
the craft, but teaching *about* witchcraft is something else again. Such courses
have been offered, sometimes at fancy prices per credit, at the New School
and New York University's School of Continuing Education in New York, at
the University of Alabama and the University of South Carolina, and
elsewhere.

THE PREVALENCE OF WITCHES

Louise Huebner in *Power Through Witchcraft* (1969): "Judging from
the mail I receive, there is at least one person in every community who
practices witchcraft. People in every walk of life are witches and wizards."
Sybil Leek once claimed she heard from "a thousand people a week" who
wanted to be witches.

"PEOPLE DON'T UNDERSTAND"

Christians used to believe that Jews kidnapped babies to be used in
murderous blood rituals. Saint Hugh of Lincoln is supposed to have been

such a victim. Black magicians have been accused of sacrificing babies, and one has at least to promise to do so to become a real Satanist.

Patty Dean Hawn, a witch, disturbed the mountain folk of Wartburg, Tennessee, by her adherence to *wicca*. But when rumors spread through the region that witch rites included the sacrificing of an eleven-year-old virgin, she denied it hotly:

> All the rumors are false. They say a devil worshipper sacrifices animals or people. We do not believe in any kind of sacrifice. Our lives are in danger because people don't understand.

Isaac Bashevis Singer recalls that as a boy he was very disturbed by the sacrifice of animals demanded in the ancient Jewish religion. Certainly Jews and Christians and "white witches" never sacrifice any living thing or person now.

POSSESSION AND EXORCISM

As the spirit of God can enter into people, making them holy, so too can the spirit of the Devil enter into them, making them evil. This is the basis of the belief in demonic possession. Diabolical possession was also thought to be the cause of madness and diseases like epilepsy, in which the victim suffers periodic seizures, or various hysterical afflictions.

Treatment of the possessed could be rough. He would surely be whipped, at least. He might be chained to a huge revolving wheel and whirled about at high speed until he lost consciousness. He might be burned or subjected to the same torture as witches were—all in the attempt to make the "demon" leave him.

If the possessed victim pointed the finger at some neighbor and accused him (or usually her) of being the person who had sent in the "demon," the accused was as good as dead. (This is exactly what happened at Salem in 1692.) In Burton-on-Trent, England, in 1596, the case of Thomas Darling occurred. Darling, a young boy, returned from a hunt one day and had a series of fits, during which he claimed to see green angels, a green cat, and a chamber pot from which flames were issuing. In his conscious moments, he produced a story of having had a run-in with an old woman with three warts on her face, and he blamed his troubles on her animosity. The neighbors thought the description sounded like one Alse Gooderidge, long suspected of witchcraft, and accordingly hauled the poor woman up before a judge.

Alse denied the charge, of course, but she was tried, convicted of witchcraft, and sent to prison, where she died before she could be hanged. Meanwhile, Thomas continued to have fits and visions, until one John Darrel, a self-appointed specialist in possession, appeared, prayed and fasted over the boy and (according to Peter Haining in *Witchcraft and Black Magic* [1972]) used ventriloquism to "converse" with the demon—and thus exorcised it.

Many churches still retain belief in the religious rite of exorcism and occasionally practice it. Recently in California, priests and doctors performed such a rite over the "possessed" boy John (the only name given) who was the original of the perturbed little girl in William Blatty's novel *The Exorcist*. John, fourteen, was exorcised more than twenty times over a two-month period.

In the eighteenth century exorcism was occasionally used by physicians in the treatment of the insane. Joseph Gassner in Germany reported remarkable results, probably with hysterics who are readily responsive to any kind of suggestion. In Germany as late as the 1830s, two leading physicians of Schwabia were treating cases of possession.

Today, vastly improved diagnosis and a broad armory of sophisticated drugs enable doctors to treat and cure many of the ailments that used to pass for possession. Medical hypnosis provides an efficient approach to cases of psychosomatic illness. But there remain a few odd cases, like John's, which—like the phenomenon of poltergeists, which they closely resemble in several particulars—remain a puzzle.

"SHALL WE JOIN THE LADIES?"

Hollywood bookshop owner Edward Gilbert recently reported that sales had tripled in the occult book market in the decade and said that "close to 90 percent of the books are bought by women."

POP GOES THE OCCULT

Coven, a pop music group out of Chicago, claim they invoke the Devil. Their lead singer is named Jinx, and they certainly raise the devil of a racket.

A MODERN CURSE

England, like America, has lost many elms lately to disease but someone stepped in to save an elm that was threatened by a planned housing development in Sussex. In March 1966 the *Evening Argus* of Brighton reported that affixed to the tree had been a public warning against cutting it down. Decorated with magical symbols, the notice read:

> Hear ye, hear ye, that any fool
> Who upon this tree shall lay a tool,
> Will have upon him a curse laid,
> Until for that sin he has paid.

Not much as poetry, but a nice idea.

JUST PLAIN FOLKS

According to Emile C. Schurmacher, author of *Witchcraft in America Today* (1970):

> In present-day America witches are of all ages and of all shades from whitest white to blackest black. Few are weird or sinister in appearance or show any physical attributes which might lead one to suspect that they differ in any way from ordinary human beings.

BLACKSMITHS

Blacksmiths in olden days were often thought to have special magical powers, for, after all, they would force the hardest of known substances, iron, to take any shape they wished. To this day in Ethiopia, Morocco, and other parts of Africa, blacksmiths are believed able to change themselves into wild animals, especially hyenas. These *boudas*, as they are called, are something like our werewolves and are thought to rob graves.

Natives say that when changing themselves into wild animals, the blacksmiths sometimes fail to remove ornaments they are wearing, and so when the magic animals are killed, they are sometimes found to be wearing necklaces or other ornaments of men.

DEGREES

There are three degrees in witchcraft, Entered Apprentice being the first. (Once you join the cult, they'll tell you what the others are.) Philip Emmons Isaac Bonewits has a B.A. degree from the University of California at Berkeley, dated June 16, 1970—"with a Major in Magic." Some doctorates in history and other subjects touch more or less significantly on magic and witchcraft.

In a coven, all members are equal. At the witches' tables the salt dish is missing, not because the witches are frightened by that symbol of preservation and purity, but because in their company no one sits below the salt. They are brothers and sisters.

UNO WHO

Jehovah's Witnesses preach that "the Great Beast" of Revelations is the United Nations.

If you want to figure this out, remember that U and N correspond (in the Tarot) to the Pope and Death and to the numbers 6 and 50 (in gematria or numerology). Good luck!

BREATH OF LIFE

AMORC (Rosicrucian) advertisements used to feature Benjamin Franklin, supposedly a member. Now they depict Sir Francis Bacon. A more recent convert to the Rosy Cross was Sirhan Sirhan; he was expelled for not paying his dues but reapplied for membership after he had assassinated Robert Kennedy.

My favorite Rosicrucian, whom you will not see in the ads or the press, was a lawyer named Heydon (born in 1629), whose odd ideas included the conviction that man's Original Sin was—eating. He recommended that people give it up. There was, stated Heydon, plenty of nourishment in the air. For those who felt they needed more on their stomachs, Heydon had a compromise: Place a plate of cooked food on your stomach and inhale the aroma.

Some people would like to deny modern Rosicrucians the right to their name. They claim that, by definition, real Rosicrucians are members of a *secret* society. One eminent authority insists they have preserved their anonymity down the centuries because they all move every ten years, and, he says, they never advertise.

What is his evidence that this supersecret Rosicrucian Order has existed for centuries? Why, no trace of them has ever been found, that's how he knows.

MASQUERADE

Kit Williams's *Masquerade* was a best-selling fairy tale that involves a bejeweled golden pendant that a moon maiden sends to her love by a messenger named Jack Hare. The thirty-two-page illustrated book was a publishing phenomenon.

Williams in real life fashioned an amulet of seven ounces of gold and studded it with gems, enclosed it in a pottery rabbit, and buried it (1979) "Somewhere in the British Isles," on public property. It is supposed to be discovered (and kept) by whoever could figure out the clues in the book.

"'Masquerade' mavens," reported *Newsweek* (March 30, 1981), "use everything from astrology to trigonometry to fathom its mystical text and complex art" and are hot in pursuit of the bauble. It is worth between $20,000 and $36,000, depending on the price of gold, and the author's royalties have reached over $500,000.

Who would have thought that a modern international quest would involve thousands seeking an amulet described in a fairy tale?

HYPNO-TECHNICIANS

These are Los Angeles (and other) cops who, after a few days of training, can hypnotize witnesses in order to get information out of them that is not available to the witnesses' conscious minds: You *do* recall the license number after all; you *can* describe the man with the gun though you thought you were too scared to notice. Your subconscious holds hidden facts.

But, in truth, your unconscious mind can lie, and distort, too, and fall prey to suggestion by the inquisitor. The International Society of Hypnotism and the Society for Clinical and Experimental Hypnotism disapprove of information taken under hypnosis, and the courts may reject it as evidence. But the police find it useful as an aid to detection. Thus hypnosis, once thought occult, now may join fingerprinting among police procedures.

OM AND THE RANGE

TM (Transcendental Meditation) used to sell people a very personal mantra, a sound to chant for emptying the mind, facilitating concentration, and aiding meditation. Then someone revealed that the mantra you got just depended on your age; there was a list.

Actually, meditation is good for you, and mantras help. You can use any one you like, provided it is a monosyllable and you are not going to get bored repeating it. You can use *krim* or *hrim* or *shrim*, *vam* or *gam* or *ram*, whatever you like. A friend on Wall Street says he uses *cash*, and it has certainly worked for him.

SATAN'S POWER

In a *People* magazine article entitled "Five Things That Would Have Made George Orwell Happy in 1984," this is the first item:

> Members of the congregation of the Cornerstone Assembly of God Church in Bowie, Md., destroyed a batch of phonograph records they said reflected "Satan's power." Among them were albums by Donny and Marie Osmond.

GREENING OF AMERICA

The old superstition that green is unlucky (because worn by fairies) has been translated into a folk belief that homosexuals wear green on Thursdays.

THE SECRET

The so-called Count of St.-Germain walks again!

In the eighteenth century he surrounded himself with a group of alchemical magicians who were supposed to have moved through various degrees (like Freemasons) until they became full-fledged adepts. At that point they were entitled to know the Secret. The count whispered to each that the secret was that there *was* no secret.

The Assassins, twelfth century followers of the murderous Hasan ibn al-Sabah, also learned at last that "nothing is true." The Tibetans are frequently told by their lamas, after a series of tests and mystical experiences, that it is all phony. But to many, as to the followers of the count, it comes as a stunning surprise.

Now, look at the group founded by Guy Warren Ballard called the Minute Men of St.-Germain. Ballard left Kansas a few years ago to start a new religion in California. It was called I AM, and the Minute Men was its paramilitary wing. The latter, claimed Ballard, was equipped with a death-dealing ray gun.

The secret is that, in Californian occult circles, anything goes.

OCCULT SUPERMARKET

The occult seems to be a thriving industry in America today. If you look in your local yellow pages, you may find magic and witchcraft suppliers, if not magicians and witches listed as such. "Magicians' Supplies" may simply mean equipment for sleight of hand, but there are warlock shops and many little sources of supply without a phone. Is there a real "magicians' supplies" store in your town, or are your local warlocks and witches creating their own equipment or making do with mail order?

A LITTLE STORY

In 1940, after Denmark had fallen to the Nazis, the great physicist Nils Bohr, still then working in his native Copenhagen on nuclear fission, telegraphed a message to British friends that concluded: "TELL COCKCROFT AND MAUD RAY KENT."

The British scientist Sir John Cockcroft was easily identified, but who or what was "Maud Ray Kent"? Some tried anagrams, and one scientist was sure it meant that U (uranium) and D (heavy water?) "may react." The British set up a MAUD Committee on the subject of atomic science and researches that might produce an atomic bomb.

Much later it was discovered there was a lady called Maud(e) Ray who lived in Kent. She had been governess to Bohr's children.

The point of this story is this: Ignorance can create mystery where there is actually none. Investigators of the paranormal and the supernatural ought to remember that, for the simplest explanation is most likely to be correct. And I feel that the simplest explanation for much magic and witchcraft is that the supernatural exists.

COMMUNIST CONSPIRACY

In 1960, a Senate Internal Security Subcommittee meeting, chaired by Sen. Thomas J. Dodd of Connecticut, heard Nigerian student Anthony G. Okotcha testify that he and twenty other African students were recruited elsewhere and trained in witchcraft at the University of Moscow. Their witchcraft professor, it was alleged, told them at the outset that the Soviet's purpose in this was "the eventual liquidation of American and British influence in Africa." Since that time it is not clear how well their lessons have been applied.

WORD WATCHING

The portable, often plastic, brightly colored cones placed in the road to divert traffic around road works are called witches' hats.

THE COVENANT OF THE GODDESS

A group of San Francisco women recently formed an organization they call the Covenant of the Goddess. It is dedicated to "Magic—the art of changing consciousness at will," which it celebrates in what it calls the Spiral Dance Ritual on "the witches' New Year," Halloween.

The Goddess, which the group describes as "the immanent life force," appears to be a kind of moon deity, worshipped in outdoor rituals. The main thrust of the the Covenant's teachings seem to be a combination of women's rights, artistic expression, and occultism.

HOLY TOLEDO!

Perhaps the city of the modern world most changed from its great days as a center for magic is Toledo in Spain, made immortal by El Greco's famous painting.

Today it still carries on some of its ancient Moorish craft of damascening metal, but it is no longer the university of sorcery that it was in the period when it brought together the magicians of North Africa, the cabalists of the Jews, and the Christian scholars who went there to absorb their knowledge of medicine, mathematics, and darker arts.

On the swords made in Toledo men used to swear the great oath, "the oath that kills." All we have left now is the slang expression "Holy Toledo!"

TRANSPORTATION

In 1969 in California, a U.S. Marine named Raphael Minichiello, en route to a court-martial for robbery, escaped from his guards, hijacked a TWA jet, and forced it to carry him 6,900 miles to Rome. He was seized by American authorties and returned to the States, but not before former friends in Melito Irpino, a village near Naples, had taken up a collection for him. They were going to pay a witch to whisk him out of the hands of the FBI and back to Italy.

The spell didn't work.

MAGIC IS BIG BUSINESS TODAY

Daniel Lawrence O'Keefe's magisterial book *Stolen Lightning: The Social History of Magic* (1982) makes a point often ignored in discussions of the subject:

Magic is big business; when practitioners succeed in avoiding taxes by having their ventures declared religions or charitable foundations they prosper. Magical products have cross-elasticities with all other goods and services in the economy; if other goods are taxed at up to 46 percent federally, and subjected also to regulation of all kinds, then magical goods may partly drive non-magical goods out of circulation. If Transcendental Meditation is permitted to sell nonsense syllables for $150.00 a morpheme in every state in the union without a single regulatory agency lifting a finger, while a manufacturing company can be prosecuted for literally thousands of infringements of six centuries of business law, which product will prosper more? Magic also obtains large infusions of capital from crazy or reactionary sections of America's rich.

OLD IDEAS

"Little is known of the religion of the early Egyptians," wrote William MacQuitty in the first issue of *Museum Magazine* (1980), "but it is probable that they were fetishists, worshippers of objects considered to have special properties—the stone or stick with which a dangerous animal had been killed, a tree that had given shelter, and so on. Gradually, religion became more sophisticated, carvings and inscriptions reveal worship of the sun-god Atum."

Many people today are mere fetishists, ascribing power to a "lucky penny" or a pen with which they have signed successful contracts, or a "winning shirt." Certainly fetishists outnumber modern sun-god worshippers. Progress?

STILL THE MODERN VIEW

Probably the best statement of how most people today feel about magic is as old as Pliny the Elder (23–79) who, in his *Natural History*, said it was "frivolous and false" and yet "still contains some element of truth in it."

BEATING WITCHES

"In 1969," writes Richard Cavendish in *The Powers of Evil* (1975), "five men and a woman were tried in Zürich and found guilty of beating a girl of seventeen to death in an attempt to drive the Devil out of her."

The young girl, Bernadette Hasler, wrote an account of how she had had sexual relations with the Devil, "all black and furry." The six accused beat her for four hours on May 14, 1966, making her eat her own excrement and otherwise humiliating and injuring her.

In witchcraft circles, the apprentice to the coven has the Devil beaten *into* him or her. Scourging is part of the initiation rite, though gentle and more or less token in many modern covens. Some witches, however, report being very severely beaten before their induction into a coven.

The Hasler incident, which made *Time* of February 7, 1969, is only one of innumerable instances, most of which go unpublicized, in which religious persons literally try to beat the Hell out of people they believe to be possessed by Satan.

THE GOLDEN DAWN

Toward the end of the last century, a group of literary men in London formed an organization for the study of magic and the occult and called it the Hermetic Order of the Golden Dawn. The Golden Dawn liked to think of itself as having arcane and unique origins, but occult groups for literary types were not uncommon in the nineteenth century, and the Golden Dawn was probably not much different from that led by playwright and novelist Edward Bulwer-Lytton.

The Golden Dawn attracted a mixed bag of literary types, including A. E. Waite, William Butler Yeats, Arthur Machen, and Algernon Blackwood, some of whose interests in the occult inevitably appeared in their work and reached the general public. It also attracted the London coroner (a strange man who also headed the Rosicrucians), the rather loony Allan Bennett (who renounced Roman Catholicism at age sixteen when it was explained to him how God had arranged for children to be born), and the crazier Samuel MacGregor Mathers (who had translated various occult works) and Aleister Crowley. These latter two consummate egoists inevitably struggled for supremacy within the organization, constantly trying to discover or devise new ceremonies and to use them for personal power. In the battle over control of the Golden Dawn, Mathers sent a vampire (among other evils) to Crowley; Crowley replied with fifty demons (including Beelzebub). It was a deadly game—at least in their own estimations.

Mathers felt he owned the Golden Dawn. Had not the basic secrets of the organization come from a coded manuscript he, Mathers, had deciphered—with some help from his wife, a clairvoyant? Crowley also intended to run any group with which he was associated. Frustrated when Mathers created new levels of "secrets" and "degrees" which he would not share with Crowley, Crowley left the Golden Dawn, set up his own group called *Argentinum Astrum* ("Silver Constellation"), created some "secrets" of his own, and began to publish the "secrets" of the Golden Dawn in his magazine, *The Equinox*. Meanwhile there appeared on the Continent Crowley's four-volume work entitled (rather preciously) *Magick*. It was denounced as full of vile rituals, and copies were extremely hard to come by, but some eventually found their way to Britain, among other places.

Ultimately, The Golden Dawn collapsed, not so much because of the internecine struggles of ambitious members or the publication of its "secrets," but because of the good intentions of writer A. E. Waite, one of the least ambitious, and most serious, members. Waite strove to make the order more Christian, and when that happened, British membership melted away.

Eventually, even the closely guarded "secrets" of Aleister Crowley and the innermost "secrets" of the Golden Dawn were published in a revealing book, *The Golden Dawn*, by Francis Israel Regardie (born 1907), who once was Crowley's personal secretary. This infuriated other occultists (especially those in California, where Regardie went to live after leaving England), who wanted to keep Crowley's *Ordo Templi Orientis* ("Order of the Eastern Temple") their private mystery. But Regardie, who authored *The Tree of Life* and other useful books on magic and mind expansion (which went over big in California), knew the significance of what he was publishing. In *The Golden Dawn*, which went through several editions, one could "read all about it."

NEW YORK STORES

New York has always been rather tolerant of witches. Ralph and Mary Hall were tried for having cast spells in New Amsterdam (1665–1668) but were acquitted, and the accusations pooh-poohed. True, Edgar Cayce and Evangeline Adams were tried here for fortune-telling, but the objection seems to have been more to suspected fraud than to substantiated supernatural activities. (Today most "fortune-telling" consists of giving people numbers to play.)

New York has plenty of occult bookstores and some courses in witchcraft for students of various levels; it is also one of the best cities in the world to get the ingredients and paraphernalia for magic and sorcery.

MAGIC TRANSFORMATIONS

David Gerrard's documentary for the Year of the Child (1979) showed young Americans exercising and chanting:

> Fee, fie, foh, fat;
> This will make my tummy flat.

GOING THROUGH CHANGES

The *I Ching* ("Book of Mutations") is identified by Louis Pawels and Jacques Bergier in *The Morning of the Magician* (1968) as the "only oracular book the rules of which have come down to us from antiquity, and is composed of graphic figures: three continuous lines, and three discontinuous lines, in every possible order."

This ancient Chinese work needs little description here, for the *I Ching*, having been taken up in the psychedelic revolution of the sixties, is still a best-seller. Most of the people who swear by it hardly think of it as magic at all.

LOCAL DEVIL

This legend, concerning the Caquende Street fountain in Sabará, Brazil, is reported by contemporary Brazilian author Fernando Sabino:

> At midnight on Fridays, a "colonial devil" is said to emerge from
> the fountain, cross the city toward the Velhas River, take a dip
> in the waters, and then disappear. That is, unless he encounters a
> woman on the road. Like all devils, he's crazy about women. He
> impregnates them, and the kids are born werewolves.

SHIVAREE

An old American custom is the shivaree, a noisy serenade to the bride and groom on their wedding night. The custom goes back to Europe, where it was called charivari and had as its original purpose not just teasing the newly married couple but actually frightening away demons who might prevent conception and the birth of a new soul.

A modern version of shivaree consists of a procession of cars following that of the bride and groom from the church to the place of the reception. The followers honk horns and create a loud and boisterous parade.

CALIFORNIA WITCHES

In 1965, during an entertainment in the Hollywood Bowl, Louise Huebner, who regards herself as a witch, offered an incantation "to increase the sexual vitality of Los Angeles," which one would hardly think was necessary.

However, Huebner's distribution of red candles, chalk, and garlic seems to indicate more familiarity with horror films than with ritual magic. Experts know that, to keep away vampires, you need garlic *flowers*; garlic only keeps away people. Nonetheless, the spell "Light the flame, bright the fire, red the color of desire," was happily chanted by the crowd, led by Huebner, dressed in a long silver robe.

Los Angeles County Supervisor Debs then jokingly gave the lady some recognition as "Official Witch of Los Angeles County." Later, when he saw the derisive press reception this was getting, he revoked her "appointment." She retaliated by revoking her spell.

Still, L.A. has many unofficial witches, so Huebner's dubious incantation can hardly be missed.

TOURIST GUIDE

In the 1970s Ernest Weatherall wrote from London for *Variety*, the show-biz bible: "For the visitor who has seen everything, the hotel concierge will probably know where you can attend the many witches' covens in town, where nude virgins will be 'sacrificed' to the spirits. The 'in-thing' in London today is to attend an exorcism ceremony, and watch one of the devil's disciples have the evil spirits knocked out of him."

But someone must have been pulling Mr. Weatherall's leg. "Nude virgins" are not all that common in London, and genuine witches' covens are Not Open to the General Public.

WITCHY BAHAMAS TODAY

In the Americas there are many places where European traditions of magic and witchcraft have been mingled with African Mumbo Jumbo (worship of an African deity) to create interesting customs, superstitions, and new religions. We may take the Bahamas as our example, for on both New Providence and the Out Islands, an active bush medicine is practiced by professors of plants (herbalists), witches involved in *fyak* (witchcraft), and medicine men with the charms and amulets of *mojo*, the fetishes and taboos of *juju* brought from West Africa. Also (though it is not a religion like the Voodoo of Haiti) there is the magic of Obeah.

A witch-man or old granny with Obeah can protect pregnant women from bad influences (with graveyard or crossroads dirt or foot-grass concoctions made from the grass growing around the house). He can fix a wayward husband or snare a lover (by putting menstrual blood in cuckoo soup and feeding it to the unwary). He can provide a guard (amulet) against other doctors' spells, or he can put a hant or ghost *on* someone or take one *off*.

You can have your house smoked to banish evil spirits or drive them away with *Petiveria alliacea* (a garlic-scented tropical American herb called Obeah bush, poor-man's strength, strong-man's weed, or guinea-hen weed). You can get an Obeah snake to protect your property from intruders or thieves, or set an Obeah trap for them, or hang a bottle or some other magic object in the trees to guard you. You can carry a good-luck bean or have someone with "the power" perform *macasee* (magic) for you, put the mouth on (curse) an enemy, drive off a plaguey spirit, or interpret your dreams for you with *King Tut* (a famous dream book that explains the significance of dreams).

Those who "live by olden days' time" keep the ancient ways inherited from British and other "massas" and likewise from slave ancestors brought to the islands from far-off Africa. Many of today's home remedies are tried-and-true substitutes for the pharmacy's products, but in the use of some of them (as when one puts a leaf in one's shoe) magic enters in.

Jumbies—evil spirits whose name is derived from African roots and resembles the Haitian *zombie*—are thought to inhabit certain caves, trees, and so on, and even those who do not believe in such things are careful, nonetheless, not to disturb them. Jumby beans (seeds of the common lead tree, *Leucaena glauca*) can be placed at the wrists of children to protect them from these "ghosts." Children continue the traditions: Even when playing a favorite game of having one of their number lie down on the ground on a moonlight night to have his or her outline traced by the placement of shining pieces of shell or white stones, they always end with the very careful removal of every last piece of the outline, lest an evil spirit come and work against the moonlight child; whose outline somehow took on something of his identity.

AMERICAN ANTICHRIST

The *Ordo Templi Orientis* that Aleister Crowley established in Europe had certain appeals to Americans, especially those interested in sex magic. These disciples formed in California a group called Agape Lodge, but the Greek word *agape* (selfless and outgoing love) had little reference to their real activities, and especially those of Jack Parsons, a brilliant physical chemist. Parsons' sex life with real women had convinced him that he would be far better off with an "elemental" woman conjured up by sex magic. For a while Parsons had to be content with Crowleyan ceremonies that involved a lot of boring ritual magic and no sex but masturbation, but in the long run— lo and behold!—the "elemental" was produced. Some people said she was a would-be poetess from New York, but Parsons was ready to believe that she was his promised magical bride.

With this attractive woman, who was red-haired and green-eyed, Parsons undertook to produce in her womb Babalon, the Crowleyan "female principle" itself. Parsons and his girlfriend advanced the cause of heterosexual sex magic to the full extent of their energies, but no Babalon was conceived.

Ultimately (1952) Parsons blew himself up in an experiment with fulminate of mercury. He is remembered chiefly not for his sexual or magical prowess but for his legal name change—from "Jack Parsons" to "Balarion Armiluss al Daijal Antichrist."

DO YOU THINK THE AGE OF MAGIC IS DEAD?

"Many people delude themselves with the belief of living in a thoroughly rationalized era," wrote the author of the article "Magic" in *The New International Encyclopedia* (1930), "until some one in the room opens an umbrella."

The ancient beliefs in magic remain very much a part of modern lives. We knock on wood in hopes of averting bad luck, we refuse to light three cigarettes with one match, we avoid ladders and are careful with mirrors. Quite apart from such practices, we say things like "if something should happen to me" instead of "when I die." Thus we show our belief in the magical dictum which says that, by naming an event, one assists in making it happen.

BLASPHEMY

The *frisson* or thrill of doing something wicked and even dangerous is one of the attractions of witchcraft. Blasphemy and sacrilege can be said to introduce what some dabblers in the occult call "electricity" into magical ceremonies.

Blasphemy was part of the stock in trade of Aleister Crowley's magic. He spread the news that he had baptized a toad "Jesus Christ of Nazareth" and then crucified it. The Sixth Degree ritual of Crowley's *Ordo Templi Orientis* is a parody of Christ's Passion, involving scourging and the Crown of Thorns, the mocking and sponge of vinegar, even crucifixion. Crowleyan sects of one sort or another still exist, and some may still perform sex-magic-related crucifixions, although none involve death so far as I know. The terrible "Texas chainsaw murders" seem clearly attributable to dementia and not demonology, but they also involved some hideous practices—such as dressing up in the skins of flayed victims—that originated in ancient Teutonic magic.

Ritual magic appears to be growing somewhat more sedate, as we see in the increasing number of "robed covens" (witches traditionally celebrated stark naked). But on the fringes they may involve what we may describe as blasphemies against both humanity and the Godhead.

LOOKING FOR SYMBOLS OF WITCHCRAFT

For 103 years Proctor & Gamble used a trademark on its products of a crescent moon and thirteen stars. No longer. A rumor started about 1980 that the symbol was drawn from witchcraft. P & G fought the allegation of Satanism in the courts and won, set up a toll-free number the public could call for an explanation of the innocuous symbol, and finally decided, in 1985, that one cannot fight the public if they are willing to see 666 in the whiskers of the Man in the Moon or credit false reports that the company publicly admitted tithing to the Church of Satan.

Perhaps those same people would care to write to Washington. What do you know about that very curious mumbo jumbo of pyramid and eye and so on, on the back of the dollar bill? Perhaps they ought to look at every committee that boasts exactly thirteen members, from the College of Heralds in Britain to some small American town's Board of Selectmen. . . .

"DO DO THAT VOODOO THAT YOU DO SO WELL"

Frank Daminger of West Virginia sued seven neighbors for $50,000 for defaming him by saying that he attracted girls by witchcraft. The case was settled out of court.

THE END OF WITCHCRAFT?

Not long before his death, Gerald B. Gardner, whom one journalist unsympathetically called "the self-appointed Pope of British Witchcraft," wrote:

> I think we must say goodbye to the witch. The cult is doomed, I
> am afraid, partly because of modern conditions, housing shortage,
> the smallness of modern families, and chiefly by education. The
> modern child is not interested. He knows witches are all bunk.

As it turns out, Gardner was wrong: The interest in magic and witchcraft increases every year. The proliferation of occult shops and various courses in the black arts, available all over the globe, make it clear that witches are getting less bunkier all the time.

GERMAN CUSTOMS

When a German peasant woman thinks she has been zapped by the Evil Eye, she instantly reverts to ancient Teutonic religious practices. She removes her dress over her head. Then she turns it around three times. (This may be a later, Christian touch, though Christians are not the only ones to find power in the number 3.) Then, holding the dress open, she drops a burning coal through it three times before donning it again.

The burning coal is one with the torches, bonfires, shafts of light illuminating the altars in temples, and all the other remnants of the old religion of the Sun God.

The dress must be, like most things in magic, turned around *wieder-schein* ("widdershins," we say in English, or counterclockwise, opposite the course of the sun through the heavens). The idea is that you are *unwinding* the spell cast on you.

TWO WORLDS

In the 1893 book, *Philosophical Studies*, one W. Wundt wrote an article entitled "Hypnotism and Suggestion." In it, he had this to say of magic and its adherents.

It is obvious that the world that surrounds us is composed of two quite different worlds. On the one hand there is the world of Copernicus, Newton, Leibniz and Kant; that is, the universe that is subject to immutable laws and where both big and small are unified in one harmonious whole. On the other hand, there exists, beside this grandiose and admirable universe, a small world of spirits, magicians and "mediums" which is the direct opposite of our great, sublime universe whose immutable laws are suspended for the profit of these most vulgar and frequently hysterical persons. So, we are led to believe that the laws of gravitation, the action of light and all the laws of our psychophysical organization must undergo a transformation as soon as they come before some "Madame Zara" [gypsy fortune-teller] . . . that they sleep a sort of magnetically-induced slumber, not so that she may predict some great universal catastrophe, but so that she may guess if some minor misfortune lies ahead of John Smith's small son. . . . Supposing all these absurdities were in fact true, can one imagine that a psychologist or a natural scientist, who is exempt from prejudice and who has free choice, would prefer the evidence of this small world of hysterical mediums to that of our great universe, whose order depends on immutable laws?

"HERE COMES THE ANTICHRIST"

To Jeffrey Burton Russell, whose books, *The Devil* (1977), *Satan*, (1981), and *Lucifer* (1985), explore the concept of God's Adversary, the modern world sounds much like that into which the Antichrist is prophesied as coming. He feels it is a world in which "a real force is actively present in the cosmos urging to evil." He concludes:

This evil force has a purposive center that actively hates good, the cosmos, and every individual in the cosmos. . . . For Christians, then, the person of the Devil may be a metaphor for something that is real, that really brings horror to the world every day and threatens to lay the entire earth waste.

In our modern world, where the nuclear means of destruction of "the entire earth" are at our fingertips, the Devil is more to be feared than ever before. For we live in an age far more genuinely terrifying than any conceived by evil witches and sorcerers of the past.

Afterword

A LL that is involved in or lies behind magical activities is too much for any single book. This one has attempted to touch authoritatively on some selected facts, chosen for their essential color and interest. To collect them, I have had to cast my net wide, and I am always ready to haul in new ones.

You may wish to write me your reactions to the book. I cannot promise to answer all your letters, but I assure you I shall read them with lively interest. I am signing below my real name and address.

Leonard is the name of the Inspector-General of Black Magic, the "great Black One" who presides at the sabbat as a giant goat with three horns and the ears of a fox and is worshipped by heirophants bearing green candles. My surname, *Ashley*, means a ring of ash trees in a field, the sacred grove where the Druids met, for the ash attracts spirits. Still, as an only child (therefore first-born), I should be immune to witchcraft, so I feel an affinity for both believers and unbelievers.

Now, hoping you have enjoyed the facts and fun of this truly marvelous subject, I conclude.

God bless you. Blessed be.

Index